WINTER WEDDING
IN VEGAS

BY
JANICE LYNN

MILLS
BOON

Dear Reader,

We've all heard that old saying: 'What happens in Vegas, stays in Vegas.' But it doesn't always… Sometimes a girl marries the wrong man who might *just* end up being the right man!

Slade Sain is about as opposite to what Taylor Anderson wants in a man as he can possibly be. Except that he's sexy as sin, makes her feel good about herself, and he's a fantastic, compassionate oncologist. Now he's her husband. So this year all she wants for Christmas is a quickie divorce and for what happened in Vegas truly to stay in Vegas.

Slade dedicated his life to breast cancer research at the tender age of twelve, when his mother died from the horrible disease. He knows the path his life is destined to take. Getting married is a bump on that road he never intended to travel over. Sure, Taylor has always fascinated him—but he's a good-time guy, not a for ever kind of man. She's vulnerable, a single mum, and still believes in Christmas. He should have known better. Only maybe his heart has been headed in the right direction all along…

I hope you enjoy their story, and that Santa stuffs your stockings with all the things you really want.

Merry Christmas!

Janice

To my favourite nurse, Joni Sain!
You rock!!!

Books by Janice Lynn

Mills & Boon Medical Romance

Dr Di Angelo's Baby Bombshell
Officer, Gentleman...Surgeon!
The Nurse Who Saved Christmas
Doctor's Damsel in Distress
Flirting with the Society Doctor
Challenging the Nurse's Rules
NYC Angels: The Heiress's Baby Scandal
The ER's Newest Dad
Flirting with the Doc of Her Dreams
New York Doc to Blushing Bride

Visit the Author Profile page at
millsandboon.co.uk for more titles.

Janice won The National Readers' Choice Award
for her first book
The Doctor's Pregnancy Bombshell

CHAPTER ONE

DR. TAYLOR ANDERSON woke from the craziest dream she'd ever had. Apparently sleeping in a glitzy Las Vegas hotel stretched one's inner imagination beyond all reason.

Married. Her. To Dr. Slade Sain.

As if.

The man was such a player, she wouldn't date him, much less consider a more serious relationship with the likes of him. Sure, he was gorgeous, invaded her deepest, darkest dreams from time to time, but the man's little black book had more phone numbers than the Yellow Pages.

If and when she married, no way would she make the same relationship mistakes she had made during medical school. Never again was she walking down that painful path of inevitable unfaithfulness from a man she should have known better than to trust.

Yet her mind warned that last night hadn't been a dream, that she had married Slade.

Last night she'd drowned her awkwardness around him. She rarely drank, but she'd felt so self-conscious surrounded by Slade and her colleagues in a social setting, that she had overimbibed. She didn't think she'd been out and out drunk, but she hadn't been herself.

These days, the real her was quiet and reserved, steady and stable. Responsible. Not the kind of woman to go to a tacky Sin City year-round Christmas-themed wedding chapel and marry a man she respected as a brilliant oncologist, had found unbelievably attractive from the moment she'd first laid eyes on him, but thought as cheesy as the Jolly Old Saint Nick who'd, apparently, also been an ordained minister. Who knew?

Mentally, she counted to ten, took a deep breath, and opened her eyes. She was in her hotel room queen-size bed and Sexy Slade Sain was nowhere in sight.

She glanced at the opposite side of the bed. The covers were so tangled, who knew if there had been anyone other than herself beneath the sheets? Just because she usually woke with the bedcovers almost as neat as when she'd crawled between them didn't mean a thing. Really.

She wasn't in denial. No way.

Neither did the fact she was in the middle of the bed, sort of diagonally, and sprawled out. Naked. What had she done with her clothes?

What had she done with her naked body?

A knock sounded on the door leading out of the room. Feeling like she was suffering a mini–heart attack, Taylor grabbed at the tangled sheets.

"Room service," a male voice called through the door.

Room service? She pulled the covers tightly around her body. She hadn't ordered room service.

The bathroom door opened and a damp, dark-haired pin-up calendar model wearing only a towel—dear sweet heaven, the man had a fine set of shoulders and six-pack!—undid the safety chain.

Slade was in her hotel room. Naked beneath the towel and he was buff. The towel riding low around his waist, covering his perfect butt, his perfect… She gulped back saliva pooling in her mouth.

Despite her desperate clinging to denial of the cold hard facts she'd been willfully repressing, she knew exactly what she'd done with her naked body. What she'd done with *his* naked body. Why her bedsheets were so tangled. The details of how she'd come to the conclusion that marrying Slade was a logical decision might be a little fuzzy, but she'd known exactly what she'd been doing when Slade's mouth had taken hers. Hot, sweaty, blow-your-mind sex, that's what she'd done. With Slade. As much as her brain was screaming *No!* her body shouted, *Encore!*

"That was quick," Mr. Multiple Orgasms praised the hotel employee pushing a cart into the room. He stopped the man just inside the doorway. "I'll take it from here."

The pressure in Taylor's head throbbed to where at any moment she was going to form and rupture an aneurysm. Slade's wife. This had to be a nightmare. Or a joke. Or a mistake they could rectify with an annulment.

Could a couple get an annulment if they'd spent the night in bed, performing exotic yoga moves with energetic bursts of pleasurable cardio?

She closed her eyes and let images from the night before wash over her, of Slade unlocking her hotel room door, sweeping her off her feet, and carrying her to the bed and stripping off her clothes. She'd giggled and kissed his neck when he'd carried her across the threshold. Then he'd kissed her. Really, deeply kissed her. Even now she could recall the feel of his lips against hers, the feel of his body against hers, his spicy male scent. Heat rose, flushing her face, ears and much more feminine parts.

They so wouldn't qualify for an annulment.

Wow at the moves the man had hidden inside that fabulous body. His hands were magic. Pure magic. His mouth? Magic. Just *wow*.

She cracked open an eyelid to steal a peek. He tipped the man from Room Service from his wallet on the dresser, closed the door, turned and caught her staring.

"Morning, Sleeping Beauty." He gave a lopsided, almost self-deriding grin. "Some night, eh?"

She groaned and pulled a pillow over her head to where she just peered out from behind it. "Tell me that wasn't real."

He shrugged his magnificent shoulders. "That wasn't real."

Dropping the pillow but hanging on tightly to the sheet, she let out a surprised sigh of relief.

"But if by 'that' you're referring to our wedding at the North Pole Christmas Bliss Wedding Chapel—" the words came out with a mixture of amusement and shock, as if he couldn't quite believe what they'd done either "—well, according to our marriage certificate, that was very real."

Keeping the covers tucked securely around her, Taylor sat up. A wave of nausea smacked her insides. He stood there looking sexy as sin and she was going to barf. Great. Just flipping great.

"One minute we were kissing in the limo surrounded by Christmas music and that crazy peppermint spray the driver kept showering us with, the next we're getting married so we could have sex. Great sex, by the way. You blew me away." His blue eyes sparkling with mischievous intent, he moved toward her and she shook her head in horrified denial.

"Get back," she warned, covers clutched to her chest with one hand and the other outstretched as if warding off an evil spirit. Sure, there was a part of her that was thrilled that he'd enjoyed their night as much as she had, but it was morning. The morning after. And they'd gotten married. "That's crazy. We didn't have to get married to have sex."

Pausing, he scratched his head as if confused. "Not that I don't agree with you, but that's not what you said last night in the limo."

The movement of his arm flexed muscles along his

chest and abdomen and sent a wave of tingles through her body, but that wasn't why she gulped again. She was just… thirsty? Parched. Still fighting the urge to barf. Forcing her eyes to focus on his face and not the rest of him, she blinked. The flicker of awareness in his blue eyes warned he knew exactly what she had been looking at, what she'd been thinking, and he wasn't immune to her thoughts.

"You told me you wouldn't have sex with me unless we were married," he reminded her.

She had said that. In the midst of his hot, lust-provoking kisses she'd thrown down her gauntlet, expecting him to run or laugh in her face. "So you married me?"

He glanced down at the cheap band on his left hand and shrugged. "Obviously."

Not that he sounded any happier about it than she felt, but someone should shoot her now. She was wearing a ring, too. A simple golden band on the wedding finger of her left hand. Because she was married. To Slade.

Slade was not the man of her dreams, was not someone she'd carefully chosen to spend the rest of her life based upon well-thought-out criteria. He was exactly what she avoided even dating because men like Slade didn't jibe with her life plans. How could she have had such a huge lapse of judgement?

The metal hugging her finger tightened to painful proportions. At any moment her finger was going to turn blue and drop off from lack of blood flow. Seriously.

She went to remove the ring, but couldn't bring herself to do it. Why, she couldn't exactly say. Probably the same insanity that had had her saying "I do" to a man she should have been screaming "I don't" at. Besides, she'd probably have to buy a stick of butter before the thing would budge.

"We should talk about this." He glanced at his watch. "But we have our presentation in just over an hour. You should eat."

She glanced at the bedside table's digital clock. Crap. She'd slept much later than normal. Then again, she'd stayed up much later than normal.

Nothing had been normal about the night before. It had been as if she'd been watching someone else do all the things she'd done, as if it had all been a fantasy, not real.

"You have to go to your room," she told him, needing to be away from his watchful blue gaze.

"I'm in my room." He shifted his weight and her attention dropped to where the towel was tucked in at his waist. His amazing, narrow waist that sported abs no doctor should boast. Abs like those belonged on sport stars and models, not white-collar professionals who saw cancer patients all day. "Last night we arranged for the hotel staff to move my things into your room while we're in class today."

They had stopped by the front desk and requested that. Wincing, her gaze shot to his.

"No." She was going to throw up. Really she was. How was she going to explain this to Gracie? She grimaced. "I don't want you in my room."

"Understood." He looked as if he really didn't want to be there either. "But we're married."

"Married" had come out sounding much like a dirty word, like someone who'd just been given a deadly diagnosis.

Guilt hit Taylor. She had told him she wouldn't have sex with him unless they were married. But wasn't marriage a bit far for a man to go just to get laid? He had a busy revolving door to his bedroom so he couldn't have been that desperate for sex. He must have been as inebriated as she had.

"How did we end up married?" she asked, pulling the bedcovers up to her neck. The less he could see of her the better. She already felt exposed.

"You told me you wanted to have sex with me, but that you wouldn't unless we were married. Our elfish limo driver said he knew a place that could take care of a last-minute license and we happened to be right outside it. We got married and had sex. You know this. You were there."

If she'd been into one-night stands, last night would have been amazing. But she wasn't. She was a mature, professional doctor who had learned her life lessons the hard way and had a beautiful little girl she was raising by herself to prove it. She'd vowed she wouldn't have sex again without being married first. Had she foolishly believed marriage would protect her from future heartbreak?

She'd wanted Slade so much. Had possibly wanted him for months, although she'd never admitted as much to herself. When their pointy-eared three-and-a-half-foot-tall limo driver had taken them to the chapel, she'd looked at Slade, expecting him to laugh at her condition.

When she'd seen him actually seriously considering marrying her just to have sex with her, a big chunk of the protective ice she'd frozen around her heart had melted, leaving her vulnerable and wanting what she'd seen in his eyes. Whether it had been the alcohol, the Christmas magic everywhere, or just Vegas madness, she'd wanted to marry Slade the night before. It made no logical sense, but she'd wanted him to want her enough to walk down the aisle to have her.

"We were drunk," she offered as an out. "We can get an annulment because we were drunk."

His expression pained, he narrowed his gaze. "Maybe."

His hands went to his hips and, again, she had to force her eyes upward to keep them from wandering lower than his face. The man was beautiful, she'd give him that.

"I wasn't sober," she persisted, clinging to the fact that she hadn't been in her right mind. She wasn't in her right mind now either. Her head hurt and, crazy as it was, she wanted him, but she couldn't tell him that. "Regardless, I want a divorce."

* * *

Raking his fingers through his towel-dried hair, Slade eyed Taylor grasping the covers to her beautiful body as if she expected him to rip them off and demand she succumb to his marital rights whether she wanted him or not. Did she really think so poorly of him? Despite the fact he'd not been able to say "I do" fast enough the night before, he didn't want to be married any more than she apparently did.

Probably less.

Sure, he'd been attracted from the moment he'd met her. But although he'd have sworn she felt a similar spark, she'd brushed off his attempts to further their relationship.

Until last night.

Last night she'd looked at him and he'd felt captivated, needy, as if under a spell he hadn't been able to snap out of.

He took a deep breath. "A divorce works for me. A wife is not something I planned to bring back from Vegas."

Or from anywhere. He had his future mapped out and a wife didn't fit anywhere into those plans. He'd dedicated his life to breast-cancer research and nothing more.

Marrying Taylor had been rash—the effects of alcohol and Las Vegas craziness—and wasn't at all like his normal self. Women were temporary in his life, not permanent figures. He preferred it that way.

A divorce sounded perfect. His marriage would be one of those "what happens in Vegas stays in Vegas" kind of things.

Thank goodness she didn't harbor any delusions of happily-ever-after or sappy romance. They'd chalk last night up to alcohol and a major lapse of judgment.

Maybe there really was something about Vegas that made people throw caution to the wind and act outside their norm. Or maybe it had been the smiley little elfish limo driver, who'd kept puffing peppermint spray into the car, telling them they were at the wedding chapel that had made the idea seem feasible. Had the spray been some type of drug?

"Good." Taylor's chin lifted a couple of notches. "Then we're agreed this was a mistake and we can get a divorce or an annulment or whatever one does in these circumstances."

"I'll call my lawyer first thing Monday morning." Relieved that she was being sensible about calling a spade a spade and correcting their mistake, he pushed the room-service cart over next to the bed and stared down at a woman who'd taken him to sexual heights he'd never experienced before. Maybe that peppermint stuff really had been some kind of aphrodisiac.

Even with her haughty expression, she was pretty with her long blond hair tumbled over her milky shoulders and her lips swollen from his kisses. Until the night before he'd never seen her hair down. He liked it. A lot.

He liked her a lot. Always had. He'd wanted her from afar for way too long. Despite the whole marriage fiasco, he still wanted her. Even more than he had prior to having kissed her addictive mouth. She'd tasted of candy canes, joy and magic. Kissing her had made him feel like a kid on Christmas morning who'd gotten exactly what he'd always wanted.

Which was saying a lot for a man who hadn't celebrated Christmas since he was twelve years old.

"Now that that's settled, there's no reason we can't enjoy the rest of the weekend. Let's eat up before this gets cold."

The covers still clasped to her all the way up to her neck, she crossed her arms over her chest. Her eyes were narrow green slits of annoyance. "Don't act as if we're suddenly friends because we both want a divorce. We're not and we won't be enjoying the rest of the weekend. At least, not the way you mean."

"Fine. We won't enjoy the rest of the weekend." He

wasn't going to argue with her. "But we're not strangers." Ignoring her I-can't-stand-you glare and his irritation at how she was treating him as if he had mange, he lifted the lid off one of the dishes he'd ordered and began buttering a slice of toast. "I've been working with you for around a year."

"You see me at work." She watched what he did with great interest. "That doesn't make us friends. Neither does last night."

She had to be starved. While satisfying one hunger, they'd worked up another. He'd ordered a little of everything because he hadn't known what she liked. Other than coffee. Often at the clinic, he saw her sipping on a mug of coffee as if the stuff were ambrosia. Funny how often he'd catch himself watching for her to take that first sip, how he'd smile at the pleasure on her face once she had. He'd put pleasure on her face the night before that had blown away anything he'd ever seen, anything he'd ever experienced.

"You make your point." He sat down on the bed and waved a piece of buttered toast in front of her, liking how her gaze followed the offering. "But as we're in agreement that we made a mistake, one we are rectifying, I don't see why we can't be friends and make the most out of a bad situation."

Scowling, she shot her gaze back to his. "You and I will never be friends."

She grabbed his toast and took a bite, closed her eyes and sighed a noise that made him want to push her back on the bed and, friends or not, taste her all over again.

Perhaps she'd prefer it if he told her how much he was enjoying how she'd just licked crumbs from her pretty pink lips? How much, now that he knew disentangling himself from their impromptu marriage wasn't going to be a problem, he was anticipating making love to her again, because for all her blustering he wasn't blind. She'd looked at him with more hunger than she had the toast. Whether she wanted to admit it or not, she was as affected by him as he was her. They had phenomenal chemistry.

She leaned toward the tray, got a knife and a packet of strawberry jam, then nodded while she spread the pink mixture on what was left of her toast. Not an easy task because she refused to let go of where she clutched the bed covers, which seemed a bit ridiculous to him since he'd seen every inch of her. Seen, touched, tasted.

Slade swallowed the lump forming in his throat and mentally ordered one not to form beneath his towel. "In case you need reminding, we had a good time last night."

"I didn't."

"Don't lie." He'd been there. She hadn't faked that, couldn't have faked her responses, and he wouldn't let her pretend she had. "Yes, you did."

"Okay," she conceded with a great deal of sarcasm. "You're good in bed. Anyone can be good if they get lots of practice and we both know you've had lots of practice."

"Lots of practice?" He hadn't lived the life of a monk, but he didn't go around picking up random women every night either. Sure, he never committed, but the women he spent time with knew the score. He wasn't the marrying kind and avoided women who were. "You want to discuss my past sex life?"

"Not really." Her face squished, then paled. "Although I guess we should discuss diseases and such."

He arched his brow. "You have a disease?"

"No." She sounded horrified enough that he knew she was telling the truth. They should have discussed all this the night before. And birth control. Because for the first time in his life he hadn't used a condom. Because for the first time in his life he'd been making love to his *wife*.

Slade's throat tightened. He'd not only gotten married

the night before but he'd had sex without a condom. How stupid could he have been?

Was that why the sex had been so good? Because they'd not had a rubber barrier between them? Because they'd been flesh to flesh? He didn't think so. There had been something more, something special about kissing Taylor.

Besides, they'd used a condom the first time. It had been their subsequent trips to heaven that had been without one. He'd only had the one condom in his wallet and they'd still been high under the Las Vegas night air—or whatever foolishness had lowered their inhibitions.

"Do you?" she asked, sounding somewhere between terrified and hopeful his answer would be the right one.

"I haven't specifically gone for testing recently." There hadn't been a need. He had never had sex without protection before her and didn't engage in any other high-risk behaviors. "It's been a year or so since my last checkup, but I do donate blood routinely and have always checked normal."

His answer didn't appease her and she eyed him suspiciously. "When was the last time you donated?"

"About two months ago."

Relief washed over her face. "No letter telling you about any abnormal findings?"

He shook his head. "No such letter. What about you?"

Her gaze didn't quite meet his. "I've only been with one man and that was years ago during medical school. I've been checked a couple of times since then. I'm clean."

As unreasonable as it was since he was no saint and they were going to end their marriage as soon as possible, the thought of Taylor being with anyone else irked him. A surge of jealousy had his fingers flexing and his brain going on hiatus.

"He didn't have to marry you to have sex with you?"

CHAPTER TWO

SLADE INSTANTLY REGRETTED his sarcastic question, especially when, with a pale face and watery eyes, Taylor glanced down at the plain gold band he'd put on her hand the night before.

"No, Kyle didn't marry me, but I did believe he was going to spend the rest of his life loving me. Silly me."

The fact that she'd been heartbroken by the jerk rankled Slade. Good thing she didn't want this marriage any more than he did. He'd hate to think he'd hurt her like that fool had. Regardless of what the future held for them, he didn't want to cause Taylor any pain. That much he knew. "What happened?"

She shrugged and the sheet slipped off one shoulder to drape mid-upper-arm. "He didn't marry me or spend the rest of his life loving me. End of story."

Hardly, but he wouldn't push. Such sorrow laced her words that his chest squeezed tighter. "I'm sorry."

"I'm not." Masking her emotions behind an indifferent expression he suspected she'd perfected over the years since her breakup with the guy, Taylor picked up a spoon and scooped up a mouthful of eggs. "He was an arrogant jerk."

Her lips were wrapped around the spoon and another jolt of jealousy hit him as she slowly pulled the utensil from her mouth.

She picked up a strawberry and bit into the juicy fruit. "Mmm. That's good."

"Speaking of good…" He watched her pop the rest of the berry into her mouth and lick the juice from her fingers, and struggled with the desire to do some licking of his own. "Last night really was spectacular, apart from the whole getting-married thing."

She met his gaze, nodded, then deflated. "Oh, Slade, what have we done?"

Hearing her say his name caused flashbacks from the night before. Until then, he'd never heard her say his first name. He liked the sound. "We got married, but we can correct that. We will correct that. As soon as legally possible."

"It's crazy that we got married. Why did we do that? We aren't in love, barely know each other and I don't even like you."

He gave a wry grin. "All this time I just thought you were waiting on me to win you over to my way of thinking."

"Professionally maybe, but not romantically."

"Professionally, I'm a good oncologist."

"You are." She winced. "I didn't mean it like that."

"Then what did you mean?"

"Just that I always thought you were a flirt and didn't take life seriously."

"I take my job very seriously." His work was the most important thing in his life and always would be. "I care a great deal for my patients and like to think I provide them the best care possible."

"You do. It's just that…" Her voice trailed off.

"It's just what?"

"I guess I let your personal life influence how I viewed you professionally."

"What do you know of my personal life?"

Her face reddened. "Not much. Just gossip really."

"Not that you should believe gossip, but what do the gossips say?"

"That you date a lot of different women."

"You think I shouldn't?"

She sighed and looked somewhere between disgusted and desperate. "What I think about your personal life doesn't matter. We'll get a divorce and no one ever need know about any of this."

Thankful that she was so practical about the whole thing, Slade nodded. "Agreed. We'll figure the legalities out on Monday and end this as painlessly as possible."

She eyed him, then gave a hopeful half smile. "Maybe we'll get lucky and there's some kind of 'just kidding, I've changed my mind because I was stupid in Vegas clause.'"

Thank goodness Slade felt the same as she did. They'd made a horrible mistake, knew it and would make the best of a bad situation.

Not that she could believe he'd married her.

The man was gorgeous, amazing in bed, could have any woman he wanted and usually did, according to her female coworkers who loved to discuss the handsome oncologist's love life latest. Why would he have married her? Taylor was admittedly a stick-in-the-mud, boring homebody. Her idea of fun was a good book while soaking in a bubble bath or playing with Gracie. Her ideal life would bore him to tears. No confetti and blow horns anywhere in her reality or her ideal future.

From what she knew about Slade, they couldn't be more opposite.

Opposites attract.

She winced at the inner voice in her head playing devil's advocate. Okay, so she'd admit she wanted to rip Slade's towel off and have that encore performance. Not that she did anything more than wrap the sheet around her, grab the cup of coffee from the tray, and, head held high, strut into the bathroom to take her shower.

Of course, that only reminded her that his naked body had been under this hot stream earlier and had she wakened in time she could have joined him. Her husband.

What a joke.

But right now she had to get her act together, because they were presenting to a group of oncologists, pharmacists, marketing representatives and others on the benefits of a new cancer-fighting drug they'd been researching.

At some point today she should probably tell Slade that not only had he become a husband the night before, he'd also become the stepfather of a precious six-year-old little girl.

She winced.

Yeah, that might shock Slade enough to have him scrambling around in hopes of finding a twenty-four-hour Vegas divorce court.

Although she had a photo of Gracie on her desk at work, she doubted Slade had ever been inside the room, that he'd ever had reason to be in her personal office. Yes, they worked in the same multifloor cancer clinic. But prior to their being chosen to go to this conference to discuss the research being done at their facility, they'd not really interacted except when he'd sent her running by asking her out.

Because she avoided men like Slade.

Had for years.

The last time she hadn't, she'd ended up pregnant and alone.

Nausea hit her. After their first time she and Slade hadn't used birth control. He'd only had the one condom, and they'd been too delirious to acknowledge the ramifications of unprotected sex.

How stupid was she? Was he?

The timing in her menstrual cycle wasn't right for pregnancy, but she wasn't so foolish as to think it wasn't possible.

Her hand went to her bare belly. Was she? Had she and Slade made a baby? Dampness covered her skin that had nothing to do with the shower water. She loved Gracie with all her heart, would do anything for her precious daughter, but she'd never planned to have more children. Not without finding a man who met all her criteria for Mr. Right, which included what kind of father he'd be to Gracie.

Then again, she'd never planned to get married to a man she barely knew either, and she'd done that.

Her parents would be so proud. Ha. Not. Her actions this weekend would just once again affirm their disappointment in her.

She finished rinsing her body, then stepped out of the shower and eyed the half-empty cup of coffee.

She picked up the cup and, with great sadness, poured the lukewarm liquid down the sink drain.

No more coffee or anything else that wasn't healthy for a pregnant woman until she knew for sure one way or the other that she and Slade hadn't created a new little life.

Slade leaned back in his chair and watched the impressive woman woo the crowd with her smiles and witty sense of humor.

Taylor went through the slide presentation she'd put together on the data their oncology clinic, Nashville Cancer Care, had collected on Interallon, a new experimental cancer-fighting drug they'd been successfully administering as part of a larger nationwide research trial. Remission rates of metastatic breast cancer had increased by 40 percent in patients who'd received the trial medication over current treatment modalities. They were hopeful FDA approval would be soon so the medication could be administered more widely.

Taylor pushed back a stray strand of pale blond hair behind her ear and pointed a laser at the current slide, referring to a particular set of data.

He'd slid his fingers through that soft, long hair last night. Not that you could tell just how long or lush her hair was with the way she had it harshly swept up. Neither could you tell how gorgeous her big green eyes were behind those ridiculous black-rimmed glasses she wore. Definitely you couldn't tell how hot and passionate her body was beneath her prim and proper gray pantsuit and blazer.

She epitomized a professional businesswoman presenting data to a crowd of health-care professionals who couldn't possibly appreciate how amazing she was.

Slade scanned the crowd, noticing several of the men watching her with a gleam in their eyes. Well, maybe some of them did see just how amazing she was, but he pitied them. She was his. His wife.

He couldn't believe he'd gone that far.

He usually had no problems with women, but Taylor had always been different. For months he'd not been able to convince her to give him the time of day and he had tried. Repeatedly, he'd struck up conversations only to have her end them and avoid him.

She made a comment, misspoke a word and poked fun at herself, getting a laugh from their audience. Slade skimmed the crowd, noticing several of the men seemed to be further enchanted by the woman on stage.

Green slushed through his veins, clogging the oxygen flow to his brain. Had to be since he sure wasn't thinking straight because his brain—or was it just his male ego?—was screaming, *Mine. Mine. Mine.*

"Now…" She flashed another smile at the crowd, pulling them further under her spell. "I'll turn the podium over to Dr. Slade Sain to present specific case studies and then we'll field any questions together."

They walked past each other as he took the podium and she returned to sit in the seat next to his at a table that had been set up at the front of the auditorium. He tried to meet her gaze, to smile at her and tell her what a great job she'd done, but she kept her gaze averted, purposely not looking at him.

Which annoyed Slade.

He stewed all the way to the podium and then did something almost as stupid as slipping a golden band around a woman's finger when he had nothing to offer her but more broken dreams.

"Ladies and gentlemen, give my wife a round of applause for the great job she just did."

Taylor's face paled.

Slade's face probably did, too. What had he just done?

Several of the people in the audience who knew them gasped in surprise. A few called out their congratulations.

When their gazes met, Taylor looked annoyed, but then she pasted on a smile for the crowd.

Their colleagues and class attendees settled down and, despite the horror bubbling in his stomach that he'd just made their mistake public, Slade got serious. He believed in the benefits of Interallon and wanted others to have the opportunity to significantly benefit from the still-experimental medication. Despite whatever was going on in their personal lives, it was his and Taylor's job to educate their colleagues, to get others involved in the medication trials, as the pharmaceutical company pushed to have the FDA expedite approval.

He went over their case studies, answered questions, then pointed to one of their colleagues whose hand was raised with a question. The doctor had started out with him and Taylor the night before, but they'd ditched him and a handful of others when they'd left in the limo.

"Sorry to change the subject off Interallon, but when did you and Dr. Anderson get married?"

"Last night." Slade glanced toward Taylor. Her green eyes flashed with anger beneath her glasses, but she kept a smile on her lovely face. No doubt he was going to get a tongue-lashing when the presentation finished. He deserved one. He wanted to scream and yell at himself for his stupid remark, too. "Next question."

The man raised his hand again and spoke before Slade could call on another person. "You and Dr. Anderson got married last night? When you left dinner, you got married?"

Taylor stood, walked over to the podium, and took the microphone. "Dr. Ryan, you'll understand if Dr. Sain and I request personal questions be saved for a later, more appropriate time. Right now, we prefer questions regarding Interallon and the success our clinic and the other clinics involved in the trials taking place are having with this phenomenal resource in our battle against a horrific disease."

Put in his place, the man nodded. Taylor immediately called on another person and fielded a question about the medication being used in conjunction with currently available treatments.

"At this time, the studies using Interallon in conjunction with other cancer-fighting modalities are just starting to take place. Nashville Cancer Care will be heading up one of those trials early next year."

Another flurry of questions filled the remaining time and no one brought up their nuptials again until after the class was over. Several of their colleagues shook their hands, patted their backs and gave them congratulations.

"I didn't see that one coming," Dr. Ryan commented, looking back and forth between them. "I didn't even know you two were seeing each other."

Slade narrowed his gaze at the other man. Cole Ryan had been one of the men eyeing Taylor on stage as if she was a piece of candy to be devoured. A growl gurgled in Slade's throat, but he managed to keep it low.

Taylor closed her laptop and picked up a file folder with her notes inside. "I prefer to keep my personal life private. Obviously, Dr. Sain and I disagree on that particular issue."

"Dr. Sain?" Ryan chuckled, then slapped Slade on the back again. "Your wife calls you Dr. Sain?"

Slade glanced at Taylor's scowl, the stiff set to her shoulders and the tight line of her mouth. He was an idiot. He deserved her anger. He didn't even know why he'd made the stupid announcement. Other than the fact that he'd been overcome with jealousy. "When she's upset."

"Trouble in paradise already. That's a Vegas wedding for you." The man laughed again, not realizing just how much he was getting on Slade's nerves. Odd, as he usually liked the doctor, who also practiced in Nashville.

"Well, congrats anyway." Cole gave them a wry look. "For however long it lasts."

Slade packed up his briefcase and followed Taylor from the conference room and down the long hallway that led out into the hotel's main lobby.

Ignoring the lush Christmas decorations and colorful slot machines scattered around the huge lobby, Taylor didn't say a word directly to him until they were alone in the elevator. Then she rounded on him, opened her mouth to speak, then stopped, closed her eyes in disgust and took a deep breath. When she opened her eyes again, anger still flickered there. "How dare you make that little announcement during our presentation?"

"I shouldn't have said anything."

"You made a joke of our presentation," she accused, practically snapping at him.

"No, I didn't." He would never intentionally do anything to take away from the importance of Interallon and the results they were getting with the medication.

"Yes, you did. Rather than paying attention to what you were saying, half the people in the room were busy Tweeting that we'd gotten married."

"You're exaggerating." He hoped she was exaggerating.

"Really?" She dug in her bag and held up her phone. "This thing has been buzzing like crazy since you made your little comment. Forget the fact that our marriage is a sham, but how dare you make a mockery of my work?"

"That's not what I was doing." Guilt hit him. She was right. They were getting a divorce as soon as it could be arranged. The fewer people who knew of their mistake the better. He'd been out of line to say anything.

"That's exactly what you were doing." She looked as if she'd like to hit him, but instead just gritted her teeth and made a sound that was somewhere between a growl and a sigh.

"You're right," he agreed with sincerity and regret. "I shouldn't have said what I did. I'm sorry, Taylor."

That seemed to take the steam out of her argument, as if she hadn't expected him to apologize. Rather than say more she just rolled her eyes upward, her long lashes brushing the lenses of her heavy-framed glasses.

The elevator beeped and the door slid open. She practically ran out. Slade followed, his eyes never leaving her as she marched to her door, dug in her bag for her room key card, then slid the card into the slot. He got there just as she pushed open the door and went inside, not waiting for him.

Slade hesitated only a second, then caught the door before it closed, and went inside to try to repair the damage he'd done.

He wasn't very good at this husband thing.

Good thing he didn't plan to be one for long.

CHAPTER THREE

TAYLOR GLANCED AROUND her hotel room and wanted to scream. Those weren't her things.

They were Slade's things.

Her blood boiled. How could he have been so stupid as to have announced that they'd married? She'd just wanted to have a quiet quickie divorce. She had not wanted anyone to know. Now everyone knew. Right before Christmas. Ugh.

She threw her bag down on her bed, wincing when she recalled her laptop was inside. She clicked on her phone to see who the latest text was from. Her parents? No doubt they'd hear of her latest "major life mistake" soon enough.

The text was from Nina. Great. Had her friend said anything to Gracie? She prayed not. No way did she want Gracie to know what an idiot she had for a mother.

Married in Vegas to a virtual stranger. Brilliant example she was setting for her impressionable young daughter. Shame on her. No doubt her parents would remind her of that over and over.

I just read that you married Slade Sain! Is that true? Hello, girlfriend, have you been holding out on me? I didn't know you two were an item and I'm your best friend!

"We need to talk."

Clutching her phone, Taylor spun at Slade's words. "You need to get out of my room."

"This is our room."

"Get out," she repeated.

"Taylor." He raked his fingers through his hair. "I'm sorry I messed up. You're right that I shouldn't have said anything. Unfortunately, I did and I can't take the words back."

"I didn't want anyone to know I married you!"

Something akin to hurt flickered across his face. "Not that I want to be married any more than you do, but am I such a loser that you're ashamed of me?"

Surprised that he sincerely looked offended, Taylor sank onto the foot of the bed and sighed. "This is crazy. I don't want to argue with you, Slade. I don't want to say hurtful things. I don't want you here. I don't want to be married to you. I don't want anyone to know. I don't want to face our colleagues at this dinner tonight, knowing that they're going to be watching us."

"That's a lot of 'I don't wants,'" he mused, his voice gentler than before. He knelt down on the floor in front of her. His eyes searched hers. "What is it you do want, Taylor?"

Although he wasn't touching her, his nearness made her insides tremble. Probably from disgust that she'd married him. "To forget this ever happened and to not be married to you of all people."

"Of all people? Ouch."

"I'm sorry if I'm wounding your ego, but don't pretend that it's anything more than that," she pointed out, wishing he'd move away from her. How was she supposed to not look at him when he was right there, kneeling in front of her? "Yes, we had sex together and it was good. But we aren't in love and we won't ever be. This was a mistake and what's worse is that it's now a public mistake." Oh, how she hated that anyone knew how big a mistake she'd made. "And above all else I don't want Gracie to find out."

Confusion furrowed his brows. "Who's Gracie?"

She might as well tell him. "My daughter."

Shock registered on his face and for a moment she thought his knees were going to give way. "You have a daughter?"

"Yes, I have a daughter." She snorted. Just as well Slade wasn't the man of her dreams, because his reaction to the news of Gracie would have killed any chance he had.

Face a little blanched, he shook his head. "You don't have a kid."

He sounded so confident in his immediate response that Taylor wanted to laugh. Only she wasn't feeling very amused at the moment. She was feeling crowded with him so close to her and annoyed at his reaction.

"Sure I do." She narrowed her gaze, hoping he'd take the hint at how much she disliked him. "Perhaps you noticed the stretch marks along my hips last night when we were…" Her cheeks heated. Crazy after the things they'd done the night before that she couldn't bring herself to say the word *sex*.

But whereas she was annoyed, his expression remained shocked. "You have a beautiful body, Taylor." His tone was as gentle as it had been before, but there was a dazed look to his eyes. "And no more stretch marks than other women have with fluctuations in weight of a few pounds."

He would know.

Ugh. She hated it that her mind went to him with other women. But, then, he did go through women just as fast as Kyle had, so why wouldn't her mind go there? He was a player. A player she had married and was going to divorce.

"Puh-lease." She didn't even attempt to hide her sarcasm. "I've given birth. I know my body changes. I don't know what game you're playing, but get real."

"You have a beautiful body, Taylor," he repeated, so matter-of-fact that something cracked deep inside even if his words only meant he hadn't really looked at her.

"The body of a woman who has had a baby. If you'd paid attention last night, you'd have realized that."

He ignored her snap, stood and paced across the room. When he turned to look at her, he didn't meet her eyes. "When?"

"Gracie is six."

The skin on his face pulled tight. His jaw worked back and forth in a slow grind. "The guy in medical school?"

She nodded and couldn't hold in her bitterness. How dared Slade look at her with accusation in his eyes? He had no right to judge her! "Give the man a prize. Of course he's Gracie's father. I told you he was the only man I'd ever been with."

"There are other ways women become mothers, Taylor," he pointed out, his voice level and patient, even though color stained his cheeks at her outburst. "A strong, successful woman like yourself may have decided to have a child and sought a fertility clinic, for all I know."

Strong, successful woman? Ha, what she really wanted to do at the moment was curl up into a ball and cry. How strong and successful was that?

"Because, like I've said, you don't know me. This just proves my point."

His jaw flexed again. "A point I tried to correct on numerous occasions, but you didn't want to let me know you."

"Of course I don't want to let you know me. You've ruined my life." She was crying now. She didn't want to cry, but from the moment he'd made his comment about his "wife" during their presentation and her phone had started vibrating in her bag, she'd wanted to cry. There was no more holding the tears back. Yep, strong and successful, that was so her. Just ask her parents.

"Please, don't cry, Taylor." He sounded almost as lost as she felt. "I want to make you smile, not cry."

The last thing she wanted was to cry in front of him, but she couldn't make the tears stop. She cried for her parents and how embarrassed they were going to be by her. Again. She cried for Gracie and how her mother's moment of stupidity would affect her. And she cried for herself, that she'd been so easily led astray after six years of living an exemplary life.

"Tell me what I can do to make things better."

"Go away," she immediately informed him.

He stared at her for long moments then gave a slight nod of his head. "I'm sorry I've upset you, Taylor. I'll go for now. I have a meeting at noon anyway, but I will be back later to change for dinner. I hope you'll be ready to talk, because whether we like it or not we are married, people do know and we need a game plan on how best to deal with this so that it has the least negative impact on both our lives."

"I heard a rumor today."

Slade winced. He should have known better than to answer the phone when he'd seen who was calling. "Hey, Dad."

"Is what I'm hearing true, son?"

"Depends on what you've been hearing."

"You married?"

How did he answer his father? The best man he'd ever known through and through. A man who cherished the bonds of marriage, a man who had lost his precious wife, Slade's mother, to cancer, and carried that bond still in his heart, despite the fact he'd remarried several years back to a good woman.

Slade couldn't lie to his father. "Guess some rumors are true."

Silence ticked over the phone line.

"Have to admit I'm surprised," his father said slowly. More silence. "She pregnant?"

Slade's face heated. Not that he could blame his father for asking. Everyone who really knew him knew he'd never planned to marry, that he had dedicated his life to medicine, to finding a cure for a disease he hated.

"Not that I know of. She does have a kid, though." Hadn't that one been a shocker? Not only had he married but he'd also become an instant father. Not that it really mattered. He wasn't likely to meet Taylor's daughter. They'd divorce, pretend as if none of this had ever happened, and that would be the end of their Vegas mistake.

Which was exactly what needed to happen, so why did the image of Taylor's tears flash through his mind and make him wish life was different? That he was different?

Then again, hadn't he learned at twelve years old that wishes didn't come true? If they did, his mother would still be alive because he'd wished more than any kid had ever wished. He was sure of it.

More silence.

"For a man who just got married, you don't sound very happy. You okay, son?"

Okay? Again, the image of Taylor's tear-streaked face popped into his mind. No, he wasn't okay. He'd married a woman he wanted physically, cared for as a person and whom he didn't want to damage emotionally. "I'm fine."

"You're not in some kind of trouble, are you?" Worry weighed heavily in his father's words. "This is just so unexpected."

Slade could almost laugh. "I'm not in trouble, Dad."

At least, not the kind his father meant.

"Well, then, congratulations."

Congratulations. Because he'd gotten married. And

become a father. Why did his tie feel as if it was strangling him?

He couldn't even respond to his father's comment.

"She must be something special," his dad continued.

Images from the night before flashed through Slade's mind, images of sharing laughter with Taylor, of holding her hand as they'd climbed into the limo to leave the hotel, of kissing her in the back of the limo, of how his heart had pounded in his chest as he'd slid a ring onto her finger and promised to have and hold her forever...

Maybe he was in trouble, because as much as he didn't want to be married, didn't want to think about the fact she was a mother, he did want Taylor in his life.

If only she weren't so complicated. If only they hadn't gotten married.

"Taylor is special," he admitted, then realized just how much he'd revealed in his three softly spoken words.

"I'm glad to hear that. After your mother died you avoided getting close to anyone. I'm glad you've met someone worth the risk."

Slade's ribs threatened to crush the contents of his chest they constricted so tightly. He hadn't avoided getting close to anyone. He'd just made a conscious decision to dedicate his life to finding a cure for breast cancer. His father didn't understand that. Maybe no one could. But to Slade, doing all he could to prevent others from going through what his family had was his number-one life priority.

"Dad, I hate to cut you short." Not really a lie. He loved his father, enjoyed talking to him normally, just not today, not when he was reeling from the past twenty-four hours, from the fact he'd woken up with a wife and a kid. "But I'm on my way to my dream job interview with Grandview Pharmaceuticals." A dream job that would give him every opportunity of achieving his number-one life priority. "I'll give you a call next week when I'm back in Nashville."

"Hello, my darling, how was school today?" Taylor said into the phone to her daughter. The first rays of happiness were shining that day.

"Good," the most precious voice in the world answered. "Aunt Nina said I was very smart."

Although she was no blood relation, Gracie had called Taylor's best friend "Aunt" for as long as Taylor could remember.

"Aunt Nina is right. You are a smart girl. And a very pretty one."

Gracie giggled. "You always say that."

"Because it's true."

"I miss you, Mommy." Gracie's voice sounded somewhere between sad and pouty. Taylor could just picture her daughter's expression, see the sadness in the green eyes that were so similar to her own.

"I miss you, too." More than words could convey.

"When are you coming home?" Gracie demanded.

"I'll be flying home tomorrow evening. You and Aunt Nina are picking me up from the airport."

"Are you bringing me a prize? Aunt Nina said if I was good while you were gone that I'd get a present."

"Aunt Nina said that, did she? So close to Christmas? Well, I'm sure if she said that, then she's right."

Gracie talked to her a few minutes more, then handed the phone to Nina.

"She's something else, isn't she?" Nina immediately said into the phone.

"I hope she's not been too much trouble," Taylor told her best friend.

"Are you kidding me? I've loved having her here. She's helped me decorate my house and you know me, I'm one of those who never has things done the week after Thanksgiving. This year, I'm way ahead of the game, and she and I have had a blast getting everything done."

Taylor understood. Gracie was a blast and loved Christmas almost as much as her mother did. No doubt the little girl had garlands and lights strung all over Nina's apartment.

"Good. When they told me I would be going on this trip, my first thoughts were what I'd do about Gracie. I've never left her before."

"Are you sure your first thoughts weren't about getting an early Christmas package from a certain sexy oncologist? Or perhaps the two of you just got carried away beneath some Vegas mistletoe?"

Taylor sighed. She had known Nina would ask about Slade. Especially since she hadn't answered a single text message from Nina or any of her other friends and colleagues. What was she supposed to say? *Yes, I messed up again. It's what I'm good at when it comes to the opposite sex.*

"You might as well tell me, because you know you're going to. Best friend, remember?"

"I remember."

"So what's up with you becoming Mrs. Dr. Sexy?"

Taylor winced. "Please tell me you didn't ask me that in front of Gracie."

"She's watching her favorite television program and is totally oblivious to what I'm saying."

"Don't count on it. She picks up on a lot more than people give her credit for."

"Fine, I'll walk into the kitchen." There was a short pause. "Now, tell me if what I read was true."

"It's true."

Nina squealed. "You and Dr. Sain got married? How romantic! Tell me everything."

"There wasn't anything romantic about it." Which wasn't exactly true. Drunk or not, he'd been sweet when he'd slid the wedding ring onto her finger, had lifted her hand and placed a kiss over the gold band. Just the memory goose-bumped her skin.

"You got married to the sexiest man we know and there wasn't anything romantic about it?"

She sank her teeth into her lower lip. "Not really."

"Which means there was at least something romantic going on," Nina concluded. "Hubba-hubba. This is huge. You got married. I can't believe it."

"That makes two of us."

"This is so unlike you. You're, like, never spontaneous. I just…" Nina paused and Taylor could just imagine her friend shaking her head while she tried to make sense of what was being said. "So, tell me the details. How in the world did you and Dr. Sain get married?"

"A bunch of us had dinner, went to watch a Christmas show and then I ended up in a limo with Slade. We drove to a cheesy year-round Christmas wedding chapel and ex-changed vows. Alcohol was involved."

Nina moaned. "Please tell me it wasn't a drive-through ceremony."

"It wasn't." Although if it had been, would it really have mattered? "Santa Claus married us."

"Santa?"

"An impersonator, but, yes, Santa. There were even elves snapping pictures and throwing fake snow at us." Ugh. Tay-lor rubbed her temple. "What am I going to do, Nina? I got married last night."

"Celebrate the fact that you married the hottest guy around and will be the envy of every female at the clinic?"

"I'm serious."

"Me, too. So, how was he?"

"Nina!"

"That good, huh?"

"That good," Taylor agreed, unable to lie. "Better than any man should be." Better than she'd thought any man could be. He'd set her body aflame and made her ache for more. "But I can't stay married to him."

"Why not?"

"We never should have gotten married in the first place. We were under the influence and made a huge mistake. Besides, he is about as opposite from what I want in a man as possible."

"You want ugly, not sexy and not good in bed?"

"You know what I mean." Would her temple please stop throbbing?

"Fine. I know what you mean, but you did get married. Show a little more enthusiasm, please. Didn't you joke last year after Christmas that you should have asked Santa for a man? Well, girl, you must have been at the top of the nice list this year for Santa to have delivered Slade Sain."

She did recall joking with Nina that she should have asked Santa for a man. She didn't want to be alone, raising Gracie without a father. But she'd much rather that than to have let the wrong man into her life. She sighed.

"We're going to get a divorce just as soon as it can be arranged." She twisted the gold band on her left hand. Why hadn't she taken it off? Why did it feel seared to her very being?

"Too bad."

Taylor pulled back her phone to stare at it. "I can't believe you said that. I made a horrible mistake last night. Can you imagine what my parents are going to say?"

"Who cares what they say, Taylor? You can't keep trying to make up for disappointing them by getting pregnant out of wedlock. These are modern times. Women have kids without being married. You finished school and have made a great life for you and Gracie. If your parents can't see what a wonderful woman you are, then phooey on them."

In theory, Taylor knew her friend was right. In her heart, she hated to disappoint her parents again. They were devoutly religious, had the perfect marriage, couldn't understand how she'd let herself become pregnant out of wedlock and although they loved Gracie, they'd never let Taylor forget how disappointed they'd been.

"I know you, Taylor," Nina continued. "I'm not sure how you and Slade ended up married. There must have been some major Christmas magic in the air last night. But quit stressing and enjoy the rest of your honeymoon before planning your divorce. Reality will set in soon enough."

"I'm not on a honeymoon and reality set in first thing this morning."

"Technically, you are on your honeymoon," Nina pointed out. "You got married last night."

Taylor dropped backward onto the bed. "Crap. You're right. I'm so stupid."

"You're the least stupid person I know."

Taylor just groaned.

"Obviously, there was something between you two last night that triggered the 'I do's,'" Nina pointed out in her ever-optimistic way. "You married a superhot guy who you had really great sex with and now he's your husband. Why not quit worrying about the details and the pending legal 'I don't's and just enjoy your honeymoon?"

If only life were that easy. "You don't mean that."

"Why wouldn't I? You never do anything for yourself, Taylor. You're always working or doing things for Gracie. For the next twenty-four hours don't worry about anyone but yourself. The act is done. You're married and on your honeymoon with a hunk. Take advantage of that, of him and his skills. What's going to happen in the future is going to happen regardless of whether or not you grasp hold of what life's presented to you on a silver platter. Or, in this case, what Santa's wrapped up in a pretty bow. I say go for it, work off some long-overdue steam, and make some memories before going your separate ways."

Ugh. Her friend almost made sense. Almost. "You're not helping."

"Sure I am. I'm just not saying what your determined-to-be-a-prude ears want to hear."

"I hate it when you're right."

Nina squealed again. "So, you're going to do it? You're going to let your hair down and rock Dr. Sain's world?"

She wasn't so sure she could rock his world, but he had seemed to enjoy the night before. They had been hot.

"I'm not sure I know how to let loose anymore," she admitted, positive it was true. She enjoyed life, but all her free time did revolve around Gracie. "And I didn't say you were right that I should let my hair down. Just that what you were saying wasn't what I wanted to hear."

"You want me to tell you that you should hightail it back home and file for divorce without indulging in some fun with your husband first?"

File for divorce. Pressure squeezed her heart. People in her family didn't divorce. They didn't get pregnant out of wedlock and they didn't marry virtual strangers in Vegas and they didn't divorce. That was her family.

But she would be three for three because she would be filing for divorce. To pretend otherwise was ridiculous. She and Slade had suffered lapses of judgement, clouded by lust and alcohol. That much she could admit to. She'd wanted him last night. When he'd kissed her, she'd melted and forgotten everything but him.

"I'm waiting for an answer."

Taylor's grip on her cell phone tightened. "I'm a mother, Nina. Regardless of what I want, I can't just go around indulging in fun whenever I want to. It's not that I don't want to indulge in fun, because I do." Oh, how she wanted to imbibe more of Slade. "He was amazing. An affair with him would be amazing, but I need to end this without doing anything that might complicate things."

"Too late. Things are already complicated."

Taylor's gaze shot to the open hotel room door and the man who stood there. Crap. When had he opened the door and how much had he overheard?

"Sorry, Nina, but I've got to go." Her gaze latched on to Slade's and she refused to look away even when that's what she wanted to do. How was it he made her feel so on edge with just a look? "My husband just walked in."

CHAPTER FOUR

FRUSTRATED, SLADE STARED at the woman lying on the bed. Clicking off her phone, Taylor slowly rose to a sitting position. Which was exactly where he'd left her.

She'd left the hotel room, though. He'd gone to a presentation, had sensed her sneaking into the meeting room and had turned to catch her sliding into a seat in the back of the auditorium. When the meeting had ended, he'd glanced her way. She'd been gone.

He'd forced himself to go to all the programs he'd marked on his agenda, even though he'd had a difficult time staying focused on what the presenters had been saying. At noon, he'd had an interview with Grandview Pharmaceuticals, the company that owned Interallon and that was renowned for their headway in the fight against cancer.

John Cordova, the older man who'd interviewed him, had commented on how they needed someone dependable, someone able to make long-term commitments, to see things through, to fill the position. The man had then congratulated him on his recent marriage.

Slade had withheld the fact that his marriage wasn't a long-term commitment but a mistake. He'd gotten the impression that a divorce so quickly following his marriage wouldn't have won him any brownie points in Cordova's eyes.

His phone call with his father played through his head. His father was going to be so disappointed in him when he told him the truth.

His temple throbbed ever so slightly. He found himself wishing he could lie on the bed beside Taylor, talk to her about the interview, about his goals and dreams, about his mother and how much he missed her, about the concern in his father's voice and how he hadn't had the heart to tell him that his marriage was over before it even started either. He wanted to talk with her the way they had the night before because talking to her, being with her, had felt so right.

Too bad Taylor was staring at him as if he were a serial killer.

Last night had been different. When she'd looked at him, he'd seen something more. That something more had triggered some kind of insanity. She'd wanted to have sex with him, and that knowledge had shot madness into his veins. She'd challenged him with her condition about marriage and, gazing into her eyes, he'd lost his mind and the ability to walk away from the temptation she'd offered.

He had the feeling that before all was said and done, his insanity was going to cost him a lot more than he'd bargained for.

She cleared her throat, reminding him that he had been staring at her for way too long.

"I need to change for the dinner program."

A semiformal conference farewell that was more socializing than anything else.

"That's fine." She watched him from behind her big glasses, which he'd really like to lift off her face so he could better read her expression.

"Not really, but I guess for the next day we don't have a choice. The hotel is sold out and I don't plan to move to another hotel."

She nodded as if she'd already known. Perhaps she'd called the front desk and asked.

Slade had never been an awkward kind of person. Usually, he could come up with something funny to say, something to smooth over any situation. This wasn't any ordinary situation, though. This was him standing in a hotel room with his wife, whom he didn't want to be his wife and neither did she want to be his wife.

He raked his fingers through his hair then, shrugged.

"I'll just grab my suit and change." He opened the closet door and removed a garment bag. "I'll hurry in the bathroom so I won't interfere with you getting ready. If you're going, that is."

"I'm going."

He nodded and turned toward the bathroom.

"With you."

He paused, but didn't turn around. "Why?"

"As far as the world is concerned, we're happy newly-weds. If we go separately, we'll have to answer too many questions. I don't know about you, but I've dealt with enough questions about our marriage already today."

Slade looked up at the ceiling, counted to ten, then turned. "That's my fault. I'm sorry. You're right. I prefer not to raise questions, but even if we're together, people are going to be curious."

"You're right, but at least if we're together we can keep our story straight."

"I won't lie to anyone who asks about us."

"You're going to tell people that you married me so you could have sex with me?"

When she said it out loud, he agreed the reason sounded ridiculous. Still…

"Isn't that why most men get married?" he said, fighting to keep his tone light. "Because they want to have sex with the woman they are marrying? I definitely want to have sex with you, Taylor."

"I suppose so," she responded, ignoring his last comment. "Or we could just tell them that we were drunk and didn't realize what we were doing."

He certainly hadn't been thinking clearly, but he distinctly recalled exchanging vows with her, promising to care for her forever, to cherish her and yet they were planning to end things before they'd even got started.

He stared at her, wishing he could read whatever was running through that sharp mind of hers. "Shall we tell them we married because we were drunk or because we wanted to have sex?"

Her gaze darted about the room as if seeking the answer somewhere within the four walls. Finally, she shrugged. "Take your pick. Both are true."

Taylor pulled her dress out of the closet. Her gaze settled on Slade's clothes hanging next to hers.

Other than her father, she'd never lived with a man, so seeing the mix of Slade's belongings with hers had her pausing, had her eyes watering up again.

What an emotional roller coaster she rode.

Her safe, secure world felt as if it was crumbling around her.

She'd quit taking chances years ago. Had quit living in some ways. Oh, she lived through Gracie, but what about for herself? Nina was right. She didn't do anything for herself, just lived in a nice controlled environment where she planned for all contingencies.

Too bad she hadn't had a backup plan for an unexpected Vegas Christmas wedding.

While Slade was in the bathroom, she changed into her dress, took her hair down from its tight pin-back and pulled it up into a looser hold. She had her contacts in her purse, but wasn't sure what it would say if she put them in when she almost always wore her glasses.

How ridiculous was she being? What did it matter what she looked like?

Still, she dug in her purse and put in her contacts. She was just blinking them into place when Slade stepped out of the bathroom.

Wearing only his suit pants.

Taylor's body responded to his bare chest like a Pavlov dog to its stimulus. The man was beautiful.

And hers.

Not for long, but at this moment Slade Sain was hers more than any other man had ever been.

Just as she was his more than any other woman had ever been his.

Maybe.

She frowned because she really didn't know that to be true. "Have you been married before?"

Her question obviously caught him off guard. "No. Why? Have you? Never mind, silly question with that one-guy thing. You haven't."

"No, I haven't," she agreed, averting her gaze from his intense blue one. "I just wondered if you had."

Despite the tension between them, he grinned with wry humor. "Wondering if I make marrying a habit?"

Exactly. "Something like that."

He slipped his crisp blue shirt on one arm at a time, then buttoned his cuffs. "I've never been married before." He paused, stared at her with a serious look. "I've never even contemplated marriage."

Her feet wanted to shuffle but she somehow kept them still. "Why not?"

Smoothing out his shirt, he shrugged. "I have other plans for my life besides a wife, two point five kids and a white picket fence."

Her chest spasmed at just how different they really were, because once upon a time she'd dreamed of being a wife with kids and that proverbial white picket fence. "I'm sorry."

"Don't be. We're human and made a mistake. People do it all the time."

He wasn't telling her anything she didn't know. So why did his words shoot arrows into her chest? "Not me. Not like this." She winced. "I mean, obviously I have made mistakes before, but I thought I'd learned better than to make this kind."

"Marrying me makes you realize you haven't evolved as far as you'd hoped?"

"Something like that. We were practically strangers and got married." Sighing, she closed her eyes. "Before last night you probably didn't even know my eye color."

"I knew."

His answer was so quick, so confident, that she couldn't question the truth of his response.

Staring at him, she asked, "How?"

He shoved his hands in his pants pockets. "I know more about you than you seem to think."

"Like what?"

"Like how much you love coffee."

She rolled her eyes. "Lots of people love coffee, so that's just a generic assumption that could be said about a high percentage of the population."

He shook his head. "You like two teaspoons of cream and one packet of sweetener."

She frowned. That was how she took her coffee. For a moment he had her, but she hadn't made it through medical school by being easily duped. "You saw me make my coffee this morning."

"You're right," he agreed, walking back to the closet to pick up his sleek black dress shoes. "I did. But I already knew how you took your coffee because I make a point to be near the lounge when you go for your morning cup at eight forty-five every day."

That he knew what time she took a coffee break was a little uncanny. Maybe she was more easily duped than she'd realized.

"What else do you know?"

"That you smile a lot at work. That your patients love you. That Mr. Gonzales has a crush on you."

"Mr. Gonzales has a crush on every female who works at the clinic," she pointed out about one of her favorite patients. The older man came in weekly for his lung-cancer treatments and the staff adored him.

"You're his favorite."

"Maybe." She watched Slade sit on the bed and slip on his socks, then his shoes. "What else?"

He lowered his foot back to the carpet but remained seated on the bed. Good. She didn't want him towering over her. "Blue is your favorite color. Not a regular blue, a turquoise blue."

"How would you know that?"

"Because you wear that color more than any other."

He knew what she wore? Why would he have noticed her clothes? Especially since she usually had her lab coat on over whatever she wore?

"You're starting to creep me out a little."

"Surely you noticed that I'd been trying to get to know you for months. I start a conversation and you end it with a few words. I walk up to you and you walk off. I ask you out, you say no."

Of course she'd said no. He wasn't her type.

"You talk to all the women at the clinic," she pointed out.

"I talk to everyone at the clinic. Not just the women."

"True, but you're a horrible flirt."

He looked amused. "I've never made any bones about

the fact that I enjoy women but that I have no intentions of settling down. I wanted to take you out, for us to enjoy our time together, and then us both move on to what we really want in life."

Taylor gulped. He sounded so much like Kyle…only Kyle had never been so honest with her, had never told her that he'd been seeing other women, that she hadn't been special. Quite the opposite. He'd made her believe she'd been his one and only.

"I date, Taylor, and I have flirted with women in the past. But for however long it takes for our lawyers to sort out this mess, I will be faithful to you. You have my word on that."

Something in his voice rang of truth, but she couldn't think straight for the heat flushing her face.

"I wasn't… I mean… I haven't slept with a man for over six years so it's a safe bet to say that for however long we're married I'll be faithful to you as well."

From his seat on the bed, he stared at her. "You're a young, beautiful woman, Taylor. Why is it that you've not had sex in six years?"

She gave him a classic "duh" look. "Because I have Gracie."

Obviously, he knew nothing about raising a six-year-old girl, about being a good mother, about trying to live up to her parents' expectations of her to be a responsible woman. Apparently.

"Being a mother doesn't make you less of a woman, Taylor. Or make you have fewer physical needs."

"Being a mother means I have to make responsible decisions because my choices don't just affect me, but her as well." With each word she said, bits of her carefully constructed facade crumbled. "She's not going to understand that I got married while in Vegas."

"Don't tell her."

Taylor bit the inside of her lower lip. He was right. She

could just not tell Gracie. She and Slade would divorce and her daughter would never know the difference. Only her daughter really did have big ears. What if Gracie found out and *she* hadn't been the one to tell her?

She didn't begin to fool herself that her parents wouldn't find out. They'd be so disappointed. Again. Not that they didn't love Gracie, but that Taylor had once again not followed their norm would earn another tsk from her mother and another sigh from her father.

"What if Gracie overheard something or someone else told her? That wouldn't be fair to her."

His expression was pinched. "I'm sure you know best."

"Clearly not."

"Or you wouldn't have married me?" His tone held wry humor.

"I'm sure for other women and under different circumstances, a woman marrying you wouldn't be considered a bad thing. But not me."

Sliding his hands into his pants pockets, he frowned. "Why not?"

Seriously? He was asking her why not? The man was the office playboy and she was the quiet mouse.

"You have to admit you aren't exactly daddy material."

Daddy material. Not that Slade wanted to be daddy material, but Taylor's words stung. So, he had absolutely no experience being a father and had no desire to learn. That didn't mean he'd be a bad one. Every guy started somewhere.

For her to judge him so unfairly irked.

"Has it occurred to you that I could already have a child on the way?"

Her face paled to an icky green shade. "We made more than one mistake last night, didn't we?"

Slade's chest threatened to turn inside out. His heart

pounded and his throat constricted at the ramifications of what they were discussing. "If you are pregnant, Taylor, I'll take care of you and our child."

Taylor surprised him by sinking onto the bed beside him. "Gracie is the best thing that ever happened to me, but I don't want another kid, Slade. Not like this."

Which meant she did want more kids someday. No doubt she was a wonderful mother. Too bad he didn't want a wife and kids because he couldn't imagine anyone better than Taylor.

He sighed at how different they were tonight with each other compared to the previous night. The night before they'd both been carefree, full of lust and passion for each other.

"I wish we could go back to last night."

"Why?" she whispered from beside him. Why she whispered he wasn't sure, but somehow her low voice seemed exactly right.

"Last night I wasn't your enemy."

Her head fell forward and she stared at her hands, no doubt at the shiny thin band on her left hand. With the way she felt, why was she still wearing the cheap strip of gold?

"You aren't my enemy, Slade."

Her words should have comforted him, but her tone wasn't complimentary.

"You're right," he conceded. "I'm your husband. That's worse."

"I'm sorry." She sounded as if she truly was.

"Tell me, Taylor, would things have been different this morning if we'd had sex without getting married?"

She shrugged. "I don't think I would have had sex without marriage. Not really. After I got pregnant with Gracie, and Kyle signed away his rights, I vowed I wouldn't give myself to another man unless he married me first."

She toyed with the gold band on her finger, then stood and walked across the room, turning to look at where he sat. "Foolishly, I equated marriage as being loved truly and completely." She laughed a little, but there wasn't any real humor in the sound. She spread her arms and gave a smile that was more sad than anything else. "Look at me now, desperate for a divorce less than twenty-four hours after getting married. Guess that old saying about being careful what you wish for definitely applies in this case."

Slade couldn't bear the self-condemnation that shone in her eyes. He crossed the room to stand in front of her. He knew better than to take her in his arms, although that's exactly what he wanted to do. Instead, he traced his finger along her hairline, then cupped her chin. Her eyes, unfettered by her glasses, glittered up at him like big and beautiful emeralds.

Guilt hit him. She wanted exactly the opposite from life. She wanted that white picket fence and two point five kids. Instead, she was married to him.

"I am looking, Taylor. I see a woman who fascinates me, a woman who is strong and good and beautiful. A woman who turns me on and makes my blood boil. We aren't enemies. We made a mistake in getting married, but we're in agreement on ending the marriage. Our mistake is a fixable one." Did he really believe his own words? He wasn't sure. He just didn't want their mistake ruining her life. "I want to spend the evening with you without what happened last night as a barrier between us. Even if just for tonight."

She considered him a few moments, emotions playing across her face. "Just for tonight? Pretend that everything is okay? Why?"

"Why not? What do we have to lose by putting forward a united front? We both want a divorce. We're on the same page. Why suffer through the evening alone when even

despite our emotional turmoil the physical is still booming between us?"

She blinked up at him. "It's what Nina said I should do…
I want to, Slade, but… Okay."

A flicker of emotion he couldn't label burned to life
within him. Crazy because the last thing he needed was
to get more entangled with Taylor. A voice in his head reminded him that he was married to her. How much more
entangled could one get?

CHAPTER FIVE

SLADE WAS THE perfect date. Maybe because he was trying so hard. Taylor knew he was trying and appreciated the effort he was exerting to make her evening as stress-free as possible, especially when she knew he wasn't any happier about their current circumstances than she was.

The meal had been the usual conference menu of a spinach salad, slightly rubbery chicken, green beans and potatoes. For dessert, they'd had a key lime pie that had been quite good.

The final speech of the conference had finished and now the attendees were mingling, with a few heading onto the dance floor and others to the main section of the hotel to gamble.

"You guys want to come with us to the blackjack table?" Dr. Ryan joined the conversation they'd been having with a couple of oncologists from Gainesville, Florida.

Slade's gaze connected with hers and she shook her head.

"Sorry, bud," Slade told his colleague. "But Taylor and I won't be doing any gambling tonight. I was just about to take her out onto the dance floor."

The dance floor? Taylor wanted to protest, but Cole Ryan was watching her reaction a bit too closely so she just smiled.

"Ha, marriage is a gamble every night," Dr. Ryan joked as Slade took Taylor's hand and led her from the group.

"I never knew he had such a sour disposition regarding marriage," Taylor mused, trying to focus on the other man and not on how good it felt for Slade to be holding her hand, on how her heart was racing at his nearness, at how her skin burned at his touch.

"Perhaps it's only your marriage to me that sours his disposition."

Taylor frowned. "You think he…? No, I mean he asked me out once, but that was a long time ago. We just didn't hit it off that way."

"That way?" Slade's face darkened and if Taylor didn't know better she'd think he was jealous. But that made no sense. They had no real ties to each other, only plans to divorce as soon as possible.

"You know, like…" She paused. She'd been going to say like she and Slade had because the biggest problem she'd had with Cole Ryan had been that there had been no sparks. Otherwise he'd been a decent guy who had met most of the criteria on her Mr. Right list.

Slade had the sparks covered and then some. Right now, with her hand in his as he led her onto the dance floor, she knew exactly how they'd ended up where they had the night before. When he touched her, fireworks went off inside her body. Last night he'd had the whole Fourth of July show exploding within her.

She swallowed, willed her body to not give in to its carnal reactions to Slade, to focus on anything but the fire between them.

Dinner had gone well. He'd had intelligent conversations with the other people at their table, had included her, asked her opinions, and sat back and let her give those opinions with admiration in his eyes. He'd been attentive, pulling out her chair, touching her frequently, smiling at her often.

When an overly pompous member of their table had gone on and on about the latest article he'd written about the denucleation of a cloned T-cell, they'd shared a look that had spoken volumes without saying a word, because they'd known what the other had been thinking. His wink had reached inside her and touched something tender.

If she hadn't known he was Dr. Slade Sain, playboy extraordinaire, if she hadn't made the mistake of marrying him, she might think he was someone she would like to date. Which was kind of silly since she was already married to him. And he *was* Dr. Slade Sain, playboy extraordinaire.

He'd said he'd be faithful for however long they were married. An easy promise since they planned to talk to divorce attorneys as soon as they returned home. Still, tonight, at this moment, it was easy to pretend that their attraction was special, that the future was full of wonderful possibilities.

What was it Nina had said? To let loose and enjoy herself? That she was married to a hunk so why not enjoy it for the rest of their Vegas stay? To worry about tomorrow... tomorrow.

Slade pulled her into his arms and, her arms around him, she buried her face into the curve of his neck. He smelled so good. So perfectly male.

He was perfectly male. His body. His mind. His sense of humor.

She wanted to cry. She wanted to forget who she was and who she had to be. She wanted to be that woman Nina had told her to be, even if only until she had to fly home tomorrow evening.

Slade drew back and looked down at her. "You okay?"

She nodded and toyed with where his hair brushed the back of his collar. "This pretend stuff isn't so bad."

One corner of his mouth lifted. "Agreed. You are very beautiful, Taylor. No pretending."

Her breath caught because he looked at her as if she were the most beautiful woman he'd ever seen. How could he look at her that way? As if she was the only woman who existed?

"Thank you. You aren't bad yourself." She attempted to lighten the heavy longing clouding her good intentions.

"If you could read my mind, you'd think every thought in my head was bad."

"Oh?"

He shook his head.

"You can't say something like that and then not tell me what you were thinking."

"Says who?"

"Me."

His lips twitched. "I'm thinking that perhaps holding you in my arms in public wasn't such a good idea, because having you pressed against my body makes me respond in a very nonpublic way."

"I noticed that."

"Kinda hard to miss."

"Did you say hard?"

His mouth was close to hers. So very close. "Isn't this about the point in our conversation where we got into trouble last night?"

"The point where we started being suggestive?" she whispered against his lips. For twenty-four hours she could let go and just be a woman who was with a man who turned her on, a woman who was with a man who wanted her.

"The point where I wanted you so badly I couldn't think of anything else but having you."

"There's only one problem." She stared into his eyes, seeing passion and something so intense it stole her breath. For twenty-four hours he was hers. Twenty-four hours and what they did wouldn't change anything. Twenty-four hours and then they'd return to reality.

"What's that?"

"I won't sleep with anyone who isn't my husband."

"And your husband?" he breathed against her lips. "You'll sleep with him?"

"Sleep? If you think we will be sleeping anytime soon, then you aren't nearly as turned on as I am."

He kissed her. Right there on the dance floor his mouth covered hers for a gentle kiss that was so potent it demanded everything she had yet gave so much more.

When he pulled back, he leaned his forehead against hers. "If we do this, nothing changes between us. We'll still end this as soon as possible. You know that, right?"

Taylor was pretty sure all that could change between them already had. They couldn't ever go back to the way things had been. With the way he was looking at her, she didn't want to. Tomorrow night they'd be back in Tennessee, reality would take over and they'd never have this moment again.

Nothing would ever be the same and if she thought about it that would terrify her.

So, instead, she clasped her hands with his and told him with her eyes what she wanted.

The night before they'd been frantic for each other.

Now, back in their hotel room, Taylor felt just as frantic, but was enjoying Slade's slow stripping of her way too much to urge him to go faster.

She wavered between eyes closed in ecstasy and open to view the fantasy of his caresses. She watched him in the dresser mirror. He stood behind her, his hand on her dress, his other at her waist as he slowly slid her zipper down her back. His mouth trailed kisses in the wake of exposed skin, causing goose bumps along her spine that scattered outward in pleasured awareness of his gentle caress.

He reached the curve of her spine and slid his hands beneath the silky material. "You aren't wearing a bra."

"There was no need. The dress has built-in support."

"Lucky dress to be next to these." His hands were now on her bare breasts, covering them, cupping them as he straightened to kiss her shoulder. His gaze met hers in the mirror as his lips spread more kisses along her nape. "Very lucky dress, but it's got to go."

He maneuvered the material to where it fell to her waist, then slipped the dress over her hips to leave her standing in her black lace panties.

His body pressed against her from behind, he examined her reflection. "You are so beautiful, Taylor."

"Don't look too close or you'll see my many flaws," she half teased, self-conscious of the changes pregnancy had left on her body. She didn't have a lot of stretch marks, true, but she did have them.

Slade spun her, knelt in front of her and brushed his lips over the small silvery streaks that marred her abdomen near her right hip.

"You are beautiful. All of you," he praised, his lips moving to her left side and kissing the tiny silver lines there.

Taylor shuddered, her hands going to his shoulders as her knees threatened to buckle.

Weak as water. She'd heard the expression used in the past but had never really understood the term until this moment. Her legs were weak as water, threatening to let her spill to the floor in a gooey gush.

His tongue traced over her belly, darting into her belly button. His hands molded her to him, helping to support her.

He moved higher up her belly, causing her breath to suck in as his face brushed against her breasts.

She closed her eyes and just felt. She felt every touch, every caress, every move of his body against hers.

She felt every emotion, every ounce of passion, every demand for more.

When she could stand no more of his sweet, torturous foreplay, she tugged on his shoulders. "Please, Slade. Please!"

He stood, took her mouth with his, and kissed her so hard that she thought they might always stay that way, that their locked lips knew something far beyond what their minds did, that they belonged together.

Not breaking their kiss, he lifted her. She wrapped her legs around his waist, not liking that his pants were in the way, not liking that he was still so dressed when she was so naked.

When he lowered her onto their bed, breaking their kiss, she immediately tugged his shirt free from his waistband. "I want to touch you."

"Good." His breathing was heavy. "I want you to touch me."

"I mean now. Before. I want to touch you the way you touched me."

His hands stilled from where he'd been unbuttoning his shirt. "I'm all yours."

Taylor sneaked a peek at the man sitting in the airplane seat next to her. He'd offered the guy who had originally had the seat a hundred dollars to swap and the guy had traded without hesitation. Currently, Slade's nose was buried in the program he was reading on his computer tablet.

"Quit looking at me like that."

"Sorry." Heat flushed her face. "Like what?"

"Like you are trying to dissect me."

"Sorry. That wasn't my intention."

Slade clicked a button on the tablet, closing the program he'd been reading, then turned to her. "What was your intention?"

"Pardon?"

"Why were you looking at me just then?"

"I…I don't know."

"Yes, you do. Tell me."

"That's ridiculous."

"You were thinking about this weekend, about all the things that happened between us, and you were wondering about what's going to happen once this plane lands," he supplied for her.

"You're wrong."

His brow arched.

"At least, partially. I was thinking about this weekend and what happened between us, but I already know what's going to happen once this plane lands."

He waited.

"Nina and my daughter will be waiting to pick me up. I'll go home with them. You and I will get divorced and will forget this weekend ever happened."

He digested her words for a few minutes, seeming to accept her prediction. His lips thinned to a straight line. "Except for the whole getting-married thing, I don't regret this weekend, Taylor."

Her heart fluttered at his words, but she tried not to read too much into his comment. Did she regret the weekend? The past twenty-four hours had been amazing. Waking up in his arms and making love first thing this morning, then again in the shower before they'd checked out of the hotel had been amazing. Dealing with the ramifications of what they'd done at the North Pole Christmas Bliss Wedding Chapel was what wasn't so amazing.

She tried not to touch her ring. She failed.

"We were in Vegas. People do silly things in Vegas. We'll be home soon and the best thing we can do is forget any of this ever happened," she whispered, even though she seriously doubted any of the surrounding passengers could hear their conversation.

"I basically agree. A wife and kid aren't on my agenda, but I'll admit—" he gave her a sexy grin "—you're going to be hard to forget."

Not nearly as hard as it was going to be to forget him.

"Maybe we could still see each other occasionally," he suggested.

Oh, how he tempted her. But to delay the inevitable would only complicate an already bad situation even further.

"We had a fun little fling this weekend, but when this plane lands everything goes back to normal. I'm a single mother with a very busy schedule. I just don't have the time or inclination for an affair with you."

"We're not exactly having an affair," he pointed out. "We're married."

"A marriage we both want ended as soon as possible. Santa Claus married us in a building that looked like a life-sized gingerbread house. Elves sold us our rings, took our picture, witnessed the ceremony. Who knows if our certificate is even real? It's probably not since it was issued after normal business hours."

Guilt hit her. She sounded crude and uncaring. But, really, what did he expect? They didn't even know each other. Not beyond the physical. That she knew quite well. She'd saved every pore on his body to memory because she'd known she'd want to pull out the memories and relive them.

"It's something to have our lawyers look into. If it's not real that would certainly simplify things.

"I don't get that lucky," she mused, thinking how great it would be if their wedding turned out to not be a legally binding union.

He took her hand into his. "You're right. Our wedding ceremony being a sham would be in both of our best interests."

She'd just said the same thing. So why did hearing him say the words cut into her chest? Make her want to hold on to his hand all the tighter?

She might have only spent two nights in his arms, but part of her felt he was hers. No doubt her feelings were just associations to the phenomenal sex they'd had. Women had been associating great sex with emotions for centuries. He'd done great things to her body in bed and out of bed. Of course she'd feel possessive of him.

What was she thinking? She wasn't thinking, that was the problem. That had been the problem all weekend.

"Physically, I still want you, Taylor. I'd like to see you again."

Physically, she still wanted him, too, but she couldn't afford an affair with Slade. "I've more to think about than just myself."

"Your daughter?"

"Yes. Gracie is my whole world. I won't expose her to this mess I've created."

"I'm really not interested in meeting your daughter or becoming a part of your day-to-day life."

"Just in meeting up with me for sex?"

"I guess that makes me sound like a jerk," he admitted, and she wasn't going to argue with him. He sounded exactly as she'd known all along.

"It doesn't make you sound like someone I want to invest more time in."

"I guess I understand that, considering you do have a kid." The look on his face said he didn't really. Or maybe it was just the prospect of her being a mother that caused the look of disgust. "I'm being selfish in that I want you in my life still."

"Just without the entanglements of marriage and my daughter?"

His grin was self-deprecating. "There I go sounding like a jerk again."

"I'll contact a lawyer and we'll divorce quietly. We both know it was a mistake, that we can chalk this weekend up to a great sexual adventure, and we can go about undoing our mistake in a completely civil way."

He studied her a moment, then nodded. "I guess you're right. I just…"

"You just what?"

"I enjoyed our time together."

His words struck deep inside her.

"That makes two of us," she admitted. She'd had such high hopes that someday she would find the right man, would marry and have a happy little family. The house, white picket fence, children, happiness.

"Seems a little sad when we are so physically compatible," Slade interrupted her thoughts.

"Perhaps." A lot sad, really. "But better we be logical and end this now than risk things getting messier."

He took her hand into his, laced their fingers and traced over her skin with his thumb. "Things would only get messier if we let them. As long as we knew the score, that we weren't long term, we could give each other great pleasure."

Taylor sighed. If Gracie hadn't been involved, she might give in to the temptation deep within her. But her daughter was involved. Gracie needed stability. Not a mother who ran out and got married in Vegas to the office playboy, planned to divorce him but wanted to keep having sex with him until the divorce was final. Slade made her act out of character, made her behave rashly. She owed it to Gracie, to her daughter's future and well-being, to make responsible choices.

Having an affair with Slade wouldn't be responsible.

"Therein lies the problem. I don't want to continue this in hopes it wouldn't get messier." When he started to interrupt her, she rushed on. "Admittedly, it would be a pleasurable mistake but a mistake all the same. We were in Vegas and got caught up in the silliness. Let's end things now while we can still be civil to each other and this, hopefully, won't ruin our ability to work in the same clinic together. I really like my job and don't want to have to look for something else."

"Mommy!" Arms spread wide, a pint-size fairy princess ran toward Taylor. "I missed you."

The moment she was off the escalator that led down to the airport's baggage area Taylor knelt down to her daughter's level and scooped her into her arms. She kissed the top of Gracie's head, breathing in the fresh baby-shampoo scent of her blond curls. "I missed you, too!"

"You shouldn't go away for so long ever again," Gracie scolded.

"It was only three nights."

"That's too long."

Three nights in which a lifetime of changes had taken place because as much as she told herself she would put the weekend's events behind her, it wouldn't be that simple. If only.

She hugged Gracie tightly. "You're right. That was way too long to be away from my best girl."

"I'm your only girl," Gracie reminded her with a giggle. "Aunt Nina and I put up her Christmas tree and she let me hang the ornaments and a stocking with my name on it. Do you think Santa will leave my presents at Aunt Nina's house?"

"Maybe Santa will leave you a present at Aunt Nina's, too, but Santa knows where to leave your presents." Taylor squeezed her daughter and kissed the top of her head again. Emotion clogged her throat at how much this talkative little girl meant to her. "That's some outfit you have going there."

Taylor raised her gaze to Nina.

"What can I say?" Nina smiled and shrugged. "She wanted to be a fairy princess. Who am I to deny her inner princess?"

"I am a fairy princess," Gracie corrected Taylor's best friend and nurse, then redirected her attention to her mother. "Aunt Nina wouldn't wear her princess clothes because she thought she might get 'rested, but I think mine are beautiful." Gracie spun as if to prove her point, curtsied, then snuggled back to where her mother still crouched down.

"Oh?" Taylor arched a brow at her friend, smothering a laugh at the mental image of Nina wearing a fairy-princess outfit in the Nashville airport.

"I figured someone would call airport security if I came in dressed like a cartoon princess," Nina admitted, gesturing to her jeans. "I tried to convince Gracie I was a princess in disguise, but she wasn't buying it."

"Princesses don't wear jeans when they're in disguise," Gracie reported matter-of-factly, her fingers going to Taylor's hair and twining beneath the pulled-back strands. Playing with Taylor's hair was something Gracie had started as a baby while nursing and something she reverted to almost always if she was in Taylor's lap or snuggled up next to her. Taylor treasured the bond with her daughter and dropped another kiss to her forehead.

"Did you bring me a present from Vegas?"

Taylor's stomach plummeted. Gracie's present. How could she have forgotten Gracie's present? She'd even mentioned to Slade this morning that she needed to stop by one of the hotel's many gift shops and pick out something special for her daughter. Instead, she'd gotten wet and wild with him in the shower and completely forgotten.

She stared into her daughter's wide expectant green eyes. Oh, yeah, she'd been irresponsible this weekend, had been a big disappointment to her child and would be mailing off her application for Worst Mom in the History of the World later this week. Yet another reason why ending things with Slade was the right decision. He made her forget things she'd never have forgotten otherwise. "I—"

"I think this is for you."

Taylor almost toppled over at the sound of Slade's voice. They'd purposely parted at the gate. He hadn't wanted to meet Gracie any more than she'd wanted him to. He'd leaned in, kissed her cheek and told her he'd had a great time, minus the whole wedding thing. She'd laughed, nodded and ducked into the bathroom to hide the moisture that had stung her eyes.

Still in a kneeling position, she glanced up at where he stood, his overnight bag draped across his shoulder, his clothes impeccable, not looking at all as if he'd been on a plane for several hours. He held a fuzzy stuffed bear wearing a pink tutu and a glitzy pink crown on her head.

Where had he gotten that? One of the Nashville airport gift shops? Had to be. He'd been at her side at the Vegas airport.

His face was pale and yet had pink splotches on his cheeks as he stared at her daughter. He eyed her as if she might morph into a monster and devour him any moment.

Gracie, never one to be too shy, spotted the bear and grinned with excitement. "I think you're right."

Her tone sounded so mature, so confident that had it not been Slade holding the bear, had he not been looking in such a shell-shocked and leery way at the little girl, Taylor would have laughed at her daughter's expression and words. Instead, all she could think was that she wanted to grab Gracie and run far away from him.

Which made no sense.

She didn't need to protect her daughter from Slade. Yet that's exactly the instinct that rose to the surface. Not that there was any need. He looked ready to bolt at any second. He should have stayed away.

"Hello, Dr. Sain," Nina greeted him, looking quite intrigued. "I hear congratulations are in order."

Taylor wanted to kick her friend, but had to settle for a warning look. Gracie's fingers left her hair and moved to hold Taylor's hand as she eagerly eyed the bear.

"Thanks," he answered, some color coming back to his face. Regaining his composure, he flashed a smile that would weaken many a female knee.

Good thing Taylor was already kneeling down because her knees wobbled.

Gracie felt her shift and frowned at her. "Mommy, are you okay?"

Not really, but she couldn't tell her daughter that because Gracie would want to know what was wrong. What could she say? That she'd spent the past two days having wild Vegas sex with this man, her husband, but now she just wanted to go back to her ordinary life and forget anything out of the ordinary had happened?

Was that what she wanted? What she really wanted? Or did she want something more? Something that made no logical sense whatsoever? Something he'd never give her and so she didn't dare even think it? If she'd had the slightest doubt, seeing his reaction to Gracie would have reconfirmed that he wasn't right for them.

"Mommy is fine, Princess Gracie." This came from Nina, who apparently took pity on Taylor's inability to talk. "She's just had a long flight home from Vegas and is a little tired."

When no one made a move, Gracie gestured toward the bear that an also silent Slade still held. "Did my mommy bring that for my present?"

Perhaps she wasn't the only one struck speechless because, despite the smile he'd flashed, Slade just stared at

Gracie as if he'd never seen a kid before, then tentatively held out the bear to her.

First getting a nod from Taylor, Gracie took the bear and cuddled it. "Thank you. I love her. I'm going to call her Vegas, Princess Vegas, because she came all the way in an airplane to live with me."

Slade opened his mouth, probably to tell Gracie the truth, that he'd bought the bear in a Nashville gift shop, but Nina stopped him.

"Gracie, that's a really cool name for a really cool bear. Can I see her?"

Gracie hugged the bear, but then showed it to Nina, pointing out a tiny pink bejeweled necklace on the toy.

"Thank you." Taylor finally found words as she straightened.

His gaze shifted to Gracie.

Taylor cast a nervous glance toward her daughter, who was still busy checking out the bear with Nina. Her friend was trying to look as if she wasn't paying attention to Taylor and Slade, but was, no doubt, soaking up every word.

His expression was serious. His blue eyes dark and intense. "I felt responsible for you not having her gift."

Taylor swallowed. "It's my fault, not yours. I let myself get distracted."

"I'm sorry, Taylor." His gaze held hers, then shifted back to Gracie. "So sorry."

"Mommy, can we go home now?" Gracie interrupted, tugging on Taylor's hand. "I want to show you the picture Aunt Nina helped me paint and we need to find a Christmas tree. Aunt Nina's is so beautiful."

Nina shot her an apologetic look at not being able to keep Gracie distracted longer.

Taylor didn't care. She didn't want to be having this conversation with Slade.

"I'm sorry, too." Taylor spotted her suitcase rolling out

on the nearby baggage carousel. "Now, if you'll excuse me, I'm going to grab my bag and go home to catch up with my daughter. Goodbye."

Just before it got too far for her to catch this time around, Taylor pulled her bag off the rolling contraption. She smiled at Nina and Gracie, and pretended everything was great. "Let's go. Not sure I'm up to going out to buy a Christmas tree tonight, but I can't wait to get home and see that picture."

First waving goodbye to a stiff Slade and thanking him again for her bear, Gracie slipped her hand into Taylor's and began talking a mile a minute, as she usually did.

Too bad Taylor wasn't able to keep from looking back when they reached the glass doors to take them out of the airport.

Slade still stood right where they'd left him.

CHAPTER SIX

SLADE LOOKED OVER his patient's labs. Her white blood cell count was too low to administer her chemotherapy.

"We'll recheck your levels next week and administer then if you're strong enough to handle the treatment."

The pale woman nodded. Twenty-three years old and fighting leukemia with all she had, Brittany Tremaine hadn't lost her hair yet, but was experiencing other devastating side effects of her therapy. "Whatever you say, Doc."

The young man beside her, holding her hand, leaned forward. "What do we do in the meantime?"

"In the meantime, she needs to rest, eat healthily, build her strength back up." Slade stood, shook the man's hand, then gave Brittany a hug that he hoped conveyed encouragement and compassion. It was what he felt for the young woman, what he felt for so many of his patients.

Oncology wasn't a profession for the faint of heart.

When his mother had died of breast cancer when he'd been twelve, Slade had become obsessed with fighting cancer. He'd held fundraisers at his school, become an advocate at raising awareness of the deadly disease, had known that he'd go into a profession where he could continue that battle and make a difference to where other kids didn't have to face the same thing he had.

Although there was a great emotional burden that came

along with his job, there was also a great deal of joy and satisfaction with each success story. He prayed Brittany would be one of those success stories.

"I'll see you around the same time next week. If anything changes negatively before then, come back in sooner," he advised, tearing off a piece of paper from a preprinted pad he kept in his pocket. A motivational quote was on the sticky note.

Slade gave a quote to each and every patient he saw each and every time he saw them. Perhaps a silly habit, but he'd had several patients comment on his messages, that they'd kept them posted on their mirrors. One survivor told him she'd kept the quotes in a scrapbook and now shared the book with others when the need arose.

Slade knew all too well about saving quotes. He had a stack of them himself. He'd not looked at them in several years, but last night, when he'd gotten home from Vegas and unpacked his suitcase, he'd pulled the shoebox he kept the notes in out from his closet. He'd flipped through the protective album he'd placed them in years ago as a young boy, and he read each and every one. Right up until the shaky handwriting had become almost illegible.

Then he'd called his dad.

When he'd gone to bed he'd been an emotional wreck in some ways, but in others he'd known exactly what he had to do. Although he couldn't stay married to Taylor, he didn't want to hurt his family, or hers. Most importantly, he didn't want to hurt Taylor.

The best way to achieve all of that was for them to pretend they were happily married, then, when he hopefully got the job with Grandview, he could leave as the bad guy, and she'd not suffer any negativity from their impromptu wedding. Should he tell her about his interview? Perhaps, but at this point, he suspected she'd use the fact that he might be leaving to be that much more on guard with him.

Taylor already aced on guard so he'd just wait and tell her if the need arose.

"Dr. Sain?" Nina interrupted his thoughts. "Sorry to bother you, but Taylor is in a room with a patient and I need someone to check a patient now, please. I believe she's having a reaction to her infusion medication."

Slade shoved his nostalgia down and followed Taylor's nurse to where a woman who appeared to be in her early fifties sat in one of the special recliners in the infusion lounge.

"Hello, Mrs. Jamison. My name is Dr. Sain. Your nurse tells me you aren't feeling well?"

"I'm itching all over." The woman scratched her neck to prove her point.

Slade skimmed his fingers over her exposed skin. Large red welts were forming. He turned to Nina. "Go ahead and stop her infusion. As long as she isn't allergic to the medications, give her an antihistamine and a shot of steroid."

"Yes, Dr. Sain."

He turned back to the patient. "Any difficulty breathing?"

The woman shook her head. "No, I just itch like crazy and feel a little light-headed."

He examined the woman thoroughly, waited for Nina to administer the medications he'd ordered. "Recheck all her vitals in fifteen minutes and pull me out of a room if you need to."

Nina nodded. "I'll let Taylor know what's going on with her as soon as she's out of her patient room."

As if she'd known they were discussing her, Taylor walked over to them. "Hi, sweetie. Tell me what's happening."

Mrs. Jamison began telling her about how she'd started itching during her infusion.

"Hmm, this is the second time you've received this

particular medication. I don't recall any problems with the last infusion. Were there any after you got home?"

Scratching, the woman shook her head. "I felt fine, but I don't now." She cleared her throat. "I feel like my skin is on fire."

Although Slade had just checked the woman, Taylor began examining her. "Heart rate is tachy."

"I gave her an antihistamine and a steroid," Slade informed Taylor. "Hopefully the symptoms will start resolving soon."

The woman hacked then cleared her throat again. "I hope so," she rasped.

"Me, too," Taylor agreed, eyeing the coughing patient with concern. "I think we're going to have to give you another shot of steroid."

"Or maybe just go to epinephrine?" Slade suggested as the woman hacked again. "I think her lips are swelling."

Mrs. Jamison's gaze lifted to them. Her lips were swelling before their eyes. Her eyes watered. Her skin became more and more blotchy. "I feel like I can't get enough air."

"Nina," Taylor said, knowing her nurse would know exactly what she wanted.

"On it," Nina replied, rushing away from them.

"Respiratory rate is over twenty," Taylor said, although Slade wasn't sure if she was speaking to him or was just thinking aloud.

"Take slow deep breaths," Slade advised, in hopes of refocusing the woman's increasing panic. He grasped her wrist and took her pulse. Running over one hundred and fifty, her heart rate was also too high.

"I...can't," the woman denied, shaking her head while coughing. She was now wheezing audibly.

Nina rushed back with an injectable pen that she handed to Taylor. Taylor popped the cap and jabbed the pen down on the woman's thigh, through her clothes, administering the medication in the process.

Slade pulled out his phone and dialed for emergency services.

"I can't…breathe."

"The reaction should be slowing very soon with the medication we just gave," Taylor informed her patient, watching as Slade checked her pulse again. No doubt the adrenaline they'd just administered would push the lady's heart rate up even higher. No matter. There hadn't been a choice. She was going into anaphylactic shock. "You're having an allergic reaction to the chemotherapy medication. It's rare for that to happen but, unfortunately, from time to time it does occur. I'm giving more steroids through your IV and I'm going to admit you to the hospital for observation tonight."

The woman just nodded between wheezes.

"Your heart probably feels as if it's racing like crazy. It is. Although the medicine I just gave can cause an increased heart rate, what I expect to happen is that once your allergic reaction is under control, your heart rate will drop back close to normal."

Taylor and Slade stayed with Mrs. Jamison, keeping her calm and stable while they waited for the ambulance to arrive. Slade soothed the lady in the chair closest to Mrs. Jamison, easing her concerns regarding her own infusion.

"As Taylor said, it's very rare that someone has a reaction to their chemotherapy, but it does happen," he assured the anxious woman, when she asked for her treatment to be stopped for fear she might also react. "You still need your medication infused. Other than prayers, the medication is the best weapon we have at our disposal to fight your cancer."

The nervous woman kept eyeing Mrs. Jamison, but did nod agreement. For a moment Slade had thought she was going to rip out her central line.

Having most of their patients' infusions occur in a common lounge area with recliners and televisions was a good thing overall. It provided support and socialization during the long infusion process. But when something went wrong it could start mayhem.

Fortunately, although the other patients had kept a curious eye on what was happening, only the lady next to Mrs. Jamison seemed spooked.

The paramedics arrived, wheeling in a stretcher.

Taylor gave them a quick report while they loaded a still wheezing and hacking Mrs. Jamison onto the stretcher.

"That scares me," the nervous woman told Slade. "What if I react to my chemo, too?"

"I don't think that's going to happen, Mrs. Smith," he reassured the woman, squeezing her hand gently. "I know putting medications into your body is scary, but there are times when not doing so would be much scarier."

"The medications make me feel so bad," the woman admitted, a little weepy. "Sometimes I feel as if I would be better off to just not take them."

"Your last scans showed a reduction in the size of your tumor. The medications are doing their job. You're doing fantastically on the medicines. To stop them halfway through would be a shame."

Taylor had stayed with her patient until they loaded her onto the ambulance. When she came back into the lounge, she came over to them.

She smiled at Mrs. Smith then glanced at Slade. "Thank you for taking care of Mrs. Jamison."

"You're welcome, but you did all the work."

"I'm not sure why Nina didn't come and get me to begin with. Mrs. Jamison was my patient."

"I had just finished with a patient and was in the hallway. It would have been silly to pull you from an examination room when I was available."

"I suppose you are right." She looked pensive, as if even though she couldn't argue with his logic she didn't really want to agree with him. "Still, I hate it that you had to take care of one of my patients."

Who did she think she was fooling? What she was really saying was that she hated that they'd had to interact. She'd avoided him all morning, including skipping her morning coffee. What was she trying to prove? It wasn't as if the entire office didn't know they'd married and was watching their every move with great curiosity. Such juicy gossip spread like wildfire and, no doubt, the entire clinic had known within an hour of Slade making his announcement during their presentation. If only he'd kept his mouth shut. If only they hadn't gotten married to begin with. If only his chest didn't feel a little like he couldn't breathe when he looked at her. Not that she was looking back. Her eyes were everywhere except meeting his gaze.

"It wasn't a big deal," he said finally, mixed emotions running rampant through him. He wanted her. But that wasn't part of the plan.

"All the same, thank you."

Taylor stared at Slade, feeling as if she should say something more, but what?

What could she possibly say to him? So much and yet, really, what was there to say?

"I had a no-show this morning—she's at home, sick. Can I help you get caught up again?" he offered, taking the pressure off her to come up with something to say.

She shook her head. "That isn't necessary, but thank you."

"I didn't think it was necessary. I just wanted to help you."

"I appreciate the offer, but I don't need your help."

Mrs. Smith was watching their interplay with curious

eyes, all concern over her infusion apparently forgotten with the minidrama unfolding in front of her. No doubt the other staff members within viewing distance were also curious bystanders. She'd gotten several congratulations throughout the morning. No doubt Slade had as well.

She'd avoided him. Something she'd gotten good at long ago. Why had Nina gone to him? They'd all worked together for over a year. There were dozens of physicians at the clinic. Never before had Nina had any reason to seek out Slade. Go and marry the man, and suddenly her nurse was asking him to see her patients. Not okay.

Taylor didn't want him seeing her patients. Not when they were having allergic reactions. Not when he'd had a no-show and offered to help her catch up.

Not that she didn't trust him in that regard. He was an excellent doctor. She'd never heard any complaints or problems regarding the care he provided his patients. Quite the opposite. Everyone sang his praises. It was just that the less she had to do with him the better. He wasn't the man for her.

"I'll talk to Nina about not bothering you regarding my patients in the future."

His brow lifted. "Why? We all help each other when the need arises. That's always been the case in this clinic."

Out of respect for the curious ears listening to their conversation and because she didn't want their patients privy to their weekend activities, Taylor just smiled. "You're right. Thank you."

Not that she wouldn't be talking to Nina. She would definitely see to it that Nina went to anyone but Slade for assistance unless a patient's health would otherwise be compromised.

As if he could read her mind, Slade just stared at her. Disappointment showed in his blue eyes. Then he turned to Mrs. Smith. "I'm going to pop in and see whoever is next, but I want to be sure you're okay before I do so. You need anything?"

Taylor didn't wait to hear the woman's response. Slade had the situation under control and the nurses were providing good care for all the other infusion patients. She was going to catch up on her morning patients.

"Do you have a minute?"

Taylor glanced up at the man standing in her doorway. Her husband.

Ugh. Could she lie and say no?

She'd managed to avoid him for the rest of the day, but had caught him watching her several times when she'd been talking to this patient or that in the infusion lounge.

The last thing she wanted was to spend time with him. Not even a minute. She just wanted to forget he existed, that she had a marriage to do away with, that she had made such a mess of her life over the weekend, that horrific sadness gripped her chest each time she thought of him.

She glanced at Gracie's photo, her greatest happiness in a gray world, and summoned up the courage to meet Slade's gaze.

"What's up?" she asked, pushing her glasses up the bridge of her nose.

He came into her office and shut the door behind him. "We need to talk."

"Not again."

"Did you call a lawyer today?"

"I did." She'd called during the lunch she'd practically inhaled while sitting at her desk. "I have an appointment to meet with her on Friday morning. Did you?"

His lips thinned. "Yes. Oddly enough, I have a Friday morning appointment as well."

Although she hadn't invited him to, he sat down in the seat on the other side of her desk and studied the photo she'd just been looking at. He sat in silence so long, Taylor cleared her throat to remind him she was in the room.

His skin drawn tightly over his cheekbones, he glanced up. "She's a beautiful little girl."

"Thank you."

His gaze drifted back to the photo. "She looks just like you."

"I am her mother." What was he doing?

"What about her father?"

Enough was enough. "Really? You want to discuss Kyle again? Because I don't."

"Does he see Gracie?" Slade persisted.

She eyed him with what had to be pure venom flowing through her veins. Really, that's what the caustic substance sloshing around inside her felt like. Venom. "He doesn't want anything to do with Gracie. He signed away all rights to her."

"Foolish man."

True. As far as Taylor was concerned Kyle had been an idiot to give up his rights to their precious daughter.

"Selfish as this may sound, I'm glad he doesn't want anything to do with her, because I don't believe he'd be a good influence or father. I'd worry about her if she had to spend time in his care and it just makes life simpler that she doesn't have to go back and forth between two houses. As much as I wish he could have been a good father to her, that's not who he is. Gracie has a lot more stability this way."

Slade's gaze met hers. "If Gracie were my daughter, I would spend time with her."

Despite the fact that he'd said he didn't want a wife or kids, he sounded so definite, she didn't doubt his claim. Irrational fear gurgled in her stomach. "Then it's a good thing she's not yours, because I'd worry about her if she was in your care, too."

She didn't add that she worried about Gracie no matter who was watching her. She supposed it was a mother thing, but she wanted to protect her daughter from all the bad things in the world. Leaving her with anyone was difficult. Even leaving her with Nina for the long weekend had been rough, and she trusted her best friend implicitly.

Slade leaned back in the chair and watched her a moment before asking, "Despite how we were this weekend, you don't like me much, do you?"

"Not really."

"Why not?"

"You're not the kind of man I prefer to spend time with."

"Yet you married me."

A vicious throb pounded at her temples. "Don't remind me."

"Why?"

She rubbed her temple, hoping to ease the pulsating pain that she'd begun to associate with thoughts of him. "Why what?"

"Why did you marry me, Taylor?"

She grimaced. "Haven't we already had this conversation?"

"Tell me again."

"I wasn't in my right mind," she said flippantly, wishing she hadn't stayed to do her charting, but had rushed straight out the door as soon as she'd finished with her last patient.

"I haven't been in my right mind since I kissed you in the backseat of that limousine."

His comment surprised Taylor and she met his intent blue gaze. "How so?"

"We're filing for divorce, which is the right thing. I don't want to get entangled in your life, yet I can't stay away from you. I can't go ten minutes without thinking about you." His gaze dropped to the photo of Gracie again, and he winced.

"There are a million reasons why I shouldn't, why I should stay away from you and just do as we decided on the plane, but I can't get past the simple fact that I want you, Taylor."

CHAPTER SEVEN

I WANT YOU. Three little words and Slade had Taylor's lungs shriveling up to oxygen-deprived uselessness.

"We don't always get what we want in life, Slade."

Not that she was complaining about her life, but she certainly hadn't.

"Besides, you just want what you can't have."

He shrugged. "We both know that if I kissed you right now, you'd kiss me back."

"I don't know that."

His brow arched. "You think I'm wrong?"

"I think you're wrong," she insisted. In theory, her claim sounded good, but she wasn't so sure he wasn't right. The man's mouth held some kind of power over her.

"Prove it."

Why was she staring at his mouth? Why were his words—"I want you"—echoing through her mind over and over and causing all sorts of jittery reactions inside her body? Want wasn't their problem. They'd wanted each other this past weekend just fine. It was everything else that had been the problem.

"W-what?" she stammered out.

"Prove that my kisses don't affect you." Was it just her or did he look inordinately confident, perhaps even a little arrogant?

"How would I prove that?" Not that she didn't immediately realize the trap he'd set. Darn him. Darn her body's reaction to him.

"Kiss me."

She crossed her arms, realized she probably looked ridiculous and dropped her hands into her lap. "I don't want to kiss you."

"Chicken."

"I'm not going to respond to such a childish taunt."

"Because you know that I'm right." His lips twitched. Oh, yeah, he'd gone from perturbed to haughty.

"You aren't right."

"Unless you prove otherwise, I am right."

Ooh, she really didn't like him.

"Fine, kiss me. But don't be offended when I go rinse my mouth out with peroxide afterwards."

He frowned but moved around the desk, took her hand and pulled her to her feet and into his arms.

The moment her body came into contact with his, she knew she was in trouble. Big trouble.

How could she have forgotten how hard his body was? How good he smelled? How could he even smell that good after working all day? But he did. His spicy male scent teased her nostrils with memories, with acknowledgment that she wanted him.

She expected him to immediately take her mouth, had braced herself for it. Instead, he slipped his fingers around her neck, slowly raking over the sensitive flesh, then pinching her hair clip and releasing her hair.

His fingers threaded into the locks, massaging the base of her scalp, every touch seducing her toward relaxation.

Just get it over with, she wanted to scream.

Or maybe it was just, *Kiss me!* she wanted to shout at him.

Either way, he was taking his dear sweet time and she was growing more and more impatient.

"I said you could kiss me, not maul me."

His eyes sparked with something akin to fire, but he didn't respond except to continue his caress of her and to lower his head.

His lips kissed the corner of her mouth. A soft, brief touch. Then he kissed the other corner.

She fought turning her mouth toward him and somehow managed to stand superstill, as if she was totally unaffected. As if she'd been telling the truth, that his kisses didn't affect her.

But he wasn't finished. He continued his soft rain of kisses, gliding across her temples, her forehead, even the tip of her nose.

"I don't have time for this," she warned.

He just smiled. Probably because her voice had wavered and hadn't sounded convincing at all. She'd sounded as if she *was* affected. Darn it.

He lowered his mouth back to hers, dipped to where only millimeters separated their lips. "My kisses may not affect you, Taylor. But kissing you affects me. My heart is racing and my lungs feel they can't drag in enough air. This weekend wasn't enough. Right or wrong, I need more."

Stop it. Please, just stop talking, her brain warned. Her mouth, unfortunately, didn't say a word. Then again, that might be a good thing because she might admit to how her own heart raced and her own lungs had deflated at his "I want you," at his tender touching of her skin with his lips.

"The anticipation of knowing I'm about to taste your sweet mouth drives me crazy, Taylor," he admitted, his voice low, husky. His gaze lifted to hers. "You drive me crazy."

He drove her crazy, too. She didn't like him and yet...

His lips touched hers. Softly at first, then not so softly,

but demanding and masterful. As if he was trying to work through the craziness to some type of satisfied peace.

Only Taylor knew there was no satisfied peace with Slade.

Even after he'd taken her to the pinnacle of pleasure and she'd thought herself completely sated, all he'd had to do was touch her and she'd been right back to craving more. Crazy. What a perfect description for the desire flooding through her.

The desire to move her lips in response to his.

The desire to wind her arms around his neck.

The desire to press her body fully to his and lean on his strength.

Yep, that was crazy.

She knew better than to lean on a man like Slade. He was a playboy. She'd seen the evidence firsthand for the past year. The fact that he kissed like a dream and his eyes promised her the world didn't mean a thing.

The fact her heart was racing didn't mean a thing.

"I don't like you," she told him the moment his mouth lifted from hers.

"I know," he conceded. "But you want me almost as much as I want you."

Probably more, but she wasn't telling him that.

But kissing him again really wouldn't hurt anything, right? After all, they'd already kissed and she'd done her best not to respond, but she'd have had an easier time stopping the earth's rotation.

Giving in to her need, she stood on tiptoe to press her lips back to his. She should have said something clever like, *Shut up and kiss me*. But talking at all just seemed unnecessary.

Feeding the hunger within her was what was necessary. Only she knew from experience that kissing Slade wouldn't satisfy her hunger. Instead, his kisses were like an appetizer that made her crave the main course all the more.

She was starved.

Then she recalled how their kiss had started. He'd been proving a point about his kisses affecting her.

She pulled back from him. "I guess I lose."

"Seriously?" Mixed emotions twirled in his blue depths. "I don't see how sharing that kiss could possibly qualify you as a loser. That kiss makes us both winners."

"If you say so." She took a step back, trying to put some distance between them. "You aren't my type."

"I think we just proved that I'm exactly your type. Do you need a reminder?"

Um, no. She wasn't likely to ever forget that kiss. "That's just sex."

"Sex is a very important part of a relationship."

She rolled her eyes. "Spoken like a true man."

"I am a man, Taylor, but I'll go on record as saying that if you believe sex isn't important to women in a relationship, you're wrong. Sex, whether it be a desire for more of it or less, is an important sharing between a man and a woman."

He was right. But both of her sexual relationships hadn't been about love, just appeasing physical attraction. Kyle had been good, but not like Slade. Not even in the same class.

"What do you know about relationships? You change girlfriends on a monthly basis," she accused, needing to establish some distance between them. "There was the one you went skydiving with, the one you hiked Everest with, the one you did the medical mission trip to Kenya with, the one you—"

"I don't need a recap. I have dated a lot of different women," he interrupted. "But just because my relationships with them didn't last long doesn't mean we didn't have a good relationship while it lasted."

She shook her head. "Again, spoken like a true man. I wonder what the women think."

"I'm still friends with most of them."

She twirled her finger in the air. "Yee-haw for you."

"Are you always so negative?"

"Always. You should stay far away." She waved her fingers at him. "Bye. See you in divorce court."

His expression serious, he said, "Actually, that's what I'm here to discuss. Have you told anyone we plan to divorce immediately?"

His question had heat infusing her face. Was she supposed to have sent out an office memo? "Only Nina."

"Good," he surprised her by saying.

"Why is that good? What does it even matter? We are immediately filing for divorce."

"But I think it's better if no one know that. At least, not until after Christmas."

"What does that matter?"

"Go to dinner with me tonight so we can discuss exactly that."

"I can't. I have Gracie."

He winced, reminding her of how he'd reacted to knowledge of her daughter, to seeing Gracie, to even looking at her photo. Had he momentarily forgotten?

"If it's the only way you'll agree, then your daughter can come, too."

She shook her head. Not going to happen. "Wow, with such sweet talk, how can I resist?"

"Do you want me to sweet-talk you, Taylor? I want you, but the reason I want to take you to dinner has little to do with that want."

"Then what does it have to do with?"

"Say yes, and I'll tell you."

Did he think he could manipulate her into going? But then an idea struck. Slade had enjoyed their sexual rendezvous where there had just been the two of them and no real-world responsibilities other than their presentation. He enjoyed kissing her and seeing her as a woman. She needed to give him a dose of her real world. In the real world she was the mother of a rambunctious six-year-old. A six-year-old whom he obviously had issues with.

She smiled a Cheshire-cat smile. "Okay. We will go to dinner."

"Okay." Surprise lit his face, and also a look that was somewhere between relieved that she'd agreed and terrified that she had. "Good. We really do have a lot to talk about. What time can I pick you up?"

"Seven." She gave him her address.

"Okay, then." He took a step back then nodded almost as much to whatever was running through his head as to their conversation. "I'll see you in a little while."

"Taylor, dear, your father's partner said he'd heard a nasty rumor this weekend."

Taylor cringed. No. No. No. She shouldn't have answered the phone. Especially since Slade would be arriving any moment.

"Craig told him that you'd gotten married over the weekend. Your father assured him that was poppycock."

Poppycock? Who said that other than Vivien Anderson?

Then again, perhaps there was no better word for the fact she and Slade had gotten married. Poppycock. Yep, that's what the whole weekend had been. What tonight was.

"Why is the idea of someone marrying me poppycock?"

"Now, Taylor, don't take this the wrong way, but you're not exactly a prize."

Trying not to be hurt, Taylor closed her eyes. Not a prize? Wasn't her mother supposed to see her as the greatest prize a man could win?

"How else is one to take her mother saying she isn't exactly a prize other than the wrong way?"

"Don't go making this about me," her mother warned. "Just tell me you didn't go off and marry someone on a wild whim in Vegas. Surely you know such a union is doomed before it's even started?"

Sure she knew that, but she wasn't admitting to a thing.

"You don't believe in love at first sight?" Why was she being so ornery? Why wasn't she just coming clean that her mother was right and that she'd made a mistake?

"Taylor! Please, tell me you didn't!"

She could lie and tell her that, but her mother's attitude rankled and for once, rather than kowtow, Taylor injected her voice with a perkiness she didn't feel. "It's hardly love at first sight, though. I've known him for a year."

"It's true," her mother gasped, her horror real and thick. "You got married. In Vegas."

Her mother made her words sound as if she had committed the most heinous crime. What else was new? Almost everything she did failed to impress her parents one way or another.

"To a doctor, Mother. He's a very successful man. You should be happy."

But rather than exclaim with joy, her mother rasped, "You're pregnant again, aren't you?"

Taylor cringed. "Do you not think a man might want to marry me just because he wants to be with me?"

Not that that was why Slade had married her, but still.

"In Vegas? Oh, Taylor, you know you wanted a church wedding!"

Had she? Taylor supposed that if she thought about it she would say she had the same wedding fantasies that a lot of women had. A day that was all about her, a gorgeous gown, flowers, a man who loved her with all his heart waiting at the end of an aisle. Not necessarily in a church, but she doubted a place named after the North Pole would have made the top one hundred.

"Vegas was much more exciting, Mom. Not everyone gets married by Santa Claus." Okay, in reality, being married by a minister in a furry red suit wasn't on her mom's top one hundred list either.

"Please, tell me you are joking."

"In a gingerbread house rather than a church. There were real elves and everything." She was bad, knew she was being bad, but she so didn't need her mother condemning her right now. She had enough of her own regrets. "It was a really unique ceremony."

"Your father is going to be so disappointed that he didn't get to walk you down the aisle."

Her mother was so disappointed she didn't get to have the huge social-club reception to show off to all her friends. Her father? She thought about the stern businessman who, although devout and good, wasn't an overly emotional man. Perhaps her mother knew a side she didn't. Perhaps her father really did want to walk his only child down the aisle. Maybe she'd stolen that experience from him, too.

Taylor felt a twinge of remorse. Her parents had been good parents, had sent her to the best schools, had made sure she'd had the best advantages in life, had always been there if she'd physically needed something. Was it their fault she'd constantly been a disappointment to them? That she'd failed them miserably when she'd gotten pregnant in medical school? That she'd accidentally gotten married in Vegas?

"I'll reserve the club for a reception." Her mother confirmed Taylor's earlier thoughts. "With the holidays, I may have to call in several favors to get the main ballroom, but I'll do my best."

"Mom, I don't need or want a wedding reception." She didn't even want the marriage.

"Nonsense. All our friends and family will be offended if they don't get to share in such an important event."

Taylor took a deep breath. Several of her coworkers had suggested throwing her a bridal shower. She'd put them off with claims of the holidays being so busy.

"Mom, it isn't fair to your club to make them shuffle around their holiday schedule to fit in a reception."

"But—"

"No buts. I have so much going on right now with Gracie, the holidays, with work."

"Fine," her mother conceded. "I'll book the first thing available for after the holidays."

Planning a reception for after the holidays was as useless as planning one for before the holidays. Unless one gave receptions to celebrate the dissolution of one's impromptu Vegas vows?

Taylor tried arguing with her mother, but to no avail as Vivien cut the conversation short. No doubt to call to book her club.

Was it wrong that she had given Gracie a glass of soda prior to Slade's arrival? That she wanted Gracie in full-chatter, full-tilt mode? That she wanted to push Slade out of his comfort zone? To play on all his worst fears about being around a kid? For him to see her as a woman who was a mother who had real-world responsibilities and not as the woman he'd slept with in Vegas?

"Mommy!" Gracie called when the doorbell rang. She jumped up and down, her blond ponytail swishing wildly. "He's here. He's here."

She'd told Gracie that a friend from work was coming to take them to Pippa's Pizza Palace. Gracie had been ecstatic because they usually only went to the designed-for-kids restaurant for birthday parties or special occasions.

Knowing she wasn't supposed to unlock the latch,

Gracie bounced back and forth in front of the foyer door. Taylor had her step aside so she could let Slade in.

When she swung the door open, he gave her a wary smile that made her question how long he had been standing out there on her porch.

"Hey."

"Hey, yourself," she flung back, moving back so he could enter the foyer. "Gracie, do you remember Dr. Sain? You met him briefly at the airport."

"I remember." Gracie beamed at him, dancing around at his feet. "He took care of Vegas."

Oh, he'd taken care of Vegas all right. Her daughter meant the bear, but Taylor couldn't help but think of the real ways Slade had taken care of Vegas. She'd hoped Gracie would rename her bear, but the name had stuck so far. Vegas had bumped Foxy as Gracie's favorite toy and she kept the bear close.

"That's right. Let's grab your coat and be off so we can get you to bed at a decent time for school tomorrow."

Gracie ran to the living room where her jacket and bear lay on the sofa.

Slade's gaze followed the bouncing little girl out of the room, then shifted to Taylor. "You look great."

Taylor laughed at Slade's compliment. She'd purposely put on an old sweatshirt and jeans, scrubbed her face clean and pulled her hair into a ponytail. Great wasn't the right adjective by any use of the word. Neither was it the adjective she'd use to describe how he looked. He looked as if he'd rather be anywhere other than here.

"Got them," Gracie announced proudly when she returned with her jacket and bear.

Her daughter handed her bear to Slade while Taylor made a great production of helping Gracie into her coat. Let him realize firsthand why she had no time for playboys.

"Be careful with her," Gracie warned him. "She is a

delicate princess and has to be treated royally. She would probably like it if you pretended to be a prince come to rescue her."

What popped out of Gracie's mouth had stopped surprising Taylor long ago. Her daughter was brilliant and readily got people to do her bidding. Slade, despite whatever was bugging him, was no exception, and whatever the problem had been he seemed to have overcome it, at least for the moment.

"Who says I'm not really a prince?" he asked, bending to Gracie's level. He held the bear to where he was staring into her painted plastic eyes. "Vegas, did you forget to tell Gracie that I am Prince Charming come to sweep the two most beautiful girls in the world off their feet?"

Gracie's eyes widened. "She did forget to tell me."

"Vegas," he scolded the bear with a gentle click of his tongue. "How could you forget something so important?"

Taylor rolled her eyes, wondering if she'd made a horrible mistake in letting her daughter spend time with Slade. She'd expected him not to want to deal with a six-year-old girl, for them to have a short evening with Slade and Gracie not having time to form any attachments. What she hadn't counted on was Slade actually playing along with Gracie's imaginings. She liked that and she didn't need anything else to like about the man.

"Let's go," she growled, irritated at herself. "I'm hungry."

"Uh-oh, Vegas." Slade's voice sounded concerned. "Princess Taylor has spoken and we must do her bidding."

Gracie giggled. "She's not Princess Taylor. She's Queen Mommy."

Good girl, Gracie. Remind him of my real role in life. The most important role in her life. That of loving and raising her daughter to the best of her ability.

Even if she had loaded her with sugar prior to his arrival.

As if she'd read her mind, Gracie started bouncing again. "Mommy let me and Vegas have soda pop!"

Hmm, maybe she should have let Gracie in on the fact that she hadn't wanted that little tidbit shared.

Slade just looked at her, raised his brow, then grinned, his stress seeming to melt away with that revelation. "Wow. It must be a special night if she let you have soda."

Gracie nodded. "It is. We're going to Pippa's Pizza Palace."

"Pippa's Pizza Palace?" Slade's gaze went to Taylor for confirmation. She nodded.

"Well," he continued, giving Taylor a look that said he knew exactly what she was up to. "It is a palace, so of course that's where princes and princesses should go."

Ha. Wasn't he in for a surprise if he expected any kind of royal treatment at Pippa's Pizza Palace. Overpriced pizza, kiddie rides and games were hardly regal.

Totally enamored, Gracie slipped her hand into Taylor's and headed out the front door. "Vegas is really excited about going to Pippa's Pizza Palace. She wants her very own crown."

"Then her very own crown she shall have," Slade promised. "After all, she is a very special princess who traveled from far, far away."

Taylor followed Slade to his car.

"Let's load you up into your chariot," he suggested to Gracie. He looked more confident than he had when he'd first arrived. Too bad he was about to have his bubble burst.

Also having figured out there was a problem, Gracie glanced up at Taylor in question. Taylor had to fight to hide her smile.

"We should take my car instead," she suggested from behind him, watching his face closely.

"Why?"

"I think you're forgetting something. Princess Gracie is only six and has to be in a children's car seat."

His expression was priceless. "Is there a seat we can just put in mine?"

Taylor hesitated a brief moment, then shook her head. "Nina has my extra seat and the one in my van is built-in."

"Your van?"

"I drive a minivan. That's what we soccer moms do."

She was driving her point home that they were on opposite ends of the spectrum. Whatever he was thinking, he didn't say anything to her, just grinned at Gracie as if he found dealing with her easier than Taylor at the moment. "You play soccer? I love soccer!"

Gracie nodded at her new hero.

"What position do you play?"

Gracie shrugged and glanced at Taylor for an answer.

"You're a forward."

"A forward," Gracie told him, puffing out her tiny chest as she did.

"That's a great position," he praised, then turned to Taylor. "Can we take your minivan instead of my car?"

She glanced toward his car. She'd seen the sporty coupe in the parking lot at the hospital, knew that's what he drove. The expensive car fit him and was perfect no doubt for impressing the women he dated.

Seven years ago Taylor would have been impressed, too. Now flashy toys and good looks didn't impress her that much. What was on the inside of a man, his morals and his character, that's what she valued. Not that Slade would have guessed that after their wild Vegas rendezvous. He probably thought deep down she was no different from the other women who had been in and out of his life.

Only as she unlocked her garage door she couldn't quite convince herself that Slade saw her the same way as the other women he'd dated.

He hadn't married any of the other women in his life.

Sure, they'd married on a silly lust-fueled Vegas whim, but they had married.

He stood next to her, taking in each step of Gracie being safely buckled into her seat. Once Taylor was confident Gracie was properly buckled in, she handed her van keys to him.

"You're going to let me drive?" he asked, obviously surprised.

"Boys are supposed to drive," Gracie piped up from her seat.

"Don't ever let any guy tell you he's supposed to drive. If you want to drive, drive."

Gracie giggled. "I don't know how to drive."

"What?" He pretended shock. "Well, I guess princesses should be chauffeured around anyway."

Taylor watched their interaction with suspicious eyes. Of course Slade was on his best behavior. She'd thought being around Gracie would make him see her as a mom and not as the woman he'd spent the weekend with in Vegas. Perhaps she'd made a mistake.

Then again, the night was young.

CHAPTER EIGHT

SLADE WRAPPED HIS fingers around Taylor's keys, watched the play of emotions across her face, then opened the passenger door for her.

"Your chariot awaits, Queen Taylor." He made a production of bowing, and earned claps and praise from Gracie. Not that he'd had much experience around kids, or even wanted that experience, but he admitted he enjoyed her honest reactions to the things he said and did.

"This is my chariot, too," the little girl informed him. "My royal chariot. For me and Princess Vegas."

"Absolutely."

Taylor rolled her eyes. She climbed into the front passenger seat and he shut the door, winked at Gracie, who winked back, then he slid her door closed, too.

So far, so good. Which he didn't think was supposed to be the case since even in his limited experience he knew sodas hyped most kids. He'd bet anything Taylor was one of those moms who limited her daughter's sweets. Tonight was not supposed to be a success. Too bad. He was determined it would be. He had a proposal to make. One that had been nagging at him from the moment it had occurred to him. One he hoped Taylor would agree to.

Gracie chatted nonstop, mostly about Santa and Christmas, on the drive to Pippa's Pizza Palace, which, despite the castle-shaped sign, didn't look like a place fit for a princess to eat. The building was a bit run-down and the parking lot needed repaving. Still, when they got inside, the interior was colorful and clean, if dated.

Gracie obviously didn't care. First getting a nod from her mother, she took off toward a row of machines and kiddie rides on the opposite side of the large open room.

Before they had placed their order Gracie was back, asking if she could have some coins.

"Let's get dinner ordered first."

"I'm not hungry," Gracie insisted, tugging on her mother's hand. "Can I play now?"

Taylor shook her head. "Not until you've eaten."

Gracie's lower lip drooped, and her shoulders sagged to where she looked like a deflated tire. "Do I have to?"

Taylor nodded, then, while Gracie ran back over to watch one of the video-game monitors, she turned to the cashier, placed an order for a small cheese pizza, a salad, a lemon water and a juice. The cashier glanced toward Slade, but Taylor shook her head.

"Our orders are separate."

"You'll have to excuse my wife. She doesn't understand the concept of 'date night,'" Slade explained to the cashier. "I will pay for their order and mine."

"No."

"Yes. Get us a table, please, and I'll finish here, wifey."

"I didn't say yes so you could buy dinner or call me 'wifey.'"

"Odd, because I did ask you to dinner so I could buy your dinner."

She pursed her lips, looking as if she'd like to argue, but instead she did as he'd suggested. He watched her walk over to a clean booth and put her purse on the seat. Then he turned back to the cashier and completed the order, along with purchasing some coins for Gracie.

"You didn't have to buy coins," Taylor said when he slid into the booth with his huge stash.

"Because we came to the Pippa's Pizza Palace to watch other kids play?"

"We came to eat."

"Pretty sure Gracie would be disappointed if she only gets to eat." As he said the words realization hit. "Unless that's your plan?" He studied her, noting her pink cheeks. "You'd like tonight to be a failure so you can add it to your reasons why we don't belong together?"

"We don't belong together." She made it sound like a disease. "I thought we agreed on that."

"We do."

"Then our being here makes no sense."

He glanced toward where Gracie covetously watched two kids whacking at clowns popping up from the top of a machine shaped like a cannon.

"Actually, our being together does make sense short-term." He needed to explain his proposal, but didn't get the chance as Gracie skipped back to their table.

"Mommy, after I eat, can I hit the clowns, too?" Gracie's eyes sparkled, her cheeks glowed and her voice held excitement.

"I'm not sure how I feel about a game where you beat up poor defenseless clowns," Taylor mused, smiling at her Mini-Me.

"Are you kidding me? Clowns are some scary business. We should both help just to be sure we get them all."

Giving Slade a beatific grin, Gracie nodded enthusiastically. "You should!"

"Don't tell me you are afraid of clowns?" Taylor asked, eyeing him with a slight smile.

"Terrified," he admitted, half-serious. He'd never been one of those kids who liked clowns. Maybe he'd watched one too many scary movies involving weirdos in clown suits.

"I'm not scared of clowns," Gracie announced, taking his hand. "Mommy's not either. We'll protect you."

"Phew. Thanks."

"Do you want to watch with me? We could look at the other games and pick out ones to play," she suggested, her eyes big and pleading.

Slade glanced toward Taylor to get her permission. Should he wait until after Gracie had eaten?

Taylor nodded. "I'm pretty sure that the games haven't changed since the last time we were here, but you should definitely show Dr. Sain all your favorite ones."

"You can come too, Mommy."

Taylor shook her head. "You two go ahead. Mommy will watch for our food. Plus, I have a phone call to make."

Gracie tugged on Slade's hand. "Come on. You have got to see the frog game! It's amazing."

Slade gave one last look toward Taylor, who, he knew, had purposely set him up to go off alone to supervise Gracie, then he devoted his attention to the child holding his hand. Something about her warm little hand gripping his, about the excitement with which she spoke, made him want to pick her up and hug her. Getting attached would be nothing short of stupid. Yet he'd jumped at the chance to spend time with Taylor. So he could ask her a favor. Nothing more. Not really.

If she'd agree to a no-strings affair, he'd jump at that chance, too. Too bad he knew she'd never offer that.

"Amazing?" he asked the girl, forcing his mind away from Taylor. "The frog game?"

Gracie nodded with great emphasis. "Amazing."

"Okay, let's go see this amazing frog game."

He let the little girl lead him over to a game where you had to squirt water onto a lily pad to make a frog move from the lily pad to where a fly was. Interesting.

But not interesting enough to keep his gaze from wandering back to the woman sitting in the booth, talking on her cellular phone. She laughed at something said, then glanced his way, caught him looking at her and frowned.

"Rolling the balls is my favorite game, but I'm not very good," Gracie informed him, tugging on his hands to take him away from the frog game and farther into the maze of games. "Mommy is really good."

She stopped in front of a row of Skee-Ball lanes.

Slade glanced over at the booth where Taylor sat, talking on her cellular phone, smiling and laughing. Her face was relaxed, beautiful, almost carefree. Who was she talking to? She'd told him she wasn't having sex with anyone, but had she been dating? He'd never asked if there was someone special in her life. There couldn't have been anyone too special or she wouldn't have married him, wouldn't have had sex with him.

Gracie continued to talk about her mother's awesomeness at Skee-Ball.

Slade smiled down at the excited little girl. "Your mommy likes to play this game?"

Gracie nodded. "It's her favorite. She's really good. She gets lots of tickets, but she always gives them to me to get the prize." The little girl gave him a pointed look, wanting to be sure he knew that giving her the tickets was the right thing to do.

Slade's gaze wandered back to Taylor. She twirled a loose strand of hair around her finger and still talked animatedly to whoever she was on the phone with. Jealousy wasn't a pretty thing and he was definitely jealous. He wanted her smiling and laughing like that with him, the way they had on the night they'd gotten married.

"That's nice of her."

Gracie nodded. "She's a nice mommy. My friend Sarah Beth, her mommy isn't nice." Gracie wrinkled her nose and looked so much like Taylor, Slade couldn't suppress the melting of his heart. There might be traits of her father present in Gracie, but when Slade looked at the little girl all he saw was a miniature version of Taylor.

"She screams and cries a lot," Gracie continued, her face and hand movements dramatic.

Slade wasn't exactly sure how he was supposed to respond, but decided a response wasn't necessary because Gracie kept right on talking and waving her hands.

"Sarah Beth says it's because she's pregnant and the baby in her belly kicks her a lot. Sarah Beth's daddy says this baby is going to be a soccer player, too. Sarah Beth is on my soccer team, but soccer season won't start back till this spring. You should come watch my games. I am very good. Mommy tells me so."

Slade took a breath for Gracie because she seemed too busy chatting to breathe. But she must have been sneaking breaths in somewhere because she kept going without being the slightest bit winded, pointing out several other games that she really hoped to play when they finished eating.

"Do you have kids?"

Gracie's random question in the middle of her rundown of her classmates caught him off guard. He shook his head.

"No, I don't have kids." For the first time in his life he almost felt as if he was lacking something by that answer. Perhaps it was the sad little look Gracie gave him, as if she was offering him comfort that he didn't.

"Are you married?"

While he racked his brain for a way to answer honestly without telling her anything her mother wasn't ready for her to know, Gracie leapt up and down.

"Yummy!" she called, grabbing his hand and not waiting for an answer when she spotted their food being delivered to the table. "Pizza. I'm a pizza-eating machine."

She made a pretense of gobbling air bites.

"Me, too," he agreed, grateful for the distraction as they headed back to the table.

"Sorry, Nina, but I've got to go. I'll talk with you tomorrow at work." She paused while the person on the other end of the phone line said something. "Okay, see you then. Have a good night."

"Nina doing okay?" he asked, to verify that she'd been talking to her best friend. He really didn't like the green flowing through his veins, the green that had flowed through his veins at the thought that there might be someone in Taylor's life. It shouldn't matter. If anything, he should want her to have someone in her life who could give her all the things she wanted for her and Gracie. All the things they deserved. It was probably some natural instinct for him to feel jealousy where Taylor was concerned. After all, she was his wife.

"She checked on Mrs. Jamison for me. They admitted her overnight for observation, but otherwise she's good."

"Mr. Slade is going to play games with me when we finish eating," Gracie announced while Taylor squirted hand sanitizer onto her tiny hands. "He's going to come to watch me and Sarah Beth play soccer this spring, too."

Slade hadn't really agreed to that, but he wasn't going to correct the child's claim. Catching Taylor's glare, he should have, though. She offered Slade the bottle and he took it, their hands brushing against each other. Zings shot up his arm. How could a single touch cause such a wave of awareness throughout his entire body?

He glanced at her to see if she'd felt the electricity that had zapped him, but she refused to look at him, her focus totally on her daughter as she put a slice of pizza onto a colorful paper plate.

"Mmm, pizza," Gracie said, continuing to talk a mile a minute.

Slade handed the sanitizer back to Taylor and found it

interesting that she managed to take the bottle without a single touch of their skin this time. Had that been intentional?

"What is on your pizza, Mr. Slade, because I only like cheese pizza." Gracie took a big bite of her pizza to prove her point.

"I got a little of everything on mine," he told her, reaching for a slice of the house special. He eyed the rather bland-looking salad Taylor had ordered. "You want a slice? I'll share."

She shook her head. "I'll finish off what Gracie doesn't eat of her pizza."

"Cheese is your favorite?"

"No, but she won't be able to eat it all."

"I will be able to eat it all," Gracie corrected her. "I'm starved." She sucked in her tiny belly and lifted her shirt to show Taylor.

Taylor smiled at her daughter and a piece of Slade's heart cracked at the love that showed in her eyes, a love he hadn't seen in years. That's what he'd lost when his mother had died, why he'd dedicated his life to breast-cancer research, why he was determined to prevent other kids from losing the same.

"Guess you better get to eating, then, before you blow away, hungry girl. But not too big bites, please," Taylor added, when Gracie took a huge mouthful, oblivious to the emotional turmoil playing out in Slade's head.

Gracie ate a slice, then eyed the games. "I'm full. Can I go play now?"

"You can, but we're not finished eating so it'll be a few minutes before we join you. Stay where I can see you."

"Okay." Gracie looked at Slade. "Hurry so I can show you how good I am at the frog game. I will beat you."

Slade watched her bounce back over to the games. "She's precious."

"I think so."

"But you didn't want me to think so?"

"I didn't say that."

"You didn't have to. You gave her soda."

She sucked in her lower lip. "So?" she challenged. "Lots of kids drink soda."

"But you don't normally give Gracie soda."

"Not usually," she admitted, impressing him that she'd been honest. He got the impression Taylor was an honest person who truly tried to live her life to a high standard. Was that something her parents had instilled in her or just who she innately was? Speaking of honesty…

"Gracie asked me if I was married."

Taylor's stomach sank. Had Slade told Gracie they'd married? "What did you tell her?"

"Not what you apparently think I did."

Which didn't really tell her a whole lot. "Then what did you say?"

He set another piece of pizza on his paper plate. "I didn't answer because we were saved by the pizza arriving."

She watched him take a bite of the loaded pizza. Her stomach growled in protest at her salad.

"I've changed my mind about telling her. I'll tell her when she's older, when she'll understand better."

He paused with his pizza midway to his mouth, an odd gleam in his eyes. "Do I embarrass you, Taylor?"

"What?"

"I'm just curious because you haven't wanted anyone to know that you married me. I was curious if you were ashamed of me."

Was that what he thought? If anything, he should be ashamed of her. She was the one who was so different from the women he'd dated. "Of course not. That's ridiculous."

As if he were no longer hungry, he set the pizza back on his plate. "Is it?"

"Of course. If I was embarrassed by you I would not have agreed to go to dinner with you tonight."

"But dinner wasn't supposed to be a success. Dinner was supposed to shove in my face that you aren't a carefree woman who can have an affair until our divorce is final."

Busted. "I didn't say that."

"You didn't have to," he pointed out, leaning slightly across the table toward her. "I have a proposal to make."

A proposal? Her stomach knotting, she eyed him suspiciously.

"Let's not tell anyone that we plan to divorce until after the holidays."

Taylor swallowed back what she was positive wasn't disappointment because she hadn't really expected him to propose they continue their weekend fling yet again.

"I can't see what the point would be," she told him, even if staring at him across the table made her want to drag him under the table and... She swallowed again.

"It would make things easier at work if we waited."

Taylor thought back on her conversation with her mother. Now there was a buzz killer. The thought of telling her that she'd been planning her divorce less than twenty-four hours after saying "I do" turned her stomach.

He picked at the edge of his paper plate then met her gaze again. "Plus, keeping the truth quiet would make things better for my family. I don't celebrate Christmas, but they do. I'd rather not ruin their holidays by having them worried that I'm facing divorce in the New Year."

He didn't celebrate Christmas? She wondered why, not liking the way her heart raced at how he was looking at her, at how her heart broke that he missed out on the joys of the holidays.

"I don't want anyone to know that our marriage isn't real," he admitted, his sincerity drawing her further into the spell he cast with such seeming effortlessness. "I know you've told Nina, but she wouldn't say anything if you asked her not to."

"You've not told anyone?"

"No. I started to tell my dad last night, but I couldn't do it. He's already worried that I've gotten married so suddenly that I just didn't have the heart to tell him."

She closed her eyes. She couldn't condemn him for not telling his father. After all, she hadn't set her mother straight. Still…

Was she strong enough to pretend they were happily married? He affected her as no other man ever had, made her heart race and her body ache, made her heart long for dreams that had been shattered long ago. He made her want and feel all kinds of scary emotions.

"I'm sorry. I just don't think I can do pretend."

"Sure you can. We did pretend in Vegas and it was amazing."

"That was different and you know it."

He considered her a moment then leaned toward her, his face only inches from hers as his gaze dropped to her lips, hesitated, then lifted back to her eyes in challenge. "Play me for it."

She couldn't breathe. Couldn't hear for the pounding of her chest. "What?" she choked out.

His grin was lethal, warning her she should just say no to whatever he was offering. "Play me to decide if we tell everyone now or wait until after the holidays."

Was it just her or had someone cranked up the heat in Pippa's Pizza Palace? Surely the thermometer was set on flaming-inferno mode. "That's ridiculous."

"Be that as it may, I'm serious." His gaze didn't waver from hers. Could he see that she was sweating? Would it be too obvious if she fanned her face?

"Why would I agree?"

"Because, if you really think about it, it's the right thing for both of us. But if you insist otherwise, if you win, I will give you what you say you want. I'll leave you alone and we'll go back to the way things were before Vegas. Plus, I will quit trying to engage you in conversation or asking you to dinner or even acknowledging that you exist."

His smile should have her running, but instead she considered what he'd said. How could she not when she could feel his breath against her lips? Or was she just imagining the soft caress that made her want to lean in and close the gap between them?

She frowned and leaned as far back in her seat as she could without looking as if she was auditioning for a human contortionist act.

"I'll quit trying to convince you to let me strip you naked and repeat all the naughty things we did last weekend, even though I will probably still be thinking about those things and wanting them, wanting you."

Her heart squeezed and she felt a little panicky at the thought of what he'd promised, of what he'd said. Not panic. Excitement. Anticipation. Slade leaving her alone was what she wanted. What she needed. She wasn't strong, and what if she gave in to the physical sparks that burned so potently between them? Especially when he kept saying he wanted her? What if he kissed her and she forgot everything but the fact that she was a woman and he made her glad of it? What if she acknowledged that he hadn't epically failed with being around her daughter tonight?

Play a game, win and he'd back off trying to convince her to have an affair destined to lead nowhere but to heartache for her. That's what she needed. Wanted. So what was the catch? "Not that I'm agreeing to anything, but what would we play?"

"Your choice."

Her choice? "Let me get this straight. I get to pick the

game and if I win, you avoid me at all costs? No changing your mind?"

"Yes," he agreed, not looking in the slightest worried. "But if I win you will give me a month of pretending to be happily married and if you happen to decide you aren't opposed to continuing our physical relationship, well, that would be an added perk."

She ignored the little voice inside her head reminding her of the last time he'd *proved* something to her, of just how tempting she found that added perk. "A month?"

"A month. That puts us at New Year."

She bit the inside of her lip. She didn't really think he could beat her at Skee-Ball, but a month…

This was crazy. He was crazy. Why was she even considering his suggestion?

"I don't want my daughter hurt."

His blue eyes twinkling, he looked more relaxed than he had all evening. "So you admit even before we start that I'd win?"

She lifted her chin a notch. "I'm not admitting anything."

His grin was wicked. "But you aren't denying that I'd win either."

She glanced over at her daughter, who was watching another child play a coin-toss game. Her gaze lit on the Skee-Ball lanes. She could do this. She could beat him, remove all temptation and just move past the events of the past weekend. It's what she needed for her sanity because being around him made her crazy.

"Any game?"

His smile broadened. "Any game."

"Skee-Ball."

He didn't hesitate, just nodded. "Best of five?"

Why had the air in the room gotten so thin?

"Best of five," she agreed, wondering what she'd just

agreed to. Not that it mattered. She couldn't recall the last time she'd lost at Skee-Ball.

"We both get a warm-up game?"

She shook her head. She just wanted to get this over with. "I don't need a warm-up game."

He looked impressed. "Okay. But don't say I didn't offer."

Taylor smiled. "No changing your mind when you lose. We'll tell everyone the truth and you'll leave me alone at all times. No looks, no flirting, no daring me into kisses, no anything. You'll stay completely away from me. Tonight will be the last time I have to deal with you."

"No changing your mind when you lose," he countered. "You agree to a month of pretending to be happily married to me, spending time with me, and tolerating my looks, flirts and dares to kiss. Although, in private, win or lose, you call the shots and I'll honor your wishes. In January, we'll announce our divorce plans and go our separate ways."

There went her throat, gulping again. "If I refuse to play?"

"Then regardless of what we tell others about our marriage, I will actively pursue what I want, which is you in my bed."

Panic tightened her throat for a brief second, then she reminded herself that he was not going to win.

"Unless you're willing to admit that you want me as much as I want you, you have nothing to lose by playing me."

No way was she admitting that to him. Sure, there was no way he couldn't know how he'd made her body explode and implode and reload over and over in Vegas, but she was not admitting a thing.

"You're right. Because I won't lose."

Not looking in the slightest intimidated by her bravado, he grinned. "Such confidence. I like it."

She picked up a piece of Gracie's leftover cheese pizza and took a bite. "I'm good at Skee-Ball."

He watched her eat, and if he was attempting to hide that eyeing her mouth gave him pleasure he failed. "Gracie mentioned that."

Yet he'd agreed. That threw her. "You knew and you still let me pick which game we played? Do you want to lose? Is this some kind of sick joke?"

"In case you haven't figured this out yet, despite how many times I've told you, I want you. And for the record I don't like to lose or fail at anything. Something we have in common."

When she just stared blankly at him, he elaborated. "Our competitive spirit."

She didn't think she had a competitive spirit, but there was something about the man that made her want to get one up on him. Plus, she wasn't 100 percent sure he wasn't just toying with her. Maybe he sensed how much she struggled with her attraction to him and out of boredom he planned to prove his point on that score as well.

Either way, all she had to do was win and, whatever his motive, it would be a moot point.

CHAPTER NINE

AT GRACIE'S ENCOURAGEMENT, Taylor and Slade played three of the frog games first. Gracie won each time. They also played several of the other electronic games, including whacking the clowns.

Hearing Gracie, seeing the joy on her daughter's face at their antics, eased Taylor's nerves.

Knowing that she would win, that Slade would quit pursuing their physical relationship, helped calm her fear of how he made her long for things she shouldn't.

He didn't seem nervous. He'd been laughing and mostly at ease with Gracie, the kiddie games and with the whole chaos of Pippa's Pizza Palace. Every once in a while she'd catch him responding a little awkwardly to Gracie's exuberance, but otherwise he'd impressed her.

"Ready to win Gracie a bunch of tickets?" His eyes sparkled with challenge.

"Oh, yeah." She was ready to get the game over so they could go home. Not that she wasn't having fun. Of course she was having fun. Slade was a fun guy. Fun wasn't the problem. But he wasn't what she wanted in a man, in a father for Gracie. He'd hurt her, hurt Gracie, if she gave him the chance. That was the problem. Why she'd needed a stronger barrier to her feelings to begin with.

That plan sure had backfired. Gracie hung on to his

every word and wanted him beside her for each game they played. She'd even caught her daughter batting her lashes at Slade. The man was a charmer. Age didn't matter. Females flocked to him and her daughter was no exception.

She ran her gaze over his handsome profile and admitted that he was definitely flock worthy. He made her want to flock, too. If only...

He turned, caught her watching him and grinned.

Taylor rolled her eyes. No need to give him a bigger ego than he already had. If he knew how much she thought about him, about their wedding night and how she wished the way he'd kissed her had been real and that he wanted a month with her to win her heart rather than to have an affair, he'd definitely tease her. Likely, he'd break her heart if given the chance. That's why she needed to accept his challenge, to beat him at his own game, so he'd back off from pursuing her and hopefully she'd walk away from their marriage without any mortal wounds.

Gracie took the center lane and they watched her play a game prior to their dropping coins into the next lane.

"You go first," she offered.

Slade shook his head. "Ladies first."

Taylor shrugged, then picked up a ball and smoothly rolled it down the lane. It dropped effortlessly into the highest point slot.

"Oh, yeah!"

Gracie high-fived her.

Slade nodded in approval. "Nice."

Unfortunately, her next two dropped into the next to highest point level slot. Frustrated that she wasn't rolling a perfect game, the remainder went into the same just-below-perfect slot until she ran out of balls.

Her score wasn't her highest, but it wasn't bad. She stepped aside. "Your turn."

"Do you want to do all five of your games first, keep a score tally and then me go?"

She shook her head. "I thought we were going to play against each other and have winners each time. The best of five, remember?"

"Either way is fine."

He dropped more coins into the slot. A new set of balls rolled down. Slade picked one up, rolled it down the lane, and plopped it into the highest point slot.

When he repeatedly dropped the balls into the same slot, Taylor began to feel clammy.

"You're pretty good."

He rolled the remainder of his balls. "I dated a girl in high school who worked in a place like this. I killed a lot of time playing this game while waiting for her shift to finish."

His rolls didn't remain perfect, but his final score was higher than Taylor's.

Gracie jumped up and down, clapping. "You're good, Mr. Slade! You beat Mommy. Look at all those tickets."

Slade tore off the long string of tickets. "These are for you, princess. We'll have you more in just a few."

"Yay," she squealed, waving the tickets around.

"Okay, then," Taylor said, her palms sweating. Of course he'd dated someone who'd worked at a place that had Skee-Ball lanes. He'd probably dated a professional Skee-Ball player and coach, too. If there was an international Skee-Ball game, he'd probably won gold. Urgh. "I guess it's my turn."

"That it is." Slade looked as if he was having the time of his life. The fink.

Taylor started the new game and took her time to make sure she sank the balls into the highest scoring slot. She did well and upped her score by forty points, which would have beaten Slade in the previous game. She smiled as she stepped back.

Excited, Gracie gathered the tickets the machine was spitting out.

"Nice job," Slade agreed, obviously not concerned. He started his game and tied her score with almost effortless ease.

"Hmmm," he mused. "We didn't discuss how to handle a tied score."

Annoyed at how calm he was, she stretched her arms over her shoulders. She just needed to loosen up a little to beat him. "We'll just keep playing. One tied game may not make a difference."

But Slade tied her next two scores. Gracie was ecstatic. Taylor was not. Three ties and he'd won the first game. She had to win this next one.

Putting all her focus into the game, she picked up her first ball and dropped it into the highest point slot. Yes. She repeated that time and again, the ball only dropping into a lower slot once. An almost perfect game. It was the highest score of the night.

Finally! Breathing much easier, she glanced at Slade. "Your turn."

"That's a pretty high score. What happens if I tie you or get a higher score?"

"You won't," she said dismissively, more for her benefit than his.

His lips twitched. "But if I did?"

"You would win because you won that first game."

"If I don't tie you?"

"We'd have to play a sixth game to break the tied score."

"I just wanted to be clear."

Slade rolled the ball and it dropped perfectly into the highest point slot. Each and every time. He only had one more to have a perfect game. He'd be up two wins to her none. If he tied her, he'd still win. Only if his ball dropped into a lower point slot would she win. Even then, they'd possibly have to play a tiebreaker. Knots twisted her stomach.

He surprised her by holding out the ball.

"Gracie, would you like to roll my last ball?"

The little girl, who had been enthusiastically gathering tickets, jumped up and down and nodded, her ponytail bouncing almost as excitedly as she had been. "I would."

He handed Gracie the ball and the little girl looked up at him, suddenly uncertain. "Will you help me, Mr. Slade? I want to do good and get more tickets."

Taylor wasn't sure anyone could resist such a sweet, innocent plea, and Slade was no exception. He stood behind Gracie, helped position her body just so, pulled her arm back and helped guide her through the motions. Gracie let go and the ball dropped into the second from highest slot, tying Taylor's score.

Taylor's knees almost gave way beneath her. No.

"That was good!" Eyes wide, Gracie jumped up and down, superenergized about her success.

Slade picked her up and twirled her around. "Princess, you are amazing!"

She giggled and patted his cheeks. "Did we win?"

He nodded. "We did win. We make a good team."

"Yea." Gracie high-fived him. "Princes and princesses always make good teams."

Taylor watched them, wondering at the doomed feeling in her gut, wondering at the emotional pangs at how her daughter was so quickly responding to Slade.

With a suddenly serious expression Gracie looked up at Taylor with her big green eyes. "You're not mad 'cause I helped Mr. Slade win, are you, Mommy?"

Oops. Her silence had gotten her daughter's attention. Oh, Slade was slick. He'd used her daughter against her. If she showed disappointment, Gracie would think her a poor sport.

Pasting a smile on her face, Taylor gestured to the long strand of tickets. "Nope. I think with as awesome as you just did you're going to run the machines out of tickets. Did you see all those?"

"Wow." Gracie's eyes grew large. "I'm going to get a stuffed monkey."

"A what?"

Gracie pointed to where the prize booth was. Hanging from the ceiling was a big green stuffed monkey with a yellow banana in his hand. "I want him."

Okay. "How many tickets does he take?"

Gracie shrugged.

"Let's find out." While Gracie and Slade ran their tickets through a counter, Taylor asked the teenaged cashier at the booth how many were needed for the monkey.

"That many?"

The boy nodded.

"Mommy, we have over a thousand tickets!"

"We're going to need them."

Slade grinned. "Takes that many for a big green monkey, huh?"

Ignoring his expression, she told him.

He whistled. "Expensive monkey."

"He's worth it," Gracie assured them, eyeing the monkey with longing. "He's the king of the jungle and has been trapped up there for months and months. He needs to get back to his kingdom."

Slade looked intrigued. "He does?"

All seriousness and in full Gracie-imagination mode, she nodded. "Plus, he has to find a princess to go to the jungle with him and lead his people."

"You're a princess," Slade reminded her, getting into Gracie's active imaginings.

"I'm a princess," Gracie agreed with a *duh* expression. "But he's going to fall in love with Princess Vegas." She took on a worried expression. "Let's hope she likes big green monkeys because not all princesses do, even though they are so cute and cuddly."

Slade's gaze lifted to Taylor's and despite still reeling inside that he'd won, that he'd brought Gracie onto his side, she smiled at his rather bewildered, overwhelmed, yet totally enamored expression.

Probably a similar expression to the one she wore that for the next month she would be pretending to be happily married to Slade and he'd be actively pursuing an affair with her.

An affair she couldn't afford emotionally.

"I want the biggest tree they have," Gracie informed Slade and Taylor as they pulled up to the Christmas-tree lot in Taylor's van the following Friday evening. "A gigantic one so I can climb high into the sky!"

"Christmas trees aren't for climbing."

Gracie scrunched her face at her mother's comment. "They should be. Christmas would be so much fun if I could climb the tree." Her face lit. "I could be an ornament."

"Or the angel at the top," Slade suggested, parking the car and not quite believing that Taylor and Gracie had convinced him to come along on this trip. The less he had to do with Christmas, the better. "You are quite the angel."

Gracie giggled, then added, "Angels fly and I can't fly. I need a Christmas tree I can climb and hang on a branch 'cause I'm a Gracie ornament."

The logic of a six-year-old had quickly come to fascinate Slade. He grinned at the miniature version of Taylor. His wife. A week ago today they'd gotten married. How crazy was that?

Was it even crazier that he'd convinced her to play along with their marriage for a month? All for the sake of not wanting news of a pending divorce to possibly reach Grandview Pharmaceuticals as it might hurt his chances of landing his dream job and because he didn't want his dad to stress over the holidays. His father had experienced enough rough Christmases over the years. Slade wouldn't be the cause of ruining this one.

Plus, he wanted Taylor so much he couldn't think of anything else but touching her again. Which was proving a little difficult since she kept Gracie between them at all times they weren't at the clinic.

Realizing her argument wasn't working, Gracie changed tactics. "I bet you'd like to climb a Christmas tree, too, wouldn't you, Mr. Slade?"

Smart kid.

Taylor sent him a warning look.

"Not really. Christmas trees aren't for climbing. But maybe someday soon I'll take you out to my dad's farm in Franklin and we'll find climbing trees."

"Really?" Gracie rubbed her hands together, then climbed out of her car seat and jumped to the ground. "Are there chickens on your farm?"

"No chickens," Slade told her. "But there are horses and cows."

"Princess Vegas has never ridden a horse," Gracie informed him very matter-of-factly. "She thinks she would really like riding a horse. Especially a white one who looks like a unicorn."

"Hmm, I'm not sure if there are any that look like unicorns, but we'll see."

Gracie nodded, then pointed out a family who were also tree shopping. "Look!" She waved at her grinning friend whose face was barely peeking out from beneath her high-collared coat, hat and scarf. "Mommy, can I go say hi to Sarah Beth?"

Sarah Beth, as in the Sarah Beth who was on her soccer team and whose mother screamed and cried a lot?

Waving at a very pregnant woman bundled up in several layers of coats and scarves, Taylor nodded. "That's fine, but walk, don't run."

Doing what could only be called a fast walk, Gracie headed to her friend and hugged her as if it had been months since they'd last seen each other.

Her gaze still on her daughter, Taylor sighed.

Slade stared at her, but she kept her gaze trained on where Gracie and Sarah Beth chatted away, waving their gloved hands around animatedly. "You shouldn't say things to make Gracie think you're going to be a part of our future. I don't want her hurt."

"Neither do I. But even after we sign divorce papers, there's a ninety-day wait before we go before the judge."

Taylor's attention snapped to him. "You talked to your lawyer today, too, then?"

"Yes. You knew I had a Friday morning appointment, the same as you." He nodded. "He said it'll be after the holidays before anything gets rolling."

Her eyes returned to Gracie. "Mine said the same. Guess it's just as well we didn't open ourselves up for more gossip at work."

He'd spent every evening this week with Taylor and Gracie. They'd eaten, played whatever games Gracie wanted to play, watched cartoons, read her stories and last night they'd pulled boxes out of Taylor's attic and stacked them in the corner of her living room in anticipation of Christmas decorating this weekend.

He could do without the Christmas decorating, but apparently if he wanted to spend time with Taylor, he'd have to endure Christmas festivities. He and his dad had quit celebrating Christmas the year his mom had died. His dad had since started again. His new wife had seen to that. Slade, on the other hand, although not a Scrooge, just didn't see the point.

Each night he'd helped Taylor straighten any mess they'd created, then, while she'd put Gracie to bed, he'd driven home to a house that really wasn't a home at all. Funny how he'd never noticed that before. He'd always liked his uptown condo with all its modern conveniences. Now the place just seemed empty. Good thing he hoped to be moving to New Jersey soon.

Half expecting Taylor to pull away, he grabbed her gloved hand and laced her fingers with his, clasping it tightly as they walked toward Sarah Beth's family. Beneath the fabric he could feel the outline of the wedding ring Taylor still wore. Just as he did beneath his gloves. For their pretend month.

Sarah Beth caught sight of Slade and leaned over to stage-whisper, "Who is he?"

"That's my boyfriend," Gracie informed them, not in a stage whisper. "He's my Prince Charming. When I grow up I'm going to marry him and we're going to live in a magnificent castle and throw grand balls for all our kingdom to enjoy."

Everyone's gazes went to Slade, including a wide-eyed, slightly amused Taylor. Stunned by Gracie's announcement, he cleared his throat.

Laughing, Sarah Beth's mother stuck out her hand. "Hi, I'm Janie. Gracie is my Sarah Beth's best friend. Together they are quite the pair. The entire family will expect an invitation to the wedding, of course. And frequent invitations to visit at the castle."

"I can only imagine." He instantly liked the very pregnant woman, even if she reportedly screamed and cried a lot. Seeing her so pregnant made Slade wonder what Taylor had looked like pregnant with Gracie, what she'd look like if she were pregnant with his child even now from their Vegas weekend. Lord, he hoped she wasn't. He glanced toward her, but she refused to meet his gaze. Her cheeks and nose were already pink from the cold. She was beautiful.

He smiled at Janie. "And, of course, on the castle invitations."

"Janie, this is Slade Sain. He's…" Taylor hesitated and Slade wondered how she would label him. Not husband, not boyfriend, not lover, but who?

"A friend of the family."

Friend of the family? That was accurate up to a point. He was friends with her and Gracie, even if about half the time Taylor treated him more as if he were her enemy. Still, she was cooperating on the pretend month and even smiled at him at work.

"Hoorah for handsome friends, eh, Taylor?" Janie laughed, then, placing a hand on her belly, glanced toward her husband. "We just got here and have to find a tree. My parents are visiting next week and they will be livid if we don't have a tree up for Sarah Beth."

"I hear you. I dread it when my parents visit on Christmas Day."

Real dread showed on her face. Did she not get along with her parents? He'd give anything to have the opportunity to spend time with his parents together again. Then again, maybe her dread had to do with her all-too-real pretend marriage. What had she told her parents?

"We'll let y'all get to it." Taylor glanced around the tree-filled lot. "Hopefully we can find a tree quickly and get in out of this cold."

They went their separate ways. Gracie latched on to Slade's free hand. "Can we put real candy canes on our tree?"

"Sure." After he answered, he realized he should have gotten confirmation from Taylor, but she didn't look upset that he'd answered Gracie's question.

"We could make paper chains to put on it, too."

"If that's what you'd like to do," he agreed.

"It is." Still clinging to his gloved hand, Gracie skipped beside him as if completely unfazed by the cold wind whipping at them. Taylor, on his other side, shivered. In the middle of them, Gracie was holding his one hand and Taylor his other. Warmth spread through Slade's chest. He felt… cozy. He swallowed and fought the feeling down. This was temporary and he was just making the best of a bad situation. It wasn't cozy. Just convenient.

"I think paper chains are beautiful," Gracie continued.

"I'm sure anything you made would be beautiful, princess." Convenient? Could he really lie to himself to that extreme? Spending time with Taylor and Gracie was more than a convenience.

"Mommy always thinks so." Gracie beamed up at him, causing Slade's heart to do a funny chest flop.

Taylor pointed to a blue spruce she spotted a few trees down from them. "It's gorgeous, but it may be too tall. Do you think we can get it inside the house?"

Would it fit through the back double doors of her house?

Slade inspected the tree, thinking that if he'd liked Christmas and had felt the need for a Christmas tree, then Taylor had made a good choice. Perfectly shaped with full branches.

"If not, we could trim some to make it work," he offered. "What do you think, Gracie?"

Gracie eyed the tree and gave him a puzzled look. "How are we gonna fit it inside the van?"

He laughed. Smart, smart kid. "You don't think it'll fit in your seat?"

Gracie giggled. "No way. We could put it on top of Mommy's van. I saw that on a cartoon."

Slade scratched his head. "I'm not sure that's going to work, princess."

"If you don't think we can get it on top of the van, we

can pick a smaller tree," Taylor suggested, but her eyes still lingered on the blue spruce.

This was the tree she wanted. The tree he suddenly wanted her to have, even though he saw no logical reason to stuff a tree inside a house and throw glittery decorations on it.

He shook his head. "This is the perfect Christmas tree."

"This Christmas is going to be a perfect Christmas," Taylor mused, almost sounding as if she really believed so.

Not that he'd celebrated Christmas in years, but he was getting sucked into the holiday by a woman so sexy she filled his every waking thought and her six-year-old princess-wannabe daughter, because he wanted to give her that perfect Christmas, to make her holidays filled with joy.

"It is," Gracie agreed, nodding. "Princess Vegas thinks so, too."

"That settles it. Princess Vegas has the best taste." Slade winked at Gracie, got a wink right back that melted him despite the cold wind. "This is our tree. We'll pay and I'll come back later in a truck to pick it up."

"You have a truck?" Taylor looked skeptical. "I can't see you driving a truck."

"No, but my dad does and of course I can drive a truck. I grew up on a farm." Granted he'd spent as much time studying, volunteering and fundraising for breast-cancer awareness as he had hauling hay or herding cattle. But he could do any job on the farm that needed to be done. He loved the land, loved riding his horse and still got a kick out of taking off on a four-wheeler for a carefree afternoon in the country. Nothing like breathing some fresh air and getting up close with nature.

"He lives close?" Taylor still didn't look sure. "We don't want to be a bother. I could call a service and have a tree delivered."

"There's no need to pay inflated prices to a service. My

dad's in Franklin. It's about a twenty-minute drive, depending on traffic. I want to do this, Taylor. Let me."

"Of course." Taylor became pensive. "What will you tell him if he asks why you need to borrow a truck?"

"I'll tell him the truth. That I need a truck to pick up a Christmas tree." Or maybe not because wouldn't that cause a slew of questions? His dad knew how he felt about the holidays, and although he and Slade's stepmom both repeatedly invited him over to celebrate the day, he always refused. "Do you want to go to?"

She immediately shook her head. "I don't think that's a good idea. He might…realize the truth."

No doubt both his dad and his stepmom would question him like crazy regardless. It would be the first time he'd seen them since returning from Vegas. Had he wanted to take Taylor as a way of curtailing their questions?

Glancing down at where Gracie was checking out a cocoon attached to a different tree, Slade whispered back, "You might be right. He does want to meet you, though."

Taylor's brows shot up. Horror paled her face. "Definitely not a good idea."

"I agree. For now."

"This is such a mess." Taylor's lower lip disappeared inside her mouth.

"Only because of Princess here. After you've told her, I think it's a grand idea." He placed his hand on top of Gracie's head and the little girl beamed up at him from beneath the hood of her coat.

"What's a grand idea?"

"Hot chocolate and marshmallows?" he suggested. It wasn't his place to tell her more. Maybe he'd just tell his dad Gracie didn't know because they wanted her to get to know him first. Once they announced their break-up, telling Gracie wouldn't be an issue. Why did the thought of their having to do that bother him so much?

"Mmm-hmm. I'm cold." Gracie wrapped her arms around her body. "Can we go home for hot chocolate?"

"I'll pay for the tree, make sure the guy marks it as sold, then come back with the truck."

"Thank you, but I'll pay for the tree. It would be silly for you to pay for my and Gracie's tree when you'll still have to get one of your own."

"I don't put up a tree, Taylor."

"No Christmas tree?" Gracie piped up, staring at him incredulously. "Are you crazy? What if Santa thinks you don't believe and he doesn't leave you presents? You've got to have a Christmas tree, doesn't he, Mommy?"

"Absolutely. So I'll pay for this one and you help pick out another for his place. We can help decorate it."

Before Slade could argue, Gracie grabbed his hand. "Come on, Mr. Slade, you gotta have a tree for Christmas."

CHAPTER TEN

"Sorry I took so long," Slade told Taylor when she opened the front door much later when he arrived with the tree.

She'd changed from her business clothes into yoga pants and a snowman sweatshirt. Her long blond hair hung in a braid. She'd scrubbed her face clean of the light makeup she'd worn to work that day. Each night was the same. She dressed down. Purposely? To scare him away? He wanted to tell her that it didn't matter what she did. He still wanted her.

"Not a problem." She moved aside so he could enter. "I got your text letting me know you'd been delayed at your dad's."

Closing the front door behind him, Slade frowned. Despite the fact his hands were cold, he grabbed Taylor's warm ones and pulled her gently to him. "Warm me up?"

"Now?" She laughed a little nervously and glanced around her foyer as if seeking an excuse to flee a crime scene.

"Can you think of a better time?"

Her hands trembled within his. "How about never?"

He laughed. "It's hard to believe a week ago I had never met Gracie or held your hand." He squeezed her hand for emphasis. "That I had never kissed you."

"A week ago you had held my hand and kissed me," she corrected, staring at their hands. "As far as Gracie goes, she adores you."

He studied her face, her pensive expression. "Does that bother you? That she likes me?"

She shrugged, making the snowman's hat bell jingle on her shirt. "Should it?"

"No, but I can see that it does." He laced his fingers with hers. "I'm not going to hurt her, Taylor."

She wouldn't meet his eyes. "I hope not."

"Surely you believe I'd never intentionally cause her pain?"

Finally, she lifted her gaze. "I do believe that."

"It's true." He glanced around the foyer and beyond to the living area. "Where is my favorite princess?"

"Asleep. She didn't want to go to bed before you got back but she was fading fast. I promised her we'd get the tree ready to decorate tomorrow." Her expression became pensive again. "I probably shouldn't have promised her that since…"

"Since?"

"Since I shouldn't make plans that include you without your permission. Especially as you don't celebrate Christmas."

He could hear the curiosity in her voice about that, but the last thing he wanted to do was have a conversation with her about his mother's death.

"I'm here, Taylor. Right where I told you I'd be."

"I know."

She refused to look at him again and he'd had enough. He cupped her chin, forcing her gaze upward. "You think I'm going to skip out on the decorating?"

"Tomorrow is Saturday. I'm sure you have other things to do."

"I've rearranged my other obligations for the next month." Normally, he spent his Saturdays with his dad and step-mother, helping out on the farm, unwinding from the week's stressors. All other spare time was spent volunteering with various breast-cancer awareness organizations. "I want to be with you, Taylor."

He wasn't sure he'd ever said truer words. Crazy how a week could change a person's life. He'd always admired her, wanted her, from afar, but now...now she was all he could think about.

"Just because you won it doesn't mean you have to be over here all the time," she clarified. "You shouldn't put off your responsibilities because of me."

He traced his thumb over the smooth lines of her face. "You need to quit trying to back out of giving me my prize."

She met his gaze full on. "You're not getting that prize."

Awareness that they were touching and essentially alone fell over them. Awareness that had her pulling her hands away from his and walking over to where she'd cleared out a corner for the tree.

"I took a pregnancy test at work today. It was negative. I know that's no guarantee and I'll probably do tests weekly until I get my period, but I thought you'd want to know."

"That's good." Because they didn't want her to be pregnant. Emotion hit him. Whether relief or something else, he wasn't sure. Just that strong emotion weighed heavily upon him.

"Yes. The timing was all wrong anyway, but I did the test just to be sure."

He nodded, feeling as if he should say something more but not really knowing what else to say.

"What do you think?" She gestured to the cleared-out corner. "This is where we put our tree last year, but it wasn't nearly as big as the one we picked this evening." She turned questioning eyes on him. Her green gaze searched his, clear, bright, full of sincerity and a good amount of uncertainty, too. "Will it work?"

He'd make it work. He planned to make a lot of things work for the next month.

* * *

"Not there, Mr. Slade. Over here." Gracie directed Slade's top-of-the-tree decorating like a miniprofessional, even framing the tree between her tiny fingers and examining it with one eye closed.

Taylor pulled another ornament out of a box. One that had Gracie's first Christmas photo inside a golden frame. Taylor's heart squeezed. My, how time flew. Not so long ago her little girl had been a precious baby.

"Hey, that's me." Gracie caught sight of what Taylor held and came over for a closer look. "I was so cute."

"And so modest," Taylor mused. She hugged Gracie to her and they both looked at the ornament.

"Not sure modesty comes into play when she's just telling the truth," Slade said, coming down the ladder and checking out what they held. "Hey, you're right. You were cute."

"I was a little baby," Gracie pointed out needlessly. "I was inside Mommy's belly just like Sarah Beth's mommy has a baby." Then she had both adults scrambling for a response. "How did I get inside your belly, Mommy?"

Slade hid a grin and waited to see how Taylor would answer.

"Babies are a special gift and once they are inside a mommy's belly they grow until they are ready to come out into this world."

The look Gracie gave her mother made Slade wonder if the girl would accept the simplified answer. With her schooling, no doubt Gracie knew a lot more about worldly things than Taylor would like. For that matter, probably more than he would like.

He glanced down at her innocent face and felt a protectiveness that made his knees wobble. He'd thought it had been figuratively, but perhaps it had been for real because Taylor and Gracie both stared at him.

"You okay?" Taylor asked.

"Fine."

Only he wasn't. He felt claustrophobic.

He didn't want this. A family. Something he'd not had since his mother had died. Maybe he shouldn't feel that way. He had his father and stepmother, but it just wasn't the same. He was glad his father had found peace. He himself hadn't. Perhaps losing his mother had left him incapable of ever experiencing those bonds again.

He had a purpose, vows he'd made on the day his mother had died, and a wife and kid didn't figure into the equation. Good thing this was only a temporary setup or he might go into a full-blown panic.

"Maybe Mommy should hang the top ornaments." Gracie brought his attention back to the present. "You look drunk."

Determined not to think about the past, or even the future, he stepped down and tickled Gracie's ribs until she pleaded for mercy amidst giggles. "Drunk? What do you know about being drunk?"

Still giggling, she gave him a *duh* expression. "I watch cartoons."

He looked to Taylor for help, but she just gave him a blank look.

"Drunks on cartoons. Who knew?"

"Well, yeah, when the mouse falls into the barrel and comes out all hiccupy and stuff," Gracie clarified very matter-of-factly.

"You think I'm all hiccupy and stuff?" He faked a hiccup for good measure, causing Gracie's eyes to widen and then for her to burst into more giggles.

"Mommy, Mr. Slade is drunk."

He scooped Gracie into his arms and twirled her around. "If I spin enough, we'll both be drunk."

Gracie begged for more when he stopped.

"You don't know what you've started," Taylor warned, watching them with an expression he couldn't quite read. And not because his brain had yet to catch up with his spinning body.

"Gracie, with you around I wouldn't need to go to the gym." Slade collapsed onto the sofa next to Taylor.

Gracie crawled into his lap and flattened her palms against his cheeks. "More. More."

"You've tuckered him out," Taylor informed her daughter. "He's old and needs his rest. Besides, you need to finish hanging your ornaments."

"I don't want to."

"Gracie."

Gracie's chin dropped so low it almost dragged on the floor. She cut her gaze to Slade. "Maybe we could spin more after I hang the rest of my ornaments?"

"Slade may have other things he needs to do today beside help you hang ornaments."

"Do you?" Gracie pinned him on the spot.

He shook his head. "Despite being old and needing my rest—" he gave a pointed look at Taylor "—I'm yours all day, princess."

"I'm glad." Gracie wrapped her arms around him and squeezed tight.

"Me, too, princess." He soaked up the goodness of her hug and ignored the panic threatening to resurface. "Me, too."

Taylor and Gracie eyed their finished product. A fully decorated Christmas tree with twinkling colorful lights.

"It looks magical," Gracie breathed.

They'd decorated the tree before Slade had left to take his dad's truck back, but had just finished decorating the rest of the room with garlands and bows and pretty knickknacks. During that time daylight had disappeared and they'd just clicked the remote to turn on all the Christmas lights in the room.

Taylor glanced at her daughter. Gracie stared at the tree with wide eyes and awe. Through the eyes of a child. Nothing had ever seemed so magical as the wonder reflected on her baby girl's face.

"You're right," she agreed. "It does look magical."

"Just wait until Mr. Slade sees it. He's gonna love it."

Slade had said he'd come back. That had been a few hours ago. It was now early evening. On a Saturday. Despite what he'd said, no doubt he would have more exciting things to do. Why would he keep hanging around when she would barely even kiss him, much less all the other things he wanted from her?

How she was holding out she didn't know. It sure wasn't that she didn't want him. With each passing day the need within her grew more ferocious. She couldn't give in. To give in would only further complicate their situation. At least on her part. She couldn't have sex with Slade and not get emotionally attached.

But wasn't that happening with spending time with him? With watching him with her daughter? Sure, he was awkward at times, but overall the man had Gracie wrapped around his finger. Or was it the other way around?

"I think you're right," she agreed with Gracie. "How could anyone not love such a magical tree?"

The song playing on the Christmas station they were listening to changed and "Rockin' Around the Christmas Tree" came on. They looked at each other. Taylor cranked the volume up several notches. Grabbing each other's hands, they began to shimmy and shake and rock in front of their Christmas tree.

Happiness filled Taylor at her daughter's laughter. The song was their Christmas favorite and one that they always stopped what they were doing and danced to. She couldn't remember when they'd started the tradition. Probably when Gracie had been two, although perhaps it had been three.

Taylor treasured those happy, silly, giggly times.

They bounced around, twisting their tushes, laughing, slinging their arms around.

"I guess you didn't hear when I knocked," Slade said, leaning against the living room door frame. "Now I see why."

Mortified that he'd seen her shaking and shimmying, Taylor felt her giddiness evaporate and she stopped moving.

Or tried to.

Gracie grabbed her hand and waved her arms as she continued to dance with all her little heart. "Come join us, Mr. Slade. We're doing the Christmas rock, Mommy-and-Gracie style. We rule."

Unable to resist her daughter's enthusiasm, Taylor began a somewhat modified version of her earlier dancing. There was nothing stylish about the way she was twisting, but she refused to let Slade ruin their fun.

She met his blue gaze, daring him to make fun of her. She wasn't quite sure what she'd do if he did, but she'd figure that out on an as-needed basis.

His eyes twinkled with mischief, but he didn't comment on her dancing skills—or lack thereof. "I'll just watch the show."

She arched a brow. "Chicken?"

About time she turned his teasing around on him.

"Come on, Mr. Slade." Gracie bounced to the beat of the music. "It's fun."

"Yeah, Mr. Slade, come on. It's fun," Taylor taunted, crooking her finger and enjoying herself more than she'd have believed possible when she'd spotted him.

Slade pushed off the door frame and strolled toward them. Strolled because walk didn't begin to describe the swagger to his gait as he crossed over to them.

"Okay, but just remember you two asked for this and I did try to spare you." His gaze locked with Taylor's, he joined in, taking one of Gracie's hands and one of Taylor's, and began moving.

Heat spread up her arm at the feel of his skin against hers. He squeezed her hand, smiled, and Taylor couldn't keep from smiling back. Darn him. She didn't want to like him or enjoy that he was touching her or to share her Mommy-and-Gracie Christmas dance with him.

Only she was and it felt so right. All of it. Everything about him.

It had only been a week and already she was weakening in ways that went beyond the tingles attacking her senses. What was she going to feel like at the end of their month? If only she didn't know he was a player, and once a player always a player. Men might be able to change for a short while, but ultimately they always went back to playing.

It's what had happened with Kyle. It's what would happen with Slade.

He'd even said as much. He wasn't promising ever after or anything more than a monthlong affair.

The song ended, but another upbeat song about a Spanish Christmas came on. Gracie let go of their hands and began wholeheartedly singing along with the words she knew.

Taylor seized the opportunity to pull her hand free from Slade's and to step away.

"Taylor?"

Feeling choked, she shook her head and walked over to a stack of plastic bins. She fiddled with the empty boxes and bags inside, rearranging items, then closing the lid.

"Taylor?" he repeated.

"Don't you have somewhere you need to be?" she snapped, hating it that her eyes watered.

"Mr. Slade, did you see the tree?" Gracie interrupted, tugging on his hand and demanding his attention.

"Yes, when I was dancing I saw the tree. You and your mom did an amazing job."

"We did. You, too."

"I only put stuff where you told me to," he reminded her.

"That's still helping, right, Mommy?"

"Right," she agreed, grateful for Gracie's interruption so she could regain her composure.

"Are you two fabulous Christmas decorators hungry?"

Gracie nodded. "Famished." She dramatically put her hands across her belly.

"Can I take you somewhere?"

"Pippa's Pizza Palace?" Gracie piped up.

"Probably not again this soon," Taylor said, thinking she couldn't stomach greasy pizza tonight.

"She's just saying that because she knows I'll beat her at Skee-Ball again."

"Sure. That's the reason I don't want to eat overpriced mediocre pizza again this soon," she assured.

"It wasn't that bad."

"It wasn't that good either," she reminded him.

Although his gaze still searched her face, Slade laughed. "So, what's another restaurant Gracie likes?"

Gracie yelled out the name of her favorite Japanese hibachi grill.

Slade's brow rose. "You like sushi?"

"She'll eat it, but she's more into the steak and the show."

"Kid after my own heart. Hibachi it is."

Three weeks had passed since Taylor had married Slade. Three weeks in which her pregnancy tests had remained negative and she'd spent an inordinate amount of time with him. He really had set aside whatever his other obligations were because he spent every moment he wasn't at work with her and Gracie.

"It's only five more days until Christmas," Slade pointed out to the little girl in his lap.

Five days. Then her month with Slade would soon be over and then…and then what? He'd wanted the month so he could actively pursue having an affair with her. The sexual chemistry was always there, burning just below the surface, simmering and threatening to rise to a boil, but other than light touches that sent her nerves into overdrive, lingering looks that made her want to both run and hide, and strip him naked, and his lightly flirtatious comments, he hadn't pushed. Why not? She was so on edge she almost wanted him to push just so she could get angry at him.

She glanced at the other end of the sofa where Gracie was curled up in his lap. They were studying a department-store sales flyer as if it contained all the secrets to the world.

"I think Princess Vegas might like this one best." Gracie pointed to an item on a particular page.

"You think?" Slade studied the page with all seriousness. "I don't know. Princess Vegas might think getting a kitchen set to be insulting. After all, princesses don't cook."

"Princesses can cook if they want to cook," Gracie educated him. "Princesses just don't have to cook if they don't want to cook. Someone else has to do the dishes. Princesses never do the dishes."

"Unless they want to," Slade added, to which Gracie frowned and Taylor fought a smile.

"Gracie, I'm not sure that toy kitchen set will fit in Santa's sleigh."

"It will. Santa's sleigh is magic. If it can fly, it can hold all the toys for good boys and girls. Besides, some people get ponies and stuff. How do you think they all fit?" She paused for effect. "Magic."

"She makes a good argument." Slade looked as if he was fighting back a smile.

Taylor nodded. Her daughter was pretty sharp. "Well,

let's hope you've been a very good girl this year, then, so Santa can bring you that."

"The kitchen is for Princess Vegas, but I have been a very good girl, Mommy."

"I think you have, but who knows what Santa's been told?" Taylor teased.

Gracie thought about that a few seconds. "Sarah Beth is getting her picture taken with Santa tomorrow at the mall. I should go and make sure Santa knows I've been a good girl."

"I think you should." Slade glanced toward Taylor. "What do you think, Mom? You up for a trip to the mall tomorrow?"

"No parking places, crowded stores, long lines waiting to see Santa? Bring it on," she agreed. How could she not at the image of Gracie and Slade on the sofa, both looking so expectantly at her?

Slade laughed. "You've obviously done this before."

"A few times."

"You two will have to humor me. I've never done the Santa-at-the-mall thing."

Taylor frowned. So he didn't have kids and didn't want kids, but what about when he had been a kid? "Where did you grow up? Siberia?"

"Here, in Nashville."

"Then how did you avoid Santa at the mall?"

"I may have been when I was really small but, if so, I don't remember. My mom got sick when I was pretty young and we just didn't do that kind of thing."

"What kind of sickness?" Gracie rubbed his cheek in what Taylor assumed was her way of trying to comfort Slade.

"Breast cancer." His eyes were focused on the flyer he and Gracie still held.

Taylor's gaze stayed fixed on him and her hands wanted to rub his cheek, too, if it would give any comfort to the raw ache she'd heard in his two words. "Breast cancer?"

"Yes."

His mother had died of breast cancer and now he was an oncologist? Coincidence? Taylor doubted it. "How old were you?"

"When Mom was first diagnosed? Five. I was twelve when she died. She put up a great fight."

"I'm sorry."

"Me, too."

"Me, too," Gracie added, just to remind them that although she hadn't been saying much she'd been taking in their conversation.

Slade pulled her to him, kissed the top of her head, then changed the subject. "So, what do you think Santa needs to bring for your mom?"

Gracie put her finger to the side of her mouth and looked thoughtful, then scooted farther up in his lap and whispered in his ear. She glanced toward Taylor and giggled, then said something else.

Slade's eyes got big. "Seriously?"

Gracie nodded. "It's what she really wants."

"Interesting." Slade gave Taylor a look that made her feel nervous. "Does Santa do that?"

A puzzled look came over Gracie's face and then she shrugged. "He's magic, remember?"

Curious, Taylor crossed her arms. "What are you two up to?"

Gracie giggled. "Plotting your Christmas present."

"She put in a pretty tall request, but since it's what you really want…"

"I guess I'll find out in five days if I've been good or bad this year."

"Or maybe you've been really good at being bad?"

Gracie giggled. Taylor arched a brow.

"I'm pretty sure Santa is going to leave a bunch of coal in your stocking, Slade Sain." She paused. "Did you ever get your tree decorated?"

He shook his head. "It's in my living room, but that's it. I'm not much on Christmas decorations."

"Gracie and I should help you decorate." Maybe it was how his voice had cracked, how he'd tried to look so unaffected when he'd said his mother had had breast cancer, but Taylor wanted to do something for him. Goodness knew, he'd done enough for her and Gracie over the past few weeks.

"I'd like that."

"Then that's what we'll plan to do tomorrow after we go to the mall."

"That'll work because I'll have to pick up some ornaments and the like while we're there."

"You don't have ornaments?" Gracie sounded stunned. "How old are you?"

He shook his head. "We won't talk about how old I am but, no, I don't have any ornaments."

"I should make you some," Gracie offered.

"I'd like that."

Taylor would swear that his voice broke and that his eyes glistened more than a little.

Gracie climbed out of his lap and headed to her room.

"She is a wonderful kid, Taylor."

"I think so." Needing to be closer to him, to bring a smile back to his face, Taylor scooted near to where he sat. "What was Gracie's suggestion for my Christmas present?"

Looking grateful for the distraction from how emotional he'd gotten moments before, he shook his head. "Ask Gracie."

"I'm asking you."

"I'm not telling."

"Why not?"

"Because it's for me to know and for you to find out."

"That is so childish."

"Guilty as charged."

She picked up a sofa pillow and tossed it at him.

He caught it. "You wanna play?"

"Not really," she denied, but her gaze stayed locked with his mischievous one. She much preferred this look to the sad one that had taken hold in his eyes.

"Then you shouldn't have started something you didn't want to finish." He scooted closer, the pillow in his hands.

"Don't do it."

"Or what?"

"Or…or…" She couldn't think of any threat that even halfway made sense, so she grabbed another pillow, whacked him over the head and shot off the sofa.

He caught her before she'd taken two steps, pulling her down into his lap. "Naughty, naughty, Taylor. Don't you know Santa is watching?"

"Santa isn't real," she told him, twisting halfheartedly to free herself from his hold, but his arms tightened around her.

"Don't you let my girl hear you say that."

"She's my girl, and I'd never say that in front of Gracie. I want her to believe in all things good."

Was he staring at her mouth? Because she really thought he was staring at her mouth.

She held her breath.

He was definitely staring at her mouth. "I want to kiss you, Taylor, but Gracie is just in her room."

"I know." She did know.

"Do you want me to kiss you?"

"I'm not going to answer that."

"Because you do?"

"I'm not going to answer that either."

He laughed.

Taylor didn't. Because she wanted him to kiss her. They'd been married for three weeks. Three weeks. They were getting divorced.

Yet she couldn't imagine her life without him.

Which really wasn't good because she didn't want to become dependent on him.

She started to rise from his lap, but he hugged her to him.

"Don't go."

"I have things to do," she argued, needing to get away from him so she could clear her head. "I need to check on Gracie."

"We'll both go."

He made everything sound so good, as if life was full of possibilities, as if they could make this work. Then again, she'd believed Kyle when he'd convinced her of that, too.

CHAPTER ELEVEN

KYLE WOULD HAVE been cursing before they'd even pulled into the mall parking lot. Taylor's father would have made one loop, declared the whole thing a disaster and told her there was no Santa but that he'd buy her one item off her list so to choose wisely.

However, Slade dropped Taylor and Gracie off at the front entrance so they could secure a place in line to see Santa. Then, still whistling a tune, he drove off in her mini-van to search out a most likely nonexistent parking space.

Twenty minutes after letting them out at the front mall entrance, Slade joined them in the Santa line.

"You're just in time," Gracie told him excitedly. "It's almost my turn."

"Glad I didn't miss it. I wanted to see you with Santa."

"Sorry this is so much trouble," Taylor apologized.

Slade just shrugged. "This isn't that much trouble. Besides, if it makes her smile and you smile, it's worth a whole lot more than the effort to find a parking space."

"How come you're so nice?"

"Because I know what's beneath your clothes and I want another peek." He waggled his brows.

Taylor's eyes widened, surprised at his reply and a little flattered, too, even though she said, "Typical male response."

"I am a man."

"So all this is about sex?" she whispered, for his ears only. "Because you haven't even kissed me."

And maybe because she didn't quite believe that his answer hadn't been a cover because he hadn't wanted to tell her why he was really so nice to her and Gracie.

His eyes searched hers. "Have you wanted me to kiss you, Taylor? I asked you last night and you wouldn't answer. If you'll recall, our agreement was that I'd only do what you wanted me to do. I want you. I've been blunt about that. What do you want?"

She was saved from answering by Gracie excitedly tugging on her hand. "I'm next."

Fortunately, her daughter's full attention was all on the Santa and, unfortunately, Slade hadn't been distracted at all. "Well?"

She shook her head. Discussing this in line to see Santa wasn't the right time or place. "It doesn't matter."

"It does."

"I was just making a point that if all this is about sex, then it doesn't make sense that you haven't, well, you know, pushed for sex."

Slade smiled and looked so smug that you'd think it was him next in line with Santa. "You've been thinking about Vegas."

"It's my turn!" Gracie grabbed their attention. "Mommy, take my picture."

"Actually, you can't," an elf informed them. "Picture packages with Santa are available for a small fee." He pointed his finger to a table on the other side of the line. "When she finishes with Santa, just head over there and they'll fix you up with all the pictures you want."

Taylor and Slade watched Gracie whisper a long request to Santa, for Santa to look their way, then her to nod and say more. The Santa looked an awful lot like the Santa who had married them in Vegas, but, then, they were both impersonating a jolly old man wearing red and having a snowy-white beard. For that matter, the elf kind of reminded her of the limo driver…but that was crazy.

She shook her head, thinking Slade's comment about Vegas must have put the notion in her mind.

"There's no telling what she's asking for," she mused, mostly to make sure the subject didn't go back to sex…or the lack thereof.

"You think she's changed her mind from the toy kitchen?"

Still studying the Santa and his elf helpers, wondering at the resemblance to the Vegas Santa and his helpers, Taylor shrugged. "Kids tend to change their minds a dozen times before Christmas actually arrives."

"I hope not."

Something in the way he said it made Taylor look at him more closely. "Why?"

He grinned. "Because this Santa went online and ordered a certain toy kitchen set."

"What if I've already bought that for her?"

"Then I will cancel my order," he immediately offered, not looking upset in the slightest.

Again, a very different response than her father or Kyle would have had if she'd done something that had messed with their plans. She knew she shouldn't compare Slade to them, but she couldn't seem to help herself.

"Have you?" he prompted.

"I haven't, but you didn't need to buy her such a big item."

"I'll keep that in mind when I buy your present." His eyes twinkled.

Heat warmed her insides. He planned to buy her a gift? Why did that mean so much more than it should? "I know you don't celebrate the holidays, so don't bother getting me a present."

"There's one to me under your tree. Gracie had me shake it and try to figure out what it was."

So maybe he was just getting her a gift in response to her gift. Still, it was the thought that counted and for a man who claimed not to celebrate Christmas to make the effort did funny things to her insides.

"It's just a little something."

"I'll get you a little something, too," he promised.

"Did you see me with Santa?" Happiness shone in Gracie's eyes. "He said I had been a very good girl and that I was going to get all kinds of presents this year."

"He did?" Taylor shot a concerned look toward Santa. Man, he looked a lot like Vegas Santa. But no way could it be the same guy. The dude really shouldn't build up kids' expectations so high. A lot of parents would do well to buy one or two of the items on their kids' lists.

"Yep, he said you were going to get what you wanted for Christmas this year, too. That he's sorry about last year, but you never said anything until Christmas Day and then it was too late."

"He did?" she repeated, yet again looking at the Santa. The man's attention had already turned to the next kid climbing into his lap, but he glanced up and winked at Taylor.

What? Taylor stared in slight disbelief at the resemblance, telling herself to stop being silly and to pay attention to her daughter.

Gracie showed them the little stocking filled with a few pieces of candy that Santa had given her and then they were ushered over to the photo table where a computer screen had pictures of Gracie with Santa pulled up.

They couldn't decide which of the three shots they liked best, so Taylor ended up buying two of them and Slade bought the other because he thought it might have been his favorite and he couldn't leave the print behind.

They shopped for a few gifts Taylor still hadn't picked up, Gracie helping to decide between several items for Nina, then they drove to her favorite hibachi grill.

By the time they got to Slade's house, had the small tree decorated with the ornaments Gracie had made him with construction paper, glitter and glue, and a string of colorful lights, Gracie was tired and curled up on his sofa to watch a movie on television. In less than five minutes she was asleep.

"I guess we should be going," Taylor said, feeling awkward in his condo now that Gracie was out like a light.

"We were so busy decorating my poor little tree that you never saw the rest of the condo. Let me show you."

"Okay," she agreed, not knowing what else to say.

His place was beautiful, airy, spacious and clean. No toys or little handprints anywhere. Everything modern, high-tech and looking like it should be featured in a magazine article on the perfect bachelor pad.

They came to his bedroom. She refused to look at the bed. Then they went into his bathroom and he had an amazing rain shower and tub. Flashbacks to that last morning in Vegas and the shower they'd shared had her face heating. Oh, my.

"That is seriously cool." She eyed the tub and tried to keep her mind off Vegas. "Gracie could swim in it."

They both stared at the tub. "It's a shame I don't use it more often."

"Just let me know when and I'll come make use of it for you." Ugh. Had she really just said that? She hadn't meant... Or maybe she had. What was wrong with her? Thoughts of Vegas? Part of her wished she could blink her eyes and they would be back to that weekend away from reality.

"Anytime, Taylor."

His voice changed, taking on a raspy quality, and her gaze lifted to his. He watched her with awareness, hot and heavy, as if his mind was filled with the image of her in his tub, of them in his tub. Was he thinking about Vegas?

Her heart rate kicked up. "Sorry, I didn't mean…"

"Taylor?"

"Mmm?"

"Shh." He grabbed her wrist and pulled her to him.

Her cheek pressed up against his chest. The material of his shirt was soft, smelled of him, made her want to snuggle in closer to the sound of his heartbeat.

His fingers were in the pulled-up tangles of her hair. His lips were brushing the top of her head. His thumbs caressed her face.

"I know Gracie is asleep in the living room, but I need to touch you, Taylor. Even if just a little. Tell me that's what you want, too."

She knew what he meant. Being pressed against him felt so good. But she couldn't forget Gracie was just a few rooms away and could wake anytime.

He gently sucked against her nape.

Taylor almost moaned. Okay, so she did moan, the sound jarring her back to reality. She bit the inside of her lip.

"I know what you say you want," he continued, his eyes flickering with emotion. "When we touch, when you look at me, your body says something completely different."

She willed her body to silence. "We both know you are an attractive, skilled man. Of course I respond to you. It doesn't mean anything."

"So if we kiss and touch, it's nothing more than appeasing our sexual appetites?" he elaborated, moving even closer to her.

"Right." Had her voice cracked?

"Which means there's no reason why we shouldn't kiss, why we shouldn't give each other pleasure, because we both know the score."

"Right." That time she knew her voice had cracked.

He spun her so she was facing herself in the mirror that ran the entire length of the massive sink and countertop. He moved close so that his body pressed against hers, so that his hardness pressed into the softness of her backside. Taylor gulped.

He shifted against her. Excited shivers shot through her body. He kissed her, thoroughly, completely, making her practically gasp for air. His hands traveled over her body, leaving a wake of awareness, of need.

"None of this matters because a few months from now it will all be as if we never happened," he continued. "We'll go on with our lives just as if Vegas never happened."

Her gaze searched his in the mirror. She was reminded of the night he'd made love to her in Vegas, when he'd stripped her in front of the mirror. He'd been full of tenderness and passion. Now his eyes burned with something different, something she couldn't quite label.

Something that made her long for things she knew better than to long for. She wouldn't be able to forget him, wouldn't be able to think of Christmas without thinking of him, of their wedding ceremony performed by Santa, of his decorating with her and Gracie, of how wonderful the past few weeks had been with him at her side.

Because he made her want to believe in the magic of the holidays, that dreams could come true, even crazy ones that seemed almost impossible, such as a playboy changing into a Prince Charming. Her Prince Charming.

Only he wasn't and that was like a bucket of cold water over her head.

"You and I did happen, Slade, and that changed everything," she admitted, so softly she was surprised he could make out her words. He must have, though, because rather than resume kissing her, as she'd expected, as she'd longed for, panted for, he stepped back, turned from her, and walked out of the bathroom with a growled comment about going to check on Gracie.

"Ho-ho-ho, merry Christmas!" Slade called out as he pushed the front door to Taylor's house closed. A house that felt more and more like home to him. Which was why he needed to forget having an affair with Taylor, see her and Gracie past the holidays, then push them from his mind.

In two days he'd be flying to Newark to tour Grandview Pharmaceuticals and negotiate the offer for his dream job.

The call had come the day before and although he'd been over the moon, he'd found himself unable to tell anyone other than his father. His father, who had asked yet again when Slade was going to bring his new family to the farm for a visit and what they thought of moving to Newark. He had hummed and hawed enough to let his dad know that what Taylor and Gracie thought really wasn't a deciding factor in his decision.

They weren't.

This was the opportunity he'd dreamed of, the perfect smokescreen for Taylor and him to quietly divorce without any holiday or life drama for either of them, without Grandview bigwigs discovering that their new clinical research director had married and planned a divorce the same weekend. A win all the way around.

"Mr. Slade!" Gracie almost toppled him over as she launched herself at him, hugging him tightly.

Forgetting Taylor and Gracie wasn't going to be easy. She'd been right when she'd said they had happened and it had changed everything. Only he refused to let it change everything. He knew what he wanted, what his life goals were, and nothing was going to stand in the way of that.

Nothing and no one. He'd enjoy his time left with them, then he'd leave and not look back.

"Hey, princess." He set the packages he held on to the

wooden foyer floor and hugged the little girl to him, loving the warmth and genuineness to her embrace. "You ready for Santa Claus to come tonight?"

Gracie nodded. "It's going to be amazing."

"That good this year, eh?"

Blond curls bounced up and down again. "Do you want a cookie? Mommy and I have been baking them for Santa."

Slade caught sight of Taylor standing in the doorway, watching them. As usual, she stole his breath.

His wife. But not for much longer. Soon he'd pack his belongings and move to another state, live the life he'd always wanted. A life where he focused on finding a cure for a disease that had robbed him of so much. That had robbed so many of so much. He had no regrets.

"Hey," she greeted him, a bit breathy sounding herself.

"Hey, yourself." He soaked in every bit of her. From her caught-up-in-a-ponytail hair, to the Christmas sweater and yoga pants, to her washed-clean face. He was leaving in two days. The thought made him want to grab her, throw her over his shoulder and lock them in her bedroom for the remainder of the time they had left.

"Come on, Mr. Slade. Come see the cookies we made. I put icing on them and sparkling things you can eat." Gracie tugged on his hand, reminding him of why he wouldn't be doing any of the things he longed to do with Taylor.

"Help me carry these to the tree." He motioned to the brightly wrapped cartoon-princess-covered packages. "Then lead me to the cookies."

Gracie giggled and began inspecting the presents. "Are these all for me?" she asked, big eyed.

He nodded. He'd gone overboard, but he'd never had a kid to buy for in the past, never would in the future and he wanted Gracie's Christmas to be special. It would be the only one he shared with her.

The thought of missing her future Christmases, of missing her, shot sadness through him. Which was ridiculous. He was getting what he wanted. He should be over the moon.

Gracie smiled at him. "That's a lot of presents."

Fingering a dangling blond curl because he needed to touch her, he pointed out, "You did say you'd been a really good girl this year."

She nodded, grabbed up a package and took off toward the living room where the tree was.

"You didn't have to get her so much."

"I had fun shopping for her." True. Even though it had been years since he'd bought more than a gift card, he had enjoyed searching out gifts for Gracie.

"I can see you now in the little-girl section of the toy store," Taylor teased.

Slade took her hand, pulled her to him for a brief kiss to the cheek. "You smell good." He breathed in the scent of her hair.

"Like cookies?" She didn't pull away. Which surprised him. Thrilled him. Made him wonder what else he could do that she wouldn't pull away from.

"Like you."

"Flatterer."

"It's the truth."

"Do you always tell the truth, Slade?"

Her question seemed an odd one. Did she know about Grandview? Was she testing him to see if he'd tell her? Or was that his guilty conscience because she didn't know? He would tell her. Tonight. He studied her expression, then shrugged. "I try to be honest."

"It's a good policy. Prevents confusion down the road."

"Yeah." If she knew he was leaving, why didn't she just say so? Then again, how could she? He'd just found out the day before.

The timer on the oven dinged.

"Time to take out the last batch. You want to help decorate? The other batches should be cool by now."

He soaked in her smile, the warmth of her expression, and wondered how many nights he'd spend thinking about her in Newark. He suspected too many.

"Sure," he agreed. "But I have to warn you, I'm more of an expert cookie eater than decorator."

"Will you read me another good-night story?" Gracie yawned and stretched out in her bed. "I'm not sleepy."

"I can see that," Taylor agreed, smiling down at her daughter. "I guess we can do one more story, since it's Christmas Eve and all."

Gracie turned big green eyes on Slade, who stood in the doorway. "Will you lie down next to me and listen, too?"

"Gracie—" Taylor began, but Slade dismissed her concerns.

"Sure."

Despite his looking a little uncomfortable, he lay next to Gracie and she snuggled into the crook of his arm, grinning up at him. "Mommy is a very good storyteller."

His expression difficult to assess, he answered, "I've heard."

"I'm not sure about that, but I can read a book." They'd just finished *The Night Before Christmas*, so Taylor reached for one of Gracie's all-time favorites about a mischievous little girl with an active imagination.

Gracie looked up at Slade. "You're going to love this. It's so good."

Taylor began to read. Occasionally, Gracie would giggle and poke Slade. "See," she'd say.

Taylor kept reading until Gracie's eyes closed, then she finished the chapter and closed the book.

She stared at the image of Gracie tucked against Slade

and her heart melted. That's how it was supposed to be, she thought. How it should be.

Her gaze shifted to his and so many emotions shot through her. Mostly emotions of longing. Not just for the physical things he did to her body but for the way he'd turned her and Gracie's lives upside down over the past weeks. She had one week left with him. Then what? They told the world they'd made a mistake and were divorcing? Would he still be a part of their lives or would he go back to how things had been before Vegas?

She set the book back on Gracie's shelf and began untangling her daughter from Slade.

"I love you, Mommy," Gracie mumbled, not really awake.

"I love you, too, sweetheart."

"I love you, too, Mr. Slade."

Taylor's gaze went to Slade's. He stared at the sleeping little girl, but didn't respond other than to lose color from his face.

She might be getting all soft and mushy on the inside, but Slade wasn't. She'd do well to remember that.

Her throat constricting, Taylor moved away from the bed and left the room. She went into the kitchen and began unloading the dishwasher. He hadn't said the words back to Gracie. Because they weren't true? Because he'd told her earlier that he tried to always be honest?

Yes, she was biased, but how could he not have fallen for the little girl as much as Gracie had fallen for him? Right or wrong, she believed he had. So why hadn't he been able to admit it?

"Do you know if you're pregnant?"

Not having heard him come into the kitchen, she jumped, startled at his presence as much as at his words. Gracie's sleepy declaration had made him wonder if Taylor was pregnant. She paused midway to the cabinet, cup in hand. "I'm not."

"You're sure?" His voice was rough. Rougher than it should be, asking such a sensitive question. Or maybe she was just being too sensitive because she'd cried when she'd started her period. Tears of relief and tears of loss. How crazy was that?

"I'm sure. I told you I wasn't after the last negative pregnancy test, and I finished my period yesterday so I know I'm not. I guess I should have told you about getting my period, too."

He nodded as if that's what he'd expected her to say. "I thought you had. You drank coffee at work this week."

The man was observant. She'd give him that. "That made you think I wasn't pregnant?"

"Despite your negative pregnancy tests, you'd not had a cup since Vegas."

Yep, he was too observant for his own good.

"I started vitamins and stopped my bad habits just in case, but nothing came of Vegas."

Nothing came of Vegas. The words ripped at her heart. What had she wanted to come of Vegas? Nothing. Nothing at all because she'd never planned for Vegas to happen.

"I'm glad," he told her. "A pregnancy would have made everything more difficult."

Taylor gulped back the stab of pain she shouldn't be feeling. "You're right."

Because they were temporary, were getting a divorce, were only together to keep from having so much life turmoil with family and at work right before the holidays. Yet she'd not met his father or stepmother. Since Slade claimed not to celebrate the holidays, she supposed it made sense, but he'd not even mentioned her and Gracie meeting his family since the night they'd bought the Christmas trees.

Why didn't he celebrate Christmas?

She put a cup in the cabinet, shut the door and dared him to look away from her. After his not responding to

Gracie, she just dared him to ignore her. "Tell me about your mother."

His face paled almost as much as it had when Gracie had told him she loved him. "My mother? Why?"

Why? Good question when they were only pretending. Only was she really? Would his comment about her being pregnant have hurt so much if she was only pretending?

"I want to understand you," she admitted. She wanted to understand why he changed relationships so often, why he felt the way he did about marriage and kids, to understand why he'd not said three simple words back to a child he obviously adored.

"There really isn't a point, is there?"

Exactly what she'd just thought, but she couldn't let it go.

"It's Christmas Eve. Humor me."

He raked his fingers through his hair. "Let's go sit in the living room. I'll tell you, but it's really not that interesting a story."

For a not so interesting story, they talked until almost midnight. Once he started talking he couldn't seem to quit. Maybe to distract himself from the panic that had gripped him when Gracie had told him she loved him. Maybe because he'd almost said the words back. But he couldn't love the little girl. Sure, he cared about her and Taylor, but he didn't love them. So instead of analyzing all the unwelcome emotions that had taken hold of him he told Taylor about when he'd first realized his mother was sick, her frequent trips in and out of the hospital, about the sticky notes she'd write him every day.

"That's why you give your patients those notes?"

He nodded. "It just feels right, like I'm keeping a part of her alive."

"You keep her alive just by being you."

Talking about his mother helped, reminded him of his

life goals, grounding him to the future he'd chosen. "She was a special lady."

"I wish I could have met her."

He pulled out his wallet and withdrew a photo. It was a family shot of him, his dad, and his mother. Slade had been about five at the time.

She'd been upset when they'd started talking, but her attitude had softened long ago. "You look a lot like her."

"Thank you."

Taylor studied the picture. "How old was she when she died?"

"Thirty-three." The words tore from his heart.

Taylor grimaced. "That's so young."

He nodded. "Too young to have dealt with the things she dealt with." He stared at the photo, lots of old memories slamming him. Good, he needed those memories to keep his mind on track. He slid the picture back into his wallet, wondering why he'd let Taylor convince him to talk about his mother. Then again, maybe he'd told her because it was the perfect lead in to telling her that he was leaving, that he was taking a job to fulfill the vow he'd made in his mother's memory. Definitely he'd wanted a distraction from Gracie's sleepy words and their shattering effect.

"You were too young to have dealt with the things you dealt with, too," Taylor mused, taking his hand. "I'm sorry."

His heart squeezed and he didn't like the jitteriness shooting through his veins. Neither did he want her pity. "It's okay."

"Not really, but I understand what you mean."

They sat there, holding hands and staring at the Christmas tree for long moments, each lost in their own thoughts. He knew where his mind was, where he needed their conversation to go, but instead they sat in silence. Finally, Taylor stood.

"I guess it's time for Santa to show."

Slade arched a brow at her. "Santa?"

"You know what I mean and, no, I'm not putting a red suit and beard on."

The image of Taylor dressed as Santa had a real smile tugging at his lips. "Too bad. You'd rock a red suit and wig."

"Maybe, but Gracie will be just as happy with Santa arriving and eating his cookies sans a wig and red suit."

"I could help take care of those cookies for you," he offered, wiggling his brows and wondering why he wasn't redirecting their conversation to Grandview.

"Have at them. She also left a glass of milk, but since it's been out of the fridge a few hours I'd recommend tossing it rather than drinking it."

Taylor disappeared into her bedroom and came back carrying some plastic bags. Wondering at himself, at his reluctance to bring up a subject that he suspected would ruin their remaining time together, Slade made haste with the cookies while she pulled out stocking stuffers and gifts from the bags.

"She's going to be so excited when she wakes up."

"I wish I could see her," he murmured, not realizing he'd said the words out loud until Taylor's head spun toward him. How much he meant the words surprised him. He really would like to be there when Gracie woke, when she stumbled half-asleep into the living room and saw her gifts.

But not because he loved the little girl. Just that he'd spent so much time with Taylor and Gracie over the past few weeks that of course he wanted to be there when she experienced Christmas morning.

He watched Taylor consider offering to let him stay. His lungs didn't seem to be working correctly. He wanted to stay, to make love to Taylor, to wake up next to her, and experience Christmas morning with her and Gracie. Part of him wanted to take her into his arms and seduce her into letting him stay. Another part had his lungs constricting so tightly he had to go.

He couldn't stay, couldn't complicate the fact he was leaving the day after Christmas by having sex with Taylor when he suspected doing so would make leaving more difficult. For them both.

"What time is too early for me to arrive?"

"It's Christmas. She'll probably be up at the crack of dawn." She met his gaze. "It's already very late. You won't get but a few hours' sleep at most. Maybe you should stay?"

"I'll be fine heading home. I can sleep when I'm old." Or when he was in Newark. Alone.

Fulfilling his lifelong dream.

Disappointment and uncertainty flickered across her face. He was doing the right thing in going home so why didn't he feel better about doing the right thing?

"Whatever time is fine, then, but I should remind you that my parents will be here about noon."

She'd mentioned that they'd be over on Christmas Day.

"They'll bring Gracie lots of frilly clothes and maybe some mutual bonds or Fortune 500 stock."

At first he thought she was kidding, but at the serious look on her face he decided she wasn't. "Interesting Christmas choices for a six-year-old."

"Six. Two. Either way, it's never too young to start preparing for one's future."

Not liking the tension now etched onto her face, he nudged her shoulder. "They sound like party animals."

"Ha." She did smile, albeit weakly. "That they are not. More like some idealistic television couple. He's an investment broker. She's a country-club stay-home wife. They live in a plastic bubble of utopia."

"And you?"

"I'm not a chip off the old block. More like the daughter who should have been a son and has been a big disappointment at every point along the way."

"I doubt that. You're a very successful woman."

She gave a wry smile. "I guess that depends on what perspective you're looking from."

"From where I'm sitting, you're accomplished, beautiful, intelligent, compassionate and a good mother to Gracie." He didn't mention sexy since he didn't think that would be a trait her parents would appreciate, but he definitely appreciated that about her. "What more could they want from their child?"

Her cheeks turned pink and he could tell his praise pleased her. Guilt hit him that he hadn't complimented her more over the past few weeks, that he hadn't realized just how much she questioned herself. He should have told her over and over how amazing she was.

"They would have preferred for me to live a bit more within the rules."

Her comment seemed hard for him to fathom. "You a rule breaker, Taylor?"

"Apparently only on the big things."

His comment had been a tease, but her slight shrug made him wonder at her past. "Such as?"

"I didn't go into investments, but a doctor was a respectable profession, so they supported me in med school. Then I got pregnant with Gracie. That didn't win me any accolades in their eyes." She took a deep breath, then gave another shrug as if what she was saying didn't matter so much, even though it obviously did. "Now I've married a man I barely knew and am going to be the first in my family to divorce."

Good thing he knew she didn't want to be married any more than he did or he'd feel all kinds of guilty. As it was, he still felt a heel that their relationship caused her grief. "They don't know we're divorcing yet, do they?"

"No, and I'm grateful I don't have to deal with that on Christmas Day, but I dread their reaction when I do tell them. They've already told me how disappointed they are yet again in my life choices. If you decided not to show tomorrow, I wouldn't blame you."

"I'll be here." As uncomfortable as it might be, he would be there for her parents' visit and would hopefully be able to show her parents a glimpse of the woman he saw.

Before heading home, Slade brought in the large box containing Gracie's toy kitchen. "Is it okay if we set this up tomorrow, or would you rather put it together tonight?"

She shook her head. "Tomorrow is fine."

"Then I'll be going."

She nodded. "Tomorrow will be a long day, full of highs and lows."

"We'll focus on the highs."

"You're right. I have a lot of reasons to be thankful." Her eyes searched his, confused, tempting. "You're one of the things I'm thankful for, you know."

He stared at her a moment, wished things were different, acknowledged that they weren't and that he would also focus on the positives. He was getting the opportunity to make a difference in a deadly disease, to strive toward his goal of a cure. He didn't acknowledge her words, because what could he say that wouldn't reveal too much of the turmoil inside him?

He grabbed his coat. "I'll be back first thing in the morning."

CHAPTER TWELVE

"TELL ME THEY weren't like that growing up."

Drying the plate she held, Taylor laughed at Slade's expression. "They weren't."

"They were worse?" Slade said, helping her dry the dishes and put them away.

Taylor just smiled. Her parents had descended on them, brought presents, criticized everything from Gracie still being in her pajamas at noon to Taylor looking tired to they really should have had Christmas at their place and Taylor should be more co-operative. They'd been polite, though barely, to Slade initially. Her father had quizzed him like a drill sergeant.

Which had seemed ridiculous since they were going to divorce anyway. Only she hadn't told her parents that and neither had Slade.

Slade had laid on the charm. Halfway through their visit her father had actually seemed to accept him. Her mother's only direct comment regarding Slade had been that, after seeing him, she at least understood Taylor's temptation, even if she didn't condone her choice.

Taylor had bitten her tongue and smiled at her parents, regardless of their words. Although not touchy-feely with her, they hadn't been bad parents, just ones caught up in their own lives and expectations to where they hadn't been able to understand when their daughter acted outside those standards.

Gracie loved her grandparents. For the little girl, they had genuinely smiled as Gracie had shown them the toy kitchen, which she and Slade had put together while Taylor had made breakfast, plus all her many toys and new clothes.

Gracie had also given Slade the presents she and Taylor had picked up for him. Not once while they'd been opening presents had he mentioned a present for her. Although a little disappointed that he'd changed his mind about picking up a little something for her, she supposed it didn't really matter. More than anything she'd been curious about what he'd choose for her.

"Mr. Slade, I made you some yummy bacon and eggs." Gracie carefully offered the plastic plate of toy food.

"Looks good." Slade pretended to eat the food as Gracie beamed at him. He might not have said the words back to Gracie, but his actions were those of deep affection.

Taylor's muscles seemed to freeze as she watched them, as she tried to wrap her mind around the man playing with her daughter, the same man who'd spent the past few weeks being the perfect guy, the same man who'd gone through at least a dozen girlfriends during the past year and who had the reputation of a ladykiller. Because he was.

Or was he?

Gracie giggled as Slade pretended to sip tea.

Taylor swallowed. A vision of him walking out of her Vegas hotel bathroom wearing nothing but a towel popped into her mind. As attractive as that image was, the image of him on the floor, playing with her daughter, attracted her in so many more meaningful ways.

Who was she kidding? Everything about the man attracted her. Because she was falling for him.

Had fallen head over heels.

Just as she'd fallen for Kyle. Only her feelings for Slade were so much stronger than anything she'd ever felt for Kyle.

Her heart ached at the knowledge and moisture blurred her vision. She wanted to believe Slade was different, that he'd changed over the past few weeks.

He glanced up, caught her eye and grinned.

Maybe, just maybe, he had fallen, too. If not, she suspected she was in for some major heartache.

Slade glanced up in time to see Taylor swipe at her eyes. Was she crying? Because of her parents? They'd been uptight but hadn't been that bad surely? He'd thought by the end of their visit that they'd started warming to him. He wanted to ask if she was okay, but she scurried away as if she'd forgotten something in the oven.

He immediately glanced up when she reentered the living area. Whatever he might have seen earlier, now she was all smiles and focused her attention on Gracie.

They spent the rest of the day playing games with her, checking out her new toys. Then, with Gracie half lying on Slade, half lying on Taylor, they watched a movie she'd gotten in her stocking from Santa. Halfway through the movie she was out like a light.

"I think she had a good Christmas." Slade watched Taylor twirl a curl around her finger as she played with the little girl's hair. Prior to dozing off, Gracie had done the same, playing with Taylor's hair, which, after her parents had left, she'd loosened and worn down.

"I know she did. She was so excited over the kitchen and all the dishes and toy food. Thank you, Slade."

"I've had a great time with her today." The perfect last day with Gracie and Taylor.

"She's crazy about you." She glanced down at her conked-out daughter. "With as early as she got up this morning, she's probably out for the night."

"Do you want me to carry her to bed?"

Surprise registered on her face. "Sure. I'll go turn her covers down."

Without waking her, they tucked Gracie in, then made their way back to the living room. Taylor picked up the remote and turned off the movie. Slade, however, went to the coat closet and dug in his pocket.

"I have a little something for you."

"You do?"

He grinned. "You didn't think I'd forgotten your gift, did you?"

"You didn't need to get me anything."

"I wanted to. I just hope you like it."

"I'm pretty easygoing so you shouldn't worry about me not liking my gift," she said with a smile. "I'm not that ungrateful a person."

"I know you're not." She wasn't. She was sweet, kind, thoughtful, passionate, beautiful and his, only not really and not for much longer.

He'd put a lot of thought into her gift. Thought hopefully she truly would understand. He'd wanted to give her a gift that meant something, a gift she wouldn't toss out after he was gone from her life. A gift she'd treasure and keep forever that was from him. Why that was so important he wasn't sure, but it was.

"Here." He handed her the present.

She opened the package, saw the jeweler's box inside and hesitated. "You said it was a small gift."

"It is a small gift."

"I thought you meant cost wise," she responded, looking uncertain.

"Just open the box, Taylor."

She did and glanced up at him with tears in her eyes. "Oh, Slade. It's perfect."

Pleasure rippled through him. Mission accomplished.

"I took the photo with my phone the other night when you had her in your lap and printed it for the locket."

She pulled the necklace out of the velvet box. "Help me."

He did, clasping the gold chain around her neck and stroking his fingertips over the smoothness of her nape because he couldn't resist the feel of her skin.

She touched the locket, which fell between her breasts. "Thank you." Then she surprised him by throwing her arms around him and hugging him.

What was Taylor doing? She knew better than to touch Slade like this. Only his gift was so sweet, so thoughtful, so perfect, she couldn't not express her gratitude.

"I take it you like it?" he asked, holding her close.

"I love it." She should move away now. Hug time was past. So why wasn't she removing her arms from around him? Why was she snuggling closer, letting the feel of him wrap around her, letting his scent envelop her, letting her body melt against his?

"I'm glad."

She nuzzled his neck lightly, knowing she should move away but needing more before she could. "What made you think to get me a locket with a photo of Gracie and me?"

"My mom used to wear one with a photo of me and her. She treasured it. I thought you might, too."

Had he just kissed her hair? He shifted. He had definitely kissed her hair. Her cheek. His lips hovered over hers, so close they almost touched, so close she could feel the warmth of his breath.

His blue eyes stared into hers, so many emotions stormed there. Emotions she recognized. Desire. Longing. Need. Confusion. She closed the tiny gap between their mouths.

A guttural noise sounded deep in his throat and he kissed her back. He held her close and kissed her over and over. Sweet, seductive, hungry kisses that cast her further and further under his spell.

When he pulled away he brushed a strand of hair back away from her face. "We shouldn't do this."

Disappointment hit her. Disappointment she shouldn't feel. She didn't want him to go. Not tonight. Not last night. Not ever. Which scared her.

She started to push him away, to tell him to leave and not come back, because truly that would be best for protecting her vulnerable heart.

Instead, said vulnerable heart pounding in her chest, she whispered, "I want this, Slade. I want you."

I want you. Had he ever heard sweeter words? More precious words? More torturous words?

He should go. He knew that. Or should at least tell her about his flight plans for the next morning before they did what they were about to do. He couldn't walk away from her. Not when he knew tonight was the last time he'd hold her, kiss her, make love to her.

He was beyond thinking about anything other than the fact that she wanted him and was giving herself to him. He couldn't walk away, couldn't do more than cherish her gift.

Hand in hand, they walked to Taylor's bedroom, pushing the door to and locking it. Slowly, in the low lamplight, they undressed each other, kissing, touching, needing, giving.

"I want you so much, Taylor." He rained kisses over her throat, her nape. It was true. With time and distance he'd get past Taylor, would move on, have other women in his life, but at the moment he couldn't imagine ever touching anyone but her. Couldn't imagine even wanting to.

"Show me," she urged, arching into his kisses.

He intended to show her just how amazing she was, and did. By the time he had pushed her back onto her bed, had prepared her body for his, Taylor whimpered.

"Please."

Please. He should be the one begging her for the privilege. Slipping on a condom, he thrust inside her, giving her everything he had to give. More. So much more because he was positive that when he left he'd be leaving behind a part of himself.

He couldn't fool himself otherwise.

Higher and higher they climbed. Heat built a sweet pinnacle that promised to topple them over the edge. So much more than anything they'd shared in Vegas. So much more than he'd dreamed possible.

Just as he reached the point he could no longer hold back the mounting pleasure, Taylor softly cried her own release and he was a goner.

Gone. Gone. Gone.

He collapsed onto the bed next to her, gasped to catch his breath, to overcome the fireworks flashing through his mind and body. Damn.

He rolled over to tell her how amazing she was, to tell her about Grandview and that he was leaving in the morning, but that maybe she could fly to Newark from time to time to see him. Or vice versa.

He wasn't opposed to a long-distance affair with her. Actually, the idea appealed a lot. There was no reason to deny themselves the phenomenal chemistry they shared.

"I don't want a divorce, Slade," Taylor told him when their gazes met. Her heart shone in her eyes and her fingers clasped the locket he'd given her. "I want our marriage to be real. For us to be real."

Oh, hell. Pain spasmed in his chest while he searched for words to say he was leaving.

* * *

If Taylor had harbored any illusions that Slade felt something for her, that he wanted the same things, the look of horror on his face quickly dispelled them. What a fool she was. What had she expected? That sex with her again would magically morph him from playboy to Prince Charming like in some fairy tale?

Just because she'd fallen for him, it didn't mean he had fallen for her. Sex was just sex to Slade. Just as it had been to Kyle. She shouldn't forget that.

"I'm sorry. I shouldn't have said that," she began, scooting away so their skin wouldn't touch. She didn't want to be touching him. Couldn't be touching him.

"Don't," he told her, grabbing her arm but not hanging on when she pulled loose. "I'm the one who is sorry, Taylor."

"You have nothing to be sorry for," she assured him, picking up her clothes off the floor and scurrying to put them back on. After all, she'd known he was a playboy, had known his reputation long before Vegas. Plus, he'd told her he didn't want to be married. For that matter, she'd told him the same thing. She'd been under no illusions except her own. Because she'd gotten caught up in their pretend relationship and wanted to believe. "This is no big deal."

"You look like it's a big deal."

Yeah, she supposed she did. Sex was a big deal to her. Always had been. She couldn't turn that off. Not the way the men in her life could.

"I've known all along that our marriage was pretend, that we were divorcing, and I had sex with you anyway. That's my problem, not yours."

"Taylor…" Her name came out as a sigh.

"It doesn't matter, Slade. I'm an adult and knew what I was doing. You played by the rules we set. This is my fault, not yours."

"I'm leaving."

She hadn't really expected him to stay the night, not after her words and his reaction, but she hadn't been prepared for his abruptness. Had she secretly hoped he'd tell her she was wrong? That he was willing to try?

Oh, God. She had.

"I know." She forced her voice to remain steady despite the pain racking her insides, making her want to curl up in the fetal position and cry at her foolish heart. "You can't stay the night. Gracie."

"That's not what I mean." He sat up in the bed, raked his fingers through his dark hair and looked so guilty she could only stare at him and wonder what he'd done. "I'm leaving as in moving."

Her knees shook and she sank onto the edge of the bed. "Moving?"

"My flight is booked for the morning."

Moving. His flight was booked. In the morning. As in he'd known he was leaving before he'd arrived this morning, before they'd spent the day together, before she'd invited him into her bedroom, before she'd told him she wanted their marriage to be real. How long had he been playing her for a fool? Was he just laughing at how easily she'd caved?

Anger hit her.

"You spent the day with me and Gracie knowing you're moving in the morning and you never said anything until *now*? Did you not think that was an important piece of information for me to have before…before what we just did?"

He had the grace to look remorseful. "Technically, I won't be moving for a few weeks, but I am flying to Newark tomorrow morning. I got the job with Grandview."

Was she missing something? "What job?"

"The one I interviewed for in Vegas."

She was definitely missing something because she'd

not known he'd interviewed with Grandview. Her mind? Her heart? Her sanity? All of the above? "I'm confused."

"I told you about my mom, about how I want to make a difference, a real difference in the fight against breast cancer. I interviewed for a position with Grandview and I got the job. This is my opportunity."

She took a deep breath. "So you've known all along that moving was a possibility, but never said anything to me? Your *wife*?" She put emphasis on the last word.

"You're acting as if you're really my wife. We've just been pretending the past month, Taylor, to make things easier at work and with our families. Nothing more. We both agreed to those terms."

He was right. It had all been pretend. But she'd gotten caught up in the pretense and had lowered her defenses. She'd fallen for him and he'd kept right on being himself. Could she even fault him for that?

"I'm sorry, Taylor. I told you from the beginning I didn't want a wife or kids. Had you been pregnant, it would have complicated our situation, but you aren't. We took precautions just then, so pregnancy shouldn't be an issue from tonight, but if so we'll deal with it."

Ugh. Hearing him talk about their making love, about a possible child they'd made, so clinically, so coldly, hurt.

"All this was to make both of our lives easier rather than face grief about marrying and filing for divorce so quickly right before the holidays, to prevent our mistake from affecting my chances with Grandview, too…"

Light finally dawned.

"That's it, isn't it?" she accused, forgetting to keep her voice down. "That's what all this was really about. Not your family or office gossip or keeping things calm until after the holidays or even sex. All this was because you didn't want Grandview finding out you'd married a woman you didn't know and planned to get divorced because you were afraid that revelation would hurt your chances with your precious dream job because they might think you flighty?"

His jaw worked back and forth. "You can't deny that this way was better all the way round, including for you."

She gritted her teeth and fought the urge to hit him. "No, you jerk, it's not better all the way round because a month ago I didn't know I loved you!"

"Taylor," he began, his expression strained. He raked his fingers through his hair again. "Please, calm down and listen to reason."

"There is no reason. You used me. The least you could have done was be honest about it so I wouldn't have bought all the looks and touches, and believed you actually cared about me and Gracie. I'm such an idiot. I knew better."

Slade pulled his jeans on and slipped his T-shirt over his head. This wasn't how he wanted the night to end. Maybe he'd known it was inevitable. Maybe that's why he hadn't told her the moment he'd found out he'd gotten the job. He'd known she'd be upset.

What he hadn't counted on had been Taylor saying she loved him. She didn't. She was just confusing unbelievably great sex with emotions.

Not that he didn't understand how she could make that mistake. He knew better, knew he was incapable of love, but he could almost convince himself he loved her, too. Almost.

The best thing he could do would be to leave. Her anger would help shield her from hurt and soon she'd realize she didn't love him. With a little time she'd acknowledge that his leaving had been the right thing.

It was the right thing.

So why did doing the right thing feel so very wrong?

CHAPTER THIRTEEN

TAYLOR MADE IT through the workday without having to answer too many questions about why Slade wasn't at work. Had Nina told their colleagues there was trouble in paradise or the truth? That Slade had left her? Either way, Taylor was grateful that the office seemed to still be on a holiday high and content to ignore her misery.

She picked Gracie up from her extended school program and focused on cooking dinner while Gracie colored a homework picture.

"I miss Mr. Slade." Gracie pouted, not looking up from where she was coloring the picture at the dining room table.

Heavyhearted, Taylor stared at her daughter. Gracie had gotten used to spending time with him every day. She'd commented repeatedly each evening that she missed Slade. No doubt this evening wouldn't be very different. Her daughter loved him. Wasn't that what she'd feared, what she'd wanted to avoid all along?

Look at what she'd allowed to happen. Not only had she failed to protect her own heart, she'd failed to protect Gracie's.

"I know, baby, but Mr. Slade is a busy man. He has important things he has to do." She'd told Gracie that Slade had gone out of town on an important trip. "He helped us a lot this Christmas, but he's not always going to be around. He has his own life, his own family."

Gracie's little face squished up. "He's married?"

That hadn't been what she'd meant. She'd been talking about his father and stepmother. Her heart thudded in her chest.

"About that..." Should she tell Gracie? What would be the point, other than that she didn't keep things from her daughter? Not usually. Why had she waited so long to tell her daughter the truth? "When I went to Vegas, Mr. Slade went with me, and we made a mistake while we were there."

Gracie stopped coloring and frowned. "What kind of mistake?"

"We accidentally got married."

"Accidentally got married?" Gracie didn't understand and Taylor fully understood that. She didn't understand any of it herself.

"I know it sounds confusing and that's because it is confusing. That's why Mr. Slade has been around so much the past few weeks. But our time with him is up."

Gracie's expression remained pinched. "Because you won't be married anymore?"

What had she done? Letting Gracie be exposed to Slade, letting her fall for his charm, letting her come to depend on him as being a part of her life? Maybe her parents were right. Maybe she was destined to always let down those she loved.

"Something like that," she admitted.

"Can't you accidentally get married again?" Gracie asked with the reasoning of a child.

Oh, Gracie! Taylor hugged her daughter to her. "Life doesn't work that way."

Gracie didn't look convinced. "Why not?"

"Mr. Slade and I didn't really want to be married."

With a wisdom beyond her young years Gracie considered all that Taylor said. "That's why it was an accident?"

"Yes."

"But why can't you want to marry him? He's really nice."

"That he is," Taylor admitted.

"Plus, he likes us." Gracie pleaded Slade's case, breaking Taylor's heart a little at how much hope she heard in her daughter's voice. "I know he likes us."

"Of course he likes us, baby," she agreed, trying to figure out how to explain her and Slade's relationship without hurting Gracie even more. "Slade especially likes you. He thinks you're wonderful."

Gracie's face took on a serious look. "Then we should keep him because I like him, too."

Taylor closed her eyes. Keep him. Sounded simple enough. Only he hadn't wanted to be kept.

"Besides, he's your Christmas present."

"What?" Taylor blinked at her daughter.

"He is your Christmas present. I know he is," Gracie insisted. "I heard you and Aunt Nina talking last Christmas when you thought I was asleep. You told her you should have asked Santa for a man." The little girl gave her a solemn stare. "At school, when we had to write letters to Santa, I asked him for a man for you, but my teacher made me write a different letter because she said she couldn't post that one on the wall."

Mortification hit Taylor at Gracie's teacher reading the letter with Gracie asking Santa for a man for her mother. Oh, my.

"So I wrote another for the wall, but Miss Gwen promised she'd send the first one to Santa. I asked him at the mall and he told me you'd gotten your present early so I knew he was talking about Mr. Slade."

"Gracie, I…" Taylor paused, not sure what to say in response.

"We should keep him," Gracie repeated. "He's a good Christmas present."

Taylor saw the longing in her daughter's eyes, knew there was a similar longing in her heart.

But she'd told him she loved him and he'd left. There was no denying that they wanted different things. Yet how did she explain that to her child? No matter what, she didn't want Gracie hurt any more than she already was. She'd known better than to let someone into her and Gracie's world, to risk someone hurting them. Lesson learned.

She pasted on a bright smile and hugged her generous-hearted daughter. "Slade was a great Christmas present, Gracie, and we got to spend Christmas with him and that was wonderful." No matter how much she ached inside, spending the holidays with Slade had been wonderful. If only doing so hadn't come at such a high price. "But now Slade gets to enjoy his Christmas present, which is to work at his dream job. As much as you and I miss him, we do want him to be happy, right?"

Taylor did. She supposed. Mostly, she just wanted Gracie not to suffer because of her mistake in forgetting who Slade really was. A playboy who wouldn't ever truly settle down.

Gracie frowned in thought. "Yes, but wasn't he happy with us?"

"He was." She believed he had been. But Kyle had been, too, at the beginning of their relationship. Men like them enjoyed life, but quickly got bored and moved on. It's just how things were. "But his new job is what he's always wanted. Because we care about him, we are happy he got what he's always wanted."

Gracie's nose curled. "I guess so."

As angry and hurt as she was by his actions, as much as she doubted she could ever forgive herself for allowing him into their lives and hurting Gracie, as much as she would never trust him again, Taylor knew so.

* * *

Grandview Pharmaceuticals was everything and more that Slade had craved for years. The clinical research director position being dangled in front of him gave him the opportunity to work directly on developing a promising new chemotherapy drug.

He'd be heading up the team.

They'd agreed to his contract terms and were having the legal documents drawn up. In the morning he'd meet with them, sign the papers and start the rest of his life.

So why was he lying in a hotel bed, staring at the ceiling and wondering if he was making the biggest mistake of his life?

Because Taylor had said she didn't want a divorce or for their marriage to be pretend? Because she'd said she was in love with him?

They never could have been anything more than pretend. He wasn't the marrying kind. He was a career man.

He thought over the past month, of the time he'd spent with Taylor and Gracie, and his insides ached.

Ached.

Because in such a short time they'd become such an integral part of his life.

Which should make him grateful the Grandview job had come through when it had. He didn't need distractions from his true destiny. He didn't need emotions blinding him to his real purpose. He'd vowed to help others, to make a difference in the fight against breast cancer, to find a cure for a disease that had taken his mother and continued to take lives.

Despite the ache inside him, that's what he needed to stay focused on. His goals. His purpose. His dreams.

Taylor wasn't a part of that.

Couldn't be a part of that.

She was better off without him.

He didn't need distractions. Just look at how thinking of her was distracting him even now.

He closed his eyes, prayed sleep would come.

In the morning he would sign his name on the proverbial dotted line and achieve a goal he'd set for himself when he'd been twelve years old.

Nothing and no one would get in the way of that.

The following evening Nina and Taylor picked up Sarah Beth to give the new big sister some playtime away from all the baby attention, and headed to Pippa's Pizza Palace. The two little girls whacked clowns, squirted lily pads and were having a great time.

Actually, Gracie had seemed much perkier when she and Nina had swung by the office to pick Taylor up. She'd had so much paperwork to wade through that she'd worked late and taken up Nina's request that she pick up Gracie and then get them dinner.

She hadn't exactly been thinking Pippa's Pizza Palace, but to see Gracie's smile, to hear her laughter, to see the sparkle in her eyes that had been missing was worth enduring greasy pizza.

Unfortunately, she couldn't stop thinking that this was where it had sort of started. Vegas was where it had truly started, but her and Slade's first real date had been here.

"You're doing it again." Nina snapped her fingers in front of Taylor's face.

She blinked. "Doing what?"

"Thinking about him to the point you totally lose touch with reality."

"Believe me, I'm in touch with reality."

"Which is?"

She stared blankly at her friend. "What do you mean?"

"What is your reality, Taylor?"

"That I lost my mind in Vegas and married a man I knew

was all wrong for me. I agreed to a month of pretending our marriage was real for Lord only knows what reason. And before long, I'll be divorced from a man I never should have trusted."

Why did her words feel like daggers in her chest?

Nina frowned. "Is that what you want?"

Taylor shrugged. "It's better this way. I told him how I felt and he left. I'm not sure why that shocked me so much. Leaving is what men I have sex with do."

Nina shook her head. "Don't compare him to Kyle. Kyle was an idiot who couldn't keep his pants zipped when there was a willing woman around. You were an impressionable young woman who'd been kept under her parents' thumb too long. He was your teenage rebellion, not the man you are in love with, like you are with Slade."

"I was in my twenties."

"You were a late bloomer," Nina quipped without missing a beat.

"Tell me about it." Taylor sighed, knowing her friend was right. Kyle hadn't been fit to spit shine Slade's boots.

"So…" Nina prompted.

"So what?"

"You completely ignored what I said about Slade."

Taylor frowned. "I've been paying close attention to everything you've said about him."

"Yet you didn't comment on the fact I said you are in love with him."

"That's not something I didn't already know so I'm ignoring that."

"Why?"

"Because it doesn't matter. Love without trust is nothing. He left Gracie and me. Honestly, it's best that he did. Better to just get his leaving over with before Gracie and I became even more dependent on him."

"I hope you don't mean that," Nina said, so oddly that Taylor raised an eyebrow.

"Why?"

But Nina didn't answer her, just indicated toward where there was a commotion in the games section of the restaurant.

Taylor turned, but didn't initially see what had caused the commotion. Neither did she immediately recognize who was causing the commotion. When she did, she almost fell out of the booth.

Slade, followed by a posse of children, Gracie and Sarah Beth included, headed toward her.

He had lost his mind. There could be no other excuse for his current foolishness.

Well, there was one other excuse.

He'd lost his heart.

To a woman who'd fascinated him long before she'd carried on a simple conversation with him and her bubbly little girl who had, along with Nina, helped him come up with a foolproof plan to win Taylor's forgiveness.

He had to pray their plan would work.

The glare she was currently giving him wasn't an indication this was going to be easy.

Recovering from her surprise at seeing him, she murmured something to Nina about leaving and stood up.

Nina grabbed her wrist and stayed her. "At least hear him out."

"I don't want to hear anything he has to say, even if he is dressed like that."

"Sure you do, and he's gone to a lot of effort so sit down." Nina's tone brooked no argument.

Looking a bit stunned, Taylor sat back down.

A good thing because otherwise he'd feel like an even bigger idiot in the Prince Charming getup Nina and Gracie had helped him choose. They'd also ensured that Taylor would show.

He turned to the little girl who was bouncing beside him. "Princess Gracie, will you take your friends over to play so I can talk to your mom for a few minutes?"

With a really big wink at him, Gracie nodded and gathered the group of kids together, shooing them back toward the games. Several times she turned back toward them, both excitement and worry shining in her green eyes.

Maybe he shouldn't have involved Gracie.

If Taylor couldn't forgive him, would it make things more difficult that he had let the little girl in on his surprise visit? No, because he refused to fail.

"I'm going to go supervise the kids." Nina stood, paused at the end of the table and gave Taylor an encouraging look. "Remember what I said about Kyle. Don't let the past color the present."

Slade didn't fully understand her comment but supposed Taylor had lumped him into the same category as her ex. As much as he hated the thought, perhaps he deserved as much.

When they were alone, Taylor gestured to his outfit. "I take it the Grandview job didn't work out and you've hired on as a local clown?"

He glanced down at his costume. "Is that how you see me? As a clown?"

Not looking directly at him, she shrugged. "I don't want to see you at all."

"Then don't look at me, but listen to what I have to say."

"What's the point? We've already said everything we have to say to each other."

Aware that other parents in the restaurant were staring at him—and no wonder—he asked if he could sit down.

"Suit yourself, but you might have more success going in search of sleeping beauties or women with fairy godmothers."

"I might," he agreed, wondering how he could ever have been so foolish as to leave. "But I'd rather spend the rest of my life convincing you to forgive me."

"Ha," she scoffed, still not looking at him. "You really would have more luck with a pair of glass slippers and a magic wand."

"Too bad, because there's only one woman whose Prince Charming I want to be."

She rolled her eyes. "What, did Grandview realize you hadn't brought your wife with you and you're here to convince me to play wifey again long enough to make the big-wigs happy?"

"Grandview doesn't care if I'm married or not married. Not really. Neither does what Grandview want really matter to me."

"Right, because that's so not what the past month was about."

"I don't work for Grandview, Taylor."

She met his gaze.

"I turned down their offer."

"They couldn't meet your demands?"

"They couldn't offer me the one thing in life I don't want to live without."

Her gaze narrowed. "What's that?"

"My wife."

His wife. Taylor bit the inside of her lower lip. What kind of game was he playing, showing up in a prince costume, spouting comments about not being able to live without his wife?

Her rib cage tightened around her lungs, making breathing difficult. Unable to bear to hear another word, she stood.

"I'm going outside."

She practically ran out of the restaurant, gulping in big breaths of cold air the moment she was outside the building.

"Taylor?"

No. He'd followed her. She ran to the van, opened the door.

"Please, let me finish."

She scrambled to open the driver's-side door and climbed inside. "There's no reason for you to finish. I don't want to hear anything you have to say."

She didn't. He'd left her. Left Gracie. Had broken their hearts and devastated their world.

"But I desperately want you to hear what I have to say. Please, let me tell you about this past week."

She shook her head. "No, because all I hear you saying is about you. So, you got to Newark and realized you missed Gracie and me? Is that what you're going to say? Well, too bad, because that ship has sailed."

"You don't love me anymore?"

She didn't want to admit to feeling anything for him, but she couldn't bring herself to lie. "I don't trust you anymore."

"You never did trust me."

"Sure I did. Christmas, when I wanted you to stay, it was because I trusted you, trusted what was happening between us."

"And I failed you horribly when I left?"

"Something like that."

"If I could go back, I wouldn't leave you, Taylor."

"Too bad that costume doesn't come with a magical pumpkin time machine, then, eh?"

"I never realized you had such a sharp tongue."

She leaned against the steering wheel, hid her face from him. Why wouldn't he just leave? Why was he here dressed like a prince when she knew he was a playboy?

"There are a lot of things you don't realize about me."

He walked around the van, opened the passenger's-side door and climbed in. "There are a lot of things I do realize about you. Like how much you love Gracie and how you devote your life to her. Like how loyal you are and you don't give your heart easily."

She didn't deny what he said, neither did she look up from where her forehead rested against the steering wheel. She did, however, pull the door closed to block out the chilly night air. Of course, that just closed her into her van with him.

"When you love," he continued from beside her, "that doesn't just go away because the person is a fool and lets you down."

"You did more than let me down. You let Gracie down. You left us."

"I had to go."

She lifted her head and glared at him. "Then why are you back here wearing that ridiculous costume?"

"I had to go to understand what I was leaving behind."

She swallowed the lump in her throat. "Which was?"

"My heart. I'm back because I love you, Taylor. I love you and Gracie."

His words stung her raw emotions. She closed her eyes. "You can't just pop back into our lives, say a few pretty words you think I want to hear and expect me to say everything is forgiven."

"It's what I want you to do, but it's not what I expect. Neither is it what I deserve. I know that. Which is why I'm wearing the outfit."

She shrugged. "I don't see the connection."

"I want to be your Prince Charming, but know I have to prove to you that I can be what you want, what you need, in a husband, in a father for Gracie." He reached across the console and took her hand, clasping it between his. "I want to make every day of your life living proof of happy-ever-after."

"You're crazy," she accused, but didn't pull her hand away. She should pull her hand away. Touching him had always taken away her ability to think and if ever she needed the ability to think it was now.

"I am crazy. About you. To leave you. To think I didn't need you. To not admit I loved you on Christmas night." He gently squeezed her hand. "But I am admitting that now. I need you, Taylor."

She couldn't answer him.

"You don't have to forgive me tonight or even tomorrow. You just have to give me the chance to prove to you that I am your Prince Charming."

"I don't have to do anything," she reminded him.

"Sure you do."

She arched a brow. "Or what?"

"Or else I'm driving you to my place and making love to you until you are so breathless you don't have the strength to argue with me anymore."

"That's just sex and eventually you'll tire of me."

He lifted her hand to his mouth, pressed a kiss to her fingertips. "You and I were never just sex, Taylor. Not even that first night in Vegas."

Their wedding night.

"In Newark I had a lot of time to think. I'm convinced I was half in love with you long before Vegas."

"That's crazy." Crazy seemed to be her new favorite word, but she was beginning to think it was the most appropriate word for the whole situation. Maybe they were both crazy.

He nodded. "But true. You fascinated me. I'd never met a woman who fascinated me so much, but you refused to let me get close. I'd catch myself looking for you at work, thinking about you after hours, and then in Vegas I'm not sure what happened other than I was on a high that you were kissing me back and wanted me. I think I would have done anything to have had you that night."

"You did. You married me."

"Something I'd never planned to do because I'd vowed to devote myself to fighting breast cancer."

"A noble cause."

"A lonely cause."

"Because you missed Gracie and me?"

"So much I felt like my insides had shriveled up and died. I had to come back."

"Because of me?" she asked, not really believing him.

He let go of her hand, leaving her with a sense of loss as he adjusted his fake crown. "Partially, but mostly because of me."

"But your mother… I don't understand."

He turned and faced her. "I didn't either at first. As little more than a kid, I set this goal to find a cure for breast cancer and made that my life's priority. Until you, I never let anything even get close to interfering with that."

"I never wanted Gracie and me to interfere with your goals." He'd come to resent them both for sure if they stood in his way. But more than that she wanted him to have his dreams, to fulfill them. Even when those dreams took him away from her.

"Neither did I, and you don't. You just updated them to the goals of a grown man rather than those of a heartbroken boy."

She waited for him to continue.

"As for tiring of you—" he shook his head "—I suppose that's a risk every couple takes, but I just don't foresee that happening. I love you and plan to spend the rest of my life showing you how much."

"You're planning to stay in Nashville?"

"I've already talked to Nashville Cancer Care. They welcomed me back with open arms."

"You're stepping back as if you never left."

"Have you not been listening? I left and I realized what I'd left and I want it back."

"You can't have me back."

"You're saying you don't love me, Taylor? Because I don't believe you."

"It doesn't matter if you believe me or not. I don't want you in my life anymore."

"Then you'll have to divorce me, because I plan to fight for my marriage with all my heart."

"Why?"

"Because we were never pretend, Taylor. I know you figured that out long before I did. We were always real, but I couldn't admit that. Maybe you couldn't at first either because we happened so quickly and you were scared we couldn't be real. But we were." He laced their fingers, stared at their interlocking hands. "We are real."

Tears prickling her eyes, she squeezed them shut. "How can I believe you? How can I know this is real and that you won't leave me again?"

"You have to trust me."

"What if I can't? What if I can't let my guard down enough to trust in you, Slade?"

He took a deep breath. "Then ultimately that lack of trust will be what keeps us apart."

She nodded.

"But don't think I'll give up. Or that I won't use every resource at my disposal."

"Gracie?" she guessed.

"She is who told me I had to wear a Prince Charming costume tonight. That you had to know what she already knows."

"I can't bear my mistakes causing her pain."

"Then you have to trust me, because she loves me."

"I know she does."

"I love her, too, Taylor. More than I thought a man could love a kid. I've never known that joy before."

"If only I believed this was real."

"Believe, because this isn't a fairy tale, Taylor. It's our real-life love story."

She was crying now. A major boo-hoo fest. "I don't want to be without you."

"Then don't be." He leaned across the console, took her into his arms, hugging her close. "I love you, Taylor. Please, don't cry because of me."

She sucked back a deep breath, swiped at her eyes. "Call Grandview first thing in the morning and tell them you've changed your mind, that you'll take the position."

He shook his head. "I haven't changed my mind. My place is right here, with you and Gracie, and working at Nashville Cancer Care. It's where I want to be."

"But your dreams?"

"Are being fulfilled in a way far beyond what I could have imagined at twelve when I made my career goals. I make a difference in the lives of my patients, Taylor. Just as you do. Perhaps not on the same scale as if I helped develop a miracle chemotherapy drug, but to the patients I see each day, to the patients I hand out my sticky notes to, I make a difference."

Her heart almost burst with warmth at what he was saying, at what she was feeling. "You're right, but if research is what you want I could go with you to Newark…"

Slade's breath caught at what she'd just said, what she'd just hinted at. Not that he'd doubted that she loved him. He'd known she had. Just that he knew she was going to have a difficult time forgiving him, trusting him.

"Newark isn't what I want. I want what I thought I never

wanted, what I've had the past month, only more. I want you to be my wife, Taylor. In every sense of the word. That's what I came here to show you tonight."

She met his gaze. Tears glistened in her eyes, on her cheeks. "I'm scared."

"Me, too, but what scares me most is the thought of not having you by my side every day for the rest of my life."

She nodded. "I do love you, Slade. So much."

"I know, honey. I'm so sorry it took me so long to cherish that gift the way I should have. The way I do," he corrected. "That reminds me." He paused, reached into his pocket and pulled out a jeweler's box. "I have something to ask you." He half knelt on her van floorboard. "Taylor Anderson Sain, will you do me the honor of being my wife?"

"I'm already your wife." More tears streamed down her cheeks.

"Humor me here. I'm trying to do this right this time."

She nodded, swiping at her eyes with her free hand.

"I love you, Taylor. Say you'll walk down the aisle to me, that we'll have your dad give you away to me, have Gracie as our flower girl, have my dad and stepmom there, all our friends and family to celebrate with us. Be my bride, Taylor. My wife. Forever."

"You really are my Prince Charming, you know," she whispered as he slipped the engagement ring on her finger.

"And you are my dream woman if only you'll say yes."

Amidst tears, she nodded. "Yes. Yes. Yes."

He leaned across the console, wrapped her in his arms and kissed her. "I'm never giving up on us, Taylor. You and Gracie are mine. You know that, right?"

She nodded. "You're mine, too. My Christmas present."

"Gracie mentioned that," he said, then grinned. "I'm thinking a Vegas honeymoon."

Happier than she'd have believed possible, she smiled at

the man who really was her Prince Charming and all her Christmases wrapped up in one delectable package.

"Sounds perfect. Last time I was there I got luckier than I dreamed possible."

"I'm the lucky one."

EPILOGUE

GRACIE ANDERSON SAIN walked down the aisle toward a flower-woven wrought-iron arbor. A few dozen people sat on each side of the aisle—friends, family, some of her parents' and grandparents' coworkers.

She dropped rose petals all along the way, taking care to space them so she'd have enough until she reached her destination.

"Hi, Gracie," Sarah Beth whispered as she passed her BFF and her family. Sarah Beth's brother was sleeping, thank goodness, because, although Sarah Beth's mom had quit crying all the time, her baby brother had picked up the slack. It was almost enough to make a girl think she didn't want a baby brother of her own.

Almost.

Gracie grinned at her friend, tossed a few rose petals her way, then proceeded down the aisle in her real-life pink princess dress, complete with real tiara.

She waved at her Grandma Anderson, who'd declared her to be the most beautiful girl in the whole world, winked at her new Grandpa Sain and then took her place next to her father to wait for who she knew was really the most beautiful girl in the world.

Her mother.

Appearing at the end of the aisle, Taylor appeared on the

arms of Grandpa Anderson, who bent, kissed her cheek and whispered something that had her mom smiling up at him.

Gracie glanced up at Slade to see what he thought of his bride and grinned. Oh, yeah. That was the right look. Perfect for a Prince Charming about to marry his princess.

The rest of the ceremony went by fast and then they were kissing. Gracie had to look away even though that seemed to be all they did these days. Even in front of Grandpa and Grandma Anderson, and Gracie's new grandparents.

She liked her new grandpa, even if he did pinch her cheeks. He was lots of fun and had promised her a pony for her upcoming birthday. A pony sounded great because she liked going out with Slade on his horse. However, when she blew out her birthday-cake candles she didn't plan to wish for a pony. That would have to wait until another holiday.

Her gaze sought out Sarah Beth in the congregation. She wiggled her fingers at her friend. Sarah Beth waved back, then reached to hand her mother something out of a diaper bag.

Yeah, Gracie knew exactly what she wanted for her birthday.

Even if baby brothers did cry a lot.

* * * * *

ONE NIGHT
BEFORE
CHRISTMAS

BY
SUSAN CARLISLE

Published in Great Britain 2015
by Mills & Boon, an imprint of Harlequin (UK) Limited,
Eton House, 18-24 Paradise Road, Richmond, Surrey, TW9 1SR

© 2015 Susan Carlisle

ISBN: 978-0-263-24742-8

Harlequin (UK) Limited's policy is to use papers that are natural,
renewable and recyclable products and made from wood grown in
sustainable forests. The logging and manufacturing processes conform
to the legal environmental regulations of the country of origin.

Printed and bound in Spain
by CPI, Barcelona

Dear Reader,

During the fall months of the year the focus in my house turns to American football. We spend hours watching and discussing it. We even attend games. While the males in my family are concerned with only what is happening on the field, I often think about what goes on behind the scenes. Who takes care of the players? What happens when a player gets hurt? During one of those games I wondered what it would be like if the team doctor was a woman, and how it would be for her to work in that man's world…

This is just what my character Melanie does in this story. For her, the game of football is a family affair. And when she has to call in an orthopaedic surgeon who cares nothing about the game for a second opinion, the fireworks explode.

I hope you enjoy reading my book as much as I enjoyed writing it. I love to hear from my readers. You can contact me at SusanCarlisle.com.

Susan

To Lacey.
Thanks for loving my son.

Books by Susan Carlisle

Mills & Boon Medical Romance

Visit the Author Profile page at
millsandboon.co.uk for more titles.

CHAPTER ONE

DR. MELANIE HYDE stood with the other chauffeurs waiting and watching passengers outside the security zone at the top of the escalators. Overhead the notes of "Jingle Bells" were being piped via speakers throughout Niagara Falls International Airport in upstate New York. She wiggled the small white sign she held back and forth. Written on it was *Reynolds*.

She was there to pick up the "go-to" orthopedic sports doctor. He'd been flown in on a private jet paid for by the Niagara Falls Currents, the professional football team and her employer. Her father, the general manager, had sent her on this mission in the hope that she might, in his words, "soften the doctor up."

Melanie had no idea how she was supposed to do that. She would have to find some way because she didn't want to disappoint her father. Long ago she'd accepted what was expected of her. Not that she always liked it.

Maybe the one physician to another respect would make Dr. Reynolds see the team's need to get Martin "The Rocket" Overtree on the field for the Sunday playoff game and hopefully the weeks after that.

As club physician, Melanie had given her professional opinion but her dad wanted a second one. That hurt, but she was a team player. Had been all her life. Just once she'd

like her father to see her for who she really was: a smart
woman who did her job well. An individual.

In the sports world, that orthopedic second opinion came
in the form of Dr. Dalton Reynolds of the Reynolds Sports
and Orthopedic Center, Miami, Florida.

She'd never seen him in person but she had read plenty
of his papers on the care of knee and leg injuries. "The
Rocket" had a knee issue but he wanted to play and Melanie was feeling the pressure from the head office to let him.
More like her father's not so gentle nudge.

Having grown up in a football-loving world, she knew
the win and, in major-league ball, the money, was everything. The burden to have "The Rocket" on the field was
heavy. On the cusp of a chance to go to the Super Bowl,
the team's star player was needed.

She shifted her heavy coat to the other arm and scanned
the crowd of passengers streaming off the escalators for a
male in his midfifties and wiggled the sign again.

A tall man with close-trimmed brown hair sporting a
reddish tint, carrying a tan trench coat and a black bag,
blocked her view. He was do-a-double-take handsome but
Melanie shifted her weight to one foot and looked around
him, continuing to search the crowd.

"I'm Reynolds," the man said in a deep, husky voice that
vibrated through her. The man could whisper sweet noth-
ings in her ear all day long.

Jerking back to a full standing position, she locked gazes
with his unwavering one.

"Dr. Dalton Reynolds?"

"Yes."

His eyes were the color of rich melted chocolate but they
held none of the warmth. He wasn't at all who she'd anticipated. Old and stuffy, instead of tall and handsome, was
what she'd had in mind. This man couldn't be more than
a few years older than her. He must be truly brilliant if he

was the most eminent orthopedic surgeon in the country at his age.

"Uh, I wasn't expecting you to be so...young," she blurted.

He gave her a sober look. "I'm sorry to disappoint."

She blinked and cleared her throat. "I'm not disappointed, just surprised."

"Good, then. Shouldn't we be getting my luggage? I'd like to see the patient this evening."

With it being only a week before Christmas, he must be in a hurry to return home to his family. After a moment's hesitation she said, "I don't know if that'll be possible. The players may have gone home by the time we get back."

"I didn't come all this way to spend time in my hotel room. I have a practice in Miami to be concerned with." That statement was punctuated with a curl of one corner of his mouth.

He had a nice one. Why was she thinking about his mouth when she should be talking to him about Rocket? The off-center feeling she had around this stranger unnerved her. She worked in primarily a man's world all the time and never had this type of reaction to one of them.

They started walking toward the baggage area. As they did, Melanie put the sign she was still carrying in a garbage can, then pulled her phone out of her pocket. "I'll try and get Coach. Have him ask Rocket to hang around. But football players sometimes have minds of their own."

"I can appreciate that, Ms...?"

Melanie stopped and looked at him. He faced her, his broad shoulders blocking her view of the other people passing them.

She raised her chin. "I'm Dr. Melanie Hyde."

A flash of wonder flickered in his eyes.

Good. She'd managed to surprise him.

"Dr. Hyde, if Mr. Overtree expects my help he'll need

to be examined as soon as possible. I have patients at home who are trying to stay out of wheelchairs."

With that he turned and walked toward the revolving luggage rack.

Melanie gaped at him. So much for "smoothing him over."

Dalton had little patience for silly games. Even when they were played with attractive women. He'd been astonished to find out that the team doctor was female and the person who had been sent to pick him up. Usually that job fell to a hired driver or one of the team underlings. He had to admit she was the prettiest chauffeur he'd ever had.

As far as he was concerned, he was here to do a job and nothing more. He wasn't impressed by the game of football. The only aspect that drew him in was that he cared about helping people who were hurting. He'd been called in to examine an injured player at great expense. The money he earned, good money, from making these types of "house calls" was what he used to support his foundation. It over-saw struggling foster children with physical and mental issues, giving them extra care so they had a chance to suc-ceed in life. He would continue to do this job as long as the teams paid him top dollar. However, he didn't buy into all the football hype.

He knew from experience that not everyone was cut out for games. He'd left that far behind, being constantly teased for being the "brain with no game." It had taken time and work on his part but he'd overcome his childhood. Now he was successful in his field, had friends and a good life. He had proven anyone could overcome their past. That was why he'd started the foundation. To give other kids a step in the right direction so they didn't struggle as he had.

The tall, athletic-looking doctor came to stand beside him. She almost met him eye to eye. He liked women with long legs. Glancing down while watching the baggage conveyer as it circled in front of him, he confirmed the length of her legs. She wore a brown suit with a cream-colored blouse. There was nothing bold about her dress to make her stand out. Still, something about her pricked his interest. Her features were fine and her skin like porcelain, a complete contrast to her all-business appearance. Not of his usual fare—bleached blonde and heavy breasted— she looked more of the wholesome-girl-next-door variety. Under all that sweetness was there any fire?

He looked at the bags orbiting before him. *Football was still such a man's world, so why would a woman choose to become a football team doctor?*

His black leather duffel circled to him. He leaned over and picked it up. Slinging it over his shoulder, he turned to her. "I'm ready."

"This way, then." She pulled on the large down-stuffed coat she'd held. As she walked, she wrapped a knit scarf effortlessly around her neck and pulled a cap over her hair. He followed her. There was a nice sway to her hips. Even in the shapeless outfit she had a natural sex appeal. He shouldn't be having these sorts of thoughts because he wouldn't be here long enough to act on them.

The automatic glass doors opened, allowing in a blast of freezing-cold air that took his breath and made his teeth rattle. "Hold up." He stepped back inside.

She followed. He didn't miss the slight twitch at the corner of her full lips. She was laughing at him. He didn't like being laughed at.

He plopped his bag on the floor and set his shoulder bag beside it before putting on his trench coat.

"Is that the heaviest overcoat you have?" she asked.

Tying the belt at the waist, he looked directly at her. "Yes. There isn't much call for substantial clothes in Miami."

"I guess there isn't. Would you like to stop and get a warmer one on our way to the practice field?"

He shook his head as he picked up his bags again. "I don't plan to be here that long."

Again they headed out the door, Dalton tried to act as if the wind wasn't cutting right through his less-than-adequate clothes. Even with a shirt, sweater and coat he was miserable.

"Why don't you wait here and I'll circle around to get you?"

"No, I'm fine. Let's get moving." He bowed his head against the spit of icy rain.

Dalton had spent a lifetime of not appearing weak and he wouldn't change now. As the smart foster kid, he hadn't fit in at school or in the houses he'd been placed in. With a father in jail and a drug addict for a mother, he'd been in and out of homes for years. It wasn't until his mother died of an overdose that he'd stayed in one place for any length of time. At the Richies', life had been only marginally better before he was sent to another home.

He'd had plenty of food and clothes, but little about his life had been easy. When all the other kids were out playing, he was busy reading, escaping. The most miserable times were when he did join in a game. He was the last one chosen for the team. If finally picked, he then had to deal with the ridicule of being the worst player. He learned quickly not to show any weakness. As a medical student and now a surgeon, the honed trait served him well.

Football, freezing weather and a laughing woman, no matter how attractive she was, were not to his taste. He needed to do this consultation and get back to Florida.

Melanie couldn't help but find humor in the situation. Dr. Reynolds' long legs carried him at such a brisk pace, she had trouble staying in the lead enough to show him where the car was parked. He must be freezing. Niagara Falls was not only known for the falls but for the horrible winter weather. What planet did he live on that he hadn't come prepared?

She pushed the button on her key fob, unlocking the car door as they approached so that he wouldn't have to wait any longer than necessary outside. Minutes later she had the car started and the heat blasting on high. She glanced at her passenger. He took a great deal of space in her small car. Almost to the point of overwhelming her. Why was he affecting her so? Melanie glanced at him. Judging by the tenseness of his square jaw, he must be gritting his teeth to keep them from chattering.

"I'm sure it'll be warm in a few minutes."

An *mmm* sound of acknowledgement came from his direction as Melanie pulled out into the evening traffic on the freeway.

Her phone rang. "Please excuse me. This may be the office about Rocket." She pushed the hands-free button. "This is Mel."

"Rocket is on his way back." Her father's booming voice filled the car.

"Great. I'm sure Dr. Reynolds will be glad to hear that. We should be there in about thirty minutes." Her father hung up and she asked her passenger, "Have you ever been to Niagara Falls?"

"No."

"Well, the falls are a beautiful sight any time of the year, but especially now with the snow surrounding them."

"I don't think I'll be here long enough to do much sightseeing."

"It doesn't take much to say you've seen the falls. They're pretty large."

"What I came for is to see Mr. Overtree, so I imagine I should focus on that." Obviously he wasn't much for small talk or the local sights. Melanie stopped making an effort at conversation and concentrated on driving in the thickening snow and slow traffic. With her heavier clothes on, she began to get too warm but didn't want to turn down the heat for fear Dr. Reynolds needed it.

They were not far from the team camp when he said, "I don't think I've ever met a female team doctor before."

She'd long ago become used to hearing that statement. With a proud note in her voice she said, "As far as I know, I'm the only one in the NFL."

"What made you want to be a sports doctor?"

His voice, she bet, had mesmerized more than one woman. Where had that idea come from? What was his question? "I wanted to be a part of the world of football."

What it did was make her feel included. She'd grown up without a mother, a coach for a father and three brothers who now played professional football. In her family if you didn't eat, drink and live football you were left out. As a girl she couldn't play, so by becoming the team doctor she took her place as part of the team. Even when it wasn't her heart's desire. "Team means everything, Mel," her father would say. "That's what we are—a team." He would then hug her. To get his attention she learned early on what she needed to do as part of the team. As she grew older the pressure to be a team member grew and became harder to live with.

She often wondered what her father would say if she confessed she didn't want to belong to a team any longer. Sometimes she'd like to just be his daughter. She was afraid of what the repercussions might be. Still she would have to say she was happy, wouldn't she?

Melanie pulled the car into her designated parking space in front of the two-story, glass-windowed building. "Leave your bag in the car. I'll take you to the hotel after we're through here."

Dr. Reynolds nodded and climbed out. He wasn't large like some of the players but he did look like a man who could hold his own in a fight. With those wide shoulders and trim hips, he appeared physically fit.

"This way," she said as they entered the lobby. The space was built to impress. With hardwood floors, bright lights and the Currents' mascot and bolt of lightning painted on the wall, the place did not disappoint. No matter how many times Melanie entered this direction, she had a moment of awe. She enjoyed her job, liked the men she worked with and loved the passion of the crowd when the Currents took the field to play.

Dr. Reynolds followed her through security and down the hall to the elevator. There they waited in silence until the doors opened and they entered. She pushed the button that would take them to the bottom floor where the Athlete Performance Area and her office were located. When the elevator opened she led him along a hall painted with different football players making moves. "Rocket should be back here."

The team had a state-of-the-art workout facility, from whirlpool and sauna to a walking pool and all the other equipment on the market to help improve the human body. She was proud of the care she was able to provide for the men. Two years ago she had instituted a wellness program for retired players who continued to live nearby.

She pushed open the double swinging doors and entered her domain. Here she normally had the final say.

Rocket was already there, sitting on the exam table. Wearing practice shorts and a T-shirt with the sleeves cut out of it, he looked like the football player he was. What didn't show was the injury to his knee and his importance to the Currents winning a trip to the Super Bowl.

She pulled off her coat. "Rocket, sorry to pull you back in but Dr. Reynolds wanted to see you right away." Turning to Dr. Reynolds, she said, "This is Rocket—or Martin Overtree. Rocket, Dr. Reynolds."

The two men shook hands.

"Thanks for coming, Doc," Rocket said. "Mel says you're the man to help keep me on the field."

"I don't know about that. I'll need to examine you first." Dr. Reynolds pulled off his coat.

"I'll take that," Melanie offered and draped it over a chair in the corner.

The doctor rolled up his shirtsleeves, revealing tanned arms with a dusting of dark hair. Using his foot, he pulled a rolling stool from where it rested near the exam table. He straddled it and rolled to the end of the table. "I'm going to do some movements and I want you to tell me when or if they hurt and where."

Melanie watched as the doctor placed his large hands on either side of the huge running back's dark-skinned knee. With more patience than he'd shown at the airport, he examined it. Rocket grunted occasionally when Dr. Reynolds moved his knee a certain way.

The doctor pushed with his heels, putting space between him and the patient. "Now, Mr. Overtree—"

"Make it Rocket. Everyone else does."

Dr. Reynolds seemed to hesitate a second before he said in a stilted tone, "Rocket, I'd like you to lift your foot as far as you can without your knee hurting."

Rocket followed his instructions. The grimace on the player's face when his leg was almost completely extended said the knee might be in worse shape than Melanie had feared.

Dr. Reynolds placed his hand on the top of the knee.

She'd always had a thing for men's hands. To her they were a sign of their character. Dr. Reynolds had hands with long tapered fingers and closely cut nails that said he knew what he was doing and he could be trusted. Melanie liked what they said about him.

He moved his fingers over Rocket's knee. "That's good. Have you had a hard hit to this knee recently?"

Rocket made a dry chuckle. "Doc, I play football. I'm getting hit all the time."

"Yeah, I know who you are. But has there been one in particular you can remember?"

"A couple weeks ago in the game I was coming down, and the safety and I got tangled up pretty good."

Melanie had learned early in her career as a team doctor that many of the players, no matter how large, were deep down gentle giants. Often they had a hard time showing weakness and fear. Rocket was one of those guys. Melanie was grateful to the doctor for his compassionate care.

"Any popping sensation, swelling or pain?"

"Not really. If Doc here—" Rocket indicated Melanie "—hadn't pulled me off the machine the other day I wouldn't have really noticed. Players are in some kind of pain all the time if they play ball. We get to where we don't really notice."

Dr. Reynolds gave him a thoughtful nod and stood. "I'd like to get some X-rays and possibly a MRI before I confirm my diagnosis."

"I'll set them up." Melanie made a note on the pad at her desk.

The double doors burst wide open. Her father entered. In his booming voice he demanded, "Well, Doc, is Rocket going to be able to play on Sunday?"

Melanie flinched. Based on what she knew about Dr. Reynolds in their short acquaintance, he wouldn't take kindly to being pressured.

Reynolds looked her father straight in the eyes. "It's Dr. Dalton Reynolds." Not the least bit intimidated, he continued, "And you are?"

Her father pulled up short. Silence ping-ponged around the room. Few people, if any, dared to speak to her father in that manner. When he was a coach he had insisted on respect and as general manager he commanded it.

"Leon Hyde, general manager of the Currents." He offered his hand.

Dr. Reynolds gave her a questioning look, then accepted her father's hand. The moment of awkwardness between the two men disappeared as the doctor met her usually intimidating father toe to toe.

She couldn't remember another man who hadn't at least been initially unsettled by her father. Dr. Reynolds's gaze didn't waver. Her appraisal of him rose.

"So, Dr. Reynolds, is Rocket going to be able to run for us Sunday?" her father asked with a note of expectancy in his voice.

"I need to look at the X-rays and MRI before I can let you know."

"That'll be in the morning," Melanie said.

"Good." Her father turned to her. "Mel, we need Rocket on the field."

"I understand." She did, but she wasn't sure her father wasn't more concerned about winning than he was Rocket's health. She just hoped it didn't come down to her having to choose between the team and her professional conscience. "But I must consider Rocket's well-being. I won't sign off until Dr. Reynolds has made his determination."

Her father gave her a pointed look. The one she recognized that came before the team player speech.

Instead he continued, "You'll see that Dr. Reynolds gets to the Lodge and is comfortable, won't you?"

As always, it wasn't a question but a directive. She nodded. "Yes."

"Good." He looked at Dr. Reynolds. "I anticipate a positive report in the morning."

The doctor made no commitment.

Her father then gave Rocket a slight slap on the shoulder. "Go home and take care of that knee. We need you on the field Sunday."

Melanie watched the doors swing closed as her father exited. She was impressed by Dr. Reynolds's ability not to appear pushed into making a decision. Her father was known for being a persuasive man and getting what he wanted. He wanted Rocket to play Sunday. Dr. Reynolds didn't act as if he would be a yes-man if he didn't feel it was safe for Rocket to do so. On this she could agree with him.

Still, it hurt that her father didn't trust her opinion.

Dalton pulled the collar of his coat farther up around his neck and hunched his shoulders. They were in her car, moving through what was now a steady snowfall. It was unbearably cold. Even the car heater didn't seem to block the chill seeping into his bones.

Dr. Hyde leaned forward and adjusted the thermostat on the dashboard. "It should be warm in here soon."

He wasn't sure he'd ever be comfortable again. Thankfully, a few minutes later he began to thaw. She maneuvered along the road with the confidence of a person who had done this many times.

"We should be at the Lodge in about half an hour. Would you like to stop for something to eat? The Lodge does have an excellent restaurant if you'd rather wait."

He looked out the windshield. "I don't think I'm interested in being out in this weather any longer than necessary."

"It does require getting used to."

He couldn't imagine that happening either. "Why is Mr. Overtree called The Rocket?"

She glanced at him and chuckled lightly. "You apparently have never seen him play. He's fast. Very fast."

"I've never seen a professional football game."

Melanie looked at him. The car swerved for a second before she corrected it.

"You might want to watch the road."

She focused on the road again. "You've never seen one in person? Or on TV?"

"Neither. No interest. I have a busy practice."

"You have to be kidding! Football is America's game." She sounded as if she was going to get overly excited about the subject.

"I think it's baseball that's supposed to be the 'all-American game.'"

"It might have been at one time but no longer." The words were said as if she dared anyone to contradict her.

He couldn't help but raise a brow. "I think there are a lot of people who love baseball that might disagree with you."

"Maybe but I bet most of them watch the Super Bowl."

Dr. Reynolds gave a loud humph. "I understand that most watch for the halftime show and the commercials." He didn't miss the death grip she had on the stirring wheel. She really took football seriously. It was time to move on to a new subject or ask to drive. "The general manager's name is Hyde. Any relation?"

"My father."

"Isn't that a conflict of interest?"

She glanced at him again. "Normally, no. We're so close to going to the playoffs that everyone on the team, including my father, is wound up tight. Anyway, most of my work is directly with the coach."

Based on the way her father spoke to her, she'd agree with him if Dalton declared Rocket shouldn't play. His being asked to consult seemed necessary just to make the team look as if they were truly interested in the player's health. So far, all he could tell they were concerned about was winning the next game.

"What made you decide to be a team doctor?"

"With brothers playing in the NFL and a father who coached, it's the family business. I always wanted to be a doctor and being a team doctor gave me a chance to be a part of football," she said in a flat tone.

Was there more going on behind that statement?

The concept of family, much less a family business, was foreign to him. His family's occupation had been selling drugs and he'd wanted to get as far away from it as he could. He'd been a loner and alone for as long as he could remember.

Thankfully she turned into a curving road lined with large trees and had to concentrate on her driving. A few minutes later, they approached a three-story split-cedar building. She pulled under a portico with small lights hanging from it. Two large trees dressed in the same lights with red bows flanked the double wood-framed doors.

"This is Poospatuck Lodge. I think you'll be comfortable here. The team keeps a suite."

"Poospatuck?" When had he become such an inquisitive person? Usually on these trips he did what was required without any interest in the area he was visiting.

"It's an Indian tribe native to New York."

As she opened the door Dalton said, "It's not necessary for you to get out."

"I don't mind. I need to speak to the management and I can show you up to your suite."

Dalton grabbed his two bags from the backseat and followed her through the door into the welcome heat of the lobby. Large beams supported the two-story ceiling. Glass filled the wall above the door. The twinkle of lights from outside filtered in through the high windows. Flames burned bright in a gray rock fireplace taking up half of one wall. Above it was a large wreath. Along the mantel lay greenery interspersed with red candles. A grand stairway with an iron handrail led to the second floor.

Christmas had never been a big holiday for him. As a small child, it had just been another day for his parents to shoot up and pass out. In fact, the last time he was taken from his mother had been the day before Christmas. It hadn't been much fun spending Christmas Day at a stranger's house. Being a foster child on that day just sent the signal more strongly that he wasn't a real member of the family. Some of his foster parents had really tried to make him feel a part of the unit but it had never really worked. Now it was just another day and he spent it on the beach or with friends.

Dr. Hyde walked toward the registration desk located to the right of the front door.

The clerk wore a friendly smile. "Hello, Dr. Hyde. Nice to see you again."

"Hi, Mark. It's good to see you also. How's your family doing?"

"Very well, thank you."

"Good." She glanced back. "This is Dr. Reynolds. He'll be staying in our suite. I'll show him up."

"Very good. It's all ready for you."

She turned to Dalton. "The elevator is over this way but we're only going to the second floor if you don't mind carrying your bags."

"I believe I can manage to go up the stairs."

She gave him an apologetic look. "I didn't mean to imply…"

"Please just show me my room." Dalton picked up his bags off the floor where he'd placed them earlier. He didn't miss her small sound of disgust as she turned and walked toward the stairs. He followed three or four steps behind as they climbed the stairs. He enjoyed the nice sway of her hips.

At the top of the stairs she turned left and continued down a wide, well lit hallway to the end.

A brass plaque on the door read Niagara Currents. She pulled a plastic door key out of her handbag. With a quick swipe through the slot, she opened the door. Entering, she held the door for him.

He stepped into the seating area. The space had a rustic feel to it that matched the rest of the building. The two sofas and couple of chairs looked comfortable and inviting.

"Your bedroom is through here." She pushed two French windows wide to reveal a large bed. "This is my favorite part of the suite."

He didn't say anything. She turned and looked at him. Dalton raised a brow. A blush crept up her neck.

"Um, I like the view from here is what I meant to say. The falls are incredible."

Dalton moved to stand in the doorway. A large window filled the entire wall. He could just make out the snow falling from the light coming from below.

"There's an amazing view of the falls from here. Now you can say you saw the falls."

"So do you stay here often?"

She glared at him. "What're you implying, Dr. Reynolds?"

"I was implying nothing, Dr. Hyde. I just thought you must have stayed overnight if you were that well acquainted with the view."

"This suite is sometimes used for meetings. Now, if you'll excuse me, I need to be getting home. I'll be here at eight-thirty in the morning to pick you up."

"Why not earlier?"

"Because the X-rays won't be ready until nine. So just enjoy your evening. If you need anything, ask for Mark."

"I shouldn't call you?" he said in a suggestive tone, just

to see how she would react. Dr. Hyde pursed her lips. Was she on the verge of saying something?

After a moment, she looked through her handbag and pulled out a card. She handed it to him. "If you need me, you may. Good night."

The door closed with a soft click behind her.

Why had he needled her? It was so unlike him. Maybe it was because she'd questioned his clothing decisions. She'd been polite about it but there was still an undercurrent of humor. Could he possibly want her to feel a little out of sorts too? He had to admit it had been interesting to make her uncomfortable.

CHAPTER TWO

MELANIE PULLED IN front of the Lodge at eight-thirty the next morning. The snow had stopped during the night but the sky was overcast as if it would start again soon. She'd left last night uncomfortable about Dr. Reynolds' suggestive manner. She wasn't feeling any better about being his hostess this morning.

When his dark shapely brow had risen as if she were proposing she might be staying the night with him, she'd been insulted for a second. Then a tinge of self-satisfaction had shot through her that a male had noticed her. She'd had her share of boyfriends when she'd been young but recently the men attracted to her had become fewer. They seemed frightened by her position or were only interested so they could meet either one of her famous brothers or one of the Currents players. The one that she had loved hadn't truly cared for her. She'd known rejection and wanted no part of it.

There had been one special man. He was a lawyer for a player. She couldn't have asked for someone who fit into her family better. He lived and breathed football. They had even talked of marriage. It wasn't until he started hinting, then asking her to put a good word in with her father when an assistant manager's job came open that she realized he was using her. When she refused to do so, he dumped her. It had taken her months after that to even accept a friendly date. After that experience she judged every man that showed any attention to her with a sharp eye. She wouldn't go through something like that again. Dr. Reynolds might flirt with her but she would see to it that was all that would happen. A fly in, fly out guy was someone she had no interest in.

She entered the lobby to find Dr. Reynolds waiting in one of the many large armchairs near the fireplace. Was he fortifying himself for the weather outside? She smiled. He had looked rather pitiful the night before in his effort to stay warm.

This morning his outfit wasn't much better. Wearing a dress shirt, jeans and loafers, he didn't look any more prepared for the weather than he had yesterday. In reality, it was unrealistic to expect him to buy clothes just to fly to Niagara Falls to see Rocket but he would be cold. However, he was undoubtedly the most handsome man she'd ever met. His striking good looks drew the attention of a couple of women who walked by. He had an air of self-confidence about him.

His head turned and his midnight gaze found her. His eyes were his most striking attribute. The dark color was appealing but it was the intensity of his focus that held her. As if he saw beyond what was on the surface and in some way understood what was beneath.

His bags sat on the floor beside him. She didn't have to ask if he had plans to return to the sun and fun as soon as possible. If Rocket needed surgery he would have to go to Miami to have it done. She hoped that wouldn't be the case but feared otherwise.

"Dr. Reynolds, good morning," she said as she approached.

He stood, picked up his shoulder bag and slipped it over his neck. Grabbing his other bag, he walked toward her.

Apparently he was eager to leave. She stepped closer. "Have you had breakfast?"

"I ate a couple of hours ago."

So he was an early riser. "Then we can go." Melanie turned and headed back the way she had come. By the time she settled behind the steering wheel, he'd placed his bag in the backseat and was buckling up.

As she pulled out onto the main road, he said, "Well, at least it isn't snowing."

"No, but the weatherman is calling for more. A lot more."

"Then I need to see Mr. Overtree's X-rays and get to the airport."

"Only eight more days. You must be in a hurry to get home to your family for Christmas."

"No family. I'll be working."

"Oh." Despite her family's year-round focus on football, they all managed to come together during the holidays. Sometimes it was around Christmas Day games, but they always found a time that worked for all of them. Her brothers had wives and children, and the crowd was rowdy and loud. She loved it. Melanie couldn't imagine not having any family or someone to share the day with. Even though much of the work fell to her. The men in her life expected her to organize and take care of them. She'd never let them know that sometimes she resented them taking her for granted.

They rode in silence for a while. He broke it by asking, "How much longer?"

"It should be only another ten minutes or so."

The sky had turned gray and a large snowflake hit the windshield. By the time she pulled into the team compound it had become a steady snow shower. Instead of parking in the front, this time she pulled through the gate to the back of the building and parked in the slot with her name painted on it. Thankfully, her spot was close to the door so they wouldn't have far to walk.

Dr. Reynolds huddled in his coat on their way to the door. With his head down, he walked slowly as if in an effort not to slip on the ice and snow. Melanie stayed close behind him. She had no idea what her plan was if he started to go down. Inside, they both took off their jackets and shook them out.

"I'll take that," Melanie said. Dr. Reynolds handed her his overcoat. Their hands brushed as she reached for it. A tingle of awareness went up her spine. Shaking it off, she hung their coats up on pegs along the wall and headed down the hall. "This way."

"I assume Mr. Overtree's X-rays will have been sent to your computer in the exam room. The MRI as well."

"Yes."

She made a turn and went down another hallway until she reached the Athlete Performance Area and pushed open one of the swinging doors and held it. She let him have the door, then continued into the room. Rocket, Coach Rizzo and her father were already there.

Her father gave her a questioning look. She shrugged her shoulder. Surely her father wouldn't push Dr. Reynolds to agree to let Rocket play if the test indicated that he shouldn't. As team doctor, she had the final say anyway. She would refuse to be a team player if it came down to Rocket's long-term health. Moving on to her desk, she flipped on the computer. She pulled up Rocket's chart. "Dr. Reynolds, the X-rays from last week and his most recent ones are ready for your review."

Giving her what she could only describe as an impressed look, Dr. Reynolds seemed to appreciate her being efficient and prepared. For some reason that made her feel good. The kind of respect she didn't feel she received from her father. She stepped away from the desk to allow him room. When the other men moved to join them, she shook her head, indicating they should give Dr. Reynolds some space. Despite that, her father still took steps toward her desk.

"Thank you, Doctor. You've been very thorough," Dr. Reynolds said to her.

It was nice to be valued as a fellow medical professional who was more interested in the health of the player than whether or not the team won. She and Dr. Reynolds were at least in the same playbook where that was concerned.

In her mind no game was worth a man losing mobility for the rest of his life. A player's heath came first in that regard. She was sure her father and the coach didn't feel the same. More than once she'd been afraid that there might be repercussions from them if she placed a player on the disabled list. Even the players gave her a hard time about her being overly cautious. As their doctor, the players' health took precedence over winning a game. Rocket had his sights set on being the most valuable player. He might agree to anything to get it. Even playing when he was injured. Sometimes she felt as if she had the most rational mind in the group.

Dr. Reynolds took her chair. He gave that same concentrated consideration to the screen as he seemed to give everything. With a movement of one long finger, he clicked through the black-and-white screens of different X-ray angles of Rocket's knee. He studied them all but made no comment.

He turned to her. "Did you have a MRI done?"

She nodded.

"Good. I'd like to see it."

She moved to the desk and he pushed back enough to allow her to get to the keyboard. As she punched keys she was far too aware of him close behind her. Her fingers fumbled on the keys but seconds later she had the red-and-blue images on the screen.

Minutes went by as Dr. Reynolds moved through the different shots.

"Well?" her father snapped.

"Let him have time to look," Melanie said in an effort to placate him. Her father shot her a sharp look.

Dr. Reynolds continued to spend time on the side views of the knee. The entire room seemed to hold their collective breath as he spun in the chair. His gaze went to Rocket. "It looks like you have a one-degree patellar-tendon tear."

That was what she had been afraid of. "That was my diagnosis."

Dr. Reynolds nodded in her direction.

"We still needed a second opinion," her father said as he stepped back.

For once it would be nice for her father to appreciate her knowledge and ability.

"Can he play?" Coach Rizzo asked.

"The question is—*should* he play?" Then, to Rocket, Dr. Reynolds said, "Do you want to take the chance on ruining your knee altogether? I wouldn't recommend it. Let it rest, heal. You'll be ready to go next year."

The other men let go simultaneous groans.

Rocket moaned. "This is our year. Who's to know what'll happen next year?"

Her father looked at Rocket. "What do you want to do? Think about the bonus and the ring."

How like her father to apply pressure.

Dr. Reynolds looked at him. "Mr. Hyde, this is a decision that Rocket needs to make without any force."

Her father didn't look happy but he also didn't say anything more.

Rocket seemed not to know what the right answer was or, if he did, he didn't want to say it.

"Hey, Doc, what're the chances of it getting worse?" Rocket asked.

"If you take a hard hit, that'll be it. Your tendon is like a rope with a few of the strands frayed and ragged. You take a solid shot and the rope may break. What I know is that it won't get any better if you play. One good twist during a run could possibly mean the end of your career."

Her father huffed. "Roger Morton with the Wildcats had surgery and returned better than ever."

"I'm not saying it isn't possible. However, not everyone does that well."

Coach Rizzo walked over to Rocket and put his hand on his shoulder, "I think 'The Rocket' has what it takes to play for us on Sunday."

Dr. Reynolds stood. "That'll be for Mr. Overtree to decide."

"You can't do anything more?" Rocket asked Dr. Reynolds.

He looked as if he wanted to say no but instead said, "I'd like to see you use the knee. See what kind of mobility you have."

Before Rocket had time to respond, Coach Rizzo spoke up. "Practice starts in about ten minutes."

"Mel, why don't you show Dr. Reynolds to the practice field?" her father suggested.

"Okay." Once again, she wasn't sure how being tour guide to the visiting doctor fell under her job description but she was a team player. She would do what she was asked. As she headed out the door she said over her shoulder, "Rocket, be sure and wear your knee brace."

She looked at Dr. Reynolds. "The practice field is out this way."

Dalton followed Melanie out a different set of double doors and into a hallway. At the elevator they went down to the ground floor. Once again she was wearing a very efficient-looking business suit. With her shapely, slender body it would seem she'd want to show it off; instead, she acted as if she sought to play down being a woman.

Her father sure was a domineering man. She seemed to do his bidding without question. He was afraid that if he hadn't been brought in for that second opinion, her father would have overridden any decision she made about Rocket. For a grown woman she seemed to still be trying to make daddy happy.

"We aren't going outside, are we?" he asked.

She grinned. "No. We have an indoor practice field. A full stadium without the stands. You should be warm enough in there."

"Good."

Melanie led them down a hallway and through two extralarge doors into a covered walkway. Seconds later they entered a large building.

They walked down one of the sidelines until they were near the forty-yard line. A few of the players wandered out on the field and started stretching. They wore shoulder pads under practice jerseys and shorts.

"Hey, Doc," a couple of the players yelled as they moved to the center of the field.

She called back to them by name. Dalton wasn't used to this type of familiarity with his patients. As a surgeon he usually saw them only a couple of times and never again.

It was still cooler than he liked inside the building. Dalton crossed his arms over his chest, tucking his hands under his arms.

Dr. Hyde must have noticed because she said, "It's not near as cold in here as outside but we can't keep it too warm because the players would overheat." Not surprisingly Melanie didn't seem affected by the temperature.

Rocket loped on the field from the direction of the dressing room. Dalton studied the movement of his leg and so far couldn't see anything significantly out of the norm.

Melanie leaned toward him. "They'll go through their warm-up and then move into some skill work. I think that'll be when you can tell more about his knee. In the past he seemed to show no indication there might be a problem until he was running post plays."

"Post plays?"

"When they run up the field and then cut sharply one way or another."

He nodded and went back to learning Rocket's movements. *Rocket*. He shook his head. It seemed as if he was picking up the slang of the game.

Would Dr. Hyde agree with him if he said that Rocket didn't need to play? As a medical doctor, how could she not?

They had been standing there twenty minutes or so, him watching Rocket while Melanie spoke with every one of the big men who passed by. The staff along the sidelines with them did the same. She was obviously well liked.

The next time a guy came by her, Dalton asked, "You have a good relationship with the team. Does anyone not like you?"

A broad smile came to her face. "We're pretty much like family around here. We all have a job to do but most of us are really good friends. I work at having a positive relationship with the players. I try to have them see me as part of the team. I want them to feel comfortable coming to me with problems. Men tend to drag their feet about asking for help." He must have made a face because she said, "Not all, but I want them to come to me or one of the trainers before a problem gets so bad they can't play."

Dalton had nothing to base that type of camaraderie on. Long ago he'd given up on that idea. Unable to think of anything to say, he muttered, "That makes sense."

She touched his arm. Her small hand left a warm place

behind when she removed it to point at Rocket. "Watch him when he makes this move."

The hesitation was so minor that Dalton might have missed it if he hadn't been looking as she instructed.

"Did you see it?"

"I did. It was almost as if he didn't realize he did it." He was impressed that she had caught it to begin with.

"Exactly. I noticed it during one practice. Called him in and did X-rays. Dad insisted I contact you. We can't afford for Rocket to be out."

He looked at her. "Afford?"

She continued to watch the action on the field. "Yeah. This is big business for the team as well as for all these guys' careers."

He looked at Rocket and made no effort to keep the skepticism out of his voice when he asked, "No life after football?"

She stepped back and gave him a sharp look. "Yes. That's the point. A successful season means endorsements, which means money in their pockets. That doesn't even include the franchise."

"And all this hinges on Rocket?"

"No, but he's an important part." She looked around and leaned so close he could smell her shampoo. "The star— for now."

He wasn't convinced but he nodded and said, "I think I get it."

Melanie's expression implied she wasn't sure he did.

They continued to watch practice from the edge of the sideline. The team was playing on the far end of the field.

"How long has Rocket...?" he began.

She turned to look at him.

Over her shoulder he saw a huge player barreling in their direction. His helmeted head was turned away as he looked at the ball in the air. Not thinking twice, Dalton wrapped his arms around Melanie and swiveled to the side so he would take the brunt of the hit. Slammed with a force he would later swear was the equivalent of a speeding train, his breath swooshed from his lungs. His arms remained around Melanie as they went through the air and landed on the Astroturf floor with a thud. The landing felt almost as hard as the original hit. He and Melanie ended up a tangle of legs and arms as the player stumbled over their bodies.

There was no movement from the soft form in his arms. Fear seized him. Had she been hurt? A moan brushed his cheek. At least she was alive. He loosened his hold and rolled to his side but his hands remained in place. Searching Melanie's face, he watched as her eyes fluttered open. She stared at him with a look of uncertainty.

"What…what happened?"

Dalton drew in a breath, causing his chest to complain. He would be in considerable pain in the morning. "We got hit."

"By what?"

"Doc Mel, you okay?" a player asked from above them.

Dalton looked up to find players and staff circling them.

A large man with bulging biceps sounded as if he might cry.

"I'm sorry, Doc Mel. Are you okay? I tried to stop." If that had been his idea of slowing down, Dalton would have hated being on the receiving end of the player's full power. Dalton returned his attention to Melanie. One of his hands rested beneath her shoulder and the other on her stomach. Her cheek was against his lips. "Do you think you can stand?"

"Why did you grab me?"

"Because you could have been hurt if I hadn't." Didn't she understand he might have just saved her life?

"Hurt?" She turned her head toward him. Her eyes were still dazed. "You have pretty eyes."

Dalton swallowed hard, which did nothing to ease the pain in his chest. She must have a head injury because he couldn't imagine her saying something so forward.

"Lie right where you are," one of the people above them commanded. "An ambulance is on its way."

Dalton shifted. "I don't think that's necessary."

The trainer said, "Yes, it is. You both need to be checked out."

"Look, I'm a doctor. I would know if I need…"

"Now you're a patient." A man with a staff shirt said, "Mel, where do you hurt?"

Dalton's hand moved to her waist and gave it a gentle shake. "Dr. Hyde, can you move?"

"Melanie…my name is Melanie," she murmured.

Three of the trainers shifted to one side of her and placed their arms under her, preparing to lift her enough to separate them.

"Melanie, they're going to move you." Dalton took his hands away.

She nodded then made a noise of acceptance and the trainers went to work. Dalton started to rise and a couple of the trainers placed their hands on his shoulders, stopping him.

A few minutes later the sound of the ambulances arriving caught his attention.

Melanie wasn't clear on all that had occurred before she woke up in the brightly lit emergency room.

"What's going on?" She looked at David, one of the trainers, who was sitting in a chair across the room.

"You were in an accident on the practice field."

Before David could elaborate, a white-haired doctor entered. "So, how are you feeling?" He stepped close to the bed and pulled out a penlight.

Slowly the events came back to her. She started to sit up. "How is Dr. Reynolds?"

The doctor pushed her shoulder, making her lie back. "First let me do my examination, then you can go check on him."

She settled back.

"I'll be in the waiting room," David said and went out the door.

"Now tell me what happened," the doctor said as he lifted one of her eyelids.

Melanie relayed the events she recalled and finished with "and Dr. Reynolds took the impact of the hit."

The doctor nodded thoughtfully. "That he did."

"How bad is he?"

"If you'll give me a few minutes to finish my exam you can go see for yourself."

Melanie's chest tightened. She hoped he wasn't badly hurt. Thankfully, the doctor pronounced her well enough to go. The time that she waited for the nurse with the discharge papers only made her anxiety grow. Because of her, Dalton was hurt.

"What exam room is Dr. Reynolds in?" Melanie asked as she pulled on her shoes.

"Next door." The nurse indicated to the right.

"Thanks." Melanie rose slowly, still feeling dazed. She sat on the edge of the bed for a few seconds. Her body would be sore tomorrow.

Minutes later, she knocked on the glass sliding door to the exam room. At a weak, "Come in," she entered. Dalton still wore his slacks but no shirt. He had a nicely muscled chest. She groaned when she saw the ice pack resting on his left rib cage. His eyes were glazed as if he were in pain and his lips were drawn into a tight line. Guilt filled her.

Another one of the trainers stood in the corner of the

room, typing on his cell phone. When she entered he slipped out, giving her the impression he was relieved to do so.

"Hey," she said softly.

Dalton's response came out more as a grumble than a word.

Melanie stepped farther into the room. She had to let him know how much she appreciated what he'd done. "Thank you."

He nodded but his jaw remained tight.

"How are you?"

"I've been better." The words were uttered between clenched teeth.

A stab of remorse plunged through her. He was here because of her. She approached the bed and moved to put her hand on his shoulder, then stopped herself. That would be far too personal. "Don't talk if it hurts too much."

A nurse entered.

Melanie didn't give her time to pick up the chart before she asked, "How is he?" She had to find out something about his injuries without him having to do the speaking.

The nurse looked at him. "Do I have permission to discuss your case?"

He nodded.

"The doctor has some bruised ribs. He'll be sore for a week or so but nothing more serious."

At least that was positive news. Melanie was already guilt ridden enough. "Then he will be released?"

"He'll be released as soon as he has someone who can take him home and stay with him. He isn't going to feel like doing much for a few days."

"I'll see that he gets the care he needs," Melanie assured her.

Dalton's eyebrows went up. "Plane…"

The nurse placed the blood pressure cuff around his

arm. "You don't need to be flying. I don't think you could stand the pain."

There was a knock at the door and Melanie looked away from Dalton to find John Horvitz, her father's right-hand man, standing there.

"How're you both doing?" Obviously he would be concerned about the visiting doctor being hurt on team time.

Melanie gave John a brief report. "He's in so much pain, it's difficult to speak." Dalton gave her a grateful look.

John focused his attention on her. "Your father wanted me to check on you both. He had a meeting. I'll be giving him a full report."

And he would. That was always the way it had been. Her father sent someone else. When he'd coached, team issues took precedence. As the general manager, it wasn't any better. His concern had always come through a subordinate. What would it be like to have him show he really cared?

"He'll call when the meeting is over," John finished.

"Who hit us?" she asked.

John grimaced. "I was told it was Juice."

"He must have been flying!"

"Not 'Freight Train'?" Dalton mumbled.

Melanie laughed. The poor guy. Maybe he did have a sense of humor. She wrapped her arms around her waist when the laughter led to throbbing.

"Are you sure you're okay?" John asked her.

"Sore, but nothing that I can't stand. Dr. Reynolds is the one we should be worried about. I think we would both like to get out of here."

As if on cue, the ER doctor came in. "If you'll give me a few minutes, I'll see you have your discharge papers. There will be no driving or flying for two days."

Dalton partially sat up, "Two days!" As if the effort was too much for him, he fell back, closing his eyes.

She owed him for making sure she hadn't really got hurt

but this was a busy time of the year and adding the Currents' play-off game didn't make it better. Now she was being saddled with taking care of him for two more days.

"The team will see that you are as comfortable as possible," John assured him.

Dalton's eyes opened but he said nothing.

John continued, "There's a driver and a car waiting to take you both home. I have notified the Lodge to do everything they can to make your stay comfortable."

"I'll see that he's well taken care of. Thanks, John," Melanie said.

Half an hour later, Melanie sucked in her breath when she looked out the hospital sliding glass door. Snow fell so thickly that she could just make out the cars in the parking lot. "The snow has really picked up."

Their driver waited under the pickup area with the engine running. Dr. Reynolds, always the gentleman, allowed her to get in the backseat first. Wincing as he bent to climb in, he joined her. He reached out to pull the door closed and groaned.

"Let me help." She leaned across him. Her chest brushed his as she stretched. His body heat mixed with the air blasting out of the car vents, making her too warm. He smelled like a fir after a misty rain. She stopped herself from inhaling. Using her fingertips, she managed to pull the door closed. His breath brushed her cheek as she sat up again, causing her midsection to flutter.

The windshield wipers swished back and forth in a rapid movement but the snow continued to pile up on the glass. She glanced at Dr. Reynolds. His shoulders were hunched and he was peering out with a concerned look on his face.

"Normal?" The word came out with a wince.

"We get a lot of snow here. We're used to it. Looks like we'll have a white Christmas, with it only being seven days off." She tried to make the last sentence sound upbeat. In pain, he took on an almost boyish look that had her heart going out to him.

He leaned back and closed his eyes. "Only thing white at Christmastime where I come from is the beach."

That didn't sound all that festive to her. Snow, a green tree, a warm fire and people you loved surrounding you was what she thought Christmas should be. She loved this time of the year.

The driver had the radio playing low and after the song finished the announcer came on. "Fellow Niagarans, it's a white one out there. The good news is the roads are still passable and the airport open. But not sure it will be tomorrow. The storm isn't over yet."

Dalton moaned.

"I'm sorry for this inconvenience, Dr. Reynolds. Maybe in a few days you'll be up to going home," Melanie said in a sympathetic tone.

And she wouldn't be nursemaiding him anymore. She needed to talk to her father about what her duties as team doctor entailed. It would probably be a waste of time; he'd never listened to her in the past and wasn't likely to do so now.

Dalton questioned if the stars were aligned against him. He was stuck in Niagara Falls longer than he'd planned. Too long for his comfort. The driver pulled under the awning of the Lodge. Dalton opened the door despite the pain it brought and climbed out. It wasn't until he turned to close the door that he saw Dr. Hyde getting out.

"What're you doing?" he muttered through tightly clamped teeth.

"I'm going to stay and see about you tonight."

"What?"

"Didn't you hear the doctor? You need someone to check on you regularly over the next twenty-four hours."

"I'll be fine."

"For heaven's sakes, can we go inside to argue about this?"

Without another word, he turned and pulled open the door to the Lodge. He had to admit it required a great deal of effort to do so.

She came to stand beside him. "You obviously need help. I feel guilty enough about you getting hurt. The least I can do is make sure you're okay."

His look met hers for the first time since they'd left the hospital. He wasn't used to seeing concern for him in anyone's eyes. He tried to take a deep breath. Pain shot through his side. He reluctantly said, "I would appreciate help."

"Then let's go try to make you as comfortable as you can be with those ribs. The elevator is over this way." They walked across the lobby.

"Not going to make me climb the stairs?" Each word pained him but he couldn't stop himself from making the comment.

She glared at him. "I thought your ribs hurt too much to speak."

He started to laugh and immediately wrapped his arms across his chest.

They rode the elevator up and walked to the room. At the door Melanie took out a room key.

"You have a key to my room?" Dalton asked with a hint of suspicion.

"I was given one when we knew you were coming so I could check on the room before you arrived." She slid the plastic card in the slot and opened the door. "I'm sure you're ready to lie down. I'll call for some food."

"Are you always so bossy?"

Melanie dropped her pocketbook into the closest chair. "I guess I am when it comes to taking care of my patients."

Dalton started toward the bedroom. "I'm not one of your patients."

"You are for the next twenty-four hours."

He wasn't pleased with the arrangements. Still, something about having her concerned for him gave him an unfamiliar warm feeling. He'd never had anyone's total focus before. Mrs. Richie had been the only foster mother who came close to doing that, but he hadn't been there long before he heard her telling the social worker that it would be better for him to move to another house. After that he'd never let another woman know he hurt or see him in need. He made sure his relationships with women were short and remained at arm's length. All physical and no emotional involvement was the way he liked to keep things.

Dalton crossed the living space and circled one of the sofas that faced each other on his way to the bedroom on the left. There was another room on the opposite side of the large living area. He would leave that one for Melanie. Giving a brief glance to the minibar/kitchen area on the same side of the suite as the extra bedroom, he kept walking.

He ached all over. His jaw hurt from clamping his teeth in an effort not to show the amount of pain he was in. He'd learned as a child that if you let them see your weakness, they would use it against you. Now all he wanted to do was get a hot shower and go to bed.

Kicking off his shoes, he started to remove his knit pullover shirt and pain exploded through his side, taking his breath. For once in his life he had no choice but to ask for help. When his breath returned he opened the door and said, "Dr. Hyde?"

Melanie jumped up from the chair. She must have been watching for him. Hurrying toward him, her eyes were filled with concern, "Are you all right?"

"I need help with my shirt."

She stepped close. "Why do you need to take it off? You could lie down with it on."

"Shower."

"Oh."

"Help?"

"Sure. Sure." She didn't sound too confident as she followed him back into the room. When he stopped at the bed she reached for the hem of his shirt. Her blue eyes met his. There was a twinkle in her eyes when she said, "You know I'm usually on a first-name basis with people I help undress. You can feel free to call me Mel."

Was she flirting with him? "You said Melanie."

She gave him a questioning look.

"That's what you told me to call you after we were hit. You can call me Dalton."

"Dalton—" she said it as if she were testing the sound of it on her lips "—hold real still." She gathered the shirt until she had it under his arms.

Pain must have really addled his brain because he liked the sound of his name when she said it. He was just disappointed he didn't feel well enough to take advantage of her removing his clothes.

"Raise your hands as high as you can. I'll be as careful as I can but I'm afraid it's going to hurt."

He followed her directions. She wasn't wrong. It hurt like the devil as she worked the sleeves off. Sweat popped out on his forehead.

"I'm sorry. I'll get you something for the pain as soon as I'm done."

Dalton was exhausted by the time she finished.

"Let's go to the bathroom to remove your pants."

"I can do that."

"What's wrong? You afraid you have something I haven't seen? I'm a doctor for an all-male football team. I think I can handle removing your pants."

"You're not my doctor."

"Just as I expected. The double whammy. Who makes the worst patient? A male doctor."

He sneered, then walked gingerly into the bathroom and closed the door.

"Just the same, I'll be right out here if you need me," she called.

If nothing else she was tenacious. With more effort than he would have thought necessary, he managed to get his pants down. In the shower he stood under the hot water until he was afraid he might need Melanie's assistance to get out. That would be the ultimate humiliation—having to ask for help again. He already looked feeble as it was.

His clothes were not right for the weather, he was hurt and now he needed her help to undress. He had to get a handle on the situation.

He turned the water off and stepped out of the shower. Melanie opened the door and entered just as he pulled a towel off the rack.

He stood motionless. "What're you doing here?"

She met his gaze with determination. "I'm going to help you dry off. There's no way you can handle that by yourself. If you're afraid I'll look, keep that bath sheet and I'll use one of the others."

Their standoff lasted seconds before he handed her his towel. He wouldn't be intimidated. Standing proudly in front of her, he didn't blink as she took the rectangular terry cloth. She circled behind him and ran the fabric across his shoulders then down his back.

His manhood twitched.

Melanie continued down his legs and up the front before she stepped around to face him. "Lean your head down."

Her voice sounded brisk and businesslike, as if she dried men off all the time. He rather liked having a woman dry him. Despite the pain he experienced with each breath, his body was reacting to the attention. Melanie briskly rubbed his hair, then went over his shoulders and down his chest. When she passed over his ribs, he hissed.

She gave him a sad look. "I'm sorry. I'm trying to be careful."

Going further south, her hands jerked to a stop and it was her turn to release a rush of air.

"I guess you weren't careful enough," he smirked.

Her wide-eyed gaze met his.

"I think I can finish from here." He didn't miss her gulp.

With a shaking hand she handed him the towel and left with the parting words, "There's a robe hanging on the back of the door."

Well, he'd won that standoff. Melanie wasn't as unaffected as she would like to make out. He let the towel drop to the floor. No way was he going to make the effort to put a robe on when he was just going to crawl into bed.

Melanie wasn't in the bedroom when he came out and he didn't pause on his way to the bed. The effort alone had his side aching. He managed to cover his lower half before there was a light knock on the door. He was in so much pain he didn't even make an effort to answer.

She pushed the door open enough to stick her head in. "You need help?"

He hated to admit again that he did. "Would you put some pillows behind me?"

Melanie hurried to him. She went around the bed, gathered the extra pillows and returned, placing the pillows within arm's reach.

Dalton groaned as he tried to sit up.

"Let me help you." Melanie didn't meet his look as she ran her left arm around his shoulders to support him. With her other hand, she stuffed a couple of pillows behind his back. The awkward process put them close. Too close for his comfort. His face was almost in her breasts. She smelled sweet. Nothing like the aroma of disinfectant their profession was known for. Too soon she guided him back against the pillows so that he was now in a half-sitting position. "Is that better?"

He nodded and made an effort to adjust the covers so that his reaction to her assistance wasn't obvious. Why was his body reacting to her so?

"Good. I'll get you that pain reliever." She stepped out of the room and soon returned with a bottle of tablets and a glass of water. Shaking out a couple of pills, she handed them to him, then offered him the glass of water.

Gladly he took the medicine and swallowed all the water. Closing his eyes, he was almost asleep when the covers were pulled up over his chest. He was being tucked in for the first time in his life...and he liked it!

CHAPTER THREE

MELANIE SETTLED IN to the overstuffed chair closest to the door to Dalton's bedroom. Dalton. She liked the name. He wasn't as much of a stuffed shirt when he was hurt. She would never have dreamed she would ever be baby-sitting the world's foremost orthopedic surgeon. Here she was spending the night and him really just a stranger. That might not be technically accurate after she'd toweled him dry. She'd been aware he was a man before, but she was well aware of how much man he was now.

Heavens, after those eventful moments in the bathroom she was almost glad he was hurt. She wasn't sure what she would have done had he leaned over and kissed her. Shaking her head, she tried to get the image out of her mind but it didn't seem to want to go. Being a professional, she shouldn't have been shocked or affected by his nakedness but somehow his body's reaction to her ministrations made her blood run hot. What was she thinking? She wasn't even sure she liked him. He'd made it clear he cared nothing about football and her life revolved around the game.

Her cell phone rang.

"Yes, Daddy?"

"How is Dr. Reynolds?"

Just like him not to ask about her. Tamping down her disappointment, she answered, "He's asleep and not too happy with having to be here longer than he planned."

"Well, try to keep him happy. We need him to sign off on Rocket."

"Dad, I wouldn't count on him doing that." Or her, for that matter. But that wasn't a battle she would have over the phone.

"Well, you never know. Since you're going to be spending some extra time with him, try to sweeten him up some."

That she *wouldn't* be doing. "I'll let you know if anything changes."

Her father hung up. She shifted to get more comfortable but that didn't seem to happen. Dalton might have taken the majority of the hit but she could tell that she hadn't escaped unhurt. She would like to sleep but she was waiting for one of the girls in the office to bring her some clothes.

While Dalton had showered, she'd called one of her friends and asked her to pack a bag and bring it by the Lodge. As soon as it arrived she would get a bath in the other room and then a nap.

As if thinking about it made it appear, there was a knock at the door. It was the bellhop with her bag. After thanking and tipping him, she closed and locked the door. She needed to check on Dalton before seeing to herself.

She set the bag on the floor next to Dalton's door and then pushed it open. It wouldn't pay for him to think she was sneaking a peek at him. She went to his bedside. He slept making a soft, even snoring sound. The covers had slipped down, leaving his chest bare. It was well developed as if he was used to physical activity. There was a smattering of hair in its center.

"Like what you see?"

Jerking back, heat rushing up her neck, her gaze flew to Dalton's face. "I was just checking on you."

"That's what they all say." His eyes closed again.

She left the room, hoping he wouldn't remember her visit.

* * *

A noise woke Melanie from where she slept on one of the sofas. She'd chosen to rest there so she could hear Dalton if she was needed. The extra bedroom was too far away.

She sat up. A fat ray of light came out of the open door. Dalton stood silhouetted in it. She sighed. At least he was wearing the robe.

"How're you feeling?"

"Hungry." His breathing still sounded difficult.

"I called for sandwiches earlier. They're in the refrigerator in the minibar. I'll get them." She stood. Pulling on the matching robe over her tailored-shirt-and-pants pajama set, she flipped on a lamp.

Giving her a critical look, he followed her to the bar. There he took one of the high stools. Melanie flipped on the light over the bar and pulled the tray of sandwiches out of the refrigerator, placing them on the bar. "What would you like to drink?"

Dalton glanced out the window. Following his gaze, she saw that the lamps lighting the falls made it easy to see snow falling.

He looked back at her. "Coffee?"

"Coming right up." She prepared the coffee machine and started it. While it bubbled and dripped she pulled out her own sandwich. "Cream and sugar?"

He shook his head.

"Does it still hurt to breathe?"

He nodded.

Pouring his coffee, she handed it to him. "Would you like more pain reliever?"

"Yes."

"I'll get you some after we eat." Despite his injury, she had a feeling he used as few words as possible all the time. She opened the refrigerator, pulled out a soda for herself and walked around the bar. Taking a stool, she made sure it wasn't the one right next to his.

They ate in silence. When Dalton finished he pushed the plate away and limped toward the window. He stood staring out. Melanie joined him. From this position the falls could be seen but it wasn't the same magnificent view as from his bedroom.

After a moment she murmured, "I want to thank you again for protecting me. I know getting stuck here wasn't what you planned."

"Not your fault."

"Still, I feel bad."

"Don't."

Neither one of them said anything for a few more minutes. Melanie was surprise by how comfortable it was to just stand next to him and look out at the snowy night. When was the last time she had spent a moment or two just being with someone?

Not that she was attracted to Dalton. She stepped away. "I need to clean up."

While she was busy behind the bar, Dalton went into his bedroom. Finished with putting everything in its place, Melanie went to Dalton's room to see about giving him some medicine. She found him sitting on the edge of the bed.

Melanie picked up the pain reliever bottle she'd left on the bedside table. Shaking out a couple of pills, she handed them to Dalton. She picked up the glass left there earlier. "I'll get you some water."

As she went by, his fingers circled her wrist, stopping her. His hand was warm on her skin. "Thank you for taking care of me."

Melanie could see the effort the words cost him, both physically and mentally. Had no one ever cared for him?

Surely as a child his mother had nursed him when he was sick?

"I'm glad I could help."

He let go of her and she continued to the bathroom to fill the glass. When she returned he was already asleep. The robe he'd worn lay on the end of the bed. He must have taken the pills dry. She left the glass on the table and adjusted the covers around his shoulders. After turning off the bedside lamp, she left the room, leaving the door cracked so she could hear him if he called.

Dalton woke to the sun streaming through the large window and the roar of the falls. He rolled over and let out a loud groan. He'd heard that having bruised or broken ribs was superpainful. What everyone said was right. If he had to sit up on a plane for three hours he wouldn't be fit to do anything for a week. Thankfully, he didn't have any cases waiting. He looked at the snow piled on the windowsill and shivered. Cold was just not his thing.

The door opened and Melanie's head appeared around it. "You okay in here? I heard you call out."

"Yes."

"You hungry again?"

He nodded. "What time is it?"

"Almost eleven."

"That late?" When was the last time he'd not been up at six?

Melanie glanced out the window. "How about some hot cereal?"

"Okay."

"Cream of Wheat okay?"

He'd not had Cream of Wheat in years. Mrs. Richie had served it almost every morning. It was a cheap way to feed a large number of children. The thing was, he didn't really mind. He, unlike most of the other children, liked the cereal.

"Sounds good."

"You seem to be breathing easier. Has some of the pain gone away?"

He shrugged. "Not really."

"I'm sorry to hear that. I'll call for some breakfast." She left, pulling the door closed.

Dalton struggled to stand. The pain was excruciating, but he couldn't lie there all day. That certainly wouldn't make it any easier to get around. He also didn't want Melanie to come back and start helping him dress. If she saw him in the nude again it had better be for his benefit as well as hers. *Damn*, where did that thought come from?

He had no interest in Melanie. Then again, he was stuck here for a few days. He had time to kill and he was attracted to her. But they really had nothing in common outside of their profession. Last night had been a normal male reaction to a woman toweling him dry and nothing more.

With great effort and teeth-gritting pain, he managed to get his clothes on. He was grateful for his loafers because those he could at least slip his feet into, even if they were inadequate for the weather.

He joined Melanie in the living area. She was dressed in another well-cut suit. The only concession to her being a woman was the ruffles down the front of her shirt.

There was a knock at the door and she went to answer it. The bellhop pushed a cart in. Melanie smiled and called him by name. How like her to have made a friend. Dalton thought how it had taken years for him to cultivate the friends he had.

After tipping the bellhop, she closed the door, then pushed the cart toward the bar area. "I thought you might like a real pot of coffee and maybe some eggs with the cereal."

"That sounds good."

She started setting food on the bar. He went to help and she said, "No. I'll get it. You're still not in very good shape."

"I need to move some or I'll get so stiff that I can't." He took the same stool as he had the night before.

"Give it a few more hours before you start getting too energetic." She poured a cup of coffee from a carafe and placed it in front of him.

"You do remember I'm a doctor?"

"I do. And I'm one too, well aware of the kind of care you need. I also feel very responsible for what happened to you. So please humor me for a little while longer." She set the food out and removed the covers. "You'll be on your own soon enough."

"How's that?"

She joined him, taking what he now considered her stool. "I work at the local hospital one day a week and today is that day."

"Really?"

"Yes, really."

He picked up his spoon. "It's just that I'm a little surprised. So you're going to trust me here by myself?"

"I think your ribs will keep you in line."

He looked out the window. The idea of being stuck in the suite all day by himself with nothing to do might be more painful than trying to breathe.

"Mind if I tag along?"

Melanie viewed at him as if he were a bug under a magnifying glass. Was he not welcome? "You want to go to the hospital with me?"

"I think it'll be a pretty long day if I stay here."

"Are you sure you feel up to it?"

"I'll make it." He took a sip of his coffee. "I'll have pain pills."

"Okay. If that's what you want to do."

Half an hour later they were getting their coats on. Melanie stepped over and helped him pull his collar up around his neck when he couldn't bring himself to attempt it. Melanie seemed to know he needed assistance without him asking. She was no doubt a caring and thoughtful doctor. Somehow it was getting easier to accept her help. "Thanks."

She smiled and headed toward the door. "If you stay around much longer you're going to have to buy some clothes or you'll freeze to death."

Dalton huffed, which brought on a stab of pain. "Would we have time to stop somewhere before going to the hospital?"

She opened the suite door. "No, but we can afterwards."

Her eagerness to get to the hospital intrigued him. The fact she made a point to work at a hospital each week was interesting. There was more to Dr. Hyde than met the eye.

The same driver who had brought them to the hospital was waiting on them in front of the Lodge. He drove them to Melanie's car at the Currents' complex. It had been sitting outside and she removed snow from the windshield before leaving. The inside of the car was so cold it seemed to never warm up. Dalton could hardly wait to buy some heavier clothes.

Melanie wasn't sure that bringing Dalton along to the hospital was such a good idea, but she didn't have the heart to leave him alone all day. Even if she had to have a shadow, it was better than leaving him behind. She'd had no idea that her assignment to pick him up at the airport would lead to her entertaining him for days.

"So where do you work when you go to the hospital?" Dalton asked.

"In the peds department."

"Wow, that's a big difference from working with the team."

"Not really. Both come in with stomachaches and injuries. The size is the only difference."

"I guess you're right."

They entered the Niagara Hospital through a staff door near the Emergency Department. Melanie loved the old stone building. There was nothing chrome and glass about it, yet it offered state-of-the-art medical care. She enjoyed her work with the Currents, but her heart was with the kids.

Heat immediately hit her in the face and Melanie started removing her outer clothes. Dalton unbuttoned his thin overcoat. She continued along the corridor to the end where the service elevator was located and he followed. As they started upward, she said, "This hospital cares for about seventy-five percent poverty level patients. Most can't pay outside of government assistance. Many only come in after they have no choice because their problem is so bad."

Dalton looked at her. "So how does the hospital stay open?"

"By support of the people who live around here and fund-raising. The Currents do a fund-raiser in the off-season each year. A get-to-spend-the-day-with-a-pro-player type of event."

The elevator door opened and they stepped out.

Dalton asked, "Is it successful?"

"Very. People come from all over the world to see their favorite player. Rocket earned the most in the bidding last year." Melanie turned to the left and walked down the wide hallway. She went by the patient rooms and stopped at the nurses' station. All the while she was conscious of Dalton beside her. He would be taking in the place with perceptive eyes. She'd seen his intense evaluation of Rocket and had no doubt he would do the same here.

The clerk sitting behind the desk said, "Good morning, Dr. Hyde. Marcus has been asking for you."

Mel chuckled. "I'm sure he's looking for a piece of candy. I'll start my rounds with him.

"Lisa, this is Dr. Reynolds. He's going to be doing rounds with me today."

Lisa gave Dalton a curious look. "Nice to meet you, Doctor."

Dalton nodded. Melanie was confident he was out of his medical element. She'd seen pictures of his shiny new clinic set in the South Beach area of Miami. No doubt he would have a hard time identifying with the type of patients this hospital typically saw.

"Well, I guess I better get started since Marcus has been looking for me." She turned and headed along another short hall. Over her shoulder she said to Dalton, "We can leave our coats in an office down here."

A few minutes later Melanie knocked on Marcus's room door and pushed it open.

"Dr. Mel!" The eleven-year-old boy had big eyes and a wide smile.

"Hi there, Marcus." She walked to the bedside and Dalton came to stand at the end. "How're you feeling today?"

"Pretty good. Are the Currents ready for the game on Sunday?"

Melanie looked at Dalton. "This guy is a walking encyclopedia of Currents statistics."

"That's impressive." Dalton sounded sincere despite his disinterest in football. She appreciated him being positive for the boy.

"This is Dr. Reynolds, Marcus. He's helping me out today."

The boy looked at Dalton. "Hi, Doc. You like the Currents?"

Dalton shrugged. "I did meet Rocket Overtree yesterday. He seemed like a nice guy."

Marcus lit up like a Christmas tree and started asking questions at a rapid pace.

Finally Melanie held up a hand. "I think that's enough questions. I need to check you out."

"Aw, come on, Dr. Mel. I want to hear about Rocket."

Dalton smiled. "We should let Dr. Mel do her thing. She might be feeling left out."

Melanie gave him an appreciative look and pulled her stethoscope from around her neck. "Okay, let me give you a listen."

Marcus swung his legs around to sit on the edge of the bed.

Melanie leaned toward him. "Heart first."

"Dr. Mel, I know the drill by now." Exasperation filled Marcus's voice.

She smiled. "I guess you do."

Melanie always hoped when she put her stethoscope to the boy's chest she wouldn't hear the swish and gurgle that said he had a bad valve. Marcus's family couldn't afford the medical care he needed. To her great disappointment, the sounds were just as strong as ever.

"Okay, deep breath time." She moved her stethoscope to his back.

Marcus filled his lungs and released them a couple of times.

"Well, you sound good," she lied. He did for someone in need of heart surgery. With every week that went by he was getting weaker.

Dalton moved to stand beside Melanie. "Marcus, do you mind if I listen to you also?"

"Sure. If you want to."

"Mind?" He indicated her stethoscope.

Pleasantly surprised that he was showing this much interest in Marcus, Melanie handed the instrument to him. She'd figured all he would do was follow her around killing time and have no direct interaction with her patients. Since his specialty was adult medicine, she'd thought he'd have no interest. Her primary practice had to do with grown men but she looked forward to the one day she spent on the pediatric floor. Difference was that he'd probably had the opportunity to choose his area of medicine while she had been told she would be a team doctor.

Melanie watched Dalton's face. His mouth tightened. He must have heard what she did. Dalton looked at her with concern showing in his eyes.

"Thanks, Marcus." Dalton handed the stethoscope back to her.

Melanie took it and wrapped it around her neck. To Marcus she said, "I'll stop by before I leave today. I forgot I have something for you. I left it in the office."

"Okay. But don't forget."

Melanie laughed. "I won't."

"I won't let her," Dalton added with a smile as he followed her out. When the door was closed between them and Marcus, Dalton demanded, "Why hasn't he had surgery?"

"Because his parents can't afford it. A couple of doctors are getting together to try to work something out. Have him moved to a children's hospital and find some financing."

"He's not going to be able to wait long."

She glared at him and worked to keep her voice even. "Don't you think I know that? I've been seeing him on and off for months. I'm well aware of how far the damage has progressed."

His expression turned contrite. "I'm used to fixing problems right away. I didn't mean to imply that you weren't doing all you could."

Was that his way of saying he was sorry? "I might have overreacted. I know we aren't supposed to have favorites, but Marcus is mine."

"That's understandable. He's a nice kid. Seems smart too."

She walked down the hall to the next room. "He's managed to have excellent grades despite being in and out of here."

"So who do we see next?" Dalton asked.

Over the next hour they fell into the routine of stopping outside the room door of the next patient while Melanie gave him a brief medical history. They saw children from two to eighteen years of age.

Only a couple of times did Dalton wince when he made a move, otherwise Melanie would have never known he'd been injured. The man sure could hold his emotions in check.

"This is our last stop. Josey Woods is a teen who has just finished chemo. She's made good progress but has pneumonia. She was admitted for a little support since she couldn't seem to shake it on her own. If all goes well she'll be going home tomorrow."

Dalton nodded and they entered the room. A young girl sat in a chair watching a music video on the TV hanging on the wall. There was a blanket lying across her legs.

"Hello, Josey. I'm Dr. Mel Hyde. You can call me Dr. Mel and this is Dr. Reynolds. We're going to be checking on you today."

"Hi," Josey said softly, not making eye contact. Blond fuzz covered her bald head.

"I hear you're feeling better and ready to go home." Melanie stepped closer.

The girl nodded.

Dalton hung back near the door. Apparently he was sensitive to the shy patient, whose mannerisms indicated she might have "white coat syndrome." Melanie was glad that neither she nor Dalton were wearing their lab jackets.

"I'd like to listen to you, if I may?" Melanie asked.

Josey leaned forward as if she was resigned to having no choice. She, like Marcus, had been in the hospital for far too much of her childhood.

"I see you like Taylor Swift," Melanie said as she prepared to place the stethoscope on Josey's thin chest.

"Yes, she's my favorite."

"I like her music too." Melanie listened to the steady thump, thump, thump of her heart. It sounded good.

"You do?" Josey seemed to perk up. She leaned forward.

"I do. Take a deep breath." Melanie glanced to where Dalton leaned against the wall just inside the closed door. He had a slight smile on his face.

Josey eagerly announced, "I have her autograph."

"You do? Another breath. I'd love to see it."

A few seconds later Josey said, "I'll show it to you." She pushed the blanket off her legs and rose. Dressed in a long-sleeve T-shirt and flannel pants, she moved around the bed. There was a limp to her stride. She took a glossy photo off the bed tray and came back to Melanie, handing it to her.

"I'm so jealous." Melanie smiled at the girl and handed the picture back.

"Taylor is too girly for me. I'm a bigger fan of CeeLo Green," Dalton said, having stepped toward them.

Josey looked at him. "I like him too."

"I'd bet you like Justin Timberlake too." Dalton's voice held a teasing note.

Josey's cheeks turned pink. "Yes. I like his music."

Dalton looked from first Josey to Melanie. "All the women I know like his looks."

"Hey, don't pull me into this conversation," Melanie protested.

Dalton came to stand beside her. To Josey he said, "Would you mind if I looked at your legs?"

She acted unsure but then she said, "I guess that would be okay. I've been told there's nothing that can be done about them."

"I'd just like to look. I promise not to hurt you."

Melanie had to give him kudos for his bedside manner with the girl. He'd found common ground before he approached the skittish patient. The man had skill.

"Josey, would you please walk to the door and back this way for me?"

She nodded and did as he asked.

When she returned Dalton said, "Please sit on the edge of your bed. I'm going to feel your legs. If at any time you are uncomfortable let me know and I'll stop."

"Okay."

Dalton went down on his heels. He felt her feet and moved along one leg and then the other. The look on his face was the same one he'd worn when he examined Rocket. Dalton used his fingers to tell him what he needed to know. A few minutes later he stood.

"I'm sorry to have to ask you this but I need you to remove your socks and pants so I can see your knees. If you have some shorts to put on that would be fine."

Josey looked at Melanie, who gave the girl a reassuring smile.

"Okay."

"We'll step out into the hall. Just call when you're ready." He started toward the door and Melanie followed.

She closed the door behind them. "I had no idea about her limp. It wasn't on the chart."

"My guess is that she and her family have just accepted it."

A faint, "I'm ready," came from inside the room.

Dalton went in ahead of Melanie this time. He was in

his element and seemed eager to see if something could be done for Josey, who was already sitting on the side of the bed with the sheet pulled over her waist.

"I'm ready."

"Great. I'm going to do something similar to what I've already done. All you have to do is sit there. If what I do hurts, just let me know."

Dalton put his hands on her right knee and manipulated it. He then moved to the left, the one with the limp. A few minutes later he stood and backed away. "I'd like to look at your left hip. All you have to do is lie on the bed and let me move your leg back and forth. You can tell me 'no' and I'll understand."

"Okay."

Just like a teen, she used only one-word answers.

Josey scooted back on the bed, lay down and adjusted the sheet. Melanie worked to control her smile. A girl was modest at that age, even around a male doctor. Melanie looked at Dalton. Especially one as good-looking as him. She couldn't blame Josey. She'd have felt much the same way if she was half-clothed in front of Dalton.

"I'm going to raise your leg up. Tell me when I've gone as far as I can." He lifted her leg slowly.

Thankfully the range of movement looked fine.

He brought the leg out to the left and then across her other leg. "Good. You can sit up." He offered his hand to Josey. She took it and he pulled her upright. "I'm glad you are doing so well and getting to go home tomorrow."

"Me too."

"We'll let you get back to your videos," Melanie said as she followed Dalton out the door as the sound of a popular song on the TV grew.

Dalton stopped when they were well out of hearing distance from anyone who might be in the hall. "I would like to see X-rays of her knee, both front and side view. I would also like to see the MRI."

"I doubt either have been done."

"You have to be kidding. Why not?" He paced three steps up the hall then turned and came back to her.

"Because there was no reason to. She is being treated for an infection as a complication to chemo. There would be no reason either should have been ordered. Here—" she gestured around her at the building "—we are treating her cancer issues. The leg issues were not on the staff radar."

His sound of disgust rubbed her the wrong way. She wasn't to blame here. If it were up to her these children would all have the finest medical care money could buy. For people like Josey and her parents it was an everyday worry about how they would pay for Josey's needs.

"Then they should be ordered," Dalton said sharply.

Now he was starting to tell her what to do. "That's easier said than done."

He glared at her. "Why is that?"

"The X-rays are doable but the MRI is a problem."

He stepped forward, his frustration written all over his face. "And I ask again—why is that?"

"Because there is no MRI machine here. She would need to be transferred to another hospital to have it done."

"Then do it."

She pulled him into an empty patient room. "Now wait a minute. You don't give me orders. You're not even on the staff here. So don't start throwing your ego around!"

Dalton looked at her calmly but the tic in his jaw gave his irritation away. "You don't want to help the girl?"

Melanie stepped back as if she had been slapped. "Of course I do."

"Okay, then. The first step is seeing that we get X-rays of her knee and a MRI if possible."

"I can order an X-ray. I'll have to see how best to proceed with the MRI."

"Good. Let's go do it."

When she didn't move Dalton took her elbow and gave her a little nudge.

Melanie pulled her arm out of his grip. Head held high, she walked down the hall. Had she ever been this angry? Who did he think he was, telling her what to do? Making demands. And, worse, implying she didn't care enough to do everything that could be done for Josey.

Stalking to the nurse's station, she went to one of the computer stations and typed in her password. She pulled up Josey's chart and ordered an X-ray with anteroposterior and lateral views.

"I'd like a skyline as well."

She looked up. Her face was inches from his. Dalton's arms were braced on the back of her chair as he leaned over her, looking at the screen.

She snapped, "You do understand that you don't have privilege at this hospital?"

"That's why I'm asking you to request one."

"Request? I missed that part." She was starting to sound childish even to her own ears. Thankfully no one was in the charting room to overhear.

Dalton sat in the empty chair next to her. He grunted as he did so, which reminded her that he still hurt. "Look, I'm sorry if I sound as if I'm telling you what to do, it's just that I think I can help Josey. Sometimes I get high-handed in my excitement." His fingertips touched her arm for a second. "Would you please also request a skyline view?"

She wasn't sure she liked his manipulation any better than being told what to do. What she did appreciate was his passion about helping Josey. He saw a problem, believed he could fix it and wouldn't stop until he tried. If only all that just didn't come with his general barking-orders attitude.

She gave him a sideways look intended to show him that she knew he was managing her, then typed in the order.

"When should those be back?" Dalton asked, standing.

"Tomorrow at the earliest. They are not a priority, so she won't have them done until morning." When he started to say something, she put up a hand to stop him. "You will just have to accept that. I will not push anymore."

"If I get a flight out tomorrow will you see they are sent to me?"

Melanie pushed away from the computer. "I will. Despite what you might think, I'd like to see Josey walk without a limp."

A heart-melting smile came to his face. "I never thought any different."

"You sure implied it."

"How about I buy you dinner tonight to make up for that?"

Melanie met his gaze. "Now you are using bribery to get your way."

He shrugged. "You have to eat, don't you?"

She did, but not necessarily with him.

"So what's next?" Dalton asked.

"I have to do some dictation. See that charts are up to date."

He groaned. "I think I'll find the cafeteria and get a bad cup of coffee. That sounds like more fun."

It hadn't been as uncomfortable as she'd anticipated to have Dalton around but it was nice to have a few minutes to herself.

For the next few hours Melanie worked her way through the charting and made sure orders were posted. While she did so she overheard a number of the nurses talking to each other about Dalton. More than once a comment was made about how good-looking he was, followed by the question of whether or not he was married, then giggles.

If they knew what a stuffed shirt he was, how demanding he could be, or that he hated sports and snow, they might not have been so impressed.

But he had been chivalrous when he protected her from getting hit, had been fair with Rocket and almost warrior-like with Josey. Maybe there was something more socially redeeming in him than she cared to admit.

She hadn't seen Dalton since he'd left for coffee. Where had he gotten to? Great, now she'd have to go hunt him down. Melanie glanced at the computer. Marcus's chart was still up. Before leaving she needed to go by and give him his present.

Returning to the office where she and Dalton had left their coats, she looked through her pocketbook and pulled out the tickets to the Currents' Sunday afternoon playoff game. She went down the hall and stopped at Marcus's door. The music from what sounded like an adventure movie came from inside the room. She knocked and received no answer. That didn't surprise her. Pushing the door open just far enough to call Marcus, she waited for an answer and heard none.

"Man, that's the best. Luke made him pay," Marcus's voice carried.

"Darth Vader is a villain's villain."

That was Dalton. Even in a few short days she had his voice committed to memory.

Melanie pushed the door open to find Marcus sitting up in bed and Dalton reclined in a chair next to him. Flashing on the TV was a Star Wars movie. A loud swish and boom filled the air. Neither male gave her any notice as she walked farther into the room.

"What's going—?"

"Shh, this is the best part," Dalton said, not even bothering to look her way.

Melanie moved around behind him and regarded the screen. Two people using light sabers slashed at one another.

Marcus leaned forward. "Wow, look at how he makes that move."

Obviously the two males had found something to bond over. She didn't say anything again until the fight was over. Even then she spoke softly to Dalton. "I'm ready to head out when you are."

He glanced at her. "This is almost over."

From that statement he left no doubt he wasn't leaving until then. Against the wall on the other side of the room was an extra hardback chair. She circled the bed toward it. Dalton and Marcus both groaned as she walked between them and the TV.

"Aw, come on, Dr. Mel," Marcus whined as he put his head one way then the other to see around her.

"Hurry up, Dr. Hyde." Dalton shifted in much the same manner as Marcus had.

She hurried by them. While pulling the chair in the direction of the bed, it made a scraping noise on the floor. Both movie watchers glared at her for a second before they returned to viewing the action.

"Sorry," she said contritely before picking up the chair. She placed it on the floor next to Marcus's bed and primly sat on it. Did she dare disturb them?

Less than half an hour later the movie ended.

"No matter how many times I see it, it's great. A classic." Dalton stood with effort and a slight grimace.

"You're right, bro, one of the best movies ever." Marcus brought his legs to the floor.

Melanie looked from one of them to the other. "Who are you two?"

"We're Star Wars fans." Marcus acted as if that was a badge of honor that had bonded him and Dalton together forever.

She nodded as if she understood what that meant. "Well, it's time for Dr. Reynolds and me to go. I just came down to bring you what I promised. It's not a trip to a Star Wars convention so I hope you still like it."

Marcus looked at her eagerly. "What is it?"

"How about box tickets to the Currents' play-off game on Sunday?"

His huge white smile stood out in contrast to his dark skin. "Man, really? Box seats! How cool."

His smile suddenly faded.

"What's wrong?" Melanie asked.

"I'm stuck in here." He looked at his bed.

"I fixed that too. You have a pass out for the day as long as you do exactly what you're told."

Marcus's smile grew again. "You can count on that." He turned to Dalton. "Will you be there?"

"No, I'll be leaving before then. But I'm sure you'll have fun."

"I can't wait. I just hope 'The Rocket' will play."

Melanie looked at Dalton, then said, "We'll have to see about that. There'll be a car here to pick you up on Sunday. You can bring one person with you. I'll stop in and say hi when you get to the stadium."

"Thanks, Dr. Mel. You rock."

"You're welcome. See you then." Melanie turned toward the door.

"It was nice to meet you, Marcus. I hope you're out of here soon." Dalton offered his hand.

Marcus placed his thin one in Dalton's and they shook.

"Later, man." Marcus put large headphones over his ears and picked up an iPad.

"That was a nice thing you did for Marcus," Dalton said.

Melanie shrugged. "No big deal. They were offered to me and I gave them to him."

"I have the feeling that you do whatever you can to make these kids happy. You have a big heart, Melanie."

She had to admit it give her a warm feeling to have him notice how much she cared. Her family wasn't even aware of where she spent her days off. She'd let this stranger into her world without even thinking. Even so, she didn't plan to let him too close—she'd seen what happened when she allowed that. Her work with the kids was her private domain.

Why had she shared it with him?

CHAPTER FOUR

IN THE PASSENGER seat of Melanie's car as they left the hospital parking lot, Dalton asked, "Where're we headed now?"

"I thought the mall might give us the most choices for men's shops." She looked over and grinned. "I didn't think you'd want to get out in the weather any more than necessary. At least in the mall it'll be warm between stores."

"You're enjoying my discomfort."

She glanced at him with a grin on her lips. "Enjoy may be too strong a word. It's more like I find it humorous."

Dalton watched as her grin transformed into a smile. Melanie's lips were full, with a curve on each end as if they were always waiting to lift in pleasure. What would it feel like to kiss them? Would they be as plush as they looked? He'd see to it she smiled with pleasure.

Where had those thoughts come from? He shifted in his seat. No doubt it came from the attraction he felt for her. "What's so entertaining about it?"

"That a man of your intelligence would come this far north in the middle of winter without the correct type of clothes."

He smirked and chuckled. "You're right. Put that way, I don't sound too smart. My only defense is that I hadn't planned to stay so long."

They both laughed. Snow continued to fall and the

traffic increased. He sat in silence as Melanie concentrated on driving.

"I hope you weren't too bored today." Melanie pulled out into the traffic along the major freeway.

"No, it was fine." Dalton hadn't spent a more satisfying day in a long time. Despite the fact that his whole body hurt, he had enjoyed working with the children and seeing different medical issues. He'd spent so long in the adult-care world, and focused on bones and tissue, it was refreshing to think small and broader.

He'd found out he and Melanie shared a common interest in children. That had come as a surprise. She kept doing that. First she was a female team doctor working in the NFL. Melanie also wasn't easily deterred from what she believed was her duty, which showed in her insisting she take care of him. And now he'd found out her real love was children. He'd never met a more fascinating woman with such diverse interests. It would be exciting to discover other aspects of her personality. At least while he was stuck there.

They hadn't traveled far when Melanie exited the freeway. She drove down a side road and turned into the parking area of a shopping mall. The lot was full and they rode up and down the aisles looking for a spot. "People are out Christmas shopping. With only six days left, the mall is packed."

"You don't Christmas shop?" He understood that women lived to shop.

"I did mine months ago. I don't like to wait to the last minute."

"I'm impressed."

Melanie turned to him. "So how about you? Do you have all your shopping done? Do you need to do some while we are here?"

What should he tell her? He didn't have anyone to buy for? "My secretary handles that for me."

She glanced at him. "Really?"

Dalton chose to ignore the question in the hope she wouldn't pursue it.

She found a parking spot about as far away from the entrance as possible. He wasn't looking forward to the frigid walk. The sun was setting and the temperature dropping. Bundling up as best he could, he started across the parking lot beside Melanie.

"I should have dropped you off at the door and then parked," she said apologetically.

"I wouldn't have allowed you to walk across this large lot by yourself." He stuffed his hands in his pockets as the wind picked up. "Not safe."

"Your mother must have taught you to be a gentleman."

Despite all the years that had passed, his chest tightened. He let her push through the revolving door first and then followed in the next partition. He said, more to himself than her, "No, that's one thing she wasn't guilty of."

"There's a men's shop down here on the right that should have what you need. I'm sorry you're having to buy clothes you won't have much use for later."

"It's better than being in the hospital for frostbite. Besides, I'm sure this won't be my only trip up north."

"Well, there is that." Melanie headed into the mall and he fell into step beside her.

They walked past the glass-fronted stores and around the next corner.

"I love to come here during the holidays. The decorations always put me in the holiday spirit." Enthusiasm filled her voice.

"I've never really thought about it."

She pointed up. "Where in the world can you see ornaments larger than a person? Or such beautiful trees?"

The wonder in her voice was almost contagious.

"You said you always have your shopping done early.

Does that mean you just come to the mall to get in the middle of thousands of people because you like the decorations?"

"I do. As long as I don't have to fight over gifts I like being in the middle of things."

"Then I'll make sure I hold you back while I'm trying to buy clothes. I wouldn't want you to get in a scuffle."

She laughed. "Thanks, I'd appreciate that. I wouldn't want to reflect poorly on the Currents' name."

"Do you always think about the team first?"

She shrugged. "I guess that's how I was raised."

"It seems to me you should think about yourself first every once in a while. I've not known you long, but you're quite a unique person. There's a lot more to you than your work with the team."

Melanie stopped walking to look at him. "Thank you—that was nice of you to say."

Her admiration made him uncomfortable. "Don't sound so surprised. I can be nice."

"Here's the shop I told you about. I think you'll find what you need in here."

"You're not coming in? What if I don't get the right stuff?"

"I was just going to wait out here for you, but if you'd like my help…"

"I could use it." He could decide on his own clothes but he enjoyed seeing her flustered. He liked teasing her and he never teased.

"Okay."

He went through the open doors of the store and she followed.

Dalton looked around. "So what do you recommend?"

She said without hesitation, "You need a couple of flannel shirts, heavy sweater, cord slacks and thick socks."

"Wow, I'm almost sorry I asked."

"You really should have a jacket but, since you aren't going to be here long, I hate for you to spend that kind of money. Especially when you might not wear it again anytime soon."

"Can I help you?" a blonde saleswoman wearing a tight dress and a smile asked.

"Yes. I'm interested in a couple of warm slacks, two shirts and a sweater."

Her smile grew. "Well, you're in the correct place. Come right this way."

Dalton glanced at Melanie and caught her rolling her eyes. She didn't seem impressed with his reception. Interesting.

Melanie tagged along behind Dalton as he followed Miss Fresh and Perky toward the back of the store. He seemed more than willing. Why it mattered to her, she had no idea.

"Right, here is our slacks selection." The clerk waved a hand toward a rack of pants, then pulled a pair out. "I think these would look great on you. I'm guessing a thirty-four/thirty-four."

Dalton nodded and smiled as if she'd given him a compliment.

No wonder her brothers said this was their favorite place to shop.

Dalton felt the material. He looked at her. "What do you think?"

Melanie was surprised he remembered she was there. She stepped forward and rubbed the pants leg. "They should do."

"Why don't you try them on so your wife can see them?" the saleswoman said.

"She's not my wife," Dalton said.

At the same time Melanie said, "I'm not his wife."

The saleswoman's smile brightened. "I'm sorry. My mistake. The dressing rooms are this way."

"Melanie, while I'm trying these on, would you mind picking out some shirts? A sweater, if you see one you like," Dalton called over his shoulder; he seemed far too eager to follow the saleswoman.

If Melanie didn't know better she would say she was feeling jealous. That wasn't something she made a habit of. Why would she care if a saleswoman flirted with Dalton? He was nothing to her. Still, he knew more about her than her own family.

She walked to the other side of the store to where the shirts hung and picked out a couple that would look nice on Dalton. Nearby on a shelf was a stack of sweaters in multiple colors. She pulled out one in burgundy and held it up. With Dalton's coloring it would suit him. Making her way back to where Dalton stood talking to the saleswoman, she joined them. They were both laughing.

"I found these. Do you want to try them on?" she said in a sharper than normal tone.

With a raised brow, Dalton asked, "What size are they?"

She told him.

"Those will do. How about a sweater?"

Melanie held it out for him to see.

"That color is perfect for you," the saleswoman cooed.

"Then I'll take it." He grinned at Melanie.

She'd had all she could take. This obvious flirtation was starting to make her sick. Why it mattered Melanie couldn't fathom, but it did. Outside of that one time in the bathroom when he'd handed her the towel, he'd treated her like a colleague. But wasn't that what she was? Why did she want him to flirt with her the same way?

Because it would be nice to feel like a woman. In her world, both at work and with her family, she was treated like one of the boys. Was she guilty of letting them do so?

The saleswoman took the clothes. "Is there anything else I can get you?"

Dalton's far-too-syrupy grin had Melanie walking off. "I think you can handle the rest without me."

Fifteen minutes later Dalton exited the store. Melanie sat on a bench in the middle of the mall, waiting. When he joined her, she said, "You seemed to be enjoying your shopping trip."

He grinned. "I was. What about a coat?"

"If you really want one there's a store down this way." She stood and started walking down the mall. "It carries a good line of coats. There may not be a salesperson in a tight dress, though."

"Do I hear a touch of jealousy in there?"

"You do not. I just don't think clerks have to wear skin-tight clothes to sell men's clothing."

"What should she wear? Something functional like your suits?"

"What's wrong with my suits? They're businesslike. Professional looking." She raised her voice.

"I think you can be professional and look like a woman too."

She turned to him. "Are you saying I don't?" Her anger grew. People were beginning to look.

"You can dress anyway you wish."

"You're right—it's none of your business." Melanie stalked ahead of him.

By the time he had reached her side, they had arrived at the coat store.

"I don't think you'll need my help here. I'm going to look next door. I'll meet you right here when you're finished."

Melanie didn't give Dalton time to answer before she walked on. She needed to get away from him for a few minutes. Stopping at the show window, she looked at the mannequins dressed in glitzy dresses in seasonal colors.

Did she really dress unfemininely? Here she was, carting him around, seeing he had warm clothes, and he was giving her fashion advice. How much nerve could the man have?

She looked down at her high-quality tailored suit. These were the kind of clothes she'd always worn. That wasn't true. Her mother had dressed her in frilly dresses, especially on holidays.

When her mom died, her father had spent little time worrying about how Melanie dressed. He'd handed money over to the housekeeper or babysitters and asked them to buy her clothing for special occasions. As she grew older her father gave the money to her. Melanie was a tomboy and that was encouraged. She looked up to her brothers, so she tended to choose shirts and jeans to wear like them.

For the prom, her friend's mother had taken her and her friend to buy their dresses. It was one of the few times she had female help with picking out clothing or with any of the other rites of passage most girls shared with their mother. A few times she'd cried herself to sleep when she heard about events like a Mother/Daughter Luncheon or when her friends talked about spending a day shopping with their mothers. She had long ago moved past feeling sorry for herself and compensated by making herself needed by her father and brothers. That was where she found her security. It would be wonderful to feel appreciated, just the same.

Why had Dalton's one comment got under her skin? Had she forgotten how to dress like a girl? Had she been living in the world of men so long that she'd given up even trying to act like a woman? When was the last time she'd bought something lacy and girly? She did like sexy underwear but few had seen that side of her.

"So which one do you like best?" Dalton's deep voice said beside her.

She jerked around. He'd caught her looking at the dresses. Now he would be pleased that what he'd said had got to her. To cover her embarrassment, she asked, "Did you find a coat?"

"You answer my question, then I'll answer yours."

She huffed. The man exasperated her. "The red one, if you must know."

The dress was mid-thigh-length and had a scooped neck. It fit tightly down to the waist then flared out into a full skirt. She'd seen fewer dresses prettier.

"Are you going to try it on?"

"You haven't answered my question."

Dalton held up a sack. "I did get a coat. I bought it on sale so you don't have to worry about me spending so much money. So are you going in?"

"No. I don't need a dress like that."

He seemed to give that remark some thought, then looked at her. "Shame. I think you'd look very pretty in it."

Melanie didn't want to admit the glow of warmth his words created.

As if he'd forgotten what they had been talking about, he said, "Hey, I'm hungry. Is there a decent restaurant here?"

"There's one down the next wing."

They made their way through the growing crowd to the restaurant. In front of the brick-facade pub, they stopped and he gave the girl standing behind a podium his name.

"Why don't we wait at the bar?" Dalton suggested.

Melanie nodded.

They took stools next to each other.

"Would you like a drink?" Dalton asked.

She ordered wine and he a whiskey.

"I haven't asked in a while, but how are you feeling?" Melanie fingered the stem of her glass.

"Let's just say that I know where my ribs are located."

"Maybe you should have stayed at the Lodge and rested."

"Are you kidding? If I had done that I wouldn't be moving now. How about you? Feeling any aftereffects?"

"When I turn a certain way I know something has happened."

Dalton nodded.

The hostess approached and said their table was ready.

Dalton placed his hand at her waist as she slid off the high stool. His fingers were warm and firm but soon fell away. She was far too aware of him following her as they maneuvered between the tables, trailing the hostess, carrying their drinks with them.

The girl seated them beside the roaring fire in the center of the dining area. The table was covered in a white cloth and a small lantern burned in the center. It was far too romantic a setting for Melanie's comfort.

"Is this table okay with you?" Dalton asked.

"Uh, sure."

"You don't sound very confident."

The man was perceptive. She'd have to watch her facial expressions around him. "No, no, it's fine."

Dalton helped her with her chair, then took the one beside her, facing the fire. His knee touched hers under the table and she shifted away.

"You have enough room?"

"I'm fine."

"I have a feeling you've said that most of your life." He picked up the menu that the hostess had left on the table.

What did he mean by that statement?

Dalton flipped through the menu. "Have you ever eaten here? Do you know what's good?"

"I've had lunch a few times. I always have either a salad or burger. So I'm not much help on the other stuff."

"I want something warm. Go-down-into-the-bones warm."

She grinned. "Now that you have clothes you're going to feel much better."

"I'm counting on that. I going to start with some soup and have a steak. How about you?"

"I'm going to have a salad and roasted chicken."

When the waitress came, Dalton gave her their order.

Dalton had been asking her questions regularly and Melanie was determined to take advantage of this time to ask a few of her own.

"So tell me, why did you become an orthopedic doctor?"

He took a sip of his drink, then placed the glass carefully on the table. Did it make him uncomfortable to answer personal questions? He certainly didn't seem to mind asking them.

"I was a good student. I took a biology class and was hooked on science. Medicine just seemed like the natural progression."

"So why orthopedics?"

"When I did that rotation, there was this man who had been crippled for most of his life. He agreed to a new procedure and now he's walking. I wanted to make that possible for people."

That answer she liked. She was glad to know he hadn't got into it for the money. With his fancy practice, she'd wondered what motivated him.

He continued, "I have a talent for what I do. The next thing I knew, I was being asked to evaluate athletes. One thing led to another."

"Seems like you have a high-pressure practice."

"It can be but I have a great staff and a couple of other doctors working with me."

"So what do you do to blow off steam when it gets to be too much?"

"Why, Melanie, are you trying to find out about my private life?" There he was with the uncomfortable questions again.

"I am not. I'm trying to have pleasant conversation over dinner."

Dalton's hand came to rest over hers for a second. "It's pleasant being here with you."

"I think you're trying to dodge the question."

Grinning, he nodded. "Maybe a little. I'm a pretty private person. I like to spend the day at the beach, swimming. I bike to and from work. I read mysteries and have been known to go to South Beach clubs on occasion. I work more than anything."

"I can't imagine biking to work. That must be nice."

"Most days it is. The weather does get hot in midsummer, but I go in so early it doesn't much matter."

The waitress returned with their soup and salad. Their conversation turned to the books he had read. Many of them she had appreciated as well. They debated the pros and cons of the plots.

By the time they'd finished their meal, Melanie found she rather enjoyed Dalton's company. He had a way of drawing her out. Really listening to her opinions. She'd felt invisible for so long, it was nice being the center of someone's focus.

He paid for their dinner and they walked back to the mall door they'd entered.

"Time to bundle up." Melanie stopped beside a bench and began putting her coat on. Dalton placed his bag on the seat and helped her when she missed a sleeve with a hand. He then pulled his new jacket out of the large bag. It was a black wool pea jacket with a double row of buttons down the center. He slipped it on.

"Looks nice. But I would suggest that you not wear the tag." Melanie removed the paper hanging from under his arm. "You'll be much happier now."

"Wait—there's more." He dug into the sack again and

pulled out a red and black scarf. Wrapping it around his neck, he flipped the ends over his shoulders and smiled broadly.

Melanie laughed. "Nice choice, but I don't think it'll keep you warm that way. Let me show you." She took the material and looped it around itself and pulled it up close to his neck, then she tucked the ends inside the lapel of his coat. Patting his chest with both hands, she met his gaze with a grin. "There."

Dalton wrapped his arms around her waist and pulled her close. "You deserve a proper thank-you for taking care of me," he whispered in a sandpapery voice as his mouth found hers.

His lips were warm and held a hint of whiskey. They were perfect. Her heart beat at record time. Her hands slid up to hold the ridge of his shoulders as Dalton pulled her tighter and the pressure of his mouth increased. Her body heated as if she were basking in the sun. His tongue traced the seam of her mouth. Her fingers seized his coat and she moaned. More, she wanted more. She returned his kiss.

Melanie had no idea how much time had passed before Dalton released her. Dazed, it took a few seconds before she realized that someone was clapping.

"I think we're making a scene," Dalton said as he picked up his bag and took her arm, leading her toward the door.

On unsteady legs, she went with him. *Wow! What a kiss.*

She glanced around to see a family grinning at them. "I guess we are." The words came out sounding shaky. The warmth of his lips still lingered on hers. A tingle lingered from his touch.

Dalton stopped on the sidewalk. "One more thing." He dug into the bag and came out with gloves.

"You thought of everything."

Pulling them on, he then stuffed the bag into the nearest trash can. He returned to her.

Not thinking about what she was doing, she ran her tongue along her bottom lip. His taste still remained.

Dalton groaned. "Please don't do that."

"What?"

He leaned in close. "Lick your lips. If you do it again I might really make a public scene."

Melanie felt hot despite the temperature being low enough for snow to fall. Dalton had been as turned on as her. "We should get out of this cold."

"I'm ready when you are."

Something about his last statement made her think it might have a deeper meaning. One she wasn't sure she was prepared to deal with.

An hour later when Melanie pulled under the portico of the Lodge, Dalton still hadn't recovered from kissing her. He wanted her.

When she'd looked at him with that sparkle of mischief in her eyes and the smile that made her lovelier than any other woman he'd ever seen, he couldn't help himself. He had to taste her. She had no idea how desirable she was. Now, he wanted more than a kiss. If that one was any indication, the electricity between them would be powerful. Why couldn't they enjoy each other while he was here?

"How about coming up?"

"I don't know…"

"Come on. We could watch a movie." He wasn't interested in a movie but he would do whatever it took to spend some more time with Melanie.

"Do you feel up to having company? I would think you'd be tired and hurting."

He was hurting but it had nothing to do with being hit. "I am but I would be doing that anyway. The pain relievers have helped. So come on."

"Okay." She pulled on through the entryway and found a parking spot nearby.

At the door of his suite she hesitated. "Maybe—"

"Look, you didn't have a problem coming in when you insisted that you needed to be here for me. There shouldn't be any big deal to spending an evening watching TV with a friend."

She stopped short.

"Don't look so surprised. I think we've become friends after today." That had been more than a friendly kiss. But he wasn't going to mention that and scare her away.

"I guess we have."

"What's the problem? Don't you think we can be friends?"

"No…yes. I don't know. I just don't spend a lot of time in men's hotel rooms."

"You could have fooled me. You were here all last night."

She pursed her lips. "You know what I mean. I think you're making fun of me now." She started down the hall toward the stairs.

He grabbed her arm, stopping her. "Maybe a little bit. Come on in. I can use the company. After all, I don't really know anyone else in town."

"Now you're playing on my sympathy." She hesitated another moment. "Okay, for just a little while."

Dalton let go of her arm and then unlocked the door. Melanie stepped into the suite. He joined her and closed the door. He walked to the coffee table and picked up the remote control to the large-screen TV and handed it to her. "Here, pick out something you'd like to watch while I put up my new clothes."

He came out of the bedroom a few minutes later, and found the TV off and Melanie sitting in one of the swivel chairs facing the window with the view of the falls. She didn't even react to his presence until he sat in the matching chair, and then only to glance at him. Neither of them said anything for a long time.

"I love the falls," she murmured. "They're so beautiful, but when the snow is on the ground and ice forms... it's magical."

"Have you always lived in Niagara Falls?"

"Heavens, no. I've lived in a number of places. You go where the football job is. Most coaches don't last but a few years if they aren't winning and only a few more if they are. Only when Dad became the general manager and I got the team physician position have I managed to stay in one place for a while."

"I hated moving around as a kid."

What had made him say that? He didn't talk about his childhood. That was a dark time in his life. Somehow Melanie made him feel safe to do so.

"I know what you mean. I don't know if I'll ever move away from here. Anyway, you can't get this just anywhere." She indicated the falls.

"You're right, but there are other wonderful places to live. Next to the beach, for example."

"It has been so long since I've been to the beach I can hardly remember what it's like."

"You're welcome to visit me anytime. My place is just across the road from the water. Take your towel and spend the day."

She looked at him for a second. "I'm sure I would interfere with your lifestyle."

"Is that your subtle way of asking if I'm dating someone?"

"Maybe. I'm not used to men inviting me to stay in their homes. I wouldn't want to step on some woman's toes."

Dalton glanced at her. He dated but never seriously. In fact, she was the first female he'd ever invited to spend any length of time in his home. With Melanie he was making a number of firsts. "I was just making a friendly offer. No pressure. You could always stay at a hotel if you wanted to."

"And I would bet you're counting on me not showing up."

"I'd have to admit I would be shocked if you did."

They sat in silence for a few minutes. Dalton found it rather interesting that he wasn't uncomfortable just sitting there. Had he ever spent time with a woman appreciating a view? He did dinner, movies, clubs and sex but never looking at something as simple as water falling. He'd never given much thought to connecting to a woman on a level as simple as enjoying her presence because he didn't want to. They met each other's mutual needs and he was gone. He always made that clear up front. Being around Melanie was doing something strange to him.

She stood. "Thanks for the offer of a movie but I'm tired and I think I'd better go. One of us slept on the sofa last night."

"That was your call, not mine. There's a big nice bed in both the rooms." The chair rocked softly as he stood.

"I guess I'm not going to make you feel guilty." Melanie moved toward the door.

"No, that's not going to happen. If you leave, who's going to make sure I can undress myself?"

"Now who's making who feel guilty? I think you'll manage."

"Is there no way I can talk you into staying?" Dalton moved closer, taking one of her hands.

"Dalton, I'm not sure what you're trying to talk me into here."

He reached an arm around her waist and pulled her close. His hand went behind her neck, bringing her face to his. "I've been thinking about nothing but kissing you again since we left the mall."

His lips found hers.

After a second her hands came to rest at his waist and started up his sides. He groaned.

She jerked away. "I'm sorry. I forgot."

"It doesn't matter." He brought her back to him. His lips found hers again. Melanie's hands went up his arms to grip his biceps. Her chest pressed against his as she leaned into him and returned his kisses. He teased her mouth and she opened for him. Their tongues mated and drove his desire for her higher.

Dalton pulled back and whispered, "Stay."

"Why?"

The question punched him in the gut. How did he answer that? *Because I want your body. Because it would be a way to pass the time.* What could he say that Melanie might accept?

She was no doubt looking for more than he was willing to take a chance on. He had only the truth. "Come on—it's not a big mystery. You're a healthy woman and I'm a healthy man. We're attracted to each other. Our kisses proved it. I thought we might have a good time together."

"So you've decided that since you're stuck here that I might be a little entertainment."

That statement didn't make him feel any better. Short-term was all he could offer. "That's not exactly accurate."

"Dalton, I'm flattered by the offer, I really am, but I'm not someone's one- or two-night stand. Let's not mess up what's becoming a nice friendship. I'll call you in the morning and see if you feel like you can fly. If so, I'll see about getting you a flight out."

Had he just been shot down? Dalton wasn't pleased with this twist of events. Melanie had turned the tables on him and taken the upper hand, made his suggestion sound like an insult. He had lost control of the situation. "Now wait a minute, Melanie, I think you've got this all wrong."

"No, I think I understood clearly. I'll call you in the morning."

She was gone before he could comprehend what had happened. If their kiss was any indication, she'd enjoyed it. But she was running from anything more. Maybe it was just as well. He wasn't looking for permanency and she'd all but told him he wouldn't do.

He'd learned long ago that having someone in his life to care and be around wasn't in the stars for him. They would only leave. He'd taken control of his life. Had built one that didn't depend on anyone but himself. Melanie didn't fit into the world he'd created for himself. Still, he enjoyed her far more than he'd liked any woman in a long time.

So why did it hurt so much when Melanie closed the door behind her?

CHAPTER FIVE

MELANIE RELIVED HER and Dalton's kiss over and over during the night. She'd been kissed before but never with the same breathtaking power, leaving her weak-kneed, heart pounding. Still she didn't know what he wanted from her.

She'd been mistaken about him when they'd first met. But she'd been wrong about another man and that mistake had taken her months to recover from. She couldn't trust her judgment, especially when Dalton's kiss had left her breathless. Her emotions had been played with once before and she refused to let that happen to her again.

When Dalton had arrived she'd questioned if he would be supportive of player care or succumb to pressure from the management to put Rocket back on the field. Thankfully, they were on the same side about what Rocket should do.

All the worrying and the angst didn't matter anyway because Dalton would be gone soon. They lived the length of the country from each other. Their paths weren't any more likely to cross than they had so far.

The wind howling made her question how bad the weather had become. Getting out of bed, she went to the kitchen and started the coffee machine before clicking on the TV. Pushing the button on the remote, she located the weather channel. A storm was affecting the entire east coast. Dalton wouldn't be pleased—he wouldn't be leaving today.

She called the Lodge and asked for his room. A few minutes later a drowsy-sounding Dalton struggled to say, "Hello?"

"I'm sorry but I have some bad news for you."

"Good morning to you too, Melanie." His voice sounded clearer. "You kept me up last night."

How could the man manage to get her heart pounding with a few simple words? It was nice to know that their kisses had disturbed him as well. She needed to get things back on a business level.

"Uh, I hate to tell you this but you're not going to get a flight out today. There's a major weather front coming in."

Melanie was surprised when there wasn't a large groan of disappointment on the other end of the line. She would miss him when he was gone.

"I figured that might be the case when I looked out the window this morning."

Imagining him still in bed with the covers tangled around his waist, his bare chest dark against the white sheets and the snow falling, had her wishing she wasn't talking to him over the phone but in person.

"So if I can't go home today, what're we going to do?"

The vision of him in bed popped into her mind again. She needed to stop thinking of him that way. They wanted two different things. "Well, I'm going to practice in a few hours. I have a couple of the players to check in with and preparations to make for the game tomorrow. Also I need to double-check Rocket."

"I think I'll go along. Better than being stuck here."

With a note of humor in her voice she said, "I missed the part where you were invited."

"Come on, Melanie, you know you enjoy having me around."

She huffed. Admitting he was right wasn't something she was prepared to do. Even after spending three full days with him, she found she'd missed him last night. "How're you feeling, by the way?"

"Stiff, but I'll live. A hot shower will help with that. Want to come over? I might need help drying off."

Now she was really having a hard time concentrating on what she had to say. "If you're going with me, be ready in an hour."

His soft chuckle filled her ear before she disconnected the call.

Dalton liked watching Melanie work. She had a real rapport with the players and staff. There was a firm but gentle manner to her care. A couple of times she'd even asked him if he was willing to give his opinion. He'd gladly done so.

It shocked him that he wasn't more upset about not being able to get a flight home. In fact, when Melanie had picked him up she'd told him he might not get out until after Christmas. He wasn't pleased but what could he do? With the snow and the holiday plane traffic, he'd be here at least another four days. More time to get to know Melanie. He'd flown in with every intention of leaving within twenty-four hours and here he was, almost glad he was stuck in Niagara Falls.

One of the players came in. "Hey, Doc, can you give my neck a look?"

"Sure, Crush, have a seat." Melanie directed the huge man to a stool.

Dalton assumed she'd asked him to sit there because she wouldn't be able to reach his neck otherwise. Melanie wasn't a tiny woman but around all the extralarge men she was dwarfed in comparison. Still she had an air of authority.

Fifteen minutes later Crush had been put under the care of a trainer for a heat compression to his neck.

"What's the deal with everyone having a nickname?" Dalton asked. "Is that the thing to have if you play football? There's Rocket and Crush and you are even called Mel instead of Melanie. Doesn't anyone go by their real name?"

She shrugged. "I don't know. In some cases it's someone's ability, in others a sign of affection and others it could be something embarrassing they have done in the past and now it's just part of them. Why? You don't like nicknames?"

He knew what it was like to have a past filled with negative names. "No, I don't."

Melanie stopped what she was doing and looked at him. "Why not?"

"I guess I was called an ugly one too many times as a kid." There he was, doing it again. He'd never told anyone that. Saying it somehow made it not feel so heavy anymore.

"I'm sorry."

"Nothing for you to be sorry about. It was a long time ago. I've gotten over it."

Melanie looked at him for a moment. Did she believe him?

A few more players came in with complaints. She checked them out and sent them to the trainers to use the exercise bikes to warm up.

At one point Rocket entered the room. "Hey, Doc Mel. Hello, Dr. Reynolds."

"You here to have your knee wrapped?" Melanie asked.

"Yeah. Not having any problems but I'm doing as you say."

"You can't be too careful," Dalton said. "Take care of it. You don't want it to get worse. I'm still unsure about you playing tomorrow."

"I've got this, Doc. I'll be fine. The team needs me."

"Tomorrow, before the game, I want you at the stadium early in the morning," Melanie said.

"Will do," Rocket said over his shoulder as he pushed through the training room doors.

Melanie looked at the wall clock. "I'm headed out to the practice field. I'll understand if you'd rather stay here."

"Are you implying I might be scared?" Dalton had long overcome being intimidated by people playing games.

"Well…" she said with a grin.

He stood. "I can handle it."

Melanie gave him a sharp look. "Okay. Come on."

They walked the same pathway as they had two days earlier and entered the practice area. Again Melanie went to the midfield line and stopped. A number of players spoke to her as they jogged onto the field.

"Hey, man, I'm sorry."

Dalton looked at the gigantic man standing beside him. "What?"

"I'm the one who blindsided you and Doc Mel the other day. Man, I'm sorry. I was looking for the ball. Are you okay?"

"I'm fine. Doc Mel is also."

The man studied Melanie. "You sure?"

She placed her hand on the player's arm. "We're both fine, Juice."

The man's concern showed in the seriousness of his eyes. "Good. I sure was worried. I'm sorry that happened."

"It was an accident. I know that." Mel smiled at him.

Juice gave Dalton a questioning look.

Dalton offered the player his hand. "No hard feelings, I promise."

Obvious relief covered his face. "Thanks, man, I really appreciate that."

"Juice, let's go," Coach Rizzo called from the center of the field.

Dalton watched as the player loped out onto the field.

"Thanks for being so understanding. Juice is one of

those tender-hearted guys I was talking about. I'm sure he lost sleep over what happened."

Dalton faced her. "Hey, I understand when accidents happen. I'm not such an ogre I can't accept that."

"I wasn't so sure about that a few days ago," Melanie murmured.

"How's that?"

"You acted pretty uptight when you first arrived."

Had he come over that way? Despite being in control of his world, owning his own practice and being a sought-after surgeon, any time the idea of a game being more important than a person came up it put him on edge. He just didn't place the same value on winning that others did. "I was that bad?"

"You were pretty inflexible."

"You still think that about me?"

Melanie smiled. "I'm learning to appreciate other aspects of your personality."

Why did he all of a sudden want to thump his chest?

For over an hour they watched the players move around on the field without any close calls.

Finally Melanie said, "I've some paperwork to take care of. So I'm going to my office for a while."

"Since I'm staying here for a few more days I need to make some calls, change around my schedule. Is there a place where I can use a computer and talk in private?"

"There's an office next to the Performance Area that isn't in use. You're welcome to it."

"Great."

He made his calls. One to an associate at his practice, telling him to request Josey's records. If they showed what he thought they would, he believed he could help the girl.

An hour later Melanie knocked on the door of the office Dalton was using. "I have to do some shopping for my family's Christmas dinner. With the game tomorrow and

Christmas Eve a few days after that, I won't have another chance. Do you want me to drop you off at the Lodge or arrange for you to get a ride back?"

Dalton couldn't remember the last time he'd been to a grocery store. Most of his meals were eaten in the hospital cafeteria or at a restaurant. Something about going to one with Melanie made it sound intriguing. It certainly sounded better than sitting in his room watching movies. "Mind if I come with you?"

Her look of shock was almost comical. "You want to go to the grocery store with me?"

"Don't act so surprised. I eat too."

She put her hands on her hips and glared at him. "When was the last time *you* went to the grocery store?"

"Okay, maybe I don't go often but it would be better than sitting in my room by myself."

"So I'm a step better than boredom."

He held her gaze. "I find you far from boring."

The air suddenly held an electric charge. "Um, you can go if you like but fair warning—it'll be a madhouse so don't expect it to be fun."

"I think I can handle it."

Melanie had to admit that Dalton was good help with grocery buying. He'd insisted on pushing the cart while she gathered the supplies she needed. It was a rather odd feeling to be spending an afternoon hour in the grocery with a man. It wasn't something she'd ever done before.

"You cook dinner for your entire family every Christmas Eve?"

"My sisters-in-law help. I do the majority of the meal but they bring the sides and desserts."

"Sounds like work."

"Not really. I enjoy it. Especially when I'm not pressed for time. This year, with the Currents in the playoffs, it will be more difficult. But I'm tickled to have the Currents doing so well. What do you usually do for a Christmas meal?"

"I go to a restaurant close to my condo for a meal with a few friends and then we spend the afternoon on the beach or beside a pool. Sometimes I'll have friends in for a catered meal but mostly it's a quiet day."

She looked at him as she placed four cans of beans in the cart. "You don't get together with family? What about your parents? Brothers and sisters?"

He was starting to think coming here with her might not have been such a good idea. "No parents. No siblings."

"I'm sorry."

"No need to be sorry. It's just the way it is."

That sounded rather sad to her. "It isn't quiet at the Hyde house. With seven kids running around, the TV on full volume, and my brothers and father armchair coaching. It is loud."

At least she wasn't asking him any more about his family.

"If you don't get to leave before Christmas you are welcome to join my family."

"I'll think about it."

Melanie moved around the turkeys, looking for the perfect one. Having picked one out, she lifted it toward the cart.

"Let me have that." Dalton took the turkey from her and placed it with the other food.

Melanie continued around the store until she had everything on her list. They loaded the groceries into the car. She offered to take Dalton back to the Lodge, but he insisted that he should help unload the groceries. She agreed. Melanie wasn't sure she was comfortable having him in her small condo. Could she resist him if he kissed her again?

By the time they had unloaded the bags at her condo, they were both cold.

"I don't see how you stand living in this winter." Dalton

joined her at her door for the second time with bags of food. "I know why we have so many snowbirds now."

"I have to admit this is rather extreme." Melanie pushed the door open and went down the short hallway to the kitchen.

After Dalton had dumped his bags on the counter he stood looking at the space beyond, which was her living area.

What did those perceptive eyes see? "Is something wrong?"

"No, I was just thinking how much this place looks like you. I like it."

Her sitting room was filled with overstuffed furniture so that it was warm and comfortable. Bright pillows in red, green and yellow were situated on the couch and chairs. Books lined one wall. A couple of floor lamps sat so they hung over one end of the couch and a chair. Modern art pictures of flowers hung on the walls. A small tree with multicolored bulbs sat in a corner. Surrounding it on the floor were presents of all shapes and sizes.

"Thank you. I spend a lot of time here so I want it to be as inviting as possible." Stepping over to the tree, she plugged the lights in. She stood looking at them for a few seconds before she walked to the kitchen. There she started taking food items out of bags. "Why don't you sit down and I'll get us something warm to drink."

"Why don't you tell me where to find the coffee—?"

"I was thinking hot chocolate."

"Okay, hot chocolate. Then we both can sit down and rest for a minute."

"If I do that I might not get up again."

"I'll see that you do. So where's a pot and that hot chocolate?"

Melanie pulled packets of hot chocolate out of the cabinet behind her. "The teapot is in the cabinet beside the oven. You can heat water in it."

Dalton found it and had water heating with the same efficiency he did everything else. While he did that, she stored away most of the food. They were still waiting on the water to get hot when she pulled out an onion and began chopping it for the dressing.

"Hey, what're you doing?"

"I can't waste time. I need to get busy with cooking this food."

"I think you can take five minutes for yourself. Go sit down. I think I can handle the hot chocolate."

She had to admit that it would be nice to sit, drink a cup of hot chocolate and close her eyes. "Okay, since you put it that way."

Melanie went to the couch, curled up in the corner, pulled her feet up and laid her head back. Her eyelids started to droop. She'd just close them for a minute.

She woke to warmth. There was a blanket covering her. The sun had set. A single lamp shone across the room. Dalton sat on the other end of the sofa reading a book. "Why did you let me go to sleep?"

He looked at her and closed the book. "Hey, I don't control that."

She threw the blanket back. "I've got to get busy."

"What's the hurry?"

"I've got food to prepare."

"What happens if you don't?" he said in a tone that implied she was overreacting.

"Then we won't have enough for the Christmas meal." She stood.

"And this would be the end of the world?"

Now he was starting to make her mad. "My family expects me to fix the turkey and dressing."

"And you wouldn't want to disappoint them." He made

it sound as if her family was taking advantage of her. He put his book down. "To keep you from going into a panic, I'll help. Just assign me something easy."

"You don't have to."

"If it will stop you from feeling guilty over a nap, then I can help out."

"How about cutting onions?" she asked, heading for the kitchen.

"Why?"

"For the dressing. I wish you had woken me."

He joined her. "You needed to sleep. Between your job with the team, working at the hospital and taking care of me, you haven't had much downtime in the last few days. I kind of liked listening to you snore."

"Hey, I don't snore!" She gave him a light swat on the forearm.

"I think the lady doth protest too much, especially when she does."

They both laughed. She'd not had this much fun in a long time. She would miss Dalton when he was gone. Too much, she was afraid. "You're so bad."

"Thank you."

"That wasn't meant as a compliment." She turned and pulled a cookbook off a shelf. "The onions are in a bag under that cabinet." Melanie pointed just past him. "Here is the knife and cutting board." She pulled them out of a drawer.

Dalton took the items from her. "I hope you don't expect my chopping to be perfect."

She met his gaze. At least he'd offered to help—something that her father or brothers wouldn't think to do. "I can't imagine you not being confident about your ability in anything."

Dalton's eyes darkened for a second, then cleared. Had she said something wrong? "I'm going to start making the cornbread." She pulled the cornmeal out from under the cabinet.

A few minutes later he ran a finger down her cheek when she came to check on his progress.

"Please don't."

Why had his simple touch made her want to lean into his heat and not leave?

"Are you scared of what I might do or is it because you're afraid of what you might do?"

If she was truthful, it was both, but she couldn't say that. "I thought we were going to keep things between us friendly."

"I was just getting your attention to ask if you had given any thought to dinner."

"No."

"Then it's a good thing that I have. I found a magnet stuck to your refrigerator with a pizza place on it while you were snoring. I ordered cheese and pepperoni. Should be here soon. I hope that's okay with you."

Melanie stepped back before she did something she might regret. Like hugging him. "Sounds perfect." Surprisingly, she was finding more and more things about Dalton that were perfect.

An hour later Dalton pushed his chair back from Melanie's café-style table and said, "It's been a long time since I've had a pizza that good."

"It's my favorite. I lived off pizza when I was a kid. The only thing my father knew to do for meals was cook frozen pizza or order in."

"It isn't easy to lose a mother when you're young."

"No. You sound like you understand."

He wasn't sure he wanted to discuss his mother in general and certainly not in particular. "I have a pretty good idea."

"You said your parents were gone. How old were you when they died?"

She wouldn't let it go. Would it really hurt him to tell his story? "Only my mother has died, as far as I know. I have no idea about my father."

"But you said—"

"They are dead to me. My father went to prison when I was a couple of months old. I never really knew him. I was taken from my mother when I was six. She died a couple of years later in jail." It wasn't as painful to tell Melanie as he'd thought it might be. Something about her made him believe she wouldn't judge.

"I'm sorry. We have more in common than I thought. We both lost our mothers."

This was getting far too personal for his taste. She made it sound as if they had a bond that would always bind them in a special way.

"So where did you live?"

"Foster homes. More than one, actually."

"That couldn't have been easy. At least I had my father and brothers. Even though they weren't around much. Mostly it was just Coach and me."

He liked that she had turned the focus off of him. "Your father wasn't around much either, was he?"

"No. But I always knew he cared about me."

"That was a good thing." He had been thirteen or fourteen before he'd thought someone actually cared about him. Mrs. Richie had been that person but she'd soon pushed him away as well. Trusting a person to have his back was something he had a difficult time doing.

She nodded. "It was. There were times I wished he understood me better. But my dad was more about guys than girls. I don't even know why I'm telling you this."

Dalton knew what it was like not to be understood. He took another swallow of his drink. "What're friends for?"

"It's not to dump the past on. I do know that." She rose and started cleaning the table. "I hate to put a man out in the cold but I need to take you to the Lodge. I have to be up early to get ready for the game."

"Do you mind me going with you? Since I'm here I might as well check on Rocket if he plays."

"No, I'd be glad to have you on the sideline but I want to warn you it'll be freezing. There's supposed to be some sun but only in the late afternoon."

"Great. I'll be looking forward to it." There wasn't much enthusiasm in his words.

"You don't sound like it. I'll stop by Coach's house early and get a few of my brother's old gloves and a hat for you. See if I can find some boots."

"Maybe that way I won't freeze."

"There are warmers you can stand beside so that doesn't happen."

When was the last time he'd not been prepared for what life brought him? Long ago he'd learned the importance of being ready. If you were prepared, then you were in control of what happened. Nothing about this trip, outside of caring for Rocket, had gone as he had planned. To his astonishment, it didn't seem to upset him as much as it should have. He was learning to appreciate the wonder of what might transpire.

His friends in Miami would hoot when he told them he'd gone to a pro football game. And probably fall on the floor laughing when they found out he'd stood in the snow on the sideline. Dalton smiled to himself. He should give some thought to whether or not to tell them about this trip. The teasing might be more than he could take.

"Come on, I'll take you to the Lodge," Melanie said as she picked up her coat off the chair where she'd left it earlier.

"Gee, I thought I might get an invite to stay the night."

His tone was flippant but he wouldn't hesitate to take her up on the offer if she made it.

"Dalton—" Her voice sounded unsure.

"I'm just kidding. I wasn't planning to spend the night." Her apparent relief pricked his feelings. "I'll call a taxi. No need for you to go out." He pulled out his cell phone and searched for a car service.

"I don't mind taking you."

"It's not a problem." He dialed the number of the service and spoke to them. After disconnecting he said, "They should be here in about fifteen minutes."

"Okay." Melanie sounded sad. She dropped her coat on the chair again and stepped toward him.

His look locked with hers.

"I'm sorry, Dalton. I'm not a very good flirt. Not like the saleswoman. I've seen too many women make fools of themselves over players. Even my own brothers. I'm not that kind of person. I don't invite men to stay. I'm not a short wow person. I'm more of the cautious, get-to-know-you-slowly type."

Dalton came closer and cupped her face. His thumb caressed the curve of her cheek. "Short wow, huh? I've not heard that before. I really was teasing about staying. There's nothing for you to feel bad about. If it isn't for you, it isn't for you."

A few minutes of uncomfortable silence filled the space between them. Why had he asked about staying? He wanted that easy interaction between them back. His phone buzzed and he answered it. "I'll be right out." To her, he said, "Taxi's here." Turning away from Melanie, he pulled his coat on, wrapped his scarf around his neck the way she'd shown him. "What time will you pick me up in the morning?"

"Eight."

"I'll be waiting in the lobby. Don't come in. I'll watch for you." He went to the door.

"Dalton…"

He turned to find Melanie right behind him. She grabbed the lapels of his coat, stood on her toes and brought her mouth to his. Her lips were damp, as if she'd just run her tongue across them with indecision. They quivered slightly. The kiss was sweet, sensuous and sincere. And entirely too short.

"See you tomorrow." She sounded a little breathless.

Wow. He had a feeling he was headed in a direction he hadn't planned to go and wasn't sure he could control.

CHAPTER SIX

MELANIE PULLED HER car into the slot designated as hers at the stadium. The other spots were slowly filling up as the players and staff arrived.

Dalton had been waiting in the lobby, just as he'd said he would. Her face turned warm as she watched him walk toward the car. That was all it took for her body to hum. It was becoming more difficult for her to keep her distance. Being impulsive was so unlike her. She still couldn't believe she'd kissed him after she'd told him they should only be friends. Had she opened the door to rejection again? Thank goodness he seemed at ease as they drove to the stadium. She was relieved he didn't mention the kiss.

Pulling a bag along with her medical one out of the backseat, she joined Dalton at the front of the car. She handed the bigger one to him. "Your warm clothes."

"Thanks." He glanced at the sky, where gray clouds gathered. "I'm going to need them."

She nodded.

"What's going on with you? It's like there is a hum of electricity about you."

"I guess it's excitement." Great—he'd noticed. This was a healthy direction. She led him through a large roll-up door opening big enough for a transfer truck to completely enter.

"What are we in, a wind tunnel?"

Melanie pushed her hair out of her face. "It's like this all the time. Even in the summer. It's caused by the air coming off the field though the tunnels."

They took a ramp and entered another door into a warm, long hallway. Melanie walked ahead of Dalton but she was aware of him close behind her. Too aware.

Never a forward person where men were concerned and still not sure she wasn't making the wrong step, Melanie was still glad she'd kissed him. When she'd told him he wasn't invited to stay she hadn't missed that dark look of rejection in his eyes. Something about his expression made her think it was a deep-seated emotion that Dalton felt more than the average person. She didn't want him to leave her place thinking she wasn't attracted to him. Who was she kidding? She wanted him on a level she'd never felt before but she had no doubt he would break her heart. They didn't want the same things in a relationship.

Today she had a job to do and thinking about Dalton wasn't the best way to do a quality one. Treating him like the visiting professional was what she needed to do.

At another door, she turned the knob and opened it. "This is the Currents' locker room."

This was her space. Next door was the training room and beyond that the dressing room. She placed her bag on the desk. "You can leave that—" she indicated the bag Dalton carried "—on that chair. Most of my time will be spent next door until the game starts. Then I'll be on the sideline. I'd be glad to have someone take you up to the Manager's box if you'd like."

"No, I'd rather see what you do."

Melanie liked the idea of Dalton being interested in her part of the medical profession. She'd had the impression when they'd first met that he didn't think too highly of it. Maybe today he'd completely change his opinion.

"Well, just know the option is always there. It's warm and there's food."

"Please don't tempt me." He grinned.

"It's time for me to check in with the trainers. They'll already be taping some ankles and caring for knees of the players that arrived early."

"I'd be interested to see how that's being done. I'm only involved in the surgery when a repair is needed, never on the preemptive side. It would be beneficial to watch it done."

"Help yourself. You can see plenty of it today."

Dalton left her for the training room. A couple of times when a player pushed through the doors to her office Dalton's voice carried as he questioned someone about why they were doing it that way. Once his laugh mixed with one of the player's.

It fascinated her that he seemed to interact with the players so well when he had no interest in the game. Or at least that was what he'd claimed. She hadn't thought he'd be comfortable with the players. Now he seemed interested in at least getting to know the team on a medical level.

Soon it was time for the team to go out on the field for the pregame warm-up. She joined Dalton in the training room.

"While they're out doing warm-ups I'm going up to say hello to Marcus. Would you like to come?"

"Sure. Do I need to put on my warmer layer?"

"That's not necessary. We'll be in the building the entire time." She went out the door and Dalton followed her. When he'd arrived less than a week ago she would have never believed she'd still be entertaining him. It was funny how life took twists and turns. Dalton might be hanging out with her because he had nothing better to do, but she was enjoying having him around. Especially when he kissed her. Melanie glanced at him. That was something she was better off not thinking about.

They took an elevator that dropped them off in a concourse carpeted in black and yellow—the Currents' colors.

A security guard stood just outside the elevator. "Why, hello, Doc. I haven't seen you in some time. It's good to see you."

"Hi, Benny. Nice to see you too. How's that new grandbaby doing?"

"Growing like a weed. Growing like a weed."

"That's great."

As they walked away Dalton asked, "Do you know everyone?"

"Don't you know the people where you work?" Surely he was on friendly terms with the people in the hospital where he did surgery. This was her place of work, just like that was his.

They walked on until they came to the Currents' staff family box that was on the forty-five-yard line.

Melanie pushed the door open and Dalton followed.

The back of Marcus's dark head was all she could see. She smiled. He had his nose pressed against the glass. A fog ring had formed in front of his mouth.

Snow fell outside to the point that in order to see the lines on the field, the snow had to be blown away.

"How's the front-row seat, Marcus?" At her question, the boy turned around.

There was a large smile on his face. "This is awesome. Thanks, Dr. Mel."

She took the chair next to him while Dalton stood nearby. On the other side of Marcus sat an older woman with gray in her tight curls. Melanie smiled at her.

"This is my grandmother," Marcus offered. "She's a big Currents fan."

The woman smiled at Melanie. "I'm Lucinda Abernathy. Thanks for doing this for Marcus. He'll remember it forever."

"You're welcome. I'm glad I could. Marcus, look who came with me?" She glanced back at Dalton.

Marcus smiled. "Hi, Doc."

"Hey, Marcus. How're you feeling?"

"Much better since I've been let out of the hospital for a while."

"I can understand that. It's been rather nice for me not to be in one all the time too."

Melanie looked at him. That was an interesting statement. He couldn't get back to Miami fast enough the other day and surgeons were known for spending large amounts of time in an OR.

She spoke to Marcus and his grandmother. "Have either of you tried the buffet?"

"Is that for us too?" Marcus asked as if he thought it might be too good to be true.

"Sure it is. Do you mind if Dr. Reynolds and I eat lunch with you and your grandmother?"

"No."

"Then let's eat." Melanie moved so that Marcus and his grandmother could come by her and be first in line. She said to Dalton, "This is our chance for a meal. We don't get another until well after the game."

"I'm hungry so this is a great time." He leaned in closer as if he didn't want anyone else to hear. "Without you spending the night and telling me what to do, I didn't get up in time to have breakfast."

"Shh," Melanie hissed as she walked to where the food was being served. Dalton was teasing her but still it made her blood flow warm just to think about *what if*.

He stood close behind her. His breath ruffled her hair when he whispered, "I'm really hungry."

Melanie poked her elbow in his ribs.

"Aww," he grunted.

She whirled around. "I'm so sorry. I forgot." She took his arm that wasn't holding his side. "Sit down. Sit down."

He settled into a nearby chair. "I'm fine. Really."

"I hurt you." She went down on a knee so she could see his face.

"I got what I deserved for picking at you."

"Are you hurt, Doc?" Marcus asked as he and his grandmother stood staring at them with full plates in their hands.

"I'm fine. Juice used me as… What are those things called that football players hit?"

"A blocking dummy," Marcus said with complete confidence. "You got hit by Juice? How cool."

"It wasn't so cool at the time." Dalton groaned as he turned in his chair. "Not so cool at this minute either."

Melanie's heart tightened. She'd have to put Dalton on the plane soon before she managed to beat him to death. "I'll get you a plate."

"I'm not going to argue."

Melanie was afraid she might cry. Dalton took her fingers in his and gave them a squeeze. "I'm going to live. Just give me a minute to catch my breath."

"Okay."

"Now, I'm going to move over to the table with Marcus and his grandmother. We'll save you a seat."

She gave him a weak smile. "Do you like your burger all the way?"

"Everything but onions. I might get up close and personal with someone before the day is out."

Melanie was glad that their lunch partners had found the table set up in the back of the room. "Do you need help getting there?"

"Melanie, I feel emasculated enough without you making me an invalid."

She bit her lip. Was she making it that bad? "All right. I'll try to show you as little concern as possible."

"Hey, don't go overboard. I like your attention."

She gave him a wry grin. "I think that's what got you into this situation."

Dalton had the good grace to give a wry smile. "That it did."

"I'll get your burger. You get yourself to the table." Melanie turned her back to him. It was tough to resist helping him, but maybe he was right, she was fussing too much.

Dalton remained at the table with Marcus when his grandmother and Melanie went to pick out desserts. "So you didn't have any guys begging you to bring them to the game?"

Marcus shrugged. "Sure, but I rather they come because they are my friend not just because I had cool seats for the game."

"So you think your friends might be using you?"

"When you're a sick kid you learn real quick who your friends are. I have a couple of good ones and couldn't bring them both. My grandmother watches every Currents game. I had to bring her or she would have killed me."

Dalton chuckled. "I guess you didn't have a choice."

"Naw."

"So when you grow up, what do you want to be?"

"I'd like to be a history teacher."

Dalton nodded. He hadn't expected that as an answer. "That sounds like a good plan."

"I like to read about history and go to forts and museums. Some of my friends make fun of me, but my grandmother says not to pay them any attention."

"Some guys just don't get it. You grandmother's right. I'm glad you have her. You'll end up being the smart guy who teaches those guys' children."

Dalton knew well the importance of having someone to cheer you on. He hadn't had anyone. Yet something deep inside him still wanted to make Mrs. Richie proud. "Keep up your studies and make your grandmother happy."

"I will."

Melanie and Marcus's grandmother returned. Placing a plate with three different desserts in front of him, Melanie then sat in the chair next to his. "I've got to go in a few minutes. If you'd like to stay here and watch the game with Marcus you're welcome to."

"Are you trying to get rid of me?"

"No, but you may wish you had by halftime."

"If I'm going to really keep an eye on Rocket, then I need to be on the field."

"That's true."

They made their way back to the Currents' locker room area. This time Dalton didn't follow. He walked confidently beside Melanie. When they arrived at the office again, Melanie said, "I keep the clothes I need in a locker in the bathroom. I'll lock the doors and you can dress in here. I found some of my brother's old long underwear. I think you'll be glad I did. Be ready to go in a few minutes."

Her tone implied that if he wasn't he'd be left behind.

He was tall enough that the snow suit she'd brought him fit well when it was zipped up the front. The boots were large but not so much so they were clown size and difficult to walk in. They were well lined and he was positive he would be glad to have them on.

Melanie came out of the bathroom dressed much as he was. "We need to get moving. It's time for the team to go to the field."

The wind pushed them backward as they made their way out of the tunnel behind the team. They ran onto the field while he and Melanie walked to the sideline.

"Feel free to stand by the warmers but don't get too close because they can melt your overalls."

By the middle of the second quarter of the game, Dalton was stomping his feet and standing beside a warmer. Snow blew as the wind picked up, producing mini tornados around his feet. Still the stands were filled with people shouting as the players moved the ball first one way and then another. He didn't understand all the penalties or the nuances of the game but he had to admit it was easy to get caught up in the excitement. He marched up and down the sideline beside Melanie as the team changed ends. She was completely into the game. Occasionally, she would holler and jump up and down. What would it take to have her that enthusiastic about him?

Rocket played well and there was no indication that his knee was giving him any problems. After a play, one of the men didn't immediately get up. Melanie and a couple of the trainers wearing medical packs around their waists ran out on the field. Soon the player was being helped to the side as Melanie gave him her complete attention.

At halftime they went into the locker room with the players. He was thankful for the warmth. The only problem was that it didn't last long enough. They had to return to the field about the time feeling returned to his toes. He hated this weather.

Melanie grinned as they made their way up the tunnel. "You sure you wouldn't rather be in the heated, glassed-in box with Marcus?"

He groaned. "Please don't tempt me." Dalton kept walking. He was determined to impress her by sticking out the game.

It was the middle of the third quarter and the Currents were winning when another player was injured. Melanie jogged onto the field once again. A group of players and staff surrounded the man lying on the ground.

For a few seconds there was complete silence in the stadium. Melanie stepped outside of the circle and waved him toward her. She didn't wait on him to arrive; instead, she returned to the center of the circle. Hurrying as fast as he could without slipping on the icy ground, Dalton made his way halfway across the field. It was much farther than it looked. As he reached the group, they opened for him.

Melanie was on her knees beside the groaning player. She saw Dalton and moved so that he could kneel beside her at the player's thigh. His cleat had been removed. A plastic sheet was beneath him. A blanket had also been thrown across the man's shoulders.

"What do you think? Broken or fractured Lisfranc joint?" Melanie asked, looking at Dalton.

"Hey, Doc," the player called, "it hurts but I can play."

Dalton and Melanie ignored the statement. He placed the palm of his hand over the top of the foot and found it was already swelling. Moving over and around Melanie, Dalton went to the feet of the player. "We need to cut the sock off."

Melanie was handed scissors by one of the trainers. With efficacy of movement she had the sock removed. While she was busy doing that, he took off his gloves. Before he touched the player Dalton rubbed his hands together to make them as warm as possible. Placing his fingers on either side of the foot, he worked his way over the bones. As he touched the top of it the man winced.

Melanie was right. "I think it's a fracture, but we need an X-ray to confirm."

"Call for the cart," she said loudly and a couple of the staff broke away from the group to do her bidding.

Dalton stood and Melanie did too as the cart arrived. She oversaw the player being loaded. When he was ready to be taken off the field, she said to Dalton, "I'm going with Mitchell to the locker room to see that he's taken care of until the ambulance arrives."

"I'll come along." Dalton started to add *if you need help*, but she wouldn't. Melanie had handled the situation with professionalism and quality of care. He'd been impressed. There was more to being a team doctor than he'd believed.

She'd seen to it that the ankle as well as the leg had been immobilized when they reached the medical area. Few he'd seen could have done it better. While she worked, the TV mounted high on the wall blared the game.

There had been another couple of touchdowns and the faint roar of the crowd reached them under the stands. Everyone, except him, reacted outwardly to each of them. He had to admit there had been a wish to throw his hands up as the Currents crossed over the line and a tug of disappointment when the other team took the lead again. By the time the ambulance arrived, there were only a few minutes left in the game and the Currents had the ball.

"Come on, Doc," Mitchell said to Melanie as she gave her report to the EMT, "let me stay until the game is over." He'd been give pain medicine and was feeling better.

"We have it on in the wagon," he heard one of the EMTs assure Mitchell.

The player was being whisked out the large roll-up door Melanie and he had walked through that morning. The TV was still on and a couple of the staff had stopped what they were doing to stand looking up at it. Melanie joined them and he stood beside her.

The Currents were on the two-yard line. If they made this play they would win the game. A thud from the pounding of feet came from above. It seemed as if everyone in the room held their breath.

The quarterback handed off the ball to number twenty-one, who Dalton had learned was Rocket. He made a move to the left, not being caught by the two men chasing him, then he cut to the right to dodge another man. He jumped a pile of men tangled up on the goal line and fell into the end zone. The crowd erupted into a roar as the last second ticked off the clock. The Currents had won the game.

"We won. We won." Melanie jumped up and down and then threw her arms around Dalton's neck and kissed him.

His arms circled her waist and he passionately returned her kiss.

Melanie broke away. "I'm sorry. I got carried away."

"I'm not." But next time he wanted her to kiss him because of him.

They looked at the TV again. His team members were slapping Rocket on the back. When they finally climbed off him and let him stand, Rocket struggled to do so.

In unison Dalton and Melanie said, "His knee."

CHAPTER SEVEN

MELANIE SHOVED THROUGH the doors and started running up the tunnel toward the arena. Dalton was right behind her. As they approached the field, people started coming in the other direction. Soon they were fighting against the tide. Dalton went past her and created a path for her to follow. It was nice to have him looking after her.

They finally made their way to the bench on the sideline where Rocket was sitting. A number of players, staff, Coach Rizzo, her father and some of the media stood close by. A couple of the heaters had been moved to either side of him and his winter game cape had been placed over his shoulders.

"Rocket, we saw it on TV. How's your knee feeling?" Melanie asked in a panting voice.

"Hey, Doc. Doc Reynolds. I thought you might be showing up."

"So how is it?" Dalton was already down on a knee in front of Rocket.

Melanie had forgotten to put on her outer clothes. Dalton wasn't wearing his coat, hat or gloves either. He must be cold. She sure was. But Dalton didn't show it. His concern was focused on Rocket.

"I'm going to have to put my hands on you. I'm afraid they aren't warm," Dalton told Rocket.

"Don't worry. I'm so cold that I probably can't feel you anyway."

"I'll make it quick. Then we'll *all* go inside."

Dalton did the same type of exam he'd done at their first meeting. Except his face grew more thoughtful this time.

Finished, he stood. "I don't want you walking on this leg. You need to have an X-ray and MRI ASAP."

"Let's get the cart back out here," Melanie told one of the staff.

"I really did it this time," Rocket said.

"I'm afraid today might be it for you this year." Dalton put his hands under his armpits and stomped the ground. One of the trainers put a blanket over his shoulders and also handed her one.

"We need him for next week," Coach Rizzo protested. "Even bigger game than this."

Her father glanced at the media, busy flashing pictures. "We don't need to make that decision until after the tests are done. This is something better discussed when we have all the information."

Dalton looked at her as if expecting her to disagree with her father.

"That sounds like a wise plan. We won't know anything for a couple of days," Melanie offered in a conciliatory tone.

Dalton gave her a disappointed look, then headed for the tunnel leading to the locker room.

The cart pulled up close to Rocket and Melanie stayed with him until he was being driven off the field. While the trainer prepared Rocket for his trip to the emergency room, she went to her office to change.

Dalton was sitting in a chair with one ankle over a knee, his outer clothes already removed. His look met hers when she entered.

"I'm freezing. That's the last time I'm running out without at least my overcoat." She pulled the blanket closer around her.

"I'm almost warm. But my toes are still burning," Dalton said flatly.

"We'll be out of here soon. I have to go to the hospital to check on Mitchell and see that Rocket gets those tests run. I'm assuming you want to go with me."

"Will you be taking any of my advice if I do?"

She stopped halfway into the bathroom. "What does that mean?"

"It means you know that Rocket shouldn't play in any more games until that knee heals. Why didn't you say so?"

"Because we don't know that for sure until after we do the tests and because you never make those type of statements in front of the media. The Currents are in the playoffs for the first time in franchise history. Rocket is an important part of making that happen. If the other team thinks Rocket won't be there, it might not give them a physical advantage but it will certainly give them a mental one. The same goes for our team. We can't have them believing Rocket is out before it's a fact. It affects them mentally as well."

"You have to be kidding. One player carries that much weight?"

"I'm not and he does." She continued on into the bathroom. Why couldn't he believe that winning the game was important?

Melanie stepped out again and looked at him. "Didn't you see how the fans reacted today? Hear Marcus talking about his grandmother's love for the Currents?"

"But is a win worth the price of a man being crippled for the rest of his life?"

What kind of a person did he think she was? "No, it isn't. I don't think so as a person and I certainly don't believe that as a doctor. All I'm saying is that we need to take it slow, know what we're talking about."

Dalton seemed to consider that. He uncrossed his leg and put his hands on his knees. "I can agree with that. As long as I know whose side you're on."

"Side? What side?"

"Rocket's or the team's."

One of the trainers opened the door and stuck his head in, preventing her from commenting. "The hospital called. They have the X-rays on Mitchell and Rocket ready."

"Good. Please, let them know I'm on my way."

She didn't have time to return to her argument with Dalton. There were patients to consider. He'd been asked here to give a second opinion and he had. Now he was butting into what he didn't understand. It insulted her that he questioned her ability to put the players' health above the team's need.

Dalton was waiting with his new overcoat on and the bag of clothes she'd brought him by the time she'd stored her game clothes and picked up her purse. "I don't have time to drop you off at the Lodge. They are expecting me at the hospital."

"I already said I was going to the hospital with you."

Melanie started out the door. "Then you need to keep in mind that I'm the team doctor and I have the final say."

"I understand that. But, just so you know, I'll give my professional opinion as I see fit."

There was that tone she recognized from when they'd first met.

She wouldn't make any headway in this conversation so she kept walking toward her car. Snow had piled up on the windshield. "Would you hand me the scraper out of the glovebox?"

Dalton opened the passenger door. "I can do that—you go ahead and get in."

"Are you trying to tell me what to do again?"

His heavy sigh made a puff of fog in the cold air. "Melanie, I'm only trying to be helpful. Let's call a truce until we have both had some rest. We've had a busy, cold day and it's not over yet. Why don't we plan to fight this out tomorrow, if we must?" He found the scraper and started removing snow as if he wasn't still sore.

Melanie settled in the driver's seat and turned the heat up high. It had been an emotional day and if the truth be known she wanted nothing more than a hot bath and bed. But that would have to wait a few more hours.

She watched Dalton as he worked. Despite their recent argument, he had been a trooper and good help during the game. She'd been glad to have him on the field to confirm Mitchell's possible diagnosis and be there with Rocket. Still, she didn't like Dalton questioning her motives.

Hours later, Melanie pulled in front of the Lodge. She'd reviewed Mitchell's and Rocket's X-rays and visited both the men in their rooms. Neither was happy about having to stay overnight, but their wives and families were handling keeping them happy. Dalton had remained beside her the entire time. They had agreed on their earlier diagnosis of Mitchell's foot and were waiting on Rocket's MRI. The hospital had promised to notify her if anything changed during the night. She'd told the nurse she would be back first thing in the morning to check on them.

A groan coming from Dalton brought her attention back to the present.

"What's wrong?"

He pointed to a sign that read "No Water."

She couldn't leave him here. He deserved running water after the day they'd had.

He'd have to go home with her even if it strained her nerves to have him close all night.

"I guess you'd better come home with me."

"Don't sound so excited about the idea. I don't want to put you out."

"And I don't think I can take a long hot shower without feeling guilty if I leave you here. And I plan to have a long hot shower."

"So you're only being nice to me to ease your conscience?"

"Something like that."

He chuckled. "At least you're honest."

"I'll wait while you get the things you need."

"I don't have but one set of clothes really." He pulled at his shirt. "If you have a spare toothbrush I should be good."

She already knew he slept in the nude. Great. What was she getting herself into this time?

As she pulled out of the parking lot she said, "I hope they have the water on by tomorrow night because the Currents are having their Christmas party here."

Dalton was fairly sure that Melanie would have been perfectly happy to go home to an empty condo and have some time to herself. But he couldn't face a night without any water. He'd try to give her space and be as unobtrusive a guest as possible.

"Why don't you shower first? I have a few phone calls to make," she said as she removed her coat and hung it up on a peg just inside the door.

He put his jacket and the large bag with the extra clothes in it on a chair. "I can't take advantage of your hospitality by doing that. You have yours, then I'll get mine."

"When I get in I'm staying until the hot water is gone. If you want any, then you need to get it now." She walked into the kitchen.

"Okay, okay. I'll make it short."

Dalton tried to make it a quick shower but he stayed longer than he'd planned. The hot water felt so good, he couldn't bring himself not to enjoy it just a few more minutes. Forcing himself to get out, he toweled off. What was he going to wear?

He opened the door a crack and called, "Melanie!"

"Yes?" she answered a minute later from outside the door.

"I hate to ask you for anything more, but do you have any sweatpants or something else I can wear?" There was a moment of silence as if she were thinking.

"Wait a sec. I do have some old sweatpants somewhere that might fit you."

A moment later a hand thrust navy material through the crack. Dalton took it.

"Pass me your dirty clothes and I'll start them washing."

Scooping up the clothes he'd taken off, he handed them to her. Careful not to let her see him nude, he pulled on the sweatpants. They were smaller than he would have liked but at least he wouldn't be wearing just a towel.

Somehow her compassionate invitation tonight after their long day and fight made him resist applying any pressure to their wavering relationship. He wanted her to know that he respected her and appreciated her willingness to share her home. What he felt now was an odd emotion. One he wasn't sure he was comfortable with.

What if he let go? Really invested himself in a relationship? He couldn't do that—she'd eventually leave, as everyone he'd truly cared about had. It wasn't worth chancing the heartache.

He entered the living area to find Melanie standing behind the bar that separated the kitchen from the larger space. The TV was on and tuned to a channel with a digital fire.

"Nice fire," Dalton said.

Her eyes went wide when she saw him and her gaze settled on his bare chest long enough that he almost forgot his resolve to keep it simple between them.

She looked away. "I, uh, needed warming up. I thought it might help."

"I left you some hot water."

"Good. I'm on my way to use it all up."

Thoughts of Melanie taking a shower had him wanting to join her. But tonight wasn't the time to push. No matter how his need for her was growing. It was becoming more difficult every second because she only wore a housecoat. For a fleeting moment he questioned whether or not she had anything on under it.

"I'm sorry I didn't have a T-shirt large enough for you."

Did she mean that? Her gaze seemed to dart down to his chest and away again every few seconds. Her interest was an ego builder.

She held a mug up. "Would you like some tea or coffee? I'm out of hot chocolate. You hungry? Want a sandwich?"

"Thanks, a sandwich and tea would be great."

"The kettle is hot. Bags beside it. You'll find sandwich meat, cheese in the refrigerator and the bread is right here." She patted the bag sitting on the counter. "I'm going to get my shower. I've put bed things out on the sofa. Sorry I can't offer you your own bedroom."

She sounded so formal. Was she nervous?

"Melanie, I'm sorry I've been thrown in your lap like I have for the last few days. I know you probably thought you would pick me up from the airport and then be done with me. I do appreciate your efforts to make me comfortable."

"You're welcome, Dalton. I feel bad that you've been stuck here."

But he'd started to enjoy it. He hadn't realized how much he needed a vacation away from his demanding practice. He'd learned a few things in the past few days, had a story to tell and met Melanie. All in all, it hadn't been that bad. In fact, he couldn't remember laughing or smiling more.

Melanie headed for her bedroom. As she went in she said, "Good night."

Dalton watched the door close between them. Disappointment filled him. He wouldn't be sharing a meal with her. The ambience of the fire and a hot drink weren't the same when the woman you wanted to share it with was in another room.

He looked at the pile of bedclothes, then back at the door. The sound of water running reached his ears and a vision of Melanie standing under a stream of steamy water had the front of the stretch material he wore tightening. Dalton sighed. He wouldn't be getting much rest tonight.

Melanie purposely pulled on the oldest and most unrevealing pajamas she owned. She was still cold after her shower and the temptation to go to Dalton and ask him to hold her was too strong. She huddled in her bed, wishing for kisses from him that she knew from experience would heat her to the core.

He'd made no advances or even said anything that could be misconstrued as an innuendo since they'd entered her home. It was as if he were putting her at arm's length. Had their fight turned his interest sour?

It was disappointing to think he no longer wanted her. When he'd walked into the living room wearing those too-tight sweats, revealing more than they should have, and his wide chest and muscular arms bare, she almost couldn't breathe. If Dalton had given any indication of interest, she would have stepped into his arms and asked if she could join him in his shower.

But he hadn't and she didn't. It was best left alone anyway. He'd made it clear any relationship between them would be strictly physical, no long-term emotion. She closed her eyes, pulled herself into a ball and shivered. Hopefully, sleep would come. Exhaustion must have finally taken over because she woke to the faint sound of movement in the other room. Who was that? What time was it?

Dalton. Morning.

Well covered in her pajamas, she opened the door to her bedroom and stepped out. Dalton stood in front of the kitchen stove. Much to her disappointment, he was wearing his own clothes. There was no bare chest for her to feast on this morning. His shirt tail was out and he'd only closed two of the buttons across his abdomen. It was a nicer view than the sun rising over the falls. She'd like to enjoy the view every morning. A wish that wouldn't come true.

"Good morning, sleepyhead."

"Hey." She moved further into the room.

"I thought I was going to have to come wake you."

Melanie tingled at the idea. What would it be like to be awakened by Dalton? Would he kiss her awake? Nuzzle her neck? Run a hand along her leg? A shiver went through her. She had it bad.

"Is something wrong? You have a funny look on your face."

"No, no, nothing's wrong." She had to change the subject. "What're you doing back there?"

"I'm making us breakfast."

"And what will that be?"

"Scrambled eggs and toast." He pushed the spatula around the pan. "Should be ready in a minute."

"I'll dress, then. I have to get to the hospital and then check on the Christmas party preparations."

Dalton gave her a quizzical look. "Since when does a team doctor become involved in Christmas party decorations?"

"Coach is the general manager of the Currents, remember? He asked me to make sure everything is correctly done."

"Have you ever thought about saying no?" He pulled bread out of the toaster.

"Why would I?"

Dalton shook his head and murmured, "I guess you wouldn't."

She stepped closer to the bar. "What does that mean?"

"Breakfast is ready. Why don't we eat it while it's hot?" Dalton scooped eggs onto plates.

He hadn't answered her question. Did she really do her father's bidding? She'd always done as he asked. Had wanted to help as part of the team. She was only being a good daughter.

"So the plan for today is to go to the hospital and then back to the Lodge?" Dalton asked as he placed the plates on the table.

"Yes, but I can drop you by the Lodge first if you would like."

"I'd like to see Rocket's MRI."

Hopefully that wouldn't bring another round of disagreement between then. She didn't doubt that they both wanted the best for Rocket but she had other issues to consider. Dalton didn't understand that. Probably never would. "You are welcome at the team party, if you would like to come?"

"I don't think so. I don't like to crash parties."

Her fork stopped halfway to her mouth and she gave him a peeved look. "You're not crashing if I invite you. If it'll make you feel better you can come as my date."

He smirked. "Why, Melanie, are you asking me out?"

The man was making an effort at humor now?

She glared at him. "I'm trying to be polite but if you're going to be a smart aleck about it, then spend the night in your suite watching TV. The guys are fun to be around. After yesterday's game they'll be in high spirits. If nothing else, the food will be worth it. We use the best caterer in town."

"Since you put the invitation so sweetly, how can I resist? Yes, Melanie, I would love to be your date for the Christmas party."

He made it sound like there would be more to it than a friendly outing.

After breakfast they visited Mitchell and Rocket. Both were clamoring to see their discharge papers, which would put them out of the hospital in time for the party. The MRI showed that Rocket's knee had become marginally worse. The decision on whether or not to let him play would be made closer to the game. Finished there, Melanie drove them to the Lodge.

In the lobby Dalton asked, "What time do I need to be ready?"

"I have to be here at seven," Melanie said.

"Then I'll be waiting in the lobby for you."

"Okay." She headed down the hall to the ballroom.

Melanie stopped. The realization of what she'd done dawned on her. She had a date with Dalton! The evening pantsuit she'd planned to wear wouldn't do, especially after his remark about her fashion sense. Suddenly she wanted to show him just how much of a woman she was. And she knew just the dress to prove it.

She checked on the party preparations and was headed to the mall by just after lunchtime. Hopefully, no one had bought that red dress. With it being two days before Christmas, it took her far longer than she would have liked to find a parking space. She walked to and through the mall at a quick pace as if someone might snatch the dress off the mannequin minutes before she arrived. Breathing a sigh of relief when she saw it still in the window, she entered the store. She went straight to the counter and waited in line. When it was her turn, she asked to try the red dress on.

"It's the last one we have," the saleswoman said as they made their way to the front of the store.

Melanie's heart plummeted.

"What size are you?"

She told her.

"I think you just might be in luck." The saleswoman smiled as she took the mannequin down and began undressing her.

A few minutes later, Melanie had the dress on and was smoothing it over her hips. She stepped outside the dressing room to look in a mirror.

"It's perfect," the saleswoman breathed.

Melanie turned one way and then the other. Smiling, she said, "It is, isn't it?" She studied her reflection. A dress was only the start. She touched her hair.

"Big Christmas party to go to?" the saleswoman asked.

"Yes. And I know this may sound like a strange question, but can you suggest some place where I can have my hair and makeup done? This afternoon?" She hated the desperation in her voice. Did the fact she was out of her element show?

"Let me make a couple of calls. My sister works at a hair salon here in the mall. The department store at the end does free makeovers if you buy makeup. I have a friend that works there."

"Thank you so much."

Melanie had the dress off and paid for by the time the saleswoman had finished her calls.

She came to stand beside Melanie. "They are both expecting you. Ask for Heather at the salon and she will introduce you to Zoe for your makeup."

On impulse Melanie hugged her. "Thank you so much."

"Not a problem. My pleasure. Merry Christmas," she called as Melanie walked away with a spring in her step.

The salon was only a few stores down. Heather, a girl of about twentysomething with a blue streak in her hair, was waiting on her. "Mary said you were on your way. What would you like to have done?"

Melanie hesitated for a moment. "I'm not sure."

"Well, since you're going to a party, why don't we try a few different ideas and see what you like?"

Melanie nodded and followed. Two and a half hours later, she'd had a wash, trim and style. It was classic and perfect for her. She'd even had her nails and toes polished while having a facial. Already feeling like a different woman, it was now time for the makeup. That item was way out of her comfort zone.

Heather walked her down to the department store and introduced her to Zoe. In no time, she had Melanie in a chair and was showing her a makeup regimen. Forty-five minutes later, Melanie left with her eyes looking smoky and sensuous, her cheekbones accented, and her lips a pouty red. In her hand was a bag of makeup goodies to try on her own. She had never felt better about her looks.

On the way out of the store she passed the handbags. Unable to control herself, she bought a tiny sparkling red evening clutch and decided she also needed a pair of shoes.

As she drove home a ripple of insecurity raced through her. Would Dalton like her new look?

Dalton scanned the lobby for Melanie as he strolled down the stairs. Thankfully his ribs had improved each day. Now he could take a breath without a sharp pain. It was a good thing because the vest he wore would have hurt otherwise.

As Melanie had disappeared around the corner to see about the party room earlier, Dalton went over to Mark, the man behind the desk, and asked for assistance renting a tux. He had been very helpful.

Now Dalton was dressed in formal wear and he couldn't locate his date.

A woman wearing a red dress stood in front of the fire with her back to him. *Must be one of the players' wives or girlfriends.* They were known for having glamorous women on their arms.

He scanned the area again. Team members were filing though the door and the lobby was becoming more crowded by the minute. Where was Melanie? She wasn't usually late. Maybe she was busy in the ballroom. He was almost to the bottom of the stairs when the woman turned around. His breath caught. This time his heart, not his ribs, hurt. *Melanie.*

He'd never seen a more beautiful or alluring woman. Her hair was pulled up on the sides, accentuating her high cheekbones. Her eyes were skillfully highlighted and there was a tint of red on her lips. She looked nothing like the no-nonsense Melanie he'd become accustomed to. No woman in the nightclub scene in South Beach could have looked sexier.

His blood ran hot. She was *his* date tonight.

Melanie walked toward him in barely there shoes the same color as her dress. He almost missed the last tread of the stairs. Heaven help him, every fiber of his being screamed to forget the party and take her up to his suite.

"Hi, Dalton," she said in a soft, unsure voice.

"You look beautiful." He couldn't take his eyes off her.

"Expecting me to be in one of my masculine suits?" There was a teasing tone to her question.

"Well, actually, yes. But I find this a very nice change." Far too nice. He was in trouble. She tempted him already but as this gorgeous vamp, he was a goner.

"Thank you. Shall we go to the party?"

Dalton offered his arm. "Yes. I'll have the prettiest woman there on my arm. Just remember who brought you."

She giggled.

It was the first time he'd heard her do that and it reminded him of bells tinkling. He planned to make her giggle again. Soon.

They walked across the lobby. With the image of Melanie in that red dress, he might start seeing the Christmas season differently. As they passed the front entrance a large man who could only be a player said, "Is that you, Doc?"

"Hi, R.J.," Melanie said.

The player stared at her. "It really is you, Doc. You look great."

A touch of pink brightened Melanie's cheeks. She stood so close, Dalton felt her stiffen. He squeezed her hand resting on his arm to reassure her. He was afraid she might bolt. She'd been invisible for so long, this amount of attention had to make her insecure.

"Thank you, R.J."

Dalton led her away and around the corner, following the other players and their women, who were dressed in festive clothes, down a wide hallway. They entered the darkened ballroom that twinkled with white lights. A huge Christmas tree stood in one corner, decorated in Currents colors and with Currents ornaments. Surrounding the dance floor were tables set for a meal with flickering candles and greenery in the center.

"Merry Christmas, Juice," Melanie said.

A quizzical expression came over the player's face. "Wow, Doc. You look sexy." Shock followed and his gaze dropped. "Uh, I'm sorry, Doc, I shouldn't have said that."

She smiled. "It's okay, Juice. Thanks."

"Why don't we get some seats at a table?" Dalton suggested.

"Okay." She led him to a table close to the dance floor. Another couple was already seated there. Dalton held the chair for Melanie and she sank into it. The man Dalton recognized as one of the trainers leaned across the table and leered at Melanie. "Doc Mel. Is that you? You look great."

"Thanks, David. Hi, Katie." Melanie introduced Dalton to both of them, then said quietly to Dalton, "This is embarrassing. I never would've worn this dress if I had known it would cause such a scene. Maybe I need to go change."

"You will not! You're a beautiful woman and it won't hurt to remind some of these people you aren't one of the guys."

She looked at him and smiled. "No, it won't."

The players and staff kept stopping by and speaking to Melanie. She seemed to take their admiration more in her stride as they commented on her looks. About thirty minutes after he and Melanie had arrived at the party, Rocket and Mitchell limped in with arms locked and their wives at their sides. There was a round of applause. The men smiled broadly and bowed.

Soon after, Leon Hyde walked to the middle of the dance floor. One of the hotel staff handed him a microphone. The crowd quietened.

"Welcome, everyone. I'll make this short and sweet so we can get down to the important stuff. Eating and dancing. Thanks for the part you play on the Currents team. You've gone above and beyond this year and we still have two more playoff games and the Super Bowl to look forward to. If they are anything like yesterday's, the road will be an exciting one. Enjoy your holiday and come back ready to work. Merry Christmas, everyone."

The crowd clapped. Soon afterward, the room became loud with conversation and music. Dalton and Melanie, along with the other couples at their table, lined up at the buffet to get their dinner.

They were still there when Melanie's father stopped to speak to them. "Mel, did you check on Rocket's test today?" he asked.

Dalton couldn't believe it. He was the first male in the room who hadn't commented on Melanie's appearance. Didn't he ever really look at his daughter?

"Yes," Melanie said.

"Well?"

He seemed impatient for her to expand on the answer, as if he were in a hurry to move on.

"Rocket needs to rest for a couple of days. Then I'll re-evaluate him," Melanie hedged.

Her father didn't look pleased with her answer. "He has to play. The team needs him."

"I understand."

Dalton's hand tightened on the plate he held. Did her father always pressure Melanie like this? What kind of situation had Melanie grown up in? He hadn't had parents around but she had, yet was her father really there for her? Maybe their childhoods hadn't been that dissimilar after all. The difference was that Melanie stayed connected to people while he chose to keep anyone he might care about at a distance. Could he have done something different?

Leon Hyde extended his hand to Dalton. "Dr. Reynolds, it's nice to have you join us tonight."

"Thank you. I appreciate Melanie inviting me. Doesn't she look amazing?"

Her father regarded Dalton as if he were unsure about what to say, then look at Melanie and offered, "Very nice."

What was wrong with him? Couldn't he see that Melanie was a beautiful young woman? Efficient, intelligent, capable, but a woman nonetheless.

When her father's attention was pulled away by another man, Dalton put a hand at her waist and gave her a light hug. "I'm hungry, how about you?"

She nodded and gave him a smile that didn't reach her eyes.

Melanie had excused herself to go to the restroom. She was making her way back up the hall on her way to the ball-room. A group of players and their dates stood outside the door. There they were able to talk without screaming over the music. As she approached, one of the players with his back to her said, "Can you believe Dr. Mel?"

"You're not kidding. I had to do a double take. I don't think I've ever seen her legs," another player added.

One of the women leaned in. "Hank talks about Doc Mel all the time. I always thought she was a he. After seeing her tonight I might be jealous."

Hank put his hand around her waist and pulled the woman close. "Hey, you don't have to worry about that. Everyone thinks of Doc Mel as one of the guys."

One of the guys. That was what she'd been, growing up. She'd even dressed the part. As an adult that hadn't changed. She had no idea she'd receive such a reaction by just wearing a dress and spending a little more time on her appearance.

She moved by the group unnoticed and stepped inside the room. There she stood to the side, watching the activity. The band had started playing and couples filled the dance floor. Other people talked in groups.

Dalton strolled toward her. He looked heart-stoppingly handsome in his tux.

"I've been looking for you."

That was all it took for her body to jumpstart to a hum.

"What's the most fascinating person in the room doing standing by herself?"

She gave him a bright smile. Dalton had always seen her as a woman. Even when he'd asked her about being a female team doctor. She'd never been one of the guys to him.

"She's waiting on the most handsome man in the room to ask her to dance."

Even in the dim light she could see his gaze intensify at her flirting. He took her hand securely in his and led her to the floor. A slow song had just begun. Dalton's arms circled her waist. Melanie placed her hands at the nape of his neck. His hair brushed against her fingers.

His mouth came closer to her ear. "You've been the talk of the party."

She looked at him. "I'm not sure I like that."

"That's because you've been hiding the fact you're a woman for too long."

He was right. She wouldn't be doing that any longer. Starting tonight.

Melanie stepped closer to Dalton, bringing her body against his. He tensed, then his arms tightened. He was warm. His breath brushed against her hair. She inhaled. *Dalton.*

The dance floor was crowded yet the only person she saw or heard was him. They were in their own world.

He kissed her temple. Her fingers teased his hair. Dalton brought his hips to hers. The ridge of his swollen manhood clearly made his desire known.

The song ended. He said, "Melanie, I think we'd better sit the next one out."

"I don't want to." Her hand caressed his neck.

"Neither do I but I don't want to embarrass you. If I continue to hold you I'm going to start kissing you and I'm not going to stop."

Melanie liked the sound of that, but she did have a reputation and position to consider. "Okay."

They returned to their table. When they were seated Dalton took her hand and held it beneath the table. A number of the players brought their wives over to meet her.

The party started winding down none too soon for her.

"Do you have to stay and see about anything?" Dalton asked.

"I just need to check in with the person responsible for handling the party."

"When you are done, how about joining me for a view of the falls at midnight?"

She whispered in his ear, "Are you wooing me to your room, Dr. Reynolds?"

Dalton leaned back and captured her gaze. "Only if you want to be."

CHAPTER EIGHT

MELANIE'S FIST HESITATED for the second time in the air as she prepared to knock on Dalton's door. Just a few evenings earlier she'd spent the night in this suite. This time her hand shook as she went back and forth with indecision. If she stepped over the threshold she was afraid her life would change forever. Maybe she was making too much of the importance. After all, Dalton had been nothing but a gentleman. Why would he be any different now?

They could have a friendly cup of hot chocolate and look at the view. He'd mentioned nothing more. But the way he'd touched her earlier said he wanted everything she would give. If she took this chance, could she stand the hurt if he promised nothing more? What if she didn't go in? Would she always wonder what could have happened between them? Know that she could have taken a chance on love and hadn't because she was too afraid? Feared rejection too much?

Her skin heated. Dalton's desire for her while they were dancing had been obvious. Being wanted was stimulating. He'd made her feel like a woman. Something she didn't know she'd been missing until he'd come into her life. Even if she were to have just this one night, she wanted it with Dalton. As a female she had power and she wanted to use it, revel in it and savor it. Loving Dalton was worth the risk to her heart. All she could do was open it. It was up to him to accept what she was giving. If he didn't, then she had at least tried.

With head held high, she rapped on the door. It opened a second later as if Dalton were standing on the other side, waiting for her knock.

"Hi." She suddenly had a longing to flee. But she wouldn't. She wanted this. She wanted him.

Dalton had removed his jacket and taken off his tie. His vest hung loose. Could a man look sexier?

"Come in. Hot chocolate is almost ready. I was waylaid by Rocket when I crossed the lobby. Took me longer to get up here than I planned."

"Rocket does that sometimes." They were having a pleasant everyday conversation. What had she expected him to do? Pull her into the room, take her in his arms and slam the door? And to think she'd stood outside like a nervous virgin. She was over that. "I'm going to sit down and take these torture devices off my feet. If you don't mind?"

"Make yourself at home."

The only light burning in the room was the one over the bar area. She took a chair in front of the window. Sitting, she worked to release the strap of her shoe.

"Here, let me do that." Dalton placed two mugs on a nearby table and sat in the other chair. "Give me a foot."

Melanie swiveled the chair toward him and lifted a leg. He cupped his hand behind her ankle and rested it on his thigh. With the nimble fingers of a man who did delicate work for a living, he undid the strap.

"Other one."

His no-nonsense tone had her relaxing back against the chair. "Now this is the life. Beautiful view, hot chocolate on a snowy day and a man at my feet." She giggled. That sounded nothing like what she'd intended to say. Too suggestive.

Dalton's hand ran across the top of her foot, no longer encased. She looked at him. Their gazes met and held. He brought her foot to his mouth and kissed her instep. Her breath caught. Her heartbeat went into overdrive. He reached for one of the mugs and handed it to her. "Just relax and let's enjoy the view."

She looked out at the falls but not for long. Her attention returned to Dalton. He was the better view. His profile in the dim light reminded her of a sculpture she'd seen in a European museum once. Her gaze followed the line of his forehead, along his nose, to his strong chin. She watched him so closely that she saw the movement of his mouth before he spoke.

"You're staring at me."

She looked at the falls. "No, I'm not."

"You were."

"Are you calling me a liar?"

Dalton wrapped both her legs with an arm and with his other hand he started to tickle the bottom of her feet.

"Stop!" She laughed.

"Admit you're a liar."

"I'm not." She chuckled again and tried to pull her legs away but he held on tighter, continuing to run his fingers over the bottom of her feet.

"You were staring at me. Say it—'I was staring at you.'" Dalton continued moving his fingers. She squirmed, causing her dress to inch up her thighs.

Melanie pulled at her hem, but it did little good. "I will not."

Dalton stopped and looked at her but still held her legs firmly. "You don't have to say it if you kiss me."

"That's blackmail!"

He cocked his head to the side and acted as if he was giving that statement a great deal of thought. "It is."

"You aren't worried about going to jail for coercion?"

He raised his chin and pursed his lips. His gaze captured hers. "You're not just any woman. So I'm willing to chance it."

"Okay, but you have to let me go."

"I don't think so." Dalton tugged her toward him. "I don't trust you." When she sat on the edge of the chair he reached an arm under her knees and one around her waist, then lifted her, bringing her to his lap. "Now it's time to pay for your lies."

He held her tightly.

Two could play this game. She shifted in his lap a couple of times, pulling on her dress as if she were trying to make herself decent. Done, she looked at him. His lips had thinned and his jaw was tight. He looked strained. She inwardly smiled.

Running her hands over his chest, she moved them up to his neckline. She slipped her fingers under the collar of his shirt. His intake of breath hissed. She brought her hands up to cup his face. Shifting again, her hip brushed against his hard length.

His eyelids lowered, hooding his eyes.

Melanie licked her lips. He groaned. She brought her face closer to his and whispered against his lips, "What was I supposed to say?"

Dalton's hands tightened on her waist as he growled, "Hell, it doesn't matter. Kiss me."

She did.

He gave her a moment of control before he seemed to lose his. His grip on her waist eased. One hand moved to the back of her neck. He pulled her lips more firmly into his. Melanie's hands went to his shoulders and gripped the fabric of his vest. Dalton eased the pressure as the tip of his tongue traced the seam of her lips. She opened her mouth and he thrust in.

Heat shot to her center. Blood pooled, hot and heavy.

Her tongue met his with a confidence she'd never imagined. The man's loving was dangerous and exhilarating.

His lips left hers and moved to nuzzle behind her ear. She purred with pleasure. She offered him more access and Dalton's lips traveled to her collarbone. There the tip of his tongue outlined its distance. His other hand cupped the top of her knee then went to the exposed expanse of her thigh. He lightly brushed her leg as his hand journeyed toward her hemline, teasing it before it went down her leg again.

Melanie turned her face and kissed him. Giving him lingering ones, then pressing her lips to his cheek before placing a kiss on his neck. Her fingers fiddled with the second button of his shirt until she had it open. She leaned over far enough for her lips to caress the skin visible in the V of his shirt.

He shifted, making her more aware of his length resting at her hip. His hand left her leg to cup her breast. She couldn't have stopped the sound of longing she made if she'd wanted to.

"Like my touch, do you?" His deep voice had taken on a raspy note.

His lips returned to hers as his hand slipped under the strap of her dress. When his fingers touched skin, she jerked.

"Shh," Dalton whispered against her lips. "You feel like warm silk."

Melanie relaxed. His hand at her waist slid up her back and pulled at the zipper. Slowly it came down as his lips found the ridge of her shoulder. With the zipper opened to the bottom of her shoulder blades, his hand returned to her neck. His fingertips tickled her skin as they trailed down her back. Melanie held her breath. Her skin was hot where he'd been, tingled where he touched and quivered in anticipation of his next move. She was a mass of sensations, all created by Dalton.

His mouth took hers in a honeyed kiss while his hand

nudged her dress strap down her arm. She wore no bra, so his fingers were free to follow the same path back. Dalton's hand brushed the slope of her breast and rested there. His mouth left hers to place kisses across her cheek to her temple as his hand cupped her breast. The pad of his thumb teased her nipple until it stood rigid.

"Perfect," Dalton murmured. Using one of his fingers he started at the top of her breast and followed the slope down to circle her tip.

Melanie moaned as heat filled her and her core contracted.

"I want to see you." Dalton's fingers returned to the dress zipper and pulled it completely open. Using a hand on her shoulder, he leaned her back, supporting her across his arm. It left her open and vulnerable. Her arm went around his neck. He pushed her dress strap from her arm until her breasts were free.

His sharp intake of breath made the blood flow to her breasts, making them tingle with heaviness. She relished the fact that Dalton found pleasure in what he saw.

He cupped her breast again. As if weighing and committing it to memory, he fondled and caressed until she wriggled.

"Baby, you're killing me." He lifted his hip. "Have compassion."

Her hand rested over his bulge. "What's wrong?"

Dalton's fingers left her breast to remove her hand and place it in her lap.

"Not yet. I want to enjoy more of you."

His hand went to her breast again and lifted. She watched as his dark head came down to capture her nipple in his wet, warm mouth. Her eyes closed in pleasure as she soaked in every ounce of sensation.

Dalton's tongue swirled around her nipple, drawing and teasing until she writhed with need. Her hand flexed and released in his hair. Dalton growled low in his throat. He released her breast and kissed her neck. His tongue flicked out to taste her.

How much more of this could she take before she was consumed by the fire he created and stoked deep within her?

Dalton dragged her other strap down her arm until her dress gathered at her waist, leaving her breasts completely defenseless to his manipulations. His mouth found the neglected breast and made it feel as appreciated as he had the other one.

Melanie ran her hands through his hair, encouraging every tantalizing movement of his mouth. She had the fleeting thought that she should have been embarrassed by her wanton position both on him and in front of a public window, but all she could comprehended was her body's reaction to Dalton's ministrations. She'd never felt more free or more like a woman in her life.

One of Dalton's hands went to her thigh and slid under the skirt of her dress. His fingers skimmed her inner thigh and moved away. Slowly his hand moved up to the edge of her panties. One finger slipped under. It traced the line of her underwear toward her throbbing core. His mouth continued to do wondrously delicious things to her breast.

His finger made slow tormenting motions. Her muscles tensed. She parted her legs in invitation. He took it and grazed the lips of her opening. The ache curling in on itself became tighter. Panting in anticipation, she waited. Dalton was bolder this time. He pushed into her opening at the same time he tugged and swirled his tongue around her nipple.

Melanie arched like a bridge in his arms. With the power of the water flowing over the falls, she burst. For spectacular seconds she remained suspended in bliss before slowly returning to reality. Dalton was there to catch her. His arms circled her waist and his lips touched the top of her head.

Dalton had done many things in his life that made him feel successful but none had given him more satisfaction than watching Melanie come apart in his arms. He'd lifted his lips from her breast just in time to see her head roll back onto his shoulder, her eyes close and her lips part as she found her piece of heaven.

He'd been afraid that she wouldn't come to his room. Feared how badly he wanted her to. Felt foolish standing by the door like a kid waiting to get into a candy store. What was happening to him? He managed to keep women in their place, at a distance where he felt no real emotion, then along came Melanie. She had his feelings so twisted, he could think of nothing but her. He'd learned long ago that to care meant hurt. He was afraid things between them had already reached that stage. Could he walk away now? Would he want to?

He gazed at her, reclined in his lap, and smiled. She was stunning.

"Dalton, kiss me," Melanie whispered with her eyes shut and the sigh of release still on her lips.

He wouldn't turn that request down. His mouth found hers. She returned a tender kiss that made him even harder than he would have believed possible. If he didn't have her soon he would explode.

His look met hers. Placing a hand on her stomach, he made small circles over satiny skin. "You are so amazing."

"You're not half-bad yourself." One of her hands went to the opening in his shirt. She flattened her palm against his skin.

He loved her touch. Something that simple from her excited him.

"It's my turn."

"Oh?" He raised a brow.

She released another button of his shirt and ran a hand over his ribs. "Does it hurt much?"

He shook his head. "Only when I'm punched."

Melanie looked at him with troubled eyes. "I'm sorry I forgot." She undid another button. "Maybe I can make it up to you." The last button of his shirt slid out of its hole. She pushed the fabric away, exposing his stomach and ribs.

She pressed her lips to his skin. His muscles quivered in reaction.

"Does it hurt here?" Her mouth touched a rib. "Or here?" She found his skin again. Moving farther around to his side, her tongue darted out.

He flinched in reaction.

With a sound of satisfaction, Melanie said, "This must be the spot." Her hand dipped beneath his shirt and caressed his side while she continued to kiss him. Her breasts rested against his chest as she kissed his damaged body.

She looked up at him. "Better?"

"No," he ground out. "Because that isn't the part of me in pain."

"So where's your problem? Maybe I can kiss it and make it better," she said in a teasing tone.

The thought of that happening had Dalton ready to take her on the floor. Melanie deserved better than that, especially with it being the first time between them. He gave her a nudge from behind and she stood.

He wasted no time in standing also. "Heavens, woman, are you trying to kill me?"

She looked unsure, standing there with her dress circling her waist and her hair tousled.

He cupped her cheek and gave her a caressing kiss. "If you were to give me a kiss where I hurt it would be more than I could stand. Hold your hands above your head."

"Why?"

"Melanie, you can trust me."

Her arms went up. Dalton took the hem of her dress and pulled it off over her head. He dropped the material to the floor. His gaze met hers and held for a few seconds before it traveled down to her breasts. They were high and the nipples taut. Unable to resist, he reached out and took one in his palm. Releasing it, he watched it bounce gently. He'd never been more fascinated. His gaze moved down to her barely there panties to follow the length of her legs. "You have gorgeous legs."

"Thank you."

"No, thank you for sharing them with me."

"You're starting to embarrass me."

"Why? I'm admiring you. You're beautiful and should be admired."

"That, and I'm standing here with almost no clothes on while you're still dressed."

He grinned and took her hand. "That problem's easily solved. Come with me."

Dalton led her across the living area to his bedroom. He turned off the light over the bar before he joined her. The only light came from the lamps shining around the falls. Shadows played over Melanie's body, making her appear otherworldly. Maybe she was. She'd certainly placed a spell on him.

He stopped beside the bed and released Melanie's hand. Taking hold of his vest and shirt, he started removing it.

"Let me help you." Melanie rested her palms on his chest and fanned them outward, pushing his clothing away. She continued over his shoulders and down his arms until the items were a pile on the floor. Coming closer, she reached for the button at his waist.

He stopped her movements with his hand over hers. She looked up at him with questioning eyes. His mouth came down to hers in a searing kiss she eagerly returned. His arms wrapped around her waist, bringing her against the ridge of his manhood. She rubbed against him. He wouldn't last much longer. He lifted her so that her feet didn't touch the floor and carried her the few feet to the bed.

Bending a knee, he laid her down on the comforter. Melanie looked at him with half-lidded eyes. She reminded him of a woman waiting on her lover in one of the old masters' paintings in the Louvre. All flesh, light and desire.

Dalton had every intention of being that lover.

His hands went to his pants button and released it and then the zipper in short order. He pushed his pants and underwear down at the same time. Stepping out of them, he stood.

Melanie's intake of breath made his chest swell. She liked what she saw. Just as she had when she'd been toweling him dry.

He moved to the bed and looked down at her. "Melanie, when I touch you again I will have to have you. I won't make any promise for the future. If you don't want that, it will kill me to let you go, but I will."

She leaned up. Taking his fingers, she tugged. "I want you. Even if it is just for tonight."

She understood him.

He came down over her, his mouth finding hers. She wrapped her arms around him and held him tight. As they kissed he pulled the covers back and then rolled to his side, taking her with him. He released her lips and said, "Crawl under."

As she brought her legs up, Dalton reached for her panties and pulled. "It's time for these to go."

Melanie lifted her hips and he slid the panties down and off her feet, throwing them to the floor. He flipped the covers over them and brought Melanie close. They lay facing each other. His gaze met hers. Her eyes were deep and luminous.

Unable to resist any longer, he glided a hand over the curve of her waist to her hip and across her behind. She blinked.

Melanie was perfect. He'd implied she should show off more of her body but now that it was his he didn't like the idea as much.

His? When had he started to think of her as belonging to him? The second she'd so freely found her release in his arms. He hadn't planned this. Hadn't been looking for it, but he would embrace it while he could…while it lasted.

She ran her hand over his shoulder and down his bicep to his elbow. The back of her hand floated over his stomach and lower. One finger trailed the length of him. His need had become a gnawing animal within him.

He leaned away and found his pants on the floor. Pulling his wallet out, he located the foil square and opened it. After covering himself, he rolled back into Melanie's arms.

She lay on her back and moved between his legs. His mouth went to her tempting breasts before he kissed his way to her mouth. Her arms circled his neck.

Melanie whimpered and lifted her hips, bringing his erection into contact with her wet and waiting center. He requested she open her mouth for him and her tongue intertwined with his.

Dalton flexed his hips and entered her. He pulled back and Melanie's fingernails dug into his shoulders. She would leave marks that he would carry proudly. He lunged again. This time taking her completely. She stiffened. He pulled away but didn't leave her. She opened her legs wider and moved with him.

"Look at me, Melanie."

Her eyes flickered open.

He raised himself up on his hands and thrust again and again. He had to control her. Her body quivered, then tensed before she fell apart beneath him. Dalton leaned down and kissed her softly on the forehead. She would have no doubt who had brought her to ecstasy.

With another deep thrust, Dalton found his rapture as well. Maybe she had the control after all.

Melanie woke to the toasty heat of Dalton against her side. She snuggled closer. The arm around her waist tightened. He'd awakened her during the early hours and made fast, hot, passionate love to her. Had she ever felt more alive?

She'd known other men, but none had such power over her with a single kiss or had created such a driving need to have him near. Mercy, the man knew how to love.

Love? That was what it had been with Dalton—lovemaking. She was in love with Dalton.

How had that happened? When he'd been so great with Rocket and Marcus? When he'd respected her boundaries? When he'd made his desire for her known more than once last night? It didn't matter when. It just mattered that it was a fact.

She loved him for standing up to her father, for knowing his own mind, for caring about sick children, for his sensitive care of Rocket—the list went on. But mostly she loved him because he saw her. The person. Not as a team member but as a woman, unique in her own right.

Melanie smiled to herself. Seconds later it slowly faded. She couldn't let him know. He'd made it clear that anything between them should have no emotional attachments. She was destined for heartache, but she would accept that when the time came.

She placed her arm over his at her waist and laced her fingers with his. Taking what she could while she could would have to be enough.

"Good morning, sleepyhead," he said in a raspy voice.

"I wouldn't be such a sleepyhead if someone hadn't woken me in the middle of the night."

His manhood, firm and long, stood against her hip. "I must not have done a good job if you are complaining about losing sleep."

"Now you're fishing for compliments."

He nuzzled her neck. "Maybe I need to convince you a little more that I rate praise."

"That's a good start." She turned to face him, interlinking her legs with his.

He chuckled, bringing a hand to her breast. "Why don't I start with...?"

Sometime later, with the sun streaming through the window and the roar of the falls outside, Melanie sat next to Dalton with a sheet pulled over her breasts, eating a grape off their room-service brunch. The sight of the sun was bittersweet. He would be leaving soon. He'd said nothing about how he felt about her. But he wouldn't; he'd made that clear. She was just a distraction while he was stuck in Niagara Falls. No way would she ruin what time she had with him by worrying about the future.

Dalton leaned over and kissed her bare shoulder. "What has you so deep in thought over here?"

"Just thinking that I've always wanted to wake up to this view of the falls."

"Have I been used?" he asked in an innocent tone.

"No more than you wanted to be."

He grinned. "I could have been used more."

"Now who is complaining?" She acted as if she were in a huff, planning to get out of bed.

Dalton took her hand, turned it over and kissed her palm. "I don't care the reason why—I'm just glad you're here."

Melanie melted. The man could charm a snake out of a basket without a flute.

"What do you have to do today?" Dalton placed their

tray on the floor and rolled toward her. The sheet slid low over his hips.

He seemed unaffected while her body heated. Did he have any idea how irresistible he was? Drawing her eyes away so she could concentrate, she said, "Nothing but a little more cooking for Christmas dinner preparations. The team has today, Christmas Eve and Christmas Day off. I don't have to be back to work until Friday."

"Great. Then we can spend the day together." He tugged at the sheet.

She held it tight against her. "That sounds nice to me."

"What would you like to do?"

The lump in her stomach eased. He wasn't talking about leaving. "If it was summer I'd say we should go out on the *Maid of the Mist*, but the river is too icy for that."

"Maid of the Mist?"

"The boat that goes out on the river and up close to the falls."

"I like the view from here." Dalton looked out the picture window toward the falls, then back at her. "This view is even better."

She leaned over and kissed his cheek. "I know what I'd like to do but I don't know if you would enjoy it. And it would be cold."

"What's that?"

"I'd like to go to the Festival of Lights and see the fireworks."

"That sounds like fun." Melanie's enthusiasm for the season seemed to be rubbing off on him. "If I may borrow your brother's clothes again."

"Of course." She gave him a quick kiss and started out of the bed, pulling the sheet with her.

"Where are you going?" He jerked the sheet out of her hands.

"Hey, give that back!"

"No."

"Why not?"

"Because I want to admire you walking across the room."

With great effort and heat on her cheeks, she strolled to the bathroom. Inside, she closed the door and leaned against it. Dalton was flipping her life over. She'd never lain around in bed with a man, and certainly not naked. But he had insisted that they have breakfast in bed. To walk in front of him, or any other man, without clothes on was far beyond her comfort zone. What would he have her doing next?

Minutes later she was in the shower soaping her body when the glass door was pulled open. He stepped in.

"Dalton!" This was another first—taking a shower with a man—one that thrilled and terrified her.

"Melanie."

"I'll be through in a minute."

"I thought I could help."

"Help?"

"Scrub your back. Then maybe you could dry me off." He wiggled his eyebrows.

"I don't think—"

He grinned. "Melanie, in some ways you're so naive. Turn around."

She did as he asked. "Why do you call me Melanie when everyone else calls me Mel?"

"Because everyone else does call you Mel. Melanie is a pretty name. A feminine name. It suits you." With soap in hand, he moved it over her right shoulder.

She turned around to face him with a smile on her face. "Thank you. That's the nicest thing anyone has ever said to me."

He slipped his arms around her and pulled her against his wet, slick body. As Dalton's lips came toward hers he said, "I meant every word."

CHAPTER NINE

DALTON WAS STILL reliving and looking forward to more hot passionate minutes in a shower with Melanie as they walked along looking at the bright flashing and twinkling lights of the Festival of Lights. Melanie was like a child, pointing and running from one place to the next in her excitement. Just watching her made him smile.

Melanie had managed to slip under his barriers. Being around her was infectious. She had a wide-open heart that embraced the young and old, the large and the small, no matter how much she had going on in her life. She had managed in a few short days to make him see the pleasure in life, find humor. Most of all she'd made him discover what he could receive in return if he trusted himself enough to open up to someone.

Melanie had a happiness in her that didn't seem suppressed by her childhood. She saw joy in a child's smile when he received tickets to a football game, or when one of the players called hello, or even in preparing supper for her family who paid her little attention. How did she come away with such a positive outlook? Could he have tried harder to fit in at his foster homes?

He had to admit the festival was rather fascinating with its blocks' worth of buildings, animal shapes and plants all outlined in lights. A number of them were synchronized to music. Even the falls' water and mist had been lit so it appeared to turn different colors. The season was beginning to grow on him.

It was past time for him to go home, but he wasn't ready. The practice was closed for the holiday and he could stay until after Christmas without ruining his schedule. A long-distance relationship would be difficult to maintain. Would they even have a chance or would she tire of him not committing? Would she be willing to even try?

They strolled hand in hand as they looked at the displays and discussed them. At a small café they stopped in to warm themselves with hot chocolate and a cookie.

"I'd like to go up on the Ferris wheel," Melanie said after taking a sip of her drink.

Despite the cold and snow, he couldn't deny her anything. Plus the idea of huddling under a blanket, looking at the falls and stealing kisses from Melanie high up in their own private world had its appeal. He had it bad. "That sounds like fun."

She put her hand over his. "I think you'll be impressed."

"It'll be nice just to be with you."

She smiled, stood and started putting on her coat. "Then let's go."

He laughed. "You're more eager to go out into the cold than I am."

Melanie leaned down and gave him a quick kiss on the lips. "Who knows, if you're nice I might keep you warm."

His body fired at the thought. He stood. "Is that a promise?"

"Come on and see." She pulled on her knit cap.

Dalton enjoyed the banter between them. He'd never had that with another woman. Somehow Melanie brought out the impulsive side of him. That part of his personality had been buried until now.

They walked the two blocks to where the Ferris wheel

turned. Each spoke and crossmember was decked out in white lights. After standing in a small line they were soon seated with a thick blanket over their laps and tucked around their feet. The chair rocked gently as they moved away from the ground. Melanie wrapped her arms around one of his, huddled close and laid her head on his shoulder. Dalton liked being the one she came to for comfort. Snowflakes drifted down around them. The lights grew smaller below them.

"Oh, look," Melanie whispered with amazement.

Dalton's gaze went to the falls, which were lit in the red and green of the season. "That is pretty amazing."

"I love it up here."

He kissed her.

"Hey, we better be careful—we might freeze together." She laughed.

"I wouldn't mind." He put his gloved hand over hers.

She clutched his arm tighter. "I wouldn't either."

They rode in silence for a few minutes, then Melanie said, "I can't believe tomorrow is Christmas Eve."

"I hadn't thought about it. I guess it is."

She shifted slightly and looked at him. "Would you like to come to dinner with my family tomorrow night?"

He'd never been very good at family celebrations. No real practice with them. He had no interest in being the odd man out. "I don't know. How would your family feel about me just showing up?"

"They'd be glad to have you. The more the merrier."

Something in him wanted to say yes while another part of him remained unsure. "Let me think about it. Christmas Eve isn't my favorite day of the year."

Melanie didn't say anything more for a few minutes. "Why not?"

"Because that's the day they took me from my mother and put me into foster care."

Her sniffle made him look at her. He brushed an icy tear

from her cheek. "Hey, don't cry. Now, I have this time with you to replace that memory."

She kissed him and didn't say anything for a while. "Will you tell me about it?"

He didn't want to talk about his past but he was one hundred feet up. There was no easy way out.

"My parents were drug addicts." Her fingers pressed his arm in encouragement.

"My father went to jail a couple of months after I was born. When my mother went to prison, I didn't have anyone else to take care of me and I went into foster care. My foster parents tried, but I didn't fit in. I liked books. I was smarter than the other kids. And they knew it. I wasn't any good at what they liked to do. So I spent most of my time by myself."

"You said the other children liked to do things? Like what?"

"Like football, baseball, whatever game was in season."

"Oh. They must have made fun of the boy who read all the time."

"They did, but that's just how kids are. I understand that now. By the time I entered high school I was no longer that awkward kid anymore, but by then I was more interested in earning money to go to college than I was in playing sports."

"The kids called you names, didn't they? That's why you don't like nicknames."

Melanie was too smart. "It is."

A boom and the opening bulb of colored sparks raining down against the black sky drew their attention.

"Fireworks," Melanie said in awe.

Another round of light flashed in the night as they continued in a slow circle. Dalton placed his arm around Melanie's shoulders and pulled her close. They said nothing. Occasionally a soft "Oh…" came from her.

Talking about his past had been difficult, but sharing it with Melanie seemed to lift a weight from him. He appreciated the moments, just as he had when he'd spent time looking at the falls with her. Just being with Melanie seemed peaceful. He would miss that when she was no longer around. The thought saddened him more than he wished to admit.

He couldn't have planned it more perfectly when the grand finale of the fireworks went off as they came to the top of the wheel. Afterward they descended to unload. Offering Melanie his hand, she placed hers in his and stepped out.

"That was wonderful," she said. "Thanks for taking me up."

Dalton smiled. "You're right—it is fun. And I think you're the one who took me."

"You might be right. Uh, about dinner. Just know you're welcome. I'd like for you to be there, but only if you want to be. I can always bring you leftovers."

Dalton squeezed her hand. It might not be that bad to spend Christmas Eve with Melanie's family. They were an important part of her life. And she had become important to him.

They headed in the direction of where Melanie had parked the car.

"I didn't mean to put a damper on the evening by telling you my life's story," Dalton said after they had walked a block.

She took his arm again and hugged it close as they continued on. "No damper. I was just thinking about how much I would enjoy a hot shower."

"That sounds great. Mind if I join you?"

"I'd be mad if you didn't."

Melanie enjoyed their shower as much that night as she had earlier. Adding to the pleasure, she'd been toweled off by Dalton and she'd returned the favor. Now it was morning and she lay next to him, listening to his even breathing as he slept. He'd woken her in the early hours of the day and made love to her again. Instead of feeling tired, she felt invigorated. The man held a sweet power over her that she had no complaints about. Other than it wouldn't last.

A finger brushed the spot where her hip and leg joined. She looked at Dalton. His eyes were still closed but there was a hint of a smile around his lips. She made a move toward the edge of the bed. A hand clasped her wrist.

"Oh, no, you don't." Dalton tugged her back to him.

"I have to get going. I've dinner to finish. And I need to bake a cake."

"That can wait." He kissed the curve of her shoulder.

"I don't think so. I've already stayed in bed far too long." She tried to remove her hand from his grasp.

"What if I agree to help you? That would give you time for…" Dalton trailed off with a suggestive look at the bed.

"Don't tempt me."

His hand released her wrist and ran up her arm. "That's exactly what I'm trying to do."

"Well, as enticing as the invitation is, I'm going to have to take a rain check. I really must get moving."

"If I can't lure you into staying, then I guess I just need to go with you. Maybe if I help I can have a second helping of dressing."

Joy filled her. "You're coming to dinner?"

"Yes, thank you for the invitation."

She smiled widely. "Wonderful. I want my brothers and their families to meet you. I would have hated knowing you were spending Christmas Eve alone."

"Wouldn't you have stopped by afterwards?"

"Absolutely."

He gave her a long slow kiss. "That's nice to know."

Hours later she and Dalton unloaded food from her car and carried it into her father's house. He'd called while they were at her condo to tell her that he was at the office and would be there in time for dinner. Her brothers and their families would be arriving soon. One had flown in and the other two were driving. Dalton had questioned her about their arrival, but he'd said nothing about the fact the airport was open.

"Just put it down wherever you can find a spot in the kitchen," Melanie said over her shoulder as she carried the dressing into her father's house.

Melanie glanced around the living area as she walked through on her way to the kitchen. Her father had a simple ranch-style home that was large enough to hold the entire family. It was done in dark colors with pictures of her father with teams he'd coached on the wall. Autographed footballs set under glass in several places. Thanks to the maid that came weekly, the place looked clean and tidy.

Every home she'd lived in growing up had looked very similar to this one. There was a marked contrast between her condo and her father's. There was nothing in her place that said she was a sports fan. Her personal space was warm and feminine, right down to the yellow throw pillows on her sofa.

Dalton followed her in and put the turkey on the counter. "I'll go get the rest of the dishes while you get things together in here."

"Thanks, Dalton. You're a great help."

He was. She was so used to doing everything by herself she'd never realized how much work it was.

"No problem. By the way, did I tell you how nice you look?"

"Thank you." He knew how to make a woman feel like a woman. In and out of bed.

She didn't have much hanging in her closet that she considered superfeminine. After searching long enough that Dalton called from the other room that he'd loaded the car, she'd decided on a blouse in a silk fabric, a sweater with pearl buttons she'd pushed to the back of the closet and her most fashionable shoes. At Dalton's look of appreciation she had no doubt she'd made the right choices.

Melanie closed the refrigerator door after putting the congealed salad inside and walked over to him. Going up on her toes, she kissed him. "You look nice yourself."

His hands tightened around her waist. She stepped back despite the longing to move closer. "I still have a lot to do and you're a distraction."

Dalton let her go. "Then I guess you better give me a job so I won't be tempting you."

"Okay. You can see about getting the plates, napkins and silverware set up on the table. We'll eat buffet-style. There are far too many of us to fit around Coach's table."

"Why do you call your father Coach? You did that at the party." Dalton looked at her with an odd expression.

"I guess that's all I really ever heard him called, so I started doing it also."

"Your father was okay with that?"

"I think he likes it, actually."

"If I ever have kids, they will call me Dad or Daddy."

What she'd seen of his interaction with kids, he'd make an excellent daddy.

Over the next half an hour she gave Dalton directions, and he followed them to the letter. It would be her guess that he didn't often relinquish control to others. It impressed her that he was willing to do it for her.

The outside door burst open and a gush of freezing air announced her oldest brother, Mike. "Hey, Mel. How's it going?"

Melanie squealed and stopped what she was doing to hug him, his wife, Jeanie, and their three children. "Mike, Jeanie, kids, I'd like you to meet Dr. Dalton Reynolds."

"You can call me Dalton." He extended a hand to Mike.

"Nice to meet you, man," Mike said. "Mel, you don't even have the TV on. What about the game?"

Mike took a seat in front of the huge TV in the living area. Jeanie came to the kitchen to help her, and the kids went to join their father. Dalton stood nearby with a bemused look on his face. A few minutes later, her youngest brother, Jim, came in with his wife, Joan, and not far behind him was her middle brother, Luke.

"Hey, guys, doesn't Mel look great? I don't know if I've ever seen you dressed so…girly," Luke said.

She gave him a slap on the forearm, then circled his neck with her arms, giving him a hug. "Good to see you too. Thanks for the compliment, I think."

Dalton looked more uncomfortable as her family grew. Had she made a mistake by asking him to come? The situation could quickly become overwhelming. While her sisters-in-law were busy in the kitchen, she slipped away to speak to him.

"Hey, how you holding up?" Melanie asked as she came up beside him where he leaned against the wall, observing the men watching the football game.

"I'm fine."

"They can be a little, uh, overpowering."

He nodded as the entire male part of the family jumped up when something happened on the TV.

She slipped her hand into one of his and squeezed.

He smiled. "Yeah, but they seem like really nice guys. I'm glad I've gotten to meet them."

Melanie let go of Dalton's hand, not wanting her family to start asking twenty questions about their relationship. Melanie wasn't sure she could answer any of them. She had no idea where she and Dalton were headed. He'd said he only did short-term. If it was up to her she'd do whatever it took to make it work between them. She'd had a full life before Dalton arrived, she thought, but now that he was in it, she wanted more. Her only hope was that when he left town, it wasn't for good.

About that time her father came through the door. Everyone but her and Dalton lined up to either hug or shake hands and slap each other's backs in welcome. With that done, her father stepped over to them. "Glad you could make it, Dr. Reynolds. Mel, I guess you have everything ready."

"Yes. It'll be on the table at halftime."

"Good." He went to join the others, who had returned to the game.

Dalton looked at her in astonishment. "Do you always plan meals around football games?"

"Not always. But this year there's a special Christmas Eve game on." Why did she feel as if she needed to apologize? She looked at her family. Was their world too wrapped up in the sport?

One of her sisters-in-law insisted they turned the TV off completely while they had their meal. There was moaning and groaning, but when all the grown females agreed the TV went black.

While she and Dalton were standing in line waiting to serve their plates, Mike said, "So, Dalton, you're the guy our sister spent the night with?"

"Mike!" Melanie shrieked in embarrassment. Did he know about the past few days?

Dalton looked at her and grinned. "Yes, that was me."

"Dalton!"

He shrugged his shoulders. "Hey, I'm just telling the truth."

Mike laughed.

"Yeah, Dad told us about you getting hit by Juice. I've played against him and I'm impressed you're out of hospital," Jim said with a chuckle.

"Thanks for taking care of our kid sister." Luke wrapped

an arm across her shoulders and squeezed. "We couldn't do without her."

"You're welcome," Dalton said. "She is pretty special."

"We would agree with that," said her brother from the other side of the table.

She and Dalton found places to sit beside each other on one of the two large couches. They held their plates in their laps. What room there was at the dining room table was given to the children.

"So, Mel, you going to sign off on Rocket playing on Sunday?" Jim asked.

She sat close enough to Dalton to feel him tense. Why had Jim brought up that subject?

"We—" she indicated Dalton "—still need to assess him again."

Her father returned from refilling his plate. "Mel's a team player. She'll see that Rocket is on the field."

Melanie felt Dalton's gaze on her, but she said nothing. She shifted on the couch cushion. Was she a team player anymore? Had she ever been? Maybe she'd just been playing the part her father wanted her to?

With the meal over as well as the game, everyone gathered around the tree. Presents were distributed. Melanie watched the look of shock on his face when her niece said, "Dalton. Who's Dalton?"

Her mother said, "Dr. Reynolds."

"Oh." Her niece carried the small present to Dalton.

He looked at Melanie.

She smiled. "Everyone gets a present under our tree."

"But I didn't—"

"That doesn't matter. Open it."

Dalton pulled the paper off and lifted the top. He reached down and picked up the lapel pin depicting the waterfall with "Currents" written across it. A smile spread across his face.

"Something to remember us by," Melanie said. She really meant *remember her by*.

"Thank you. I can't tell you the last time I got a Christmas present. I'm sorry I didn't get you anything."

She leaned close. "I'll take a kiss later."

He captured her gaze. "You can count on that."

Soon after the presents were all opened, her brothers and their families left to stay in rooms at the Lodge. She and Dalton were loading the last of the dishes into her car when her father said, "Mel, I've called a press conference for the day after tomorrow at nine a.m. I'll expect you to be there to reassure everyone about Rocket."

"Coach, I still need to reevaluate him." She wished she'd sounded firmer.

"Then have it done before the press conference."

"Mr. Hyde, with all due respect, I don't think it's in Rocket's best interest to even consider playing."

"Dr. Reynolds, I appreciate you coming all the way up here and I'm sorry that you've had such a difficult and long stay, but you've given your opinion. Mel has the final say as the team doctor."

When Dalton started to say more she placed a hand on his. "It's Christmas Eve. Let's not get into this tonight. Day after tomorrow will be soon enough."

Her father said, "Mel, I've taught you what's expected when you're a member of a team."

Melanie knew that all too well. *Do what's best for the team.* She resented the pressure he was applying. Was uncomfortable with Dalton seeing how her father treated her. Maybe she should be a team player and go along. She always had before. No, she couldn't face Dalton or herself if she didn't do what was best for Rocket. Disappointing her father would be hard, but lowering her medical and personal standards would be worse.

She kissed her father on the cheek. "Merry Christmas, Coach." The words were flat, even to her own ears.

Dalton said little on their drive back to her house and neither did she. The proverbial two hundred and fifty–pound football player in the car kept them quiet. That was pressure of its own. Now she felt as if her father was pulling her one way and Dalton the other. They carried in the dishes with few words spoken. Melanie went to the kitchen and started putting leftovers into storage containers.

"I'm glad you came tonight," she said as she cleaned out the dressing pan. She meant it, but would he ever be the kind of guy that would enjoy going to her family's get-togethers? "I know my family can be a bit much."

Dalton moved away from where he stood looking at her Christmas tree and came to stand on the other side of the bar facing her. "I'm glad I went. I better understand you."

She met his gaze. "How's that?"

He shrugged. "Just that now I know why you work with a professional football team but spend your days off at a children's hospital. Or why you were so surprised at the party the other night that they thought you are an attractive woman. And why you are letting your father manipulate you into doing something you know isn't right."

"My father is not manipulating me."

"You don't call what he said tonight manipulation? Your reaction was to say nothing. Classic control method. You didn't even tell him there's a good chance that Rocket will not play."

"I don't know that for sure." She was starting to get annoyed.

Dalton's chin went down and he gave her a look that said, *You have to be kidding.* "Oh, come on Melanie. You do too. You know as well as I do that it isn't in Rocket's best interest to play. You called me in as an expert when you already knew he shouldn't play. But you are letting you father push you into believing differently. It's more important to win than for a man to maintain his health and mobility. What it boils down to is, you want to make your father happy so he'll notice you."

"How dare you?" The spoon she held fell from her fingers and clinked on the floor. She ignored it. Anger fired in her chest.

"I dare because…"

"Because why?"

"It doesn't matter. It doesn't take much to see that your father has always treated you as one of the guys in your family instead of a daughter who needed a father's attention. That extends to your professional life and now he sees you as a puppet he can manipulate."

That was how her ex-boyfriend had treated her when he was trying to get a job with her father. She'd been his puppet for months. When he didn't get what he wanted he threw her away. Her fingers gripped the edge of the counter. "That's not true!"

"I disagree."

She hated the calm smug way he spoke to her.

"If I was willing to bet, I'd put my money on it that it wasn't your idea to become the team doctor."

He was right. It hadn't been. She wanted to be a pediatrician.

"I'm right. I can see it on your face. You care too much about what your family expects. Your father is so focused on football he hardly recognizes you as the wonderful, remarkable woman you are. In many ways you're guilty of fostering that. You wanted to be a pediatrician but did what would keep you included by the family and noticed by your father. You're a caring and bright doctor with a large heart, and you are all woman when you let it show. Stand up to your father. Stand up for Rocket and yourself."

Dalton watched as Melanie stood straighter. She glared

at him. The wild look in her eyes said he'd pushed too far. He'd almost told her he cared for her, but if she rejected him, he didn't know if he'd recover. Having gone years without letting someone have that kind of power, he couldn't risk doing so now.

"How dare you presume to tell me how a family works? You know nothing about family dynamics."

He flinched. She was cutting deep.

"What qualifies you to judge mine?" she all but spat.

He held up a soothing hand. "You're right—I don't know about families. But what I do know is medicine and knees. If you let your father or anyone else on the Currents staff pressure Rocket to play on Sunday, they are wrong. He could damage his leg permanently."

"But we don't know that for sure."

"I do."

"How, Dalton? Because you're the go-to man for leg injuries? Because you are all-knowing and all-seeing. You're not any better than you think my father is. You want to oversee every decision. Be the final word. You're so used to being right or having the ultimate say that you can't stand the thought that someone might disagree with you or want to do it differently."

"I'll have you know that I always put my patients first." Dalton stepped back. He was starting to lose control of the conversation and Melanie.

"And I always put my players first. Still, it's not as cut-and-dried as you think it is. You have a practice where you're the king of the mountain. You've spent all your life standing alone. Trying to prove to yourself and others that you're worthy of being wanted, or asked to join the team. Even when you could have been chosen you remain by yourself. You are so afraid of being rejected you are scared to let go. So don't tell me about what I should do when you have no idea what it's like to carry so many others on one decision."

What she said smarted.

"I think I should leave before either one of us says something they might regret."

"That figures."

"What?"

"Running and hiding when it gets too hard. Anytime you lose the upper hand or feel the situation slipping out of your control you leave. Is that what you have been doing all your adult life? That way you don't have to worry about ever feeling like you did as a kid. Of all people, you're the one telling me to stand up to my father. But you haven't left your past behind. It follows you like a chain with a ball attached. You even made it clear that what was between us would be only temporary because you were afraid you might feel too much. Might have to stay in one place and commit.

"You're highly successful, top in your field, yet you still think like the little boy who wasn't picked to play ball. You fear that anyone you have a real connection with will turn you away. Not want you. No one likes to be rejected. I certainly didn't."

"How is that?"

She glared at him. "My old boyfriend used me to get a job with my father. When I said I wouldn't help him, he dumped me. Everyone gets rejected, so don't think you are so special in that regard. How others feel and act isn't under your control. You're afraid they will disappoint you or hurt you. You don't give them a chance to show you anything different. It's time to trust you're worth having."

Now she was starting to throw mud. "Don't take the high road here, Melanie. I may have to be in control because of my past, but you're controlled in the present. I'm not sure one is better than the other. You think I can't say what I feel, but I can." He pointed to her and back to himself. "There is something special between us."

Her eyes widened.

"Don't act so surprised. You know as well as I do that what has happened over the last few days is rare between a couple. I wanted us to figure out how to make it work. Now I think that's not possible until you can make a decision for yourself, out from under you father's thumb."

"And I think you need to revisit your past so you can face the future. Learn to be a part of a relationship wholeheartedly. Find value in yourself, not through your profession."

Dalton shook his head. "I'm sorry things ended this way between us. It's not what I had hoped for. I'll call for a taxi and wait at the store down the street."

It took a few seconds before she sighed, then said, "Don't do that. I'll drive you to the Lodge." She walked to the coatrack.

He didn't argue. The idea of walking down the street in the cold did nothing to improve his spirits. They rode in silence to the Lodge. Dalton was afraid to say more for fear he'd make the situation worse. Melanie pulled to a stop at the front door.

He climbed out. "Goodbye, Melanie."

"Goodbye, Dalton."

CHAPTER TEN

MELANIE TOOK A deep breath and adjusted the collar of her shirt. Looking into the mirror in the bathroom of her office one more time, she saw only the red rimming her eyes. Hopefully the cameras wouldn't be on her that long. She had the press conference to get through, then she would have a few days to compose herself before the game. And she would collect herself—she had to.

It had been the longest drive of her life back to her condo after dropping Dalton off. Back home, she'd not even stopped to finish storing the leftovers from dinner. Instead, she'd gone straight to her bathroom and turned on the shower. Climbing in, she'd let her tears flow with the water until it was cold.

How had things turned so ugly between her and Dalton? She'd never spoken to another person with such venom before. Why him? Because she cared so much.

She'd called the Lodge the next morning, asking for him. Mark was on duty and he told her that Dalton had already left for the airport.

Christmas morning. Merry Christmas. He must have been really angry with her.

Melanie had spent the rest of the day vacillating between wallowing in pity and eating every piece of candy she could find. By the middle of the afternoon, she'd called her father and told him she wouldn't be by, but would see him at the press conference. With her brothers in town, she wouldn't be missed.

She went over her conversation with Dalton again and again. Their upbringings had been miles apart—him by himself and her with people to answer to all the time. They were too different to understand each other. But they had no trouble communicating in bed. So much so that she missed him with a pain that was almost breathtaking. Surely with time that would ease. If it didn't, she had no idea how she would survive.

Now it was time to put on a happy face to the sports world. She'd done a few press conferences but they still weren't her idea of fun.

A knock came at her office door. "Hey, Doc, Mr. Hyde sent me down to tell you it's time."

"Thanks, I'm on my way."

Her father was eager for this press conference to go his way. There hadn't been time to do new tests on Rocket. She had spoken to him earlier that morning and he'd said his leg felt fine.

Ten minutes later Melanie was sitting at a table in front of the press with her father, Rocket and Coach Rizzo.

Her father started the conference by making a statement about his hopes for victory on Sunday. "And now we will take a few questions."

The people in the room all started talking at once. "Dr. Hyde, Dr. Hyde."

Her father recognized the man.

Melanie forced a smile. "Yes?"

"What is your professional opinion regarding Rocket playing this Sunday?"

She took a deep breath. "Rocket has been resting his leg. Closer to game day, I will put him through a battery of tests and make the final decision about whether he plays or not."

Her father leaned toward the microphone, "All plans are for Rocket to be on the field Sunday. I'm sure you agree, Dr. Hyde."

She couldn't believe that her father was now putting words in her mouth on national TV. Could he undermine her professionally any more effectively?

It seemed to take forever for the press conference to end. She spoke to Rocket, telling him she wanted to see him in her exam room in thirty minutes, and she left.

Dalton had been right. She was letting her father push her around about Rocket and that had to stop today. Back in her office, she called her father's secretary and asked to see him that afternoon.

Rocket showed up on time and she did her exam. She sent him for an X-ray and told him to spend some time with the trainers working on the machines. Rocket seemed up-beat and talked of nothing but playing in the game. Tension and excitement filled the building with everyone in high spirits about the Currents' chances of winning.

At the time slot Melanie had been given, she arrived at her father's office. She was announced over the phone by his secretary. Her father waved her into a chair in front of his desk as he continued his phone conversation. Just like at his home, football memorabilia filled every shelf. There were a few old pictures of her brother's children but nothing of the entire family together or of her.

A few minutes after she'd arrived, he hung up and said, "Mel, I think the press conference went well."

"Coach, that's what I want to talk to you about."

"Is something wrong?"

"I wish you hadn't said Rocket would be playing on Sunday. It isn't a sure thing. It's my job to make those determinations. I would appreciate it if you wouldn't put words into my mouth."

Her father leaned forward in his chair and gave her a

pointed look. "And my job is to keep the franchise making money. Part of that is putting the correct spin on the situation. I want Rocket on the field. Give him steroid shots, pain relievers—I don't care what. But it's your job to see that he plays."

"That's where you are wrong, Coach. It's my job to see that the players remain in good health. That their lives now and later aren't put in jeopardy. I can't stand by while anything different happens."

"You will do as you are told."

Dalton had called it. She'd been so caught up in being noticed by her father she'd compromised who she was. She blinked. But no more. She would no longer be anyone's puppet. It was time for a drastic change. One that was overdue.

"Father—" at her use of that unfamiliar address he cocked his head and gave her a questioning look "—I won't."

"Mel—"

"It's Melanie."

"What has gotten into you?"

"Nothing that shouldn't have happened sooner. I won't agree to Rocket playing on Sunday or any other Sunday until next season. His leg will not improve enough in the next few days for him to play. I'm not going to sign off on him. Dr. Reynolds was right and I should have agreed with him when he gave his opinion. The team will have to win without Rocket."

"Mel, you are part of the team. You need to act like a team member."

"No, Father, I need to do what is best for Rocket and that is for him not to play."

Her father stood. "This is more than just about one person."

"That's where you are wrong. It is about a person. You never have seen the individual. It has always been about the team—in your professional and private life. I no longer want to be a part of a team. I want to be your daughter. That is all. I love medicine but I have always wanted to work with kids. I'm thankful for all you have done for me but it's time for Melanie Hyde to be herself. I'll be turning in my resignation after the season is over."

"Mel, I think you should give this more thought." His voice rose.

"No, sir, I think that's the problem. I've been using my head instead of my heart for too long. I'm going with my heart now."

"Mel—"

"Melanie, please."

Her father's face had turned red. "Melanie, we'll talk again when you're more rational."

"I won't be changing my mind about Rocket or leaving. I love you, Father, but it's time for me to live the life I choose. Not the one chosen for me."

Her father wore a perplexed look on his face as if he hadn't comprehended a word she'd said. His phone rang and, to his credit, he paused a second before he answered it. As he did, she left the office.

Dalton flapped the file he'd been reviewing down on his desk. It had been two weeks since he'd left Niagara Falls. It was a new year but it hadn't been a good one. He missed Melanie to a degree he would have never thought possible. It was almost a physical pain that didn't seem to ease.

He fingered the file he'd just put down. It was Josey Woods's—one of the patients he and Melanie had seen on the day they went to the children's hospital. His colleague had spoken to him about Josey being a good candidate for a new procedure they were doing on children her age with long-term bone malformation. The only complication was her recent chemo. When she was far enough out, they would bring her in for the surgery. Josey was just one more reminder of Melanie. As if he needed one.

As soon as he had returned to the Lodge, he'd called to see if he could get a flight home. There had been one early the next morning. More than once he'd started to call Melanie but had pushed Off on his phone. As he'd watched her interaction with her family he'd felt her pain that they took her for granted. Worse than that—how could a man pretend to care about Melanie to get to her father? She deserved better. He was furious on her behalf.

What if he and Melanie had tried to make it work? Their backgrounds were so far apart, would they have made it a month, six, a year? Would he have ever fit into her family? Yet he and Melanie had been so close. Their bodies in sync with each other.

She'd accused him of running away. Maybe he had but he needed a chance to think. Give her space as well. It was time he went home anyway. He'd opened himself to her more than he had to anyone in his life. Even gone so far as to tell her he cared about her on a level he didn't clearly understand at the time. He'd returned to the world he knew and understood, yet he was out of control. Something was missing. That something was Melanie.

He'd unfastened the part of his heart he'd guarded so carefully for so many years and let her in. She'd ended up capturing his entire heart and he'd left it behind in Niagara Falls with her. He couldn't deny it. He'd fallen in love with Melanie.

But even that knowledge didn't make his life any better—if anything, it made it worse. He'd told her it was up to her to come to him. She had to break away from her father. See herself as Dalton did. As a strong woman who was special in her own right, not because she was just part of a group. It was for her own good. He only hoped she realized it before the pain of losing her killed him.

He'd watched the game on Sunday for two reasons. One—to see if Melanie agreed to let Rocket play. And the other—to see if he could catch a glimpse of her. To his displeasure, he hadn't seen Melanie. To his frustration and disappointment, Rocket was dressed in his game uniform ready to play. The sports announcers said that Rocket was being held in reserve in case he was needed. If the team fell behind, he'd be sent in. Because the Currents were winning for most of the game, Rocket never had a chance to play. The announcer went on to say that they were saving Rocket's leg for the Super Bowl. Still, Melanie must have given her okay for him to play or he wouldn't have been on the sideline in his uniform. Nothing had changed.

The Currents won the game, but Dalton didn't see it as a victory.

Now, he looked out the window of his second-floor office at the top of a palm tree that blew gently in the south Florida breeze. A statement that Melanie had made during their argument continued to haunt him. She'd said he needed to face his past, make peace with it so he could understand relationships. Was that what he'd been doing all these years—hiding from people? If his affair with Melanie was an example, hiding might have been a good thing. If you let go and showed weakness you could get hurt.

In his adult life he'd made sure he was always in control. While he'd been in Niagara he'd not had that luxury and he'd never been happier. Did he want to go back to being the old Dalton? Now that he knew what it felt like to have someone care about him, and to care about them in return, he wasn't so sure.

If Melanie came looking for him, would he be the man she wanted if he didn't reconcile with his past?

Three days later he turned right into the street where he'd lived when he was ten and eleven. He'd already visited two places of the five where he had lived as a child. One of the houses had been boarded up and the other had a different family living in it. He hadn't expected to speak to anyone when he'd started his road trip northward to a town in central Florida, but something pushed him to knock on the door.

Dalton drove slowly down the street, watching for the all-too-familiar yellow house in the middle of the row. He pulled to the curb across from it. Toys still littered the yard. There was a car in the drive. Someone must be home. What was gone was the empty lot next door where everyone had gathered to play. Did his foster parents still live here?

He climbed out of his car and started toward the house. Some of his hardest years had been spent here. This was where he'd lived when he'd made up his mind he would be a doctor, make something of himself and leave who he had been behind. He'd managed to do that until Melanie came into his life.

Standing on the porch, he knocked on the screen door. He waited a few seconds and knocked again. The shuffle of feet came from inside and then the door was open a crack.

"Can I help you?"

"Mrs. Richie?" Dalton asked, peering through the screen to see the old woman's features.

"Yes."

"I don't know if you remember me, but I'm Dalton Reynolds. I lived here for a while. I was one of your foster kids."

She pushed the screen door open. "Dalton Reynolds! Of course I remember you. How're you doing?"

"I'm fine. I'm a doctor in Miami."

"Do tell. But I'm not surprised. I always knew you would make it. You were a tough one. Come in and tell me about yourself."

She turned and headed down the hall he remembered as longer and wider. Not given a choice, he followed her to the kitchen. It hadn't changed much. Some of the appliances looked new, but otherwise it was the same.

"Have a seat, Dalton. I'll get us some iced tea." She went to the cabinet and pulled two glasses out.

Dalton sat in the chair he had as a child. It creaked, just as it had then.

Mrs. Richie walked to the refrigerator, removed a pitcher and filled the glasses. She came to the table and placed one in front of him and the other down next to the chair she eased into.

"It's nice to hear you're so successful." She took a sip of tea.

"Why? You didn't think I would be?"

"Heavens, no. I could see you were smart. You made good grades even though you were so unhappy. You didn't let that stop you."

He met her look. "You knew I was miserable?"

"I could tell from our talks you were unhappy. I knew how the other kids treated you."

"Why didn't you do something to stop it?"

"Because it would have only made it worse. If I had stepped in for you every time it would have been harder for you when I wasn't around. I had confidence you would find a way around it. You did. You concentrated on being a good student."

"I read all the time."

"You did. I knew you were trying to escape, so I saw to it that there were plenty of books around on your level and above."

And there had been. Dalton had never questioned why there was a steady stream of books available to him. Or why Mrs. Richie loaded everyone up to go to the library every Saturday when he was the only one willing. In her own way she had given him a wonderful gift.

"But I didn't have any friends."

"That's why I suggested to your caseworker that you might be better off moving to another home. I could see things were getting hard for you around this neighborhood."

He'd seen the move as a betrayal when she'd been trying to help him. Life had been better for him in the next home. He'd stayed there until he'd graduated from high school. "Thank you, Mrs. Richie."

"You're welcome. Now tell me about your life. Do you have a wife and children?"

"No. But I hope to soon." Dalton spent the next few minutes telling her about himself. When he left, she made him promise to keep in touch, even if it was a yearly Christmas card.

"You're one of the success stories, Dalton. Be proud of yourself. I am."

Dalton wasn't proud of the way he'd left things with Melanie. That he planned to remedy right away.

Melanie didn't stay for the Super Bowl celebration. The Currents had won by a wide margin. Without Rocket. She'd already cleaned out her office and said her goodbyes. She would miss the players and staff. They had become like family, but it was time to move on and find another family. With any luck, maybe create one of her own.

She smiled as she stepped out of Miami Airport and the heat of the sun touched her face. Just a few hours ago she'd been knee-deep in snow. She was trading that for sand. Pulling the strap of her small bag over her shoulder, Melanie raised her hand for a taxi.

Two hours later, she stood in front of what she hoped was the door to Dalton's apartment. It had taken some web surfing, phone calls to colleagues and one heart-to-heart with Dalton's secretary to find out the address, but she hadn't given up. She just hoped another woman didn't answer the door.

Pushing the doorbell, she waited. Nothing. Pushing it again, she listened for footsteps. None. Fumbling around in her purse, she found her business card and a pen. On the back of the card she wrote: "Came for that visit. I'm at the beach."

She took the elevator down from the penthouse floor and crossed the street to the beach. Despite it being the middle of January, there were a number of people enjoying the water. Pulling her new towel out of her new beach bag, she laid it out on the sand near the water. She removed her cover-up and sat on the towel. It was a beautiful spot.

Looking over her shoulder, she searched what she believed were Dalton's windows for movement and saw none. Her nerves were getting the better of her. Would he be glad to see her? Worse, ignore her note? She just had to hope that she hadn't been imagining what had happened between them in Niagara. He had said he cared. Surely that hadn't changed in a month.

It was a workday, so he probably wouldn't be home for another two or three hours. She could enjoy the beach for a while and worry later. Pulling her bag to her, she reached in and brought out a romance novel she'd bought in the airport. It would have a happy ending even if she didn't get hers.

Melanie woke with a sense that someone sat beside her. She opened one lid to see a shadow across the bottom half of her body. It was a big person. She opened both eyes. It was a man, but she was looking into the sun and she couldn't see his face but she did recognize those shoulders.

"Dalton…"

"What are you doing here, Melanie?" He didn't sound excited to see her.

She sat up. "You said I should come visit."

He wore a shirt with a too-heavy-for-the-climate sweater over it and long pants, socks and boots. The man had a serious problem with wardrobe decisions.

"No, I meant here on the beach. You're burnt. You should

know better than to stay in the sun too long when you're not used to it."

Melanie looked down at the tops of her feet. She would be unhappy soon as the sunburn set in.

Dalton stood in the shifting sand with all the grace that she'd remembered him having. He offered her his hand. "Come on—let's go get some aloe on you before you start hurting."

She took his hand and he helped her stand.

He handed her the cover-up. "Pull this on while I put the rest of your stuff in your bag." He picked up her book and raised a brow before placing it inside.

Melanie slipped on the oversize T-shirt. Dalton didn't seem pleased or upset to see her. She wasn't sure how to take that.

He carried her bag as they walked across the sand toward his place. Not once had he touched her. Fear started to seep in that he never would again. He was being too civil after all the harsh words she'd said. They seemed never to be on the same wavelength except in bed. Even now she was half-clothed and he was dressed as if he was headed to snow country. *Snow country.* Had he been coming to see her?

"Uh, Dalton, aren't you a little overdressed for this part of the world?"

He glared at her. "The only time I seem to have the correct clothes on when I'm around you is when we are in bed…"

Thinking about Dalton in bed had her almost as hot as her burned skin. "Why do you have those on now? Going somewhere?"

"I was."

"Well, don't let me hold you up. I can take care of my burn myself."

"I'm not going now. There's no reason to."

"Why?"

They crossed the street and entered his building. "Because I was coming to see you. I was at the airport and I forgot something important. I had to come back and I saw your note."

She reached out to him as the elevator door closed with them in the car.

"Don't touch me, Melanie. If you do, I'll forget that we need to talk. And we *need* to talk."

Melanie let her hand drop. What exhilaration she'd felt at learning he was coming to see her died. This wasn't an open-arms welcome.

The elevator opened and they walked down the hall to his door.

"I know I said some hasty things to you and I'm sorry."

Dalton unlocked the door and pushed it back so she could enter first. "I'm not sorry you did. They were things I needed to hear."

"Still, I didn't have to be so horrible when I said them." She looked around. His place was unbelievable. Ultramodern, with a one-eighty view of the ocean—it was like being outside all the time. One of the windows was a sliding door that was pushed back and a breeze flowed through.

Dalton went into the all-white kitchen and said, "Would you like a glass of iced tea?"

"That would be nice."

He fixed the drinks while she wandered around the living area. It was done in different shades of sand colors with an occasional pop of color.

"Nice place."

"Thank you. I don't spend as much time here as I would like to."

She turned to look at him. "Why is that?"

"It's not much fun to come home to an empty house. I hope to change that, though."

He was making her nervous. Was he trying to tell her that he'd found someone else?

"Look, Dalton, I just came by to say I was sorry about what happened between us. I tried to call you the next day but you were already gone. I just wanted to apologize. I won't keep you any longer." She started for her bag but he stepped between her and it.

"You said Rocket couldn't play."

She looked at him, surprised at the change of subject. "How do you know?"

"I watched the championship game. Even watched the Super Bowl."

"Wow! You have changed."

He moved closer. So close she could feel the heat of his body. "I was so desperate for a glimpse of you I'd sit through anything."

Moisture filled her eyes. She still had a chance.

"I'd like to cash in my rain check. Please kiss me."

Dalton couldn't allow that request to go unfilled, even though they still had things to sort out. He gathered Melanie into his arms and held her tightly as his lips found hers. Damn, he'd missed her with every fiber of his being. She wrapped her arms around his neck and held on as if she would never let go. Her mouth opened for him and she brought her legs up to encircle his hips. Her core called to his hardening manhood.

She pulled her mouth away from his and said, "I've missed you."

"I've missed you too." Dalton carried her to the couch and he sat down. She faced him as she remained in his lap. "We have to talk before this goes any further."

"What's there to talk about?"

"The fact that I love you and want you in my life forever." She cupped his face and smiled at him. "I love you too."

Dalton's heart soared as he gathered her into his arms again. "Please say it again. I was afraid I'd never hear it."

She looked directly into his eyes. "I love you."

He kissed her. Long, wonderful minutes later, he released her mouth. "When did you decide to come down here?"

"Two days after you left."

He gave her a look of disbelief. "Why did you wait so long?"

"Because I had to wait until after the season was over. Had to work out my contract. Plus I needed to be around to make sure Rocket didn't sneak onto the field or was pushed."

"How did he take not getting to play?"

"Pretty hard at first, but he accepted it was in his best interest. He'll be ready for the next season and not lose his chance to ever play again. I agreed to let him suit up for the Championship game only because I was convinced it would mentally hurt the other team. For the Super Bowl I took no chances. Rocket wore his street clothes on the sideline."

"How about your father? Is he speaking to you?"

"He and Coach Rizzo didn't take it too well. I think winning the Super Bowl, Rocket or not, eased the pain. I quit my job and told my father I was going to work with children. That I wanted to be my own person."

"How did he take that?"

"He's coming around to the idea slowly. But I left on good terms. He gave me a glowing recommendation that helped me get a position at the children's hospital here in Miami. I start next week."

"You do? You were that sure of me?"

"No. Just hopeful."

"Well, I have some confessions of my own."

Her eyes had turned serious. "What are those?"

"You got me thinking about how I've dealt with what

happened to me. I went to visit some of the places I lived and thought about how I felt when I lived there. I talked to one of my foster mothers, the one I felt closest to for a time. It was the home where I was the happiest…and the unhappiest. It turns out that the time I lived there in many ways made my life better. She knew what the other kids were doing to me. In her own way she protected me and gave me the groundwork to go on to school and become successful."

"You will have to take me to visit her sometime so I can thank her for the wonderful man I know today."

A knot lodged in his throat at how easy Melanie saw the picture that he'd painted with such broad strokes. "I would love for you to meet Mrs. Richie. I also have a surprise for you."

"What?" Melanie squirmed in his lap and he almost forgot what he was going to say.

"I had a colleague in my practice who specializes in young adults look at Josey Woods's chart. You remember Josey from the day we visited the hospital?"

Melanie nodded.

"Well, there's a new procedure and he thinks she's a perfect candidate. She'll be coming down in the summer to have her legs straightened. She'll be dancing at her prom the next spring."

"Have you talked to her family? Do they have a way to pay? Do I need to do something to help?"

How like Melanie to want to support people.

"That's taken care of. My foundation is covering all their expenses."

She leaned back and studied him. "You have a foundation?"

"I do. Most of the money goes to making foster children's lives better. But since it is mine, I can also use the money for other good causes. All those high fees I charge for my consults go into the foundation."

She kissed him and pulled away. "You really are wonderful."

"Thanks. Coming from you, I consider that the highest of compliments. Now, you mentioned something about a rain check a few minutes ago. If I remember correctly, that was for lovemaking. I'd like to cash that now, if you don't mind."

Melanie rubbed against him. "I don't mind at all. But I just need you to promise that I can come to the bank anytime."

"The doors are always open for you. Now and forever."

MELANIE INTERTWINED HER fingers with Dalton's as they sat on her father's couch. He leaned over and kissed her temple.

She looked at the Christmas tree and then around the room at all the people she loved. It was hard to believe that an entire year had passed.

"I hope we don't get snowed in," she said.

Dalton smiled. "If we do, I'm prepared this time. I won't have to borrow your brother's clothes."

"The only reason you are is because I did your packing."

Dalton squeezed her hand. "That's one of the perks of having a wife."

Her father came to sit beside her. "Hey, I saw a piece on the TV about the boy you helped have heart surgery. Smart kid and a big Currents fan."

Melanie squeezed Dalton's hand. His foundation had seen to it that Marcus was able to travel to Miami for the necessary surgery, which was at Melanie's hospital. He had even arranged for his grandmother to come and found them a place to stay for a couple of months afterward. "Marcus is doing great."

She and her father were closer than ever. He had seen to it that she'd had a beautiful wedding with all the trimmings. Her brothers and their families were in attendance. Even Mrs. Richie was there, proudly sitting in the mother of the groom's spot. Things weren't perfect between Melanie and her father, but they did speak every week on the phone and often talked about things other than football. She and Dalton had also made it up to one of the Currents' games during the year for a visit.

"Present time," one of her nephews called.

As usual it was loud and boisterous as the group unwrapped their presents.

Melanie was handed a box. She looked at the tag and then at Dalton. "We agreed no presents so all the foster kids would have a good Christmas."

"I didn't give you one last year so I owed you. Open it."

Melanie tore the paper away to find a snow globe with Niagara Falls inside.

"I couldn't pass it up."

She smiled at Dalton. "It's perfect. And so are you."

"Uncle Dalton, here's one for you."

He took the small box and looked at the tag. "We said no gifts."

"I couldn't help it either," Melanie said.

Dalton unwrapped the box and opened the top. He lifted the baby's rattle in Currents colors out. "What?"

The room quieted. Melanie watched as question, disbelief, wonder and then pure happiness settled on his face.

"We're having a baby?"

Melanie nodded.

"We're having a baby!" Dalton's arms encircled her as his lips met hers.

Her father said, "Great. Another for the team."

Melanie smiled softly. *No, a family for Dalton.*

* * * * *

MILLS & BOON®
Christmas Collection!

Unwind with a festive romance this Christmas
with our breathtakingly passionate heroes.
Order all books today and receive a free gift!

MILLS & BOON®

MEDICAL ROMANCE™

THE ULTIMATE IN ROMANTIC MEDICAL DRAMA

A sneak peek at next month's titles...

In stores from 4th December 2015:

Available at WHSmith, Tesco, Asda, Eason, Amazon and Apple

Just can't wait?
Buy our books online a month before they hit the shops!
visit www.millsandboon.co.uk

These books are also available in eBook format!

1115/03